AF001276

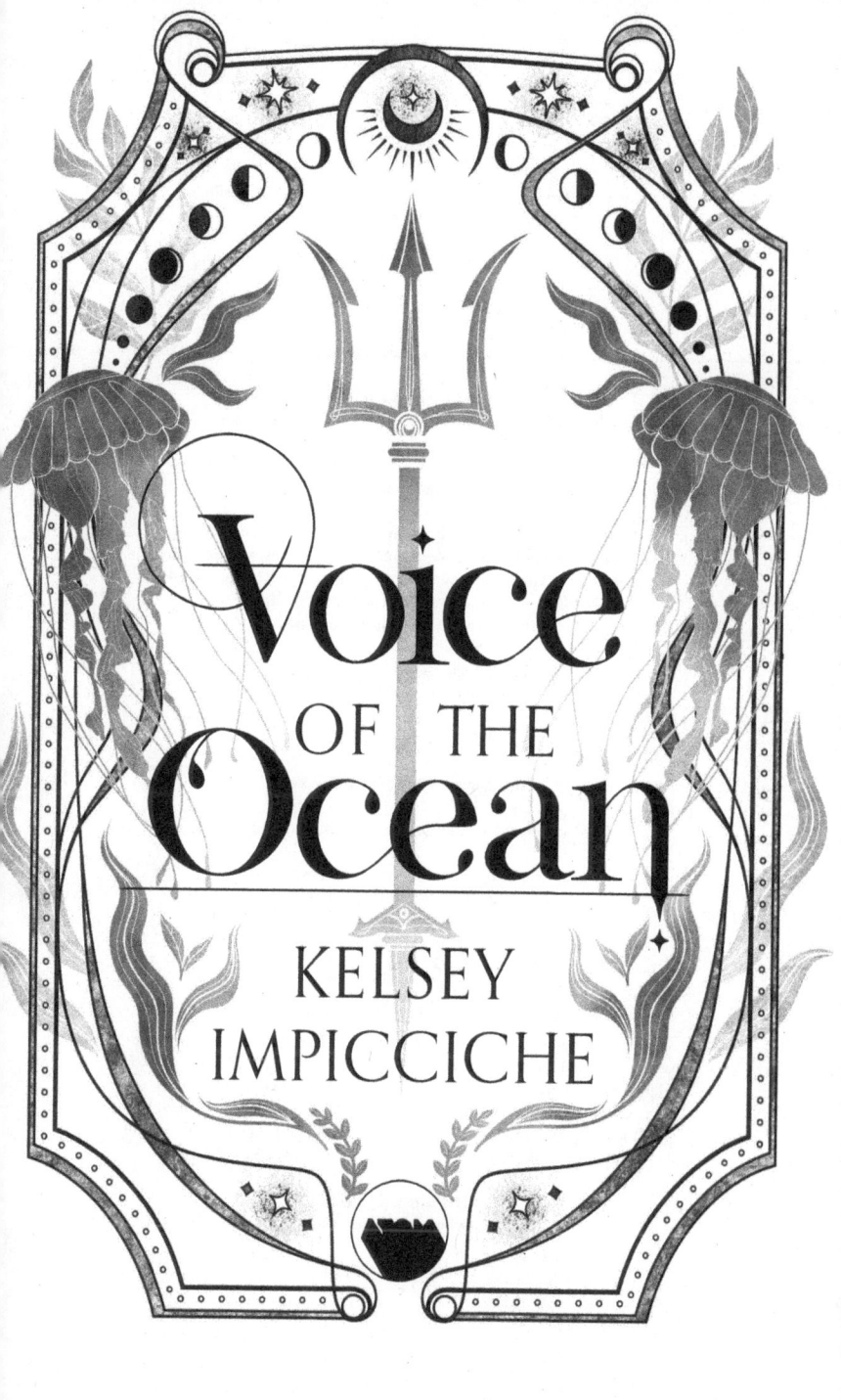

ATOM

First published in the United States in 2025 by Blackstone Publishing
First published in Great Britain in 2025 by Atom

5 7 9 10 8 6 4

Copyright © Kelsey Impicciche, 2025

The moral right of the author has been asserted.

*All characters and events in this publication, other than those
clearly in the public domain, are fictitious and any resemblance
to real persons, living or dead, is purely coincidental.*

All rights reserved.
No part of this publication may be reproduced, stored in a
retrieval system, or transmitted, in any form or by any means, without
the prior permission in writing of the publisher, nor be otherwise circulated
in any form of binding or cover other than that in which it is published
and without a similar condition including this condition being
imposed on the subsequent purchaser.

A CIP catalogue record for this book
is available from the British Library.

ISBN: 978-0-3491-2565-7

Cover and book design by Larissa Ezell

Printed and bound in Great Britain by Clays Ltd, Elcograf S.p.A.

Papers used by Atom are from well-managed forests
and other responsible sources.

Atom
An imprint of
Little, Brown Book Group
Carmelite House
50 Victoria Embankment
London EC4Y 0DZ

The authorised representative
in the EEA is
Hachette Ireland
8 Castlecourt Centre,
Dublin 15, D15 XTP3, Ireland
(email: info@hbgi.ie)

An Hachette UK Company
www.hachette.co.uk

www.littlebrown.co.uk

To the girls who are told they cry too much,
and to my dear friend who helped teach me it's okay.

But a mermaid has no tears, and therefore she suffers so much more.
 —Hans Christian Andersen, "The Little Mermaid"

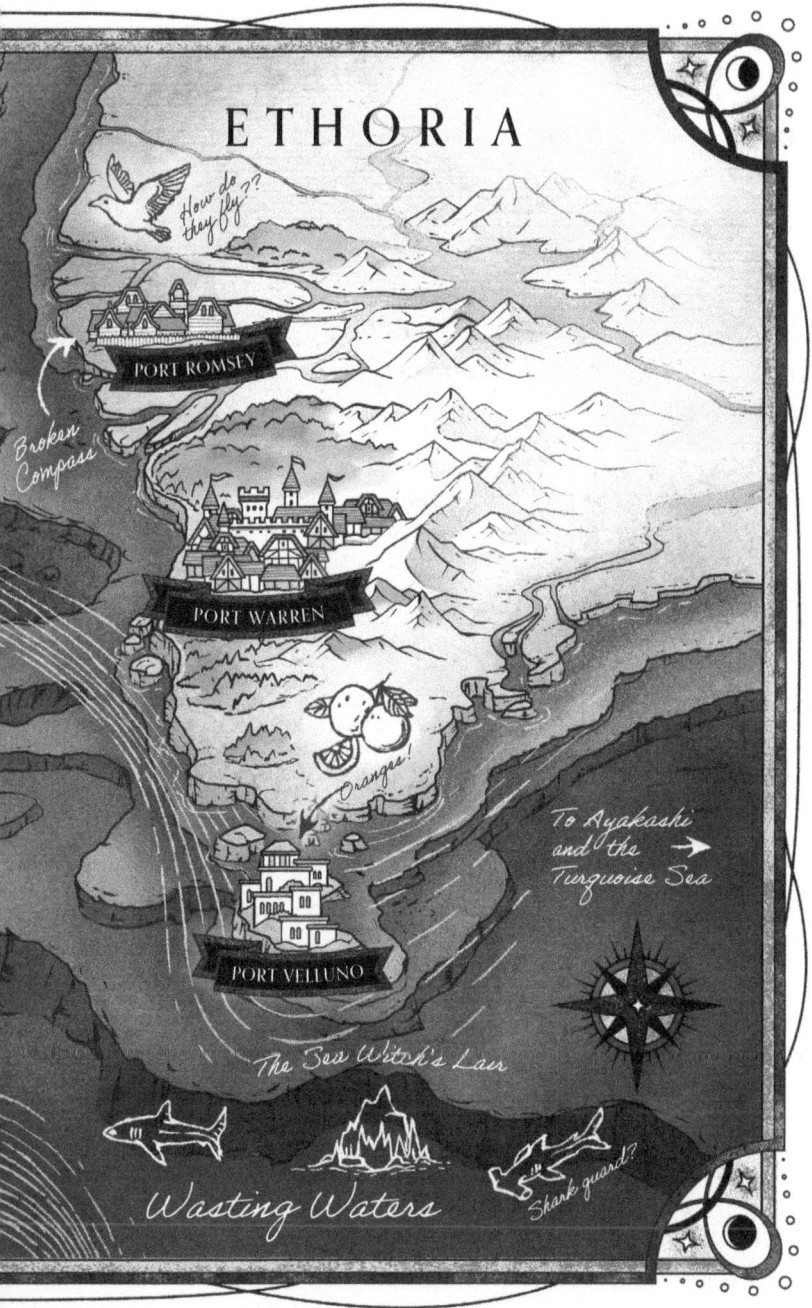

CHAPTER 1

When Celeste's head breached the surface of the water, the ringing stopped. She took a gasping breath, filling her lungs with salt air. It was the first deep breath she'd taken in weeks. In fact, it was the *only* breath she'd taken in weeks. For sirens had no need for deep breaths. Their gills ensured they never needed to surface. Furthermore, in the Kingdom of Staria, breaching the surface was strictly forbidden.

Unfortunately, the surface was where the young princess felt most at peace.

Celeste laid back into the water, letting her body bob up and down in the space where the air and water met. A wide grin grew upon her lips, and she closed her eyes, enjoying the feeling of the air kissing her wet skin. The *nothing* of it all. Dawn approached above her, its first embers glittering on the sea's horizon. Here she no longer heard the echoes of her argument with her mother ringing in her ears. The argument that had been building for the past cycle.

The argument about her initiation.

In four phases of the moon, Celeste was to complete her final test to be inducted into the ranks of the Chorus. A distinction her mother, the queen, did not think she was ready for despite it being the very thing she'd been training to achieve. It had been such an honor to become an initiate. When Celeste began training at thirteen cycles, her parents were so proud. She hadn't even expected them to approve. But they surprised her. Deciding it was the perfect opportunity for their youngest daughter to learn to control her Voice. To learn discipline. Structure. Respect for the rules of Staria. It was all her father talked to her about for the next month. In fact, it was one of the only things her father ever *did* talk to her about.

Celeste drew her tail of silvery blue through the water, wondering why breaching the surface was forbidden in the first place. She had never seen anything out of the ordinary. Her kingdom's waters were so far removed from shore that no creature born of land could survive. Not even human trade routes traveled so far. And if the rare ship ever did journey into siren waters, the Chorus ensured no threats remained.

A splash sounded to her left, and Celeste bolted upright, scanning the waves. It was only a fish jumping through the swells. Not a Chorus scout, the only sirens occasionally permitted to surface and who worked in pairs. Although Celeste was certain the scouts patrolled seas further east, she remained vigilant. If she were caught above, she'd be stripped of her rank. The one thing she had ever truly earned. Her only hope to make her parents proud. She'd be restricted to the palace or shipped off to another kingdom for marriage, like her sister Sephone, who departed five cycles ago.

Celeste could practically hear Sephone's voice in her head, ever the voice of reason. *Come on, little star. It's not worth the risk.* But Sephone hadn't been around to talk her baby sister out of things for quite some time. Not since Celeste was twelve cycles old. A pang of longing filled Celeste's chest, as it always did when she thought of her sister.

But I know what I'm doing, she assured herself. Celeste wasn't a fool. She never surfaced far from home and never stayed out too long. Besides, she'd needed this. Needed to get away from the palace. From her mother. She'd almost lost control again.

But as Celeste scanned the sky, drinking in the vivid strokes of sunrise, her eye caught on something. A shadow, hardly discernible along the northwest horizon.

She froze, eyes widening. It was much too large to be a scouting pair. *Swim home*, Sephone insisted in her head. *Stay safe.* But Celeste could not move. She'd never seen anything on the surface before. And wasn't it her duty as a future Chorus member to investigate? Celeste chewed at the inside of her cheek. The excuse sounded weak even to her own ears. *But still...*

With the grace of a predator, Celeste swam toward the shadow. Though she was nowhere near the deadliest predator in the sea, she'd been trained in combat. Even the choppy surface water didn't slow her, despite how foreign it felt. Far below, where she lived, the sea was calm, constant. Here the water was always changing. A threat. A challenge.

At half the distance, Celeste fell still, not daring to swim closer despite her curiosity screaming to keep going. Surely she was close enough to make out what the shadow was, but far enough to avoid detection. There were countless dangers the shadow could be. She emerged, her crystal eyes finding the pall almost immediately. It looked like ... a *ship*. Instinctively, she sank back into the water, heart shuddering. Whether from panic or something else entirely, she could not tell.

There was a ship in Staria's waters. A human ship.

Why? This vessel was farther south than any she'd heard of before. There was nothing out here for humans to explore. No countries. No islands. No land whatsoever. And yet, impossibly, there it was. Glimmering like a mirage against the dawn.

Go home! her sister's voice demanded in her head. But Celeste remained, squinting to discern the shape of it. She'd seen sunken ships before. The decaying corpses of once great vessels that littered the ocean floor. Sirens often scavenged them for materials. But those were leagues away. Celeste would know. Foraging was the one activity that brought her outside the confines of the kingdom—not that she was allowed to do it often or without supervision. And with so few freedoms available to her, the hobby grew into an obsession in her youth. Every time Celeste heard a new ship had gone down nearby, she begged her sisters to take her to rifle through it first. They teased her, assuming she liked having first pick of the best things. But it wasn't true. What Celeste liked most was seeing the ships before the ocean took them. To see them as the humans might have: whole and sturdy. Well, as whole and sturdy as a sunken ship at the bottom of the ocean could be. After she joined the Chorus initiates, those trips became few and far between.

But here one was. Celeste sighed. It was impossible to see any details from so far away. She could not glean the color of the sails or any significant markings. Every fiber of the princess yearned to draw closer. There would be real humans on board. What would it be like to see one up close? Were they as monstrous as all the stories said? When she was a child, her eldest sister, Shye, wove tales of their rows and rows of sharklike teeth. Teeth to rip out their victims' throats. They had eyes the color of blood, clawed fingers as long as seaweed, and legs that ended *in a second pair of hands*. Celeste endured nightmares of endless hands for weeks after that.

But some cycles later, the young princess found a ship with a statue of a human on it. The statue's mouth was closed, so she could not ascertain the shape of its teeth. But much to her disappointment, the fingers were the same as any siren's. In fact, the human looked surprisingly similar to a siren. Except that just below the hips, where a tail should have been, the human had *legs*. And they were even more horrible than Shye had described them. Three times the width of an arm and nearly twice as long, legs looked disgusting to Celeste at first, but she supposed they had to use something to walk.

The ship was drawing closer, heading directly toward her. But as much as Celeste longed to see the humans for herself, she couldn't. The punishment for being seen by a human was banishment. Not only was that a death sentence for a siren; the shame it would bring to her family would be immense. Sirens would sing Songs about the day the princess was cast out of her kingdom. Although Celeste dreamed of doing something worthy of being sung about, that wasn't what she had in mind.

And yet...

Human sightings were so rare, even for the Chorus. If her mother had her way, who knew when—or even *if*—she'd have a chance to see one again. *Just one look won't hurt anyone*, a small voice said. Her own voice. And before she realized she'd decided, Celeste was hurtling forward. Excitement thrummed in her veins, pushing her faster until she could feel the force of the ship in the water. She paused, the weight of her decision settling in. There was a reason the punishment was severe. Not only would this endanger herself but she'd be in violation of a treaty among all siren kingdoms. To humans, sirens were a myth. And it was in everyone's best interest to keep it that way. Revealing the existence of sirens to humankind was punishable by death. Was she really willing to risk death?

Just one little look, she assured herself. *Then I'll accept my fate. Whatever it may be.* And with a beat of her tail, she rose so her eyes were just above the surface.

Music?

She wouldn't have believed it, except the sound was unmistakable. It never occurred to her that humans could do such a thing. The strumming of strings filled the air, drawing her in. And just as it was about to repeat its refrain, a voice joined it—deep, velvety smooth, and decidedly male. The song was inviting, but not in the way sirens' Songs were. To the sirens, Songs were tools. Weapons. Healers used the Song to manipulate bodies. The Chorus used the Song to manipulate minds. And storytellers used the Song so their history would not be forgotten. There were Songs to teach and Songs to tear down, to celebrate and to mourn, but every Song was magic. An echo of the Goddess herself.

But this human music had a magic all its own. The voice calling to mind tender heartbreak and bittersweet longing.

As the melody reached its chorus, it shifted. The mournful

singing became loud and rough, more of a shout than a melody. Other voices joined in, mixing together like sand, smooth and coarse all at once. The leader sang first. The others responded in unison. Call-and-response.

Celeste rose further from the water, tilting her head up to gaze along the side of the ship. A chill raced down her spine. It was massive, black and looming like a great beast. Large masts rose from the deck, carrying crisp white sails. Long, weathered scratches covered the wooden sides like a wrinkled face, betraying its long history. At the front of the ship, Celeste could just make out an ornate golden figure of a woman with feathered wings, her long arms tucked against her sides, as if preparing to spring into the air. The ship groaned as it rocked back and forth, the waves moving Celeste right along with it. Fearing an undertow, she swam away from its pull.

And that's when she saw him.

The singer.

He stood atop the railing of the ship, leaning casually over the water with one hand gripping a rope. His hair, dark as night, swept over his forehead as he turned his sharp jaw into the wind. To her annoyance, his eyes were simply brown. Not even a hint of blood. But his voice. It poured from his full pink lips as easily as breathing. And somehow the song was made better from watching him perform it. There was something about him, as if he was the center of a whirlpool, and Celeste found herself sinking into his gravity. He wore a dark shirt, left partially open to reveal the sculpted top of his chest. And on top of it, a long leather coat hugged his wide shoulders, swaying against his legs. Celeste stared at the strange leather. It was too thin to be armor. Why wear such a thing? Did it not simply get in the way?

He smiled, and his teeth—Celeste let out a huff of exasperation. His teeth were ordinary, rectangular and straight. *I should have known Shye was lying*, she thought bitterly, embarrassed she had believed the childhood story for so long. But the human did not need rows of sharp teeth. There was still something dangerous about him. It was more than the countless weapons strapped to his body. It was something hiding behind his eyes. Behind his wide smile. Dangerous yet beautiful.

And if he looked down, he'd see her.

Celeste sucked in a breath, yet she remained frozen in place, all sense of self-preservation and training lost. Everything about him fascinated her. From the way he moved, so much clumsier than any siren and yet full of confidence and purpose, to the way he sang. His song was simple and repetitive, nothing like the complex magic of the sirens. But to her surprise, she found herself fighting the urge to sing along.

A small creature appeared beneath the ship's railing. Its beady eyes scanned the waters below, tongue lolling. Celeste dove forward, hiding closer to the ship. Was that an animal from land? She'd never seen any before. Not any alive, anyway. Its face looked similar to a seal, but it was covered in fur like an otter. And on either side of its head, long flaps swung back and forth. Even from her place beside the ship, she could see the animal give a shake, sending the flaps flopping. The effect of it was surprisingly adorable, given its strangeness. The animal gazed up at the singer, body wriggling with barely concealed excitement. And the singer brightened, dropping down to the ship's floor and causing Celeste to swim out a bit more to keep them both in sight. The man ran his fingers through the animal's curling hair, and in spite of herself, Celeste's heart gave a little tug at the sight. There was a kindness to him. A gentleness.

A cry rang out as the humans finished their song, dissolving into cheers and shouts of goodwill, and the singer turned away from her. From her new vantage, Celeste could see more of the ship. A smile lit her face as she recognized things from her explorations. Mysterious objects now whole and in their proper place. An instrument she'd seen in pieces was now strummed by a human's deft hands. She frowned. Somehow Celeste always pictured them playing it with their creepy leg fingers.

"Bastian," called the handsome singer, his tone commanding

and warm. "I need an update on our supplies." He spoke in the common human tongue. A thrill went up Celeste's spine at hearing it used by a native speaker for the first time. Although not generally known by sirens, the language was required learning for every member of the Chorus.

Another human moved into view, a wide white smile contrasting beautifully with his rich brown skin.

"We are on schedule in terms of our store," the other man, Bastian, replied. "Food will last until we make port, and our stock of ale and wine is more than enough to keep us going as our water supply diminishes."

The leader nodded, half listening while he scratched behind the animal's ear. Then, with a great bark, the creature scampered off in chase toward something Celeste could not see. "Well then! Good day," the singer called after it in mock offense. He turned to Bastian. "Do you think the Admiral is cross with me?"

Bastian shrugged. "Have you done anything to incur his ire?"

"The problem is, dear Bastian"—his lips quirked up wickedly—"that I incur so much ire that one couldn't possibly keep track."

Bastian laughed and shook his head. "Then we may never know."

A new song struck up. Feet slammed against the ship's surface, and crewmates sprang into movement, weaving around each other, shouting the song back and forth.

The prince arched an eyebrow. "Care for a dance, Quartermaster?"

Amusement passed across Bastian's face. "Far be it for me to keep you from your birthday celebrations, My Prince, but shouldn't we keep an eye out?"

"Let Ol' Gunner keep watch for all the nasty creatures of the deep." He grinned as he gestured to a hulking man with a downturned mouth who, to Celeste, resembled a blobfish. "I think we're prepared for anything that may come our way." Without waiting for Bastian to respond, the man—a prince, apparently—leaped into the center of the dance, the crew roaring in approval.

Celeste watched in awe, captivated by the liveliness of it all. Sirens danced in graceful movements performed at special ceremonies, clear and calm. The humans moved like a raging current. And in the center of this whirlpool danced the prince.

There were so many humans on the ship. At least a hundred, by her estimation, and that was only those above deck. Their skin tones were various shades of pale pink, soft gold, or brilliant brown. Where were the greens? The purples? The blues? Where were the flaming reds and burning oranges? Even their hair only ranged from light brown to black. *How boring*, she thought with awe. She looked past the ship to the horizon, wondering if this ship was traveling in a group like sirens did. But all she saw were dark storm clouds moving in and the sun climbing higher in the sky. *The sun!* If she didn't leave soon, she'd be caught. And although she dearly wished to stay and learn more, Celeste knew that she had already risked too much.

If only she knew how right she was.

CHAPTER 2

Something was wrong. Celeste had swum only a few miles toward home when she felt it. A disturbance in the water. Halting, she willed her racing heart to calm before it alerted any predators. How she wished for her spear. It had been a risk not to bring it, but leaving the palace armed would surely draw too much attention if she were seen. She lifted her hands, rolling them into fists.

She cast a look around at the endless turquoise vastness, but her eyes only fell upon a freshly born sea turtle. The little body was so small that if Celeste hadn't been training as often as she did, she would have missed it. The newborn flapped its arms adorably, rocking its shell side to side through the rippling water. So small in the great vastness of the open ocean. She swam down a little closer to look.

But then she felt it again. Something else was near.

From the dark depths a hulking body cut through the water like a knife. A massive blue shark, nearly twice the size of Celeste from head to fin. The shark was still far enough for Celeste to make an escape; it was no match for the speed and dexterity of a siren. The turtle would not be so lucky.

The gills across Celeste's neck fluttered in indecision.

It's not our place to intervene with other creatures. This time the voice inside her head was of her instructor Madam Auralia. And it was true. In the wilds of the ocean, no creature was safe. It was stupid to risk your life for an animal, let alone a turtle. Each second that ticked by was a risk in itself.

But she could not tear her gaze away from the toddling newborn.

With a growl of frustration, she dove. The turtle, who'd seen Celeste and knew her as a predator, attempted to flee. But its little limbs were too clumsy. The shark gained, but the siren was closer. With outstretched hands, she scooped the turtle into her arms and bolted.

Behind her, she felt the shark follow. Could feel it drawing closer by the second. The frightened turtle struggled in her arms, desperate.

"Stop wiggling," she hissed, clutching it tighter. "I won't eat you. *I'm saving you.*"

But when they reached the sandy floor, her stomach dropped. There was nothing but delicate coral as far as she could see. No place to hide. Celeste let out a curse. She wouldn't dare touch the sacred reef. And even if she could bring herself to break off a piece as a weapon, it would be too brittle to use for long.

Panic tightened her chest, and she fought to keep her breathing even. Her fear would only send the shark into a frenzy. The hesitation had already cost her dearly. The shark shot toward her, jaws open wide.

Celeste spun, throwing her body in an arch at the precise moment the shark went sailing off beneath her. The trick only gained her moments. In an instant, the shark whipped around, ready for a second attempt. It was fast. Much faster than she'd anticipated. Fleeing was out of the question. And she doubted she was strong enough to beat a shark in a fistfight, especially while holding the very thing she was trying to protect.

One option remained. And yet she wavered, dodging the shark again to buy time. *You won't hurt anyone,* she tried to reassure herself, *and you are out of options*. And so as the shark dove for her tail, Celeste focused and opened her mouth.

The Song poured from her lips, haunting and beautiful. A soft, clear sound that beckoned and caressed like a lover. It was a sound that could shatter hearts and bring hundreds to their knees.

Celeste's body began to glow. Silvery-white light pulsed from the tips of her hair to her tail. The siren stiffened, eyes widening in alarm as she looked upon herself. *No. This isn't right. Stay calm. Stay in control.* If she lost focus, the magic of the Song would be undone. That was why sirens ordinarily sang in groups.

As if in response, the Song slipped further from her grasp. But instead of the magic falling away, as it should have, it became a writhing and wild thing all its own. And although the water hardly moved, her moon-white hair billowed around her head, swirling and fluttering. Clouds circled in the shark's fathomless black eyes, swallowing them whole. Its body slowed to a halt, so close its nose bumped against her tail. Celeste's shoulders sagged in relief. The Song continued, wrapping around the predator's frozen form. Holding. Dominating. The shark's stillness was eerie to behold. Like a moment preserved in ice. In her hands, the baby turtle had stilled as well. She winced. *Not again.*

Celeste swam forward, beckoning the shark to remain with her. As much as she wished to flee, she had to keep her target within eyesight to maintain the connection. It trailed behind her like a shadow, an extension of herself, obeying her every thought.

Now what? Celeste needed to get to her lessons. Madam Auralia had kicked initiates out for being late. But she couldn't swim home. That would lead the shark straight to her kingdom. She'd just have to find somewhere to leave the shark.

It took some time, but at last she found the perfect opening in the side of a cliff far from Staria's entrance. With one gesture of her hand, the shark swam headfirst into the crevice, burrowing deep inside. She backed away, still singing until she was certain the shark was far enough inside. Then she turned tail and darted away.

But it turned out she shouldn't have bothered. Celeste was in sight of home when she at last felt the turtle's wriggling begin again. The Song had taken over ten minutes to fade. She cursed beneath her breath. *Why did it linger?*

Celeste stared down at the tiny turtle, rubbing her thumb against its smooth shell. She could keep it. It'd be nice to have a little friend to take care of. But Celeste's parents would never allow it. Not since *the dolphin incident*. But who knew dolphins were so contemptible? And even if Celeste *could* bring the turtle home, she'd have to explain where she had gotten it. If only she weren't such a terrible liar.

With a sigh, the siren found a small rock formation beside a busy reef, safe enough for a young turtle to make its home. She unfurled her fingers, enjoying the sweet feeling of victory as the little creature swam free.

"All the blessings of the Goddess be with you, little one," she whispered with a smile. "Until the tides turn." Then, with a proud swish of her tail, she made for home.

The Kingdom of Staria was built in the embrace of a vast cave system in the Southern Ocean. At its front, one small entrance was guarded day and night. Thousands of cycles ago, Celeste's ancestor, Queen Isla of House Neris, constructed it so she could control all movement in and out of her kingdom. But having one entrance and exit also meant those inside could be easily trapped. And so, secret tunnels had been constructed. Well concealed and hardly used, they certainly came in handy if you were a princess with a secret.

Celeste reached a pile of rocks and pushed them aside to reveal a hole slightly wider than her hips. She swam through, making sure to sweep the rocks back in place behind her with her fin. Beneath, the hole widened into a long, deep cave. She rushed along, the light growing dimmer as she went. Siren eyes were adapted to limited light, but she'd know each twist and turn even in darkness.

The tunnel ended in a wall. Celeste felt along the flat rock until she found a small fracture, and she pushed. The stone gave, sliding to reveal the back gardens of the palace. She slipped through the opening, turning to replace the rock.

A hand clamped down upon her shoulder. "What do you think you're doing here? The palace is not open to visitors."

Celeste's heart plummeted into her stomach. She'd been rushing and hadn't noticed the guard. They hadn't recognized her yet, but if she bolted now, they'd pursue her. How would she explain herself? *If the queen found out...*

With a jerk, the guard swung her around to face them. Celeste winced. She hadn't had time to think of a lie. Perhaps *that* was what she should have been doing during the swim home. But her mind had been flooded with thoughts of the human ship. No, not the ship. *The prince*. His dreamy song still echoed endlessly in her ears, a call waiting for her response.

Celeste met the guard's eyes, knowing full well that her guilt was likely written across her face. But as the guard looked at her, realization dawned. They dropped their hand from her shoulder as though she had burned them.

"Princess!" they exclaimed, lilac skin flushing deep red.

Celeste knew most of the sirens who worked within the palace grounds, but she did not recognize this one. Perhaps they were new? Maybe luck was still on her side.

"Good tides!" Celeste chirped, flashing a too-bright smile. "I apologize, but I don't believe we have met."

The guard blinked before inclining their torso, dark hair falling into their face.

"Please accept my apologies for touching you, Highness. I did not recognize you."

Celeste threw a glance around to see if anyone else was watching but found no one. "Do not worry yourself," Celeste said graciously. "But I do have somewhere to be..." she trailed off, hinting that she didn't know their name.

"Maris, Your Highness." The guard flushed, pleased that she cared enough to ask their name.

"A pleasure to meet you, Maris," Celeste said with a wink. "I look forward to seeing you again!"

The guard blinked, staring even as she swam out of sight.

That had been close. *Too close.* She had been lucky. If she had been caught by a guard who knew where she was meant to be, they'd have gone straight to the queen. But now that she was safely on her way, a little thrill ran through her at the victory. *I got away with it.*

Buzzing with energy, Celeste dashed through the palace halls to her rooms. She grabbed her spear and leather armor. Her lips hummed the human prince's tune, echoing behind her as she swam through the halls. But when she reached the palace entrance, her mother's voice stopped her.

"You're late," the queen said. "And you haven't eaten."

Celeste paused. She considered swimming away, pretending she hadn't heard. But there was no use ignoring the queen of Staria. With a sigh, Celeste entered the dining room.

The white stone ceilings were cavernously high in every room of the magnificent palace, arched, and covered in shimmering mother-of-pearl. Small shafts of light illuminated the room from deep cuts circling the domed roof. They were too narrow for sirens to travel in and out of, but they let in enough light. The effect was a little claustrophobic, in Celeste's opinion. Especially when she knew how the sun shone above.

Queen Halia reclined at the head of a long stone table, fixing her youngest daughter with a questioning stare.

"Good morning, Mother," she said tightly. She tried to ignore the pit in her stomach from her mother's worry. The queen cared greatly how the family appeared to others. "You look very regal today, Father."

King Tidus responded with a grunt that made Celeste smirk. A man of few words. Her father did look rather striking that morning. Dressed with his formal stingray leathers strapped tightly across his wide chest. The masculine balance to the queen's sovereignty. They were the perfect pair. Him battle ready and her in a delicate pearl crown and elegant shelled finery.

"Why aren't you at training?" The king lifted a golden shell filled with shining red fish eggs to his lips. He was a large siren with stiff, sizable muscles beneath his sand-colored skin. Atop his head rested a large silver crown with rare pointed shells rising like spears. Beneath the crown, his hair was long, braided, and golden blond.

"I'm on my way there now." Celeste was anxious not to be late. She tried, and failed, to avoid glancing at the tempting piles of sea grapes that sat upon the table. Her stomach growled.

"Don't leave hungry. We wouldn't want you fainting during drills in front of the others," her mother chided.

Celeste sighed, knowing there was little sense in fighting. She was already going to be late, so she grabbed a fistful of sea grapes and popped one into her mouth.

"Your sister has already come and gone this morning," the queen informed Celeste.

Of course she had. Shye, the heir apparent, was nothing if not punctual.

The queen tucked a strand of coral-red hair behind a delicately webbed ear. It was the same color that Shye, her eldest sister, shared. Sephone's hair was soft and pink, a mix of their parents. Only Celeste's hair was white. The House of Neris was once known for their white hair. It came from the Queen Mother's lineage, descended from the Goddess of the Sea. But it had been over a century since anyone in their family had been born with the white hair of their ancient house. Having it should have made Celeste feel special. But growing up, she would have done anything to have her mother's hair.

"Any news of Sephone?" Celeste asked, hope rising in her chest.

"Not today, Celeste."

Celeste nodded, deflating a little. They hardly received news of her sister since she had left the kingdom in search of a royal marriage. In fact, Celeste couldn't remember the last time she'd received a letter from her sister. It'd been nearly a cycle now. Still, she couldn't help but ask anyway.

"Why *are* you in your armor today, Father?" she asked, curiosity getting the better of her.

"Meetings," he said.

"What about?"

"They pertain to the protection of this kingdom," he said, before returning to his food, signaling the conversation's end. Celeste wasn't sure why she expected anything else. Her father was never one to give many details.

A server swam into the room, carrying a fresh silver tray of oysters. But the queen surveyed only her daughter, a tight expression on her face. Echoes of their argument rang in Celeste's ears. Certain her mother wished to reignite the dispute, she dove toward the oyster shells.

"Please excuse me. I really must go," Celeste told them, swimming from the room.

"We will speak after," the queen called after her.

But Celeste was already flying down the hall, shoving an oyster into her mouth and trying not to focus on how late she was or what exactly her mother wished to say. A task she quickly failed at, as she squeezed the now empty shell in her hand. *Madam Auralia is going to kill me.* Swimming past the dining room had been a mistake. She should have thought to go another way. She shouldn't have saved the turtle. She should not have gone to the ship. Her mind should be on the upcoming initiation, not returning to that handsome prince.

He was a human. She was a siren. Their kind had been at war since their creation.

She was certain she would never see him again.

And he would never know she existed at all.

CHAPTER 3

"Good tides, Helena!" Celeste said, waving at the guard at the palace entrance.

"Good tides, Princess! Aren't you late?" Helena called back with a knowing wink.

The young princess grinned. "I've got to give Madam Auralia something to complain about!" Helena's familiar laugh followed behind her as she swam across the palace's colorful front gardens. Delicate purple coral and red algae swayed as she passed.

Buildings and shops climbed as high as the eye could see, lining the sandy paths through the kingdom. Sirens wove in and out as they went about their daily tasks, stopping occasionally when they saw her and lowering their heads in deference. Celeste darted left, finding herself at the city's center. In the middle of the plaza sat a grand statue of Staria's founder: Queen Isla, eldest daughter of the Goddess and first of the Neris line. The sight made Celeste's rhythm falter.

As a child, Celeste believed the statue might come to life. Her huge tail circled beneath her like a coil ready to spring. In one hand Isla held coral, a symbol of the fragility of peace. While in the other she held a sharpened spear—a symbol of war, defense, strength. Although Isla wore nothing save for her crown, it was Celeste who felt naked under the statue's fierce gaze. The princess could almost feel her ancestor's piercing eyes in her back as she turned away. The same eyes as her mother.

With a flick of her tail, Celeste put as much distance between her and the statue as possible. But as the Chorus headquarters loomed into view, white-hot dread filled her stomach. Its tremendous archways stood high above the surrounding buildings, like the edge of a scalloped shell. Depictions of victorious battles and legendary sirens were carved into each column. Beautiful and imposing, the building was where all members trained and conducted business. And, unfortunately for Celeste, it was all too quiet.

Celeste gathered her courage and pressed on, entering the grand atrium. She swam up to the third floor and down the hall until she heard Madam Auralia's familiar alto.

"Fish guts..." Celeste cursed under her breath.

The instructor obviously felt her movement in the water, because the next thing Celeste heard was as clear as a moon jelly.

"It seems Princess Celeste has not been eaten by a shark on her way to class today." Madam Auralia turned, towering over her as she entered the room. The instructor's yellow eyes flashed with unrestrained disgust. Celeste felt herself shrivel.

"Please accept my deepest apologies, Madam." Celeste bowed her head. "You see, I—"

Auralia cut her off with a look. It was a shame. The lie she'd manufactured on her way over was one of her best yet.

The princess noticed her instructor's dress armor. Strange, on such an ordinary day of lessons. But her stingray leather was polished and shining. And in it, Madam Auralia looked downright lethal. Her obsidian hair was braided into a severe crown atop her head, complementing the stripes that covered her from neck to tail.

Celeste glanced down at the sand floor and swallowed, throat dry, hands shaking. *Please*, she sent up a little prayer to the Goddess, *please don't let her throw me out*. She should have stayed within the palace. Should have calmed herself some other way.

"This is the second time you've been late, *Princess*," Madam Auralia spat the title as if it were an insult.

Celeste's cheeks burned red, the gazes of her fellow initiates crawling up the back of her neck. Traitorous tears pricked in the corners of her eyes. *Master yourself. Stay calm.* She couldn't risk having another breakdown. But the oxygen felt as though it had been sucked from her lungs. Her mother's words echoed in her head. *"I just don't want you to get your hopes up, darling."* And suddenly she was back in her room. Suffocating.

"Forgive me, Madam. It won't happen again," Celeste said, fighting the tears in her eyes.

Madam Auralia paused for a moment, considering. "For your sake, I hope that is true, Your Highness. I do not give third chances."

Celeste remained still, keeping her gaze downcast. Was that all? Had Madam Auralia actually allowed her to remain? *Don't cry*, she told her watering eyes. *Not in front of all of them.*

"Compose yourself," Madam Auralia said, a flicker of disgust in her eyes. "And take your place." Then, without another look, she launched back into her lecture.

Celeste's shoulders eased. Why hadn't she been expelled? Others had been for less... Perhaps Madam Auralia was in a good mood. Or perhaps she didn't feel the need to remove Celeste. Not when the final test might do that job for her. But Celeste couldn't dwell on it now. Still trembling, she ducked her head and headed to her place beside her best friend, Maeve. The cecaelia looked at her with concern in her dark brown eyes. She raised a brow and covertly poked Celeste in the side with her magenta tentacle as if to say, *Where were you? Everything okay?*

Celeste smiled and nodded, attempting to furtively blink the tears away. As children, the two had been inseparable. Close enough to read each other's moods. To communicate without a word. But Maeve only nodded, not inquiring further.

Celeste looked down at her hands. "Did I miss anything important?" she whispered.

"Not particularly."

Good, Celeste thought, the tightness in her chest softening. She thought to ask Maeve about her crush. What was her name again? She was sure it started with an L. *Lylia? Leanna?* It had been ages since they'd caught up. But the question died on her lips when she noticed Madam Auralia's yellow gaze flick in their direction. Fine. Celeste could live vicariously through her friend's love life *after* lessons, then.

The water shifted, alerting them to a presence in the hall.

"That must be our guest," Madam Auralia said brightly.

Celeste and Maeve exchanged a glance. Neither of them had ever heard her say *anything* brightly before.

The mystery was quickly solved as the king entered, royal armor gleaming.

Immediately the energy in the room shifted. Backs straightened. Eyes became alert. Celeste's stomach clenched. *Why is he here?* She hated that he caught her by surprise. Hated how she now understood why Madam Auralia hadn't kicked her out, given her father was on his way. And she hated that she wasn't the least bit surprised he hadn't mentioned anything to her about this at breakfast. The king probably didn't want to appear to give his daughter *preferential treatment*.

"It is my honor to introduce you all to His Majesty, King Tidus of House Neris. Your Royal Highness, thank you so much for coming to speak personally to our initiates. It is our great pleasure to have you," Madam Auralia said, a smile on her face. Although the instructor maintained her usual stoicism, Celeste could see excitement twinkling in her eyes. Even if it was more common for the king to make public appearances than the queen, it was still a rarity. Staria's queen was the head of the kingdom and military, but the king was her right hand. Her counterpoint. Her balance. Wherever he went, he represented the kingdom, same as the queen.

Her father smiled and bowed. "The honor is mine, Madam. I thank you for your most gracious welcome and for allowing me to interrupt your day." He turned and scanned the group, never meeting Celeste's gaze. She felt herself sink a little lower. "I have the privilege of presenting your first official mission with the Chorus. And your final test."

At those words, the room thrummed with energy. No one spoke or moved, but they buzzed with nervous excitement. The initiation was supposed to be phases away. And yet suddenly the moment they'd been training for was unexpectedly here.

Before Celeste could wonder why, the king went on in his booming voice. "A ship was spotted today in the waters surrounding our kingdom."

Celeste stiffened. That meant a Chorus scouting pair was on the surface that morning as well.

"It was reported that the human Raiden Sharp is aboard, son of King Leonidas."

King Leonidas.

No... it couldn't be. Cycles ago, King Leonidas had done something Queen Halia could never forgive. Of all humans, he was the one the Kingdom of Staria hated most—and feared. The last time a team of the Chorus went in search of him, none of them returned. Over the last cycle, several other Chorus scouts had gone missing, and reports of a ship with dark sails stalking their borders had become frequent. King Leonidas's ship.

Celeste didn't know much about the human king and his son, but she did know they were dangerous. Her eyes widened. The prince. *Raiden Sharp.* His name sang through her. But the human she had seen couldn't have been the son of the bloodthirsty King Leonidas.

No wonder her father was here to deliver the news. The majority of the time, Chorus members simply patrolled the waters for threats. Encounters with a human ship were rare and unheard of so close to Staria. Celeste wished her father had mentioned any of this at breakfast.

"I will let your madam explain further." King Tidus nodded to Auralia, and a small blush appeared on the siren's face as she bowed.

"I expect nothing but perfection from this team. Thank you for protecting the kingdom, and may the Goddess protect and keep you." His speech finished, Tidus turned fully to Madam Auralia and bowed his head. "Thank you for your work, Madam. Good tides." With that, he left the room as quickly as he had entered.

The restrained atmosphere of the room shattered into excited murmurs and gossip.

"Initiates!" Madam Auralia's sharp tone cut through the noise, silencing the group. "You understand the importance of this mission. Every Chorus member has been called to join the Song. We need every siren we have to ensure this opportunity is not wasted. You all will be paired with a current member of the Chorus, who will be your guide. Missions like this are rare; we have time to mount an attack, and it's important for you to get this experience. It will be dangerous, but it is the prince and not the king himself, and I think you're ready. Don't disappoint me."

"Yes, Madam," they responded in unison.

Madam Auralia took a moment to scan the initiates, her sharp yellow eyes pinning each one. "The Song is a gift. Tonight you join the Chorus for the first time. The safety of Staria rests upon your shoulders. Remember what you're doing this for."

CHAPTER 4

"I can't believe we're going to the surface today!" Maeve pulled her spear from her back. "At last we get to see action, you know?"

After Madam Auralia dismissed them to their combat training early, no one had been able to stop talking about the mission.

"I know." Celeste looked at her own spear, passing it from one hand to the other. "I'm surprised they're inviting us at all. They must be certain nothing will happen, right?"

They swam together to an open section of the courtyard to begin their warm-up. Although they'd done this countless times, everything suddenly felt new again.

"I thought you'd be more excited," Maeve said, brows knitting. "You love going beyond Staria's walls. What's wrong? Are you worried?"

"No! No, I am excited. What's there to worry about?" Celeste pushed memories of Raiden Sharp's ink-black hair from her mind as she readied her spear. "Especially when you'll be there, *best in class*."

"Right!" Maeve grinned, lowering into fighting position. "They will sing songs of us for generations! The day the human prince was lured to his doom by the Chorus and their *princess*."

Celeste had no time to react, for suddenly Maeve's spear was flying at her head. She shifted, knocking the weapon away with her own.

Then she pulled her spear to her body before lunging at Maeve. Her friend ducked out of the way, but barely.

"Distracting me with flattery will not work," Celeste snarled in jest.

Maeve laughed, and they began again, running through their usual routine until their chests rose and fell from the effort. While Celeste had never been very confident with her Song, her skill with the spear was the one place in which she shone.

"Initiates, in line," Captain Io interrupted.

At once the sirens stopped, swimming into line before their instructor, a large siren with cropped green hair. Io wore a bright smile as they gazed upon the initiates before them. Behind them, five sirens entered the courtyard, each dressed in armor with spears strapped to their backs. Although Celeste had never met them, she'd recognize them anywhere. Members of the Chorus.

"General Xandra, these are our current initiates. Initiates, I would like to introduce you all to General Xandra and our team," Captain Io said proudly. "This specific team is tasked with missions involving errant ships."

The general swam forward, radiating dominance. Even Captain Io looked small in comparison to her large blue frame and roping muscles. General Xandra's black eyes scanned each initiate, pausing for a moment when she reached Celeste. The princess lowered her gaze, and soon the general moved on.

"Good tides, recruits," Xandra said, her tone deep and gravely. "While we still do not know why this ship entered our lands, it is our job to stop them before they can pose a threat. No survivors."

The feeling of Maeve's gaze on her made Celeste aware that she was picking at her scales. She dropped her hands to her sides, embarrassed. She'd expected to feel excited. Proud. After four cycles of training, it was hard to believe her chance to prove herself was here at last. But all she felt was tense.

"We will swim in pairs," the general continued, swimming up to the first of the initiates. "Your name, Recruit?"

"Nautica," the siren answered, bowing their head in respect.

"You will be with Officer Zale." She gestured to a siren with skin striped in orange and cerulean. Zale bowed his head in response, and Nautica fell in line beside him. "Your name?" Xandra asked the next initiate, who turned a brilliant shade of red.

"Analora," she said, twisting her soft purple hair tightly around her fingers. Analora was paired with Officer Wrasse, a very slender siren with sharp features and pale blue skin. And Leif was paired with Captain Io, their regular drill instructor. When Leif swam up to join Io, the instructor clapped him on the back so hard it made Leif cough. Celeste and Maeve covered their mouths, stifling laughter.

"Your name, Recruit?"

Under General Xandra's hard gaze, the cecaelia dropped her hand as though it'd bitten her. "Maeve, General."

"You'll be paired with Officer Rae." Xandra nodded to a silvery siren. Celeste's eyes widened. She'd heard stories of Rae. Of how she'd led the rescue of two sirens from a human fishing boat after they'd been caught in a net. After they were safe, Rae drowned the entire crew in a matter of minutes. A living legend.

"And last, Princess Celeste," the general said, not needing to ask her name and not pretending otherwise. "You will be paired with General Echo."

Celeste nodded, trying not to let the surprise show on her face. *General?* Echo was beautiful, as all sirens were, but she'd stand out in any group. Her skin was a soft peach, like Celeste's, but she was covered from head to fin in red and white stripes. Spiky fins protruded from her hips, fanning around her like a lionfish. She appraised Celeste, her bloodred hair billowing around her heart-shaped face. Beyond her beauty there was an intensity that made Celeste recoil. Why would someone so highly ranked be on this mission? Each squad only required one general to lead. Was it the mission? Or was it *her*? Did Madam Auralia think Celeste needed someone to watch over her? Or . . . did the queen have something to do with this? Celeste's stomach twisted.

"If there are no questions," General Xandra said with a look that didn't invite questions, "then let us move on to the subject of your final examination."

This was it. The final thing that stood between Celeste and her future.

"This evening you will be judged on four metrics: how you follow instruction; how you blend within the group; your knowledge of procedure; and, of course, your Song. In every mission, a siren must have each of these qualities to be an asset to their unit. As you know, each Chorus unit is made up of five members. And tonight all five units will be in attendance.

"It is of the utmost importance that you can work together as a team. The Chorus is a blend of many. An unbreakable force. Pay attention to those around you. Fill in gaps. Keep your formations tight, and above all else, listen to your superior." General Xandra scanned each initiate. "You have already been tested in your strength, agility, speed, endurance, and knowledge of human language, geography, ship structure, and weaponry."

Several heads nodded in agreement.

"Tonight is your chance to prove you deserve to be a member of this team. So take a good look at your assigned Chorus member"—she gestured toward them—"for they will be the ones examining you this evening. It will be their decision whether you succeed or fail."

Celeste glanced toward Echo, whose expression was unreadable. Stoic.

"Now," Xandra said, clapping her deep blue hands together, "I'll pass things to Captain Io, who will be running our drills in preparation for this evening."

"Thank you," Io said, bobbing up to the front beside the general. "Let's begin by breaking into pairs—a Chorus's harmony is more than just vocal." They winked.

Numbly, Celeste followed Echo to a space in the courtyard. It was happening. She had her chance to join the Chorus, permanently. *So why did she feel sick?* She looked over toward Maeve in hopes of sharing the feeling but saw her friend was already deep in conversation with her new mentor, Rae. The cecaelia's eyes glimmered with excitement as the officer gave her pointers about her spear grip.

Celeste turned to Echo. "It's an honor to have you as my mentor," she said, head dipping.

The siren looked her over and nodded graciously. "The honor is mine, Princess."

"Do you—" Celeste paused, trying to pick which question to ask first. She had so many. But she knew she couldn't ask anything about the humans. Even if it was the one subject she wished to speak about the most. "Is there anything I need to keep in mind as I prepare for this mission? Something you wish you'd known as an initiate?"

"As long as you listen to General Xandra and follow her command, you will be fine, Princess," Echo assured her. "There is no need to worry yourself."

Celeste frowned. Although the words gave the impression Echo was confident in Celeste's abilities, something about it felt off. Echo made no further effort to converse, and Celeste stifled her questions. It was clear she did not intend to answer them.

In the awkward silence, Celeste overheard Leif and Io arguing about strategy behind them, smiles on their faces.

"Why wait and attack at night? Wouldn't it be better to strike as soon as possible?" the young initiate asked.

Io shook their head. "Daylight offers little protection. The element of surprise is paramount, and it's better for the Chorus to be in position and focused before any humans raise the alarm. Not to mention it's easier for humans to see and use their weapons during the day."

"Right, of course," Leif replied, nodding. "I hadn't thought about how the dark might protect against their cannons and guns."

A sigh escaped Celeste's lips. It seemed all the others were gaining useful knowledge from their mentors. And despite having the highest-ranking member assigned to her, Celeste gained nothing more than assurance that she should listen to her superior. A fact she already knew.

"All right," Io called after a moment, "I hope you all feel a little more comfortable around your new companions. Let's fall into line and practice our formations. This will feel different, especially with a larger group. The key is to think as a group. Don't leave any gaps."

The sirens swam into position, Celeste and Echo falling into line at the end.

"Ray!" Io bellowed, making the accompanying hand signal.

As quick as a sudden storm, the group arranged into a perfect diamond.

"School!"

On and on, Captain Io tested them on each and every formation, reminding the initiates which ones would be used on their mission that night. It was strange to adjust to the senior members, who responded so quickly Celeste had to focus to keep up. Each movement was completed wordlessly.

"The Chorus must move as one mind," Io shouted. "More often than not, you won't use your spears. The Song is your true weapon."

Staria had a large military, but the most elite and specialized of those formed the Chorus. As children, sirens were schooled by their family members. Only at the age of seven did they begin a more formal education. Celeste and Maeve, like most children of prominent families, were taught in a private school on the palace grounds. When a siren reached the age of thirteen cycles, they underwent a series of tests to help align them with a job or role within the kingdom. It was tradition and ensured that each siren had a place in society. A way to contribute.

After testing, young sirens were given two or three options for their role in Staria from which they could choose. Celeste, however, was not tested. Royal children within the House of Neris did not have the option to become such things as a teacher, a storyteller, or a craftsiren. At birth, Celeste's future was decided for her: to be a figurehead and perform royal duties. A role that didn't suit her at all. Celeste always talked too much during social appearances, making speeches that were entirely too long or went off topic. But when she didn't speak, she found it difficult to sit still. To focus on what was happening. So many times the queen suggested she stay at the palace. Focus on her studies.

"A princess's first priority is to her people," Queen Halia had told Celeste on her thirteenth birthday, when she'd cried and begged to be given a test like Maeve. "Our role is to protect the kingdom."

Which had given her an idea. For it was true, her family had a long tradition of fighting to protect their people. Why, even Queen Isla herself was known for her strength. So when Celeste asked if she could join the Chorus, to fight for her people as Queen Isla had, her parents agreed. Having a member of the royal family join the military had happened before, and having one in the most esteemed division looked good. For the Chorus protected the kingdom from humans. They were heroes. And it didn't hurt that her best friend, Maeve, had planned to join as well.

They'd done everything else together, after all.

After finishing the final test, Captain Io dismissed the ragged initiates. Maeve and Celeste fell into rhythm, swimming together toward the atrium. A nagging feeling tugged at Celeste's heart. She felt guilty lying to her friend about why she'd been late. She wished more than anything to tell Maeve about the ship she had seen. The human prince. Their music. Celeste didn't have many friends. It was only ever her, Maeve, and Sephone. Halia preferred to keep her daughter's group small. But now with Sephone gone, Maeve was the only one Celeste could talk to, the only one she might tell.

And it had been a while since the two had time together. Maeve was busy with her new girlfriend, and Celeste—well, she was practicing. Or with her family. Or sneaking out to get some air. She missed the times when the two had been inseparable. When they would stay up late together trying to catch seahorses with their hands or swapping stories of the human world they had overheard.

But now they were soldiers.

Celeste looked at her friend, lips pressed closed. What would Maeve say if she told her about the prince? Would she be curious? Angry? Did she ever have doubts about the humans too? Time was running out to ask.

"Care to float around a bit?" Celeste said, bumping her shoulder into her friend.

Maeve's face fell. "I have plans with Serafina."

Serafina. *That* was her name. *Not an L name, then.* Serafina, the weaponsmith's apprentice. They must have been seeing each other for quite some time now.

"Oh! Oh, of course," Celeste said, then added in a singsong tone, "*sounds serious.*"

Maeve whacked Celeste on the shoulder. "Don't say it like that!"

"Are you in *loooove*?" Celeste teased, batting her eyelashes. But instead of laughing, Maeve froze. As she averted her eyes, bright blue rings appeared all over the cecaelia's body. Celeste let out a gasp. "Wait—are you?"

"I—let's talk later, all right? Maybe tomorrow! After the mission," Maeve stammered as they continued out of the building, catching sight of Serafina.

"All right," Celeste said, shoulders sagging a little.

She watched as the two of them swam off, Maeve sharing the news of their new mission. Celeste's heart squeezed a little in her chest at the sight. If Maeve was in love, why hadn't she told her? Celeste hadn't expected that anything serious was going on. Maeve was always dating someone, after all. She flitted between love interests so regularly it was hard for Celeste to keep track. Celeste never thought Maeve would be the one to settle down. Many sirens never partnered. But this—she'd never seen Maeve react that way before.

Celeste wasn't a stranger to romance. She was merely a stranger to it being reciprocated. When she was seven, her first love was a siren boy whose family worked in the palace. She saw him almost every day and fell madly in love with him. It took her three cycles to confess her feelings. But when she did, he admitted he loved her older sister, Sephone. The little blowfish then proceeded to tell the tale to every siren their age, boasting about how he turned her down. Celeste had cried herself to sleep for a week.

None of her other dalliances had fared much better, and now, at the age of seventeen, Celeste had all but resigned herself to a partnerless life. Not that seventeen was all that old for a siren. In many ways, she was still a child, given how long sirens lived. Although they aged similarly to humans, their magic made their life cycles nearly twice a human's. *Once I'm a full member, I'm sure I'll have time to make plenty of other friends in the Chorus*, she told herself, the pang of loneliness creeping under her skin. *I will have no time to worry about romance.*

Along the journey home, Celeste's mind turned over all that she had seen. The humans had been nothing like she'd imagined. They laughed. Took care of animals. Made jokes. They even had music like sirens. Were they hiding their murderous tendencies? Was there something she hadn't seen? Everything she'd wanted was falling into place. But it all felt wrong. As childish as it sounded, Celeste had always pictured being a member of the Chorus like a heroic ballad. Epic battles against bloodthirsty monsters with nothing but her Song and spear. Protecting the innocent and punishing the evil. But evil didn't look the way she had imagined.

She couldn't recall any mention of Raiden before. Only his father, King Leonidas. And Celeste knew that a parent's decisions often had little to do with their children. Still, if the Chorus decided to take these measures, then he must be a threat. And hadn't she known firsthand what horrors humans could do? In the past fourteen cycles, since King Leonidas had become a threat, a few sirens had been captured. Killed. It wasn't common, but that was because of the Chorus. Missions like the one tonight kept them safe.

But weren't they passing judgment before any wrong was committed? What if the Chorus killed innocents too? *Were* there any innocent humans?

Celeste's stomach turned as she sped toward home. These thoughts felt like treason. And what did this say about her? She had trained so hard to be a member, and on the first mission she got cold fins? Yet somehow she couldn't erase the vision of the prince. His dark hair and smile as he kicked up his feet and danced. The tenderness he showed to that small animal.

Nerves. That's all it was. *I'll feel differently tonight*, she assured herself as she swam into the halls of the palace. Training and lack of sleep had made her tired. A good nap would help restore her jumbled thoughts. Celeste passed the familiar tapestry of the Goddess's daughters. Queen Isla the Protector, first of House Neris and founder of Staria, floated at the center. Around her, her three sisters gathered. Queen Suna the Wise, who founded the Kingdom of Ayakashi, stared straight at the viewer, wearing nothing but a large pearl necklace. Queen Klara the Strong, of Skalvaske, wore a crown of stars. And seated along the sand floor was the fourth daughter, Lyra the Beautiful. In her hands, Lyra held the Goddess's legendary three-pronged trident.

Celeste was still gazing at the intricate plant-woven tapestry when her shoulder collided with another.

"Apologies," Celeste said, righting herself in the water before recognizing her eldest sister, Shye, before her. "Good tides!" she added, rubbing the back of her neck.

Shye, the perfect image of their mother, wore an annoyed expression. The red hair of House Neris was cropped short on her head, hanging into piercing silver eyes. "Good tides, Celeste," she said simply, tucking her harp beneath her arm before continuing in the opposite direction. It wasn't a surprising reaction from Shye. The sisters were fifteen cycles apart. Although they grew up together in the castle, there had always been a great divide.

"Coming from lessons?" Celeste asked, following. "Where are you headed?" She was rather thankful for the distraction. It was rare to see Shye in the halls, given she was almost always with Halia, studying to become the next great queen of Staria.

"Yes. And I am on my way to Mother's quarters," Shye answered, then glanced sideways at her sister. "I presume you have heard about the Chorus's mission this evening."

"I have," Celeste responded, lifting her chin. "In fact, my class is going as well."

A flicker of surprise crossed Shye's face for a moment, before it fell back into her mask of calm. "You know, Celeste," she said, as if she were picking each word carefully, "you must listen to whatever the senior members tell you. This is a very serious and important mission."

Celeste stiffened. It was the same advice Echo had given her. "Of course, Shye. I have been training for this for the last four cycles. I know what to do."

Shye sighed. "I know you have, little star. I'm giving you some sisterly advice."

Face burning, Celeste crossed her arms over her chest. However well-intentioned, the comment stung. *Why does everyone keep telling me that?* She was seventeen! But no matter how hard she trained and worked, she still somehow couldn't escape being a silly little girl in their eyes. *I'm probably just being sensitive*, she told herself, pushing away her feelings.

"I understand," she replied instead.

Shye gave her sister a smile and then continued on her way, leaving Celeste floating listlessly behind. For most of her life, Celeste had enjoyed being the youngest daughter. There was very little responsibility, and her parents gave her everything she ever wanted, so long as she stayed in line. But somewhere along the way, Celeste had begun to realize that no one expected anything from her. Which also meant no one trusted her with anything.

She turned back toward her rooms, attempting to calm herself and failing. Whenever she felt like this, the only thing that always soothed her was going to the surface. But since that was out of the question at present, Celeste decided the next best thing would be finding some peace among her collection of treasures.

CHAPTER 5

Lying upon the warm, sandy floor of her bedroom, Celeste stared blankly above. She did not see the glorious iridescent shells that were intricately hand-placed across the vaulted ceiling. Her mind was leagues away, on the surface watching the human prince laugh. She replayed it in her mind, every detail burned into her memory. His dark hair falling over his forehead. His high cheekbones and his dark round eyes. His smile. Without noticing, she hummed, and it was the song he'd sung.

The water around her drifted. She felt someone coming.

"Celeste!" a voice echoed up the spiraling path that led to the princess's rooms.

The siren bolted upright. "In here, Mother!" she called, perhaps too brightly. Firmly Celeste put aside whatever confusing feelings she had and focused on the mission. It was her first real assignment with the Chorus, and she couldn't wait to tell someone about it.

The queen swept into the room, the shells across her back tinkling like little bells. "I wished to see you before you left with the Chorus," she said with a smile, coming to rest on a stone chair next to her daughter.

"It was certainly a surprise that the test was moved to today. But I feel ready," Celeste said, placing her hands in her lap.

The queen smiled. "Good. General Echo came by not too long ago and told me you were to be paired with her."

Celeste's stomach clenched. Why was General Echo reporting to her mother about her? Wouldn't Xandra be the one to give the official report? It was her mission, not Echo's.

Halia's eyes roamed over her daughter, stopping at the top of her head. "Your hair is a mess. You should comb it, little star," she tsked.

Celeste's hand jumped to the spot her mother looked at. She tried to straighten the tangled knots with her fingers, but the action felt pointless in the water.

"Are you nervous?" the queen asked, getting up and moving toward the mother-of-pearl comb on the shelf.

"I—" Celeste began, hand dropping from her hair. She wanted so desperately to ask her mother about the prince, but she was certain it was a bad idea. "No."

The queen glided back to her daughter's side, eyes unreadable. With a gentle touch, she placed her hand on Celeste's chin, turning her daughter's face away. Then she carefully ran the comb through the tangles, each stroke smooth and soft. The touch was soothing. Calming. It reminded her that she wasn't speaking only to the queen of Staria. She was speaking to her mother. The siren who raised her.

"Did you know humans sang songs?" Celeste hedged.

The comb paused, then continued.

"Their songs aren't like ours."

"Right! I know," Celeste agreed, heart hammering. Why did she say that? What if her mother asked how she knew about the human songs? But the queen said nothing, only finished brushing and set the comb down. "Are—are all humans bad?" Celeste turned to face her mother, knowing full well she was swimming in dangerous waters. But she couldn't stop herself.

The water around her felt as though it had dropped several degrees.

"They would kill you as soon as they laid eyes on you. You know this," the queen said, her brow knit in confusion.

"I know, but—" Celeste's words died in her throat. She wanted to ask about the animal. About the dancing. To ask why sirens hated these creatures who made the things sirens pillaged. Surely there was more to them than violence. But she couldn't say any of what she'd seen without revealing that she had been to the surface that morning. Instead, she said, "What if they're not all dangerous?"

The queen looked as though Celeste had slapped her.

But Celeste pushed on. It was as if her thoughts were water, rushing out at once. "I'm sure you have good reasons for not trusting them... but couldn't there be some humans who are good too? Just because their king is a monster doesn't mean his son—"

"That's enough, Celeste."

"But, Mother—"

"Humans are dangerous and violent, even to their own."

"I know," Celeste said, knots forming in her stomach.

The queen shook her head, hurt plain on her face. "Then how can you say such things? Just because you discovered they have songs you think they're civilized?"

Tears pricked at Celeste's eyes. "I don't know—"

"You don't." The queen sighed, rubbing her temples with her long fingers. "You don't know anything about them."

This landed like a blow. "That's why I'm asking you!" she said. "I only want to understand, Mother. You haven't told me anything about them. Everything I know has come from gossip or through training. I know their language and their ships and their geography. We even collect their *things*! I just—" Celeste stopped at the look on her mother's face, angry enough to boil water.

"That's enough," the queen said, straightening.

"Please, Mother. I just want to talk about this." But as the words left her mouth, her voice began to waver. Then the tears grew in her eyes, until they released, unbidden, mixing with the water around her and disappearing as quickly as they formed.

"Calm down," the queen said. "Crying about it is not going to help."

Celeste wiped at her eyes, embarrassment white-hot in her chest. It only made things worse. The tears did not listen.

"Don't act like this," the queen said, "like *one of them*."

The words sucked the air from her lungs. Sirens considered humans irrational creatures, led by their emotions and incapable of reason or control. Celeste gasped, the tears falling faster. *Stop crying*, Celeste begged her tears, but they ignored her silent pleas. The feelings inside her felt too big, too confusing. *This is foolish. Why am I crying over this? Why can't we just talk? How did this go so wrong?*

But this was not the first time. Celeste had always been emotional, unlike her family. She'd never seen her mother or father cry. Shye hadn't cried since their grandmother died, and Sephone... Sephone only cried when no one was looking. But it seemed as though Celeste cried all the time. She couldn't control it. And even having someone present wasn't a deterrent. Despite her and her mother's wishes, the Chorus hadn't trained it out of her. She wished she could handle her emotions like other sirens. She wished she didn't cry when she was angry or sad or frustrated. But she did. She always did. And she hated herself for it.

The queen took a deep breath and reached for Celeste's hand. "I don't think being a member of the Chorus is the right fit," she said. "I fear this is too much pressure for you."

It was as though Celeste had been doused in the icy waters of Skalvaske. "What?"

Her mother rose, moving toward the door. "I know you went to the surface today. The guard told me," she said, voice low. Celeste looked down at her fin, embarrassed. "You're not ready. I hoped you could learn from General Echo, but—I don't think you should be making any more trips to the surface anytime soon. Clearly, they're leaving a bad impression on you."

With those words, the queen swam from the room.

"No!" Celeste shouted after her through her tears. "Mother, wait!"

No answer.

In frustration, Celeste slammed her fist into the floor, sending bits of sand swirling into the water. Then she crumpled, tears blurring her vision. It poured from her. All the confusion about the humans, the prince. All the anger at her sister, at her mother, at the Chorus for assigning her a babysitter, at Maeve, who was always too busy. But most of all, at herself. For thinking for one second things would be different. That her mother might understand. Or at least talk to her about it. She should have never spoken of these things. She knew better. And now she had no future.

What was she if she were not a member of the Chorus?

What would she do?

Nothing. The answer hit her all at once. *She'd do nothing.*

It took time for the sobs to slow, the tears to lessen, her vision to clear. She looked around the room, gazing at the things she'd collected over the cycles. Colorful glass bottles. Shiny human coins. Sparkling jewels. Silver combs upon a shelf. Celeste pushed herself from the floor and picked up an object she'd found on a ship that had sunk after a siren raid. She moved her fingers over the smooth golden surface before pressing a little knob at the top. It sprang open, revealing a glass-covered face with two arrows, one long and one short, connected in the center but pointing outward. The arrows didn't move on their own, but if she turned the knob, they spun around. She wished for the hundredth time that she knew what it was.

It was on one of her rare trips out to sea that she had found the object. For her eleventh birthday, her parents gave Maeve, Sephone, and Celeste permission to leave the castle grounds after significant begging. Sephone had been sixteen, so it was her responsibility to keep an eye on Maeve and Celeste. Other sirens their age were allowed to leave home unchaperoned. But, of course, their mother had sent along a royal guard, Helena. She was fun to be around, so it didn't bother the girls. The summer waters were warmer than usual, if you swam high enough. Maeve and Celeste took turns daring each other to swim up a little toward the surface, each one trying to get closer than the other. They didn't make it far before Helena suggested another game.

When they came upon the shipwreck, Celeste squealed with joy. The ship was lying on its side like a carcass of a great whale. The wreck was recent, so there wasn't much growing on the ship yet, but already fish and other small creatures had made the husk their home. Shrieking battle cries, Maeve and Celeste raced each other to the vessel. Shipwrecks happened every so often, but Celeste had never scavenged a ship before. The little princess reached the ship first but hesitated before entering. What dangers lurked inside? Whatever had happened to the ship, it had been violent. Large pieces of the walls were missing or damaged. Had the Chorus done that?

"You look like you've seen the Sea Witch," Sephone teased.

"No," Celeste said, swatting at her sister. "I'm not afraid." And with a deep breath, Celeste plunged inside. No door was left unopened. No secret undiscovered. She didn't even take much; she only wanted to see it all. Thick rope too heavy to move. A collection of tiny blunt knives; little tridents; and small, shallow bowls attached to some handles. Waterlogged books. At the time she hadn't known what they were. Their warped covers and delicate pages looked like clams. Sirens didn't have a common written language. But the Chorus later taught her of books, and how humans used words to keep their stories instead of Songs.

In the ship, Celeste felt like an investigator, collecting clues about human life. And in a back room, she saw something shining on the floor. The golden object. Solid and smooth in her hands. And when Sephone entered the room, Celeste tucked the item away into her satchel so her sister wouldn't fight her for it.

Sephone and Celeste had been close for a time, despite their age difference. But as those final two cycles went on before Sephone left, her sister's fascination with shipwrecks and stories faded. Interests the sisters once shared. Instead, Sephone began taking lessons from tutors. So many that Celeste hardly saw her. When she asked, their mother told her that Sephone was preparing to become a wife to someone from another kingdom. The king and queen said it was Sephone's choice. She did not have to marry a foreign siren royal if she did not wish. But Sephone accepted the role with grace. And when the day came for her to visit the other siren kingdoms, she left.

It had been five cycles since Sephone had gone, but somehow Celeste still felt her absence everywhere. Her mother tried to spend time with Celeste when she could, but she was so busy being queen that even with her father's aid it was too much work. And they wouldn't let Celeste go visit Sephone.

"We cannot use such immense resources for a simple visit, little star."

The oceans were just too vast. Too dangerous. It was rare for sirens to journey through the Wasting Waters between the kingdoms, where most didn't survive for long, though it was said the Sea Witch lived there, deep in a cave.

The ice kingdom of Skalvaske lay to the north, founded by Queen Klara, the third daughter of the Goddess. There sirens grew to be the size of whales, though it was the smallest siren kingdom in population.

Celeste had only met one siren from another kingdom. A diplomat from Ayakashi, in the east. Founded by the second daughter, Queen Suna, it was the second-largest kingdom to Staria and home to the most renowned storytellers. Sirens would risk swimming the ocean just to hear their tales. But the encounter with the diplomat was short, and Celeste was not allowed to ask them questions. She was left with only her lessons to give her the answers she sought.

Pulling herself from her memories, Celeste placed the golden object back on her shelf. The overwhelming tide of feelings had ebbed, but she could not shake her sadness. Soon it would be time to leave for the mission.

A mission she could not miss.

Setting her jaw, Celeste took up her spear from its place against the wall. A gift from her father on the day she joined the Chorus's initiates. She remembered wanting to hug him after seeing it. It was the most beautiful spear she'd ever seen. The shaft was wrapped in stingray leather, and around the top near the wings—the part of the spear that protruded from the sides like a cross guard—black pearls were inlaid. Celeste placed the spear reverently upon her lap and began to sharpen it. With each rhythmic scrape, she felt herself sink into her routine. She could do this. She was ready. She had worked too hard for too long to give everything up now. After tonight she would be a full-fledged member of the Chorus, and her mother wouldn't be able to keep her locked up in the palace any longer.

Rising from her chair, she secured the weapon to her back. She smoothed her hair with her hands, weaving it into a long white braid and securing it with a bit of fish leather. Then, with a steadying breath, she exited her room and made her way down toward the main hall.

"Where do you think you are going?" The queen's voice halted her. She stared at her daughter, eyes wide with shock. Around her, two members of the council exchanged glances.

"I am leaving for my mission so I will arrive early," Celeste said, respectfully nodding toward each council member, one of whom—the head of the council—was Maeve's mother.

The queen left her company, barreling down upon her daughter. "No, you are most certainly not. You are forbidden from going to the surface." She kept her voice low, tossing a glance toward the council members behind her.

"I am an initiate of the Chorus," Celeste said, lifting her chin and refusing to lower her voice. "I am required to go. My absence from this mission will result in my removal."

"Perhaps that is for the best," her mother said quietly, moving into her daughter's path.

Celeste's eyes pricked with tears, the careful calm she had cultivated shattering like thin ice. "I am not a child, Mother!" she exclaimed. "You cannot order me around like—"

"Then stop acting like a child," the queen retorted, all effort to hide the dispute gone. The words struck hard. "How am I to trust you when you come home spouting nonsense! It is too dangerous. If you fail to control yourself, you could hurt someone."

Celeste squeezed her eyes shut. "I won't—"

"Forgive me," the queen said, cutting off her daughter as she turned to the council members behind her. "I must speak with my daughter. I will rejoin you in the pearl room."

They nodded, bowing low before excusing themselves. But Celeste did not miss how they whispered to each other as they went. And neither, apparently, did the queen.

"Celeste, you are not going on the mission, and that is final," Halia said.

Tears blurred Celeste's vision as they mixed with the water around her. "You don't want me to try, because you're afraid I'll fail. That I'll embarrass you." She threw the word *embarrass* like a curse. As if it was the worst thing in the world.

"No," her mother said. "I don't want you to try because you might hurt someone else."

The words hurt more than Celeste thought they would.

"I can control it now," the princess pleaded. "I know I can. Please just trust me."

"My answer is no, Celeste. I'm sorry."

The words resounded with utter finality. Celeste should have known. Known her mother wouldn't understand. Known to keep her mouth shut. It was clear to her that Halia would never have let her join the Chorus. Not really. Perhaps she'd never believed her daughter would get this far. If it hadn't been this, it would have been something else.

Celeste sank to the stone floor beneath her, the spear on her back clattering as it hit. Four cycles... four cycles undone. She had only wished to talk. To tell someone—anyone—about her doubts instead of holding it all inside. Shame and anger rolled down her in waves, crashing over and over.

She had nothing now.

"Why don't you calm down in your room," her mother said, reaching for her daughter's hand in sympathy.

Celeste flinched away and pushed herself off the floor. When she looked into her mother's face, there was no surprise there. Only pity. It was as if she had been waiting for this moment to come. Celeste looked away, not wanting to see it any longer. Without another word, she swam down the hall toward her room. Her mother did not stop her or offer comfort. Instead, the queen watched as the space between them grew. Then Celeste turned the corner and left her mother alone in silence.

Sephone had always been the better daughter. She never asked questions or spoke out of turn. Sephone did as she was told. And Shye was like their father. Hardheaded, straightforward, and ambitious. But strong. So strong. Doing everything by the book.

Celeste was the foolish one. The curious one. Too silly. Too loud. Too emotional. Once, when she was six, she swung her arms around when she was telling a story at dinner and knocked her mother's favorite crown from her head. It fell, and one delicate piece of coral snapped from it. Her mother hadn't reprimanded her. She hadn't needed to. The crown had been in the royal family for generations, and in one sweeping gesture, Celeste had ruined it.

She was tired of ruining things.

She was tired of everyone treating her as if she were some problem to solve.

Without the Chorus, she would be destined to rot away in the palace alone or be wed off to some foreign prince, like Sephone. Her life would never be her own. So when Celeste reached the end of the hall, she did not turn to swim up the circling tower to her rooms. Instead, she swam straight through the side exit and into the night.

CHAPTER 6

The belly of the human ship cut through the dark waters, its lanterns casting a faint glow around the vessel. Beneath the surface, a small army of sirens in perfect formation awaited, dressed in battle armor with sharpened spears strapped to their backs. Celeste floated among them, her heart pounding in anticipation. She kept her mind focused on her mission, ignoring any thoughts of doubt that tried to slip in through the cracks.

"Initiates, stay with your assigned officer and do not engage with any humans," General Xandra said. "Officers Zale, Wrasse, and Captain Io will use water to extinguish their lanterns. If they cannot see us, they cannot use their weapons effectively against us. Then we shall begin the Song. Our main target is the prince, but we shall leave no survivors."

Celeste tried to ignore the churning in her stomach that started at the mention of the prince. *It is not your job to question. It is your job to serve,* Celeste reminded herself as the general finished explaining the details of the mission. They were to spread out along the starboard side, remaining close enough to help each other but far enough to keep out of each other's way. Celeste had studied ships with the Chorus for the last several cycles. *Port is proven left, and starboard is surely right, so long as you are facing the fight*, she recited in her head the little song she had created to remember the difference between the two.

"Initiates, if I give this signal"—the general raised her arm so that it was bent at an angle and her hand was level with her head—"you are to join the Song and sing with us. Understood?" Her piercing purple eyes scanned the group, making eye contact with each initiate until she landed on Celeste.

"Yes, General," they responded in unison.

"Good," the general said with a smile. "May the Goddess look upon us with favor and guide our Song this night."

It was time. Celeste twisted around to catch Maeve's eye, but her friend was already turning away with her officer, falling into line. *You can do this*, she reminded herself, but inside she was nervous. Everything was happening so quickly. It felt as though she had blinked, and she was here. She should have felt excited. She should have felt proud. But instead she felt sick. Her mother's words continued to ring in her ears. *You're too emotional. If you can't control yourself, you could hurt someone.* She had never disobeyed a direct order from the queen before. Everything about tonight felt wrong.

But this was her chance to make things right. To prove she was capable. Celeste let her body go through the motions, following behind General Echo as they ascended. When they were just below the ocean's surface, the sirens stopped.

"Ray," Xandra called. And like a school of fish, the sirens moved into formation. The senior members of the Chorus floated beside their initiates, watching their every move. Judging how well they took command. Celeste straightened beneath Echo's gaze, keeping her eyes focused on Xandra. Waiting for their next command.

With a gesture from the general, Zale, Wrasse, and Io shot toward the surface, breaching so smoothly they didn't make a sound. Celeste watched with awe. The first lantern flickered out. Then another. When the final light winked out, and the ship was plunged into darkness, General Xandra let loose a single note.

A call.

And the Song began.

Together the sirens cut through the water, smooth as silk. Celeste did not have a moment to think as the surface drew closer and closer. As one, they emerged. At first Celeste saw nothing but white. It was startling, and confusing, until she recalled the name for this phenomenon. *Fog.* It surrounded them, thick and rolling. In the distance, a streak of light flashed. There, then gone. After several beats, a rumble sounded. Like tumbling rocks. The sound sent a shiver down Celeste's spine. Within the thick mist, the Chorus drifted like ghosts, letting their lungs and eyes adjust. After a moment, the outline of the black ship appeared. The gold of it looked dull in the darkness. Zale, Wrasse, and Io drifted into their positions. Ocean waves hissed against the side of the ship, mixing with the hushed voices of the few sailors who remained awake.

"They all went out! S'like magic," one said, fear coloring their voice.

"Just get 'em lit again," said another.

One of the humans stepped through the fog toward the nearest lamp. Then General Xandra began to sing.

From deep within the ocean, we sisters rise in song.

Her voice was low, rolling across the waters and echoing eerily back. Although Celeste had heard the Song sung countless times over the cycles, it had never sounded like this. The water always muffled the sound, distorted it. But in the crisp night air, the Song was clear and enchanting. The waves beneath them slowed, as if the sea itself calmed to hear her.

Above, the human stilled.

Come closer. Hear us calling. In our arms you belong.

The initiates listened silently as members of the Chorus joined their voices to hers, harmonizing as though the one voice had split into many. Xandra reached her long arms toward the human who stood along the banister, curling her fingers, beckoning.

"Sirens!" a shout called out from the ship.

"They're real!" another called, this one in a tone of awe.

"Help! Captain!" The voice cracked as it sounded the alarm. At once, the ship burst into noise. Feet pounded against wooden floors. They called out to each other, shouting orders and rousing sailors from sleep.

It would not matter.

Come rest your weary bones, love. Come join us in the sea.

The Song was a caress, a young lover calling out to their beloved. Along the bow of the ship, another sailor joined the first, moving slowly as though in a trance. Milky-white eyes looked blindly upon the water. Their lips curled into a lovesick smile.

Let the gentle waves consume you, for your heart belongs to me.

"Man the cannons!"

"Where do we aim? I can't see a damn thing!"

"It's coming from everywhere!"

Each man talked over the other. They needed to see to use their weapons. It made them weak. Sirens did not need such things.

I'll fulfill your every longing. I am everything you crave.

The Song drifted, circling the ship. It came from everywhere and nowhere, a cool touch on a fevered head. The notes glided, slithering toward the humans, around them, into them. It held them in its gentle embrace. It guided them. More humans joined the others at the railing, their sightless eyes gazing upon the sirens.

"They're on the starboard side!" a booming shout called.

The sound made Celeste's heart shudder. *The prince.* But despite his cry, the chaos on the ship was quieting as they sang. Sounds of movement slowed until Celeste could make out a unified tap of feet moving in rhythm to the Song.

Let me kiss away your sorrows as I lay you in your grave.

A human began to climb the railing. His feet were sure-footed as they planted themselves upon the banister, and as he pushed himself up to standing, it looked as though he had appeared from a cloud. His body was unnaturally still as he stood in the wind, looking out over the water with murky white eyes. Echo opened her arms wide to him, and like a child, he opened his in response. The Chorus grew louder.

"Bastian? *Bastian!*"

The shout was startling amid the song, like a rock thrown into a still pond. Celeste had been certain all the humans had fallen under its spell by now. To her left, Maeve's eyes widened, and Leif stole a glance sideways at Nautica. But the Chorus members remained unperturbed. The only sign they had noticed the disturbance was their growing volume. But Celeste could still hear one pair of offbeat footfalls against the wooden deck.

"Bastian, stop!"

Another bolt of lightning sang across the sky. Much closer than before. Light flashed across the ship. Celeste's stomach rolled as she gazed upon the lifeless face of the man who had danced and laughed with his prince not hours ago, the one he'd called "quartermaster." Others began to climb the railing as well. Their expressions all looked the same: soft and happy. But there was nothing alive behind their eyes.

Thunder rumbled as the mist parted, and the prince strode into view. His dark coat billowed behind him with each pounding step, looking like Death incarnate. But his face was not soft. It was tense.

Angry. Afraid. The prince was awake. Untouched by the Song. He reached the railing, and with one hand, he hauled the nearest crewmate backward. He reached for the next, throwing this one, too, to the ground. Celeste couldn't look away as he went through his crew one by one, working his way to the quartermaster.

This shouldn't be happening. Celeste had never heard of a human who could resist the pull of the Song before.

Take my hand and let me guide you as you listen to our song.

The Song swelled, but the prince remained unaffected. General Xandra stiffened. Then, to Celeste's surprise, she raised her arm, bending it into a right angle. *The signal.* Celeste's throat tightened. The initiates were being called into the Song. Around her, voices rose, entwining. Bastian's left foot slipped from the banister. With a shout, the prince made a break for the quartermaster. But beneath, Echo beckoned, achingly beautiful. And it was as if Celeste could see the siren's voice rolling up from the water and wrapping around Bastian's throat.

My sisters have been waiting, and in our arms you belong.

He dove.

"No!" cried the prince, his hands grasping at air as Bastian tipped over the ledge with a smile. The quartermaster fell headfirst, landing with a sickening splash. One by one, the other crew members climbed upon the railing, arms opening wide. Even the few the prince had pulled away were crawling back, white eyes unblinking. The sight of them made Celeste's stomach sour. She looked to Maeve, searching for a similar look of horror upon her friend's face, but instead she saw a warrior. Her gaze was cold as ice as her lips moved in sync with those around her.

We are doing what is necessary. It is for our protection, Celeste reminded herself as her eyes found the prince again. He was no longer trying to stop the tide of crew members, but instead stared down where Bastian had disappeared. Any resolve Celeste had crumbled when she caught the look on the prince's face. The horror and sorrow as he searched for any sign of life from his friend.

Finally, Bastian's body emerged from the ocean. His arms flailed not in distress but in desperation. As if he would die should he not reach his beloved Echo. The general beckoned to him again, long arms pale in the darkness. And he began to close the distance between them.

Bring me all your fears and sorrows. I will wash them all away.

Bastian moved like an animal, pure instinct. He paddled, arms smacking the water again and again. The gap between them lessened, until he was halfway between the boat and her arms.

Splash! Celeste looked toward the sound to find the prince breaking through the surface of the water. Her heart hammered. Why would the prince willingly dive into the ocean? He knew there were sirens in the water. Now he'd sacrificed his only advantage. Horror climbed up her throat, stealing the breath from her lungs as she watched him swim after his friend, each stroke clumsy to Celeste's eyes.

This wasn't the action of a monster.

Bastian frantically flapped through the water, and Celeste saw the turtle from that morning.

Does that make us the shark? She felt as though she might be sick.

Xandra dove forward, her powerful tail launching her at the prince. She could pull him under, Song or no.

The prince did not see her. His head was underwater as he swam forward. Toward Echo. Toward Celeste. The dark fabric of his jacket pulled at him, dragging him backward. Xandra gained. Above them, the storm approached, threatening rain. *He will die.* Celeste had known this, and yet facing it was quite another thing. *And I will watch him as he dies trying to save another.*

It was then that she noticed she was not singing. She had never started.

And I'll hold you in my arms, my dear, as you perish and decay.

Without thinking, Celeste plunged. There was nothing in her head. No thoughts or questions or doubts. There was only instinct, moving her toward Bastian. Beneath, she could see how his legs flailed without rhythm. The sirens around her did not move. They were a trained system. They did not act without orders, and with the general taking care of the prince, the one human who avoided their Song, there was no need to change tactics.

Within seconds, Celeste had reached Bastian. He was now only a couple of lengths away from Echo. Celeste grabbed at his ankle, hoping to pull him away without being seen. But he was stronger than she expected. His foot kicked at her and collided with her wrist, knocking her arm away. She grunted and reached again and again, until her hand at last grasped his ankle. But his unreasonable thrashing made it hard to keep hold of him, and once more her hand slipped.

There was no way she could save him like this, and she was wasting time. Time the prince didn't have. Pulling her spear from her back, she flipped the weapon around. *Sorry about this*, she thought as she jabbed the flat of the spear into his temple. At once, Bastian fell still. Returning her spear to her back, Celeste grabbed the human's ankle and began to drag his limp body along the surface. She was careful to keep his nose and mouth above water, for the Chorus had taught them that humans—like seals—needed to be on the surface to breathe. How strange that now she used this information not to drown one but to save him. The sight could have been funny—Bastian floating away from the sirens as Celeste towed him from beneath the dark waves. But although Celeste was trying her best to hide, the charade was clearly in sight of Echo and the others.

A commotion rose, the water distorting most of the sound. Celeste ignored it, searching for any sign of the prince. And when she found him, several lengths away from her, General Xandra had reached him.

"Celeste!" Celeste spun to see Maeve floating in the darkness behind her, confusion apparent on her face. "What are you doing?"

Celeste stared at her friend. If she did this, there would be no turning back. She looked toward the prince, resolution wavering. Xandra grasped his leg and dragged him down. He was fighting, but he was staring at *her*.

He saw her.

There was fear in his eyes as they flicked between her and Bastian's unconscious body floating above. The prince twisted, trying to break free, and she realized he did not have any weapons. He must have abandoned them on the ship before jumping. Bubbles escaped his lips as he fought to free himself from Xandra's grip. But she was too strong. And they were descending deeper and deeper into endless nothingness.

With utter certainty, Celeste knew that if she let these humans die, this moment would haunt her for the rest of her life.

"I'm sorry," Celeste whispered to Maeve, before she raced toward him.

CHAPTER 7

Lightning cracked, revealing the churning world below. Celeste towed Bastian along the surface with one hand, pulling her spear free with the other. When he was far enough away from the others, she released him. Then she dove straight for the general and the prince. Her spear spun around in a graceful arc, dull end connecting with Xandra's back. The general jerked, her grip on the prince releasing. Thunder cracked. And it was as if time slowed and held its breath. Her head turned, meeting the princess's eyes. Xandra froze, a spear tip at her throat. For the first time, Celeste saw surprise on the general's face.

"Princess, what are you doing?"

"Staria is peaceful," Celeste's voice cracked. "This is... slaughter."

"Get back in formation."

Behind the general, the prince kicked his legs, propelling him toward the surface. Toward Bastian.

"But... what have these humans done wrong?" Celeste kept her gaze on her general, afraid to alert her. "There must be another way to—"

"I am not arguing with a *fry* in the middle of the Song." Xandra's jaw tightened. "You knew what you signed up for."

It was true. She *had* known what she signed up for. She grew up knowing the Chorus drowned sailors. But these humans didn't match the descriptions she had heard in the stories. Humans were bloodthirsty, murderous, depraved, emotional creatures. These people looked as though they were merely in the wrong place at the wrong time. Maybe her mother was right. She wasn't cut out for this.

A body fell into the water. Then another. And another.

"I don't care who your mother is. Get back in line."

"No."

Humans rained down. Five, then ten, then fifteen. Until the water was churning with them. A mass of writhing limbs. They fell upon each other, kicking and clawing to reach the calling sirens. Celeste lowered her spear, moving to help them somehow.

She heard the weapon before she saw it. A faint whistling just behind her head. Celeste twisted and knocked Xandra's spear away. The general's nostrils flared, black eyes glinting. There was nothing of her leader in that gaze. Only rage. Celeste was now another threat to be eliminated. Regaining control of her spear, Xandra thrust toward Celeste's stomach. This time the princess was not quick enough. It struck against the leather of her armor, stealing the air from her lungs. Celeste doubled over, gasping.

She would not win a fight against Xandra. The general was nearly twice her size and had three times her training. She had to think of something. Quickly. But the blows kept coming. Celeste swept her spear over her head. Although she blocked the impact, pain shot down her arms.

"Look at them, Celeste," Xandra said, yellow eyes flashing as she pointed at the lovesick men above. "You would betray your people for these animals?"

That only reminded Celeste of—

Without warning, Celeste launched toward the surface, disappearing into the chaos and tangle of humans. As she emerged, one reached for her, grabbing as if to use her to propel himself forward. She dodged him easily. Her eyes remained on the ship, searching for a pair of floppy ears.

She found none.

Heart plummeting, Celeste scanned the water. There was no sign of the animal. Instead, she found the prince. His head rested against Bastian's chest, face tense until at last his shoulders sagged in relief. *Alive.* Celeste's shoulders fell as well, drawing closer. The prince looked up, catching her eyes with his. But there was no fear. Only a question. *Why?*

Celeste wished she knew the answer.

Around them the humans blindly thrashed until they reached the siren calling them, only to disappear beneath the waves. *I can't save them all.* The thought was a stone in her stomach. *I can't stop this. They won't listen to me.*

And so she did the only thing she could think to do.

She fled. Taking the human prince and his friend with her.

The human prince kicked and struggled, shouting words she had not learned in training but could surmise were rather rude. She should have expected it. She was a siren. Her folk were attacking his ship. But had they not shared a moment before? Surely he understood she did not intend to drown them. Apparently, that wasn't enough for him to trust her.

Despite the prince's protests, her grip did not loosen as she pulled them by their shirts. Bastian, luckily, did not fight, but only because he was still very much unconscious. She swam with abandon. Fleeing the very sirens she'd sworn to obey. Somewhere along the way, it started to rain. Fat drops fell upon the sea, so numerous they drowned out the distant sound of the Song.

Eventually, the prince ceased his fighting, choosing to stare at her darkly instead. She supposed he was waiting to see what she would do next.

That made two of them.

This was so much worse than breeching the surface. Then she'd only risked losing her place in the Chorus. In saving the prince after he'd seen them, she'd committed treason. Broken the treaty between siren kingdoms. The penalty was death.

She continued to swim.

She swam until she could no longer see the ship in the storm. And then she stopped. They were not followed. *Good.* Her hands, stiff from gripping the humans, released. *Now what?* There were others. So many others. Could she go back and save more? She looked at the prince and his friend, floating in the sea before her. Would they drown if left to their own devices? Bastian was floating, despite being unconscious. But that fact wasn't terribly reassuring.

She bit her lip, keeping her focus on the problem before her instead of allowing the shock of what she had done sink in. Their safety remained uncertain regardless of what she did. Xandra or Echo could come for them at any moment. But no ideas came rushing to her. Nothing but endless water surrounding them. From the dark waves beneath to the pouring rain above. She pushed her wet hair from her face, trying to think. These humans were helpless. It would likely take all night to reach the closest human island from here; she wouldn't have time to get them there if she wanted to save the others. And there were no small islands nearby to leave them on.

The prince looped his arm under Bastian's shoulders, helping to hold his head above water as they bobbed. But his gaze remained on her, appraising beneath long, dark lashes. He was so close she could see his eyes were as dark as his hair. They turned downward at the corners and were framed by full, arched brows that were nearly hidden beneath his wondrously tousled wet hair. His full lips, which were topped with a rounded cupid's bow, pulled into a smirk. Were they as soft as they looked?

"Eyes up here, love."

He pointed to his eyes with his free hand. Celeste tore her gaze away, wishing the Goddess would smite her. And yet there was something thrilling about hearing that low voice, which had run through her mind all day, speaking to her. Still, she didn't respond.

Although she understood the common human language well enough, she hardly spoke it. Her accent was thick. It struggled against the human's hard consonants, and the sentences always formed wrong. Instead, she gestured with her hands spread wide, palms facing down toward the water.

Stay here.

"Where else would we go?"

She rolled her eyes. If he was well enough to make jokes, he was well enough to keep them both afloat until she returned. She dove into the water and swam in the direction of the ship. She couldn't see it in the storm, but she knew where it was. The journey without the humans took less time. And before she had time to question what in the Goddess's name she was doing, she'd arrived.

The storm raged. It was no longer the idle threat she remembered but a violent, terrible thing, wreaking vengeance upon the ship. The vessel looked small beside the rising waves that crashed against its sides. The woman at its bow no longer looked as if she were taking off in flight. Instead, she appeared as though she were tied to the ship, forced to meet its fate. Fear grew within Celeste, and she tore her gaze away to search for the other humans. But the water was too rough. It took her time to find them.

Her hands flew to her mouth. Her stomach roiled as she looked upon the hand of death for the first time. The humans floated together along the starboard side, nearly twenty in total, bobbing and tossing face down in the angry waves. The sirens were nowhere in sight. *They must be underwater with the others.* The thought made her stomach twist tighter. She had arrived too late.

A howl pierced through the storm, the sound its own painful music, desperate and raw. Celeste searched for the source until she found it. The floppy-eared animal paced back and forth on the ship, whining. The Song was only sung for the humans. This creature could not speak. Could not reveal the existence of sirens. It was unaffected. And now the poor thing was left all alone.

A wave crashed against the ship's side, sending the deck tilting.

The creature's thin legs tangled beneath it as it attempted to find purchase, but it slipped on the slick floor and slid with a yelp out of sight.

Celeste let out a cry and swam toward the ship, careful to keep herself away from the bodies. She dove deep into the water, reaching a spot far enough beneath before turning and racing upward. She built up speed, moving faster and faster, until she launched from the water and into the air. Her arms reached above her head, stretching for the railing. But although her jump was high, the deck was higher. Fingernails scraped wood as she began to fall, sliding down until she fell into the water below.

Reemerging, she searched the side of the ship. There had to be a way that the humans could climb up. But Celeste didn't find anything low enough for her to reach. If the humans used something to come and go, it wasn't there. Maybe they never left the ship. That would make sense, given their disastrous excuse for swimming.

The ship gave a great surge and began to tip sideways, away from her. She heard the animal howling a sorrowful note.

A thought struck her.

The sirens hadn't sung to the animal. But that didn't mean she couldn't. Still, Celeste hesitated. Her command over her Song was uncertain at best. What if she lost control? What if she hurt the animal? What if she hurt someone else?

But there was no other way. She had to try.

With a deep breath, Celeste began to sing. *"Take my hand and let me guide you as you listen to my song."* Her words danced along the roaring waves, slipping up and through the storm circling around them. In her voice, the words sounded soft and sweet. Almost playful. She focused on the picture of the animal. Ears flopping. Tail wagging. *"Come closer. Hear me calling. In my arms you belong."* The howls stopped. Celeste swept her eyes back and forth along the deck of the ship. *"Come rest your weary bones, love. Come join me in the sea."* Her voice crescendoed as she sent a little prayer to the Goddess that her Song wouldn't alert the Chorus. That it would not slip from her grasp. "*Let the gentle waves consume you, for your heart belongs to me.*" She lifted her arms, reaching for the ship and beckoning gently. Ears flopping. Tail wagging. Legs jumping.

A little black nose appeared beneath the railing. Her heart lurched in relief. The animal stared down at her with cloudy white eyes. A rush of victory thrummed through her, and Celeste had to stop herself from spinning around in glee. Still, this little victory cost her. Her focus wavered. The animal's eyes blinked, clouds fading. No... Another wave crashed upon the deck, sending the dog sliding once more out of sight. Celeste squeezed her eyes shut, fear like yellow bile choking her. But she suppressed it; she had to focus.

"*I'll fulfill your every longing. I am everything you crave...*" Celeste beckoned. "*Let me kiss away your sorrows as I*"—from the corner of Celeste's eye, she saw something move, but she had to stay focused—"*lay you in your—*"

A blinding bolt of lightning struck. Celeste watched in horror as the pretty white sails were set ablaze. The ship was on fire. But she didn't have time to gawk. The animal appeared, running. She swam down just for a moment so she could gather enough speed. Then she launched herself into the air, arms flung wide. The animal leaped, skinny legs stretching and ears flapped back as it sailed through the rain. The body collided with her chest, throwing her off-balance. But her arms circled the creature, clutching it to her as they fell backward into the raging sea.

For a moment, she did not know up from down. Not until she saw the flames roaring, guiding her back. She surfaced, checking the animal for injury. But she found none. Nothing but docile white eyes where her magic still lingered. Holding the warm, furry body close, she swam away from the ship, careful to keep the creature's head above water. She didn't know much about land animals, but she guessed they were similar to humans in this way.

She didn't look back. She already knew how it all ended. It had been there all along. She had known those sunken ships had once belonged to humans. But she hadn't thought much about what had happened to them. Each happy memory of searching sunken ships soured. Mustering all her strength, Celeste pushed herself to swim faster, beating her tail behind her. Seeing the destruction firsthand was too much to bear.

A wall of heat and sound crashed into her back. Celeste cried out. She curled around the dog protectively as the impact sent them flying. Shards of wood mixed with the pouring rain. She turned. *What was that?* Black smoke spread like squid ink above the sinking remains of the once glorious vessel. Celeste could feel herself holding back tears. *Had that been their home?* If it had, it would not be mourned. Its inhabitants were dead. All but three.

The prince was waiting. But instead of leaving, she straightened. For just at the back of her neck, she felt an unmistakable feeling. She was being watched.

She held the enchanted creature close as she searched for the source. It did not take her long to find them. The Chorus. They had surfaced just on the other side of the ship. Her hands grew cold. It wasn't over. They wouldn't let the prince escape that easily.

And then she saw Maeve looking right at her.

Maeve would tell them. Celeste did not blame her. Initiates were trained to obey, not question. Celeste was the one who was too curious. Too wild. Too foolish. And look where that had gotten her.

Without hesitation, the princess bolted, racing back to where Bastian and his prince waited. As they swam, the poor animal drifted from its stupor, shaking in fear and cold. It whined softly.

"I'm sorry," Celeste said in her language, knowing it wouldn't understand.

She began to feel the humans nearby in the water. They flailed around like prey. Any siren with half a sense could pick them out easily, even in the storm. Her tail pushed faster. She had to reach them first, swim them somewhere safe. If she could somehow get the humans on land, it'd be impossible for the others to reach them.

Just as she spotted the two dark shapes of the humans on the horizon, Celeste felt the Chorus in the water behind her. That meant they felt Celeste too. The Chorus would follow wherever they went. Track them and leave no survivors. She knew their tactics well. But she had never pictured this. She had always believed the Chorus acted in defense. That's why the Goddess gave them their Song. To protect.

When had that changed? Or had she just been naive?

The prince scanned her face as she approached. Beside him, Bastian floated, still unconscious.

"What happened?" he asked.

The creature wriggled in her arms, yelping and scratching.

"Admiral!" the prince gasped. The animal broke free and paddled happily to him, tail smacking the water. The prince pulled it into his arms and buried his head in its fur. He lifted his eyes and looked at her. "You—you saved my dog?"

Celeste nodded, flushed.

"The others." He paused. "They're gone."

It wasn't a question.

She nodded again in response.

The water beneath moved, shifted as the Chorus closed in. They were out of time. Everything inside her wanted to grab him and swim, but it was no use. They had no chance of escape. She was out of options. So she pulled her beloved spear from her back and turned to face the consequences.

CHAPTER 8

The sirens broke through the surface several lengths away, General Xandra at the front. A blind rage distorted Xandra's face. But beside her, Echo was as calm as clear water, which was a great deal more frightening. Celeste expected them to say something. To ask her why she had done this. To ask her to stand down. Instead, General Xandra raised her spear in challenge. The others fell back. Celeste positioned herself in front of the prince and his companions. She eyed her competition, not liking her odds in this rematch.

Xandra launched herself at Celeste. The princess fell back, attempting to knock away the blow. But the general had more force. They collided like a thunderclap. Celeste just managed to deflect the blade away from her shoulder, but the wings just below the weapon's tip made contact. Pain lanced through Celeste. Sharp and then dull at once. Xandra pulled back, but Celeste was quicker this time. The smaller siren used both hands on the shaft of her spear to swing up. She knocked the second blow out of the way. In the time it took Xandra to recover, Celeste dove.

Celeste knew her strengths and her weaknesses well. As initiates, sirens had weapon training every day. Xandra may have been larger, but Celeste excelled at using her surroundings. Before the general had time to react, Celeste grabbed the fin of her superior's tail and pulled her under. Xandra sputtered, her lungs taking a moment to adjust. And in that moment, Celeste thrust her spear toward Xandra's temple. The blunt end. For even now, she couldn't bring herself to injure this siren she respected.

Xandra saw the blow coming. She evaded to the left, grunting. Celeste let the swing of her spear spin her around and brought the weapon around back toward the temple again. But once more, Xandra's training was unmatched. The general blocked, the clash nearly knocking Celeste's spear from her hands.

Celeste swam back, adding distance between them. But as she did, her attention was drawn above. The other sirens were not waiting for their leader to finish her. The fight was a distraction to lure Celeste away and leave the humans unprotected.

"*No!*" the princess cried. She darted toward them but was knocked off course. Hard. Pain bloomed again in her shoulder, and she turned to see blood clouding the water. The general lunged again, and this time Celeste did not hold back. With a grunt, the little siren parried and then moved into a thrust of her own. Xandra dodged, but not fast enough to avoid it. The tip of Celeste's spear sliced across the side of her superior's arm.

"You can't win," the general said.

She was right, of course. Even if Celeste managed to best Xandra, she couldn't beat them all. Above her, the prince and his companions were surrounded. Feinting another thrust, Celeste used the distraction to flee. She surfaced between the humans and Echo. Despite having the upper hand, the sirens did not move on the humans. Like perfect little soldiers, they awaited instruction from their superior. Celeste pointed her weapon toward Echo, blood and water dripping from her.

"Get back!" Celeste shouted.

Just behind, Maeve floated beside Officer Rae. Celeste avoided her friend's gaze. She did not want to see how her Maeve looked at her now.

"That's enough," Echo said. "Lower your weapon, traitor."

Celeste wished she knew the perfect thing to say, like her sister Sephone always had. How could she make them understand? But even if she found the words, she knew they wouldn't listen. Goddess's fins, she wished she even felt confident she was making the right choice. This wasn't a simple rule break. *This was treason.*

The gazes of her fellow initiates felt heavy upon her. It was unbearable. Did none of them feel as she did? Why was Celeste so horrified by what had happened when no one else reacted? *You're acting like a human*, her mother's voice echoed in her head, ringing. She was too much like them. Too emotional. Tears sprung to her eyes. How did she let this happen? Fear and shame simmered inside her, overwhelming her.

General Xandra emerged, and the circle of sirens widened to make room.

"Chorus"—the general sheathed her spear—"drown the humans and capture the traitor."

"Yes, General," they responded in unison.

The Chorus closed in, weapons drawn. Celeste no longer recognized them, these sirens she'd known for cycles. She didn't even recognize herself. *Traitor.* The pressure inside her built, and she looked at the prince. He held his companions close, jaw tight. Her heart was beating too fast. Her mother's words shouting at her over and over.

"How am I to trust you?"

"Stop acting like one!"

"That's enough."

The ringing in her ears swelled. She could feel herself slipping. It was happening again. Her hands flew to her ears, but she couldn't block the sound. Echo reached to restrain her. Celeste couldn't breathe. Her heart raced. *I should have never come.* Tears pricked her eyes. *What have I done? What have I done? What have I done?*

Echo's hand clamped over Celeste's shaking wrist.

"Calm down," she said.

It was an order.

Celeste looked into her eyes. And screamed.

The sound poured out of her, vibrating throughout her body. She couldn't control it and couldn't stop. Echo's hand slipped from her wrist. The world tilted. And darkness fell.

Celeste awoke to the feeling of someone's hand on her shoulder. The rain had stopped, but it was dark. The hand shook her again.

"Please, wake up."

She opened her eyes and saw the prince staring at her. His dark eyes seemed to be scanning her, as if looking for an explanation. Her arm burned hot where he touched her, and she tilted her head to look down at it. The other shoulder, which was still bleeding, burned for an entirely different reason.

Sighing with relief, the prince released her, and Celeste sank back into the water. She felt empty and tired.

"That was—" He paused, looking over his shoulder, then reconsidered. "Thank you," he finished instead. At his side, his pet was held in his free arm, but it hung there, body limp. Celeste's eyes widened, and she reached toward the Admiral.

"He's fine. Just unconscious," the prince assured her. "They all are."

A cold dread settled upon her as she lifted her head and looked past him. It was hard to see. Black smoke seemed to have descended upon them, and Celeste wondered if it had somehow come from the burning ship. She pushed past him and saw bloodred hair. A gasp escaped her throat. General Echo's body floated belly-up in the water. It was almost serene, how her hair circled her pale face. She looked as if she were sleeping. Maeve slept beside her, tentacles moving gently with the waves. The Chorus floating motionless was almost a twisted copy of the humans she had seen not hours before. Celeste placed a hand against her friend's chest. After a second, she felt the gentle beating of her heart. *They were alive.* Her hands shook, and she turned away, squeezing her eyes shut. *At least they were alive this time.*

The tears came anyway. Her body shook with them as they pooled in her eyes and overflowed. But unlike any other time she cried, they did not simply mix with the water and disappear. They trickled and poured and flowed, leaving salty tracks down her cheeks until they were dripping along her chin. The experience was unnerving.

The prince said nothing. He turned his face away to give her privacy and focused on making sure Bastian, who was still unconscious, did not float too far.

Celeste heated with embarrassment. She hated crying. Hated that this human had seen her utterly fall apart. In haste, Celeste dove into the sea. The water rushed up to meet her, mixing with the tears and washing them away. Soon it was as if they never existed. *This isn't helping*, she told herself. *You need to get it together and swim these humans to land. You can't undo what you've done, so the least you can do is finish what you've started.* Clenching her jaw, she took a deep breath and resurfaced.

The prince turned, meeting her eye. And the siren paused. Why hadn't her voice put him to sleep too? Why hadn't anyone's Song affected him? But she didn't have time for such questions. The Chorus could wake any second. Flushing, she reached her hand out to the human.

Let's go, it said.

"Well, I suppose *I* can't swim to Velluno," he said, taking her hand.

In spite of herself, Celeste laughed. She wrapped her arm around the prince, who held the Admiral and Bastian. She tried to keep her face expressionless as she felt the warmth of the prince's body pressed against her. Her wounded shoulder still throbbed, but it wasn't too bad. It was the least of her worries at this point. She didn't seem to be losing too much blood, and she knew how to avoid attracting predators.

With their party ready, Celeste swam off. She'd need to swim fast if they wanted to make it to Port Velluno before the Chorus could catch them. Luckily for them, she knew the ocean, and although she had never seen them, she knew the locations of the human lands very well. She knew exactly where they were going. Still, the journey was awkward. Despite her being both strong and fast, carrying two grown human men and their dog through the water was a challenge. Bastian was no better than deadweight, and many a time she would feel him slipping and would have to stop to allow the prince to readjust his grip. The prince—she mainly tried her best to ignore him. But his right arm had laced itself around her, large hand pressed against her abdomen, and she couldn't help but notice what felt like every firm muscle of him.

Above them, stars shone brightly, helping to guide her way. The sea, which had grown still and dark, reflected the glittering sky, and it was as if they were swimming through galaxies. In spite of all that had happened, Celeste couldn't help but be swept away by the beauty of it all. Their journey was quiet, except for the gentle sound of the waves and Celeste's tail moving them forward in a repetitive rhythm.

Time lengthened and shortened in equal parts. The journey felt like an eternity, and yet Celeste was somehow shocked when she saw the faint shadow of a human city appear on the horizon just before dawn. Her pace quickened, and her shoulders relaxed for the first time since that morning. The prince didn't seem to see it for another good hour.

"Velluno."

He turned his head to look at her, and her heart skipped a beat. This close, she could see he had a tiny mole on his left cheek. One that pulled as his lip curled up. She met his gaze. His beautiful dark eyes and—he turned his face away to look toward the city. They were fast approaching it now. Which, mercifully, gave Celeste something to think about beyond that mole of his. She had never seen a human city before. Even with her excellent vision, she could only make out parts of the port town, which was built into a cliffside. Despite the late hour, there were still many lanterns lit around the town, revealing winding stone streets and short square buildings. But she didn't dare let her curiosity get the best of her. She couldn't stay long. The Chorus would awaken and be looking for her soon, if they weren't already.

She slowed her pace, searching for a dark stretch of beach to drop them. After traveling all night, her arms and tail were sore and tired. The wound in her shoulder had stopped bleeding, but it was still painful. Even her face felt sore. Perhaps from the wind and ocean spray. This surprised her. She never expected the wind to hurt.

A little north of the port, Celeste found a darkened beach and headed in that direction. But the closer they got to the land, the better she could see the human city. There were no humans, as far as she could see. Perhaps they were sleeping. But floating in the waters just beyond the city were many ships, like the one the prince and Bastian had been on. Most of them were significantly smaller, and some didn't have sails and looked to only fit one or two humans, but all were connected with rope to wooden platforms that jutted out from the land. *So that is how they get on their ships.* There were so many things Celeste didn't recognize or understand. It was overwhelming and thrilling all at once. Tall green plants sprang up between clusters of buildings, fat and full, but she didn't know what they were called. They made her want to leap from the ocean and run her fingers over them. Would they be soft like algae or hard like coral?

Celeste swam into the shallows of a darkened alcove until she could feel the sand brush against her fin along a sandbar. She stopped and unwound her arm gently from the prince. Her body felt cold in his absence, but she ignored it. Wordlessly, she helped him get ahold of Bastian and the dog, both of whom had begun to stir. It took a moment for him to find his footing, but eventually the prince was able to stand, the water coming up to his chest. He looked at her, about to say something, when the quartermaster let out a long groan.

"Bastian!" he said, watching in obvious relief as the quartermaster rubbed his eyes with the back of his hand. "You bastard. You slept through the whole thing." The prince laughed, pulling Bastian into a hug.

Celeste fell back, watching the celebration from the outside. The waves pulled her, drawing her out to sea. She didn't fight it as the two humans found their legs and stumbled to land. They raised their knees up high with each laborious step. When they finally reached the shore, they collapsed into the sand. The two gasped and laughed until they grew still. And Celeste wondered if the effort had killed them after all. So she stayed for a while, watching until she could see the gentle rise and fall of their chests. They were alive, and yet she remained. The Admiral, at last fully awake, untangled himself from the prince's arms and shook the water from his body. He circled the men, sniffing them with his little black nose. When neither stirred, the animal paced back and forth until he, too, tired and curled up beside them.

The waves pulled and pulled, and the two humans became smaller and smaller. After a time, Bastian roused from sleep. The sky had just begun to brighten—dawn mere moments away. He turned, waking the prince beside him. The two spoke to each other, but Celeste couldn't hear what they said. They looked around themselves, as if taking in their surroundings for the first time. And when they finally peered out to the ocean for a sign of their rescuer, she was too far gone.

Maybe it was better this way. After a day or two, they would look at each other and wonder if it hadn't just been a bad storm. If perhaps the sirens had been a dream. And if they had any sense, they would stay well away from the ocean for the rest of their short human lives. Over time they would forget she existed. But even if they did, the Chorus wouldn't forget. She knew what awaited her when she returned to Staria.

Her body felt numb as she bobbed listlessly in the waves. She'd had a future with the Chorus. Her family loved her, despite her flaws, and she had thrown it all away. She thought of Sephone's laugh and her mother's embrace. Her father's steady presence. Shye with her fierce protectiveness and how she would braid Celeste's hair every morning growing up. Even if Celeste was right about the humans, did it matter? It wasn't as though anything would change. The Chorus would continue to hunt them to protect their kingdom from discovery.

Floating in the open ocean, with Velluno growing smaller and smaller in the distance, Celeste considered her options. She didn't have many. If she chose to go home, death surely awaited. Perhaps she should flee, although it wouldn't increase her chances of survival by much. At least she could keep her pride. She wouldn't have to look into the disappointed eyes of her father. And her mother—a stab of sorrow pierced her heart. How could Celeste face her mother, knowing how she had betrayed her? Perhaps she deserved to rot in the Wasting Waters. Maybe the legendary Sea Witch would take pity on her and—Celeste sighed heavily. From what she knew of the Sea Witch, she wasn't exactly one to take pity. Or help.

When Celeste was little, her favorite of her mother's stories was always the one about the Sea Witch. She'd beg and plead to hear the tale, and eventually her mother would relent.

"Deep within the Wasting Waters, where no siren dared to go, lived the Sea Witch," Queen Halia would say, combing her daughter's moon-white hair. "But, once, she lived in Staria, as you and I do. She was the most powerful healer in the Southern Ocean. There was no ailment she could not cure and no wound she could not sing closed. But the Sea Witch grew tired of such simple Songs. She began to experiment."

"And then she became a witch!" Celeste would pipe in, grinning.

"Be patient, little star," Halia chided, but there was no bite to it. "The Sea Witch invented new Songs. Songs to change a siren's body into anything she wished. Songs to make sirens fall in love against their will. Songs to grant dreams." Celeste wasn't sure she believed such things were possible. "Such experimentation was—and still is—forbidden, and so the Sea Witch was cast out, doomed to wander the Wasting Waters for eternity. But banishment did not stop her. Desperate sirens who heard of her magic went in search of her deep-sea grotto, seeking a miracle. In exchange, the witch would take things. The color of your hair"—her mother tugged gently at Celeste's hair, making her laugh—"a cycle of your life. The texture of your lips. Or even your voice."

Celeste broke from the memory. It was at that moment she felt them. Her reckoning. A part of her had been waiting for this. She took one last look at Port Velluno. The city hummed to life as the sun rose above it. Humans opened their doors, and fishermen readied their boats. A new day was here. Swallowing, Celeste turned her face away and dove into the waters to meet her fate.

CHAPTER 9

"Celeste?"

The sound of her mother's voice stirred Celeste from her deathly sleep. She felt wrung out. Despite the fact Celeste had gone with the Chorus willingly, Xandra still felt the need to bind and gag the princess, if only to keep her from knocking them all unconscious again. They had left her in the palace cell, where she cried herself to sleep. Apparently, after swimming as fast as she could for an entire night, her body simply gave up.

Days had passed. How many, she did not know, for the cells were dark, and she'd slept through most of them.

"Mother?" Celeste croaked, looking up from her place upon the sandy floor.

"You're finally awake. Praise the Goddess." Her mother sighed, tension leaving her shoulders. Then her brows knit in concern. "Oh, my little star. What have you done now?"

It was a phrase Celeste had heard all her life. The words were never a firm reprimand and always said with great affection. But the sound of it now cut her deeply. Celeste's heart twisted as she gazed at her mother. Halla's usual pristine appearance was gone. No crown or glittering shells adorned her. Behind Halia, King Tidus lingered, his face unreadable. Celeste's hand went to her shoulder and found her wound was gone. A healer must have visited.

"Keep watch," Halia said to her husband, resting a hand on his chest.

Celeste's father nodded and swam down the hall, leaving his wife to unlock the prison door. It swung open with a creak, and Celeste rushed into her mother's arms.

"I'm sorry. I'm so sorry," Celeste cried, body trembling. Halia's grip tightened around her daughter.

"I told you not to go," she said into her hair.

"I'm sorry."

Halia pulled away, holding her daughter at arm's length. "You disobeyed me," she said, anger flaring. The queen let go of her daughter and started swimming back and forth. "What were you thinking? You could have died! You injured General Xandra and endangered the Chorus. And, of all things, you exposed our kind to humans! Do you understand what that means? We could be held in breach of our treaty with Skalvaske and Ayakashi. I told you no, and you did it anyway."

Celeste rubbed her eyes with the heels of her hands. She loved her mother, but she knew Halia couldn't possibly understand why she had done it. And how could she explain herself? Was she to tell her mother that she couldn't watch the prince die after he tried to rescue his friend? That they looked *too much* like sirens? Her reasons sounded ridiculous to her own ears.

"And then, instead of listening to your general, like you were told, you risked your life to rescue two humans, one of whom is the son of the man who *killed your grandmother.*"

The words were a spear to the gut. Halia had only been a couple of cycles older than Shye was now when Queen Celeste had been killed. And even though Celeste had been but three when her namesake died, it was a day she couldn't forget.

"And"—the anger in her mother's voice waned—"and the council are considering your actions as treason against the kingdom."

"I'm sorry," Celeste repeated, her voice breaking.

Queen Halia, the strongest siren Celeste had ever known, crumpled to the floor. Her eyes shone with restrained tears as she grabbed her daughter's hands. Celeste froze, watching with wide eyes. She had never seen her mother cry before. Not even the night of her grandmother's death. Something inside Celeste shattered at the sight. She couldn't handle seeing the pain she had caused her mother. Yet another wave of tears filled her own eyes, and she wished there was something, anything, she could do to ease her mother's pain.

"Please listen," Halia said, her hands shaking. "We don't have much time. They have not yet reached their verdict. But there can only be one outcome: execution. If you stay here, I will not be able to stop it. But—" She paused, considering her next words carefully. "I have arranged for Helena to escort you safely out of the kingdom."

Celeste nodded, hope rising in her chest. "So I am to be banished?"

"Not exactly."

Unease crept down Celeste's spine.

"I am still queen." Halia lifted her chin. "The council and I work in tandem, but they are not the rulers of Staria. Before they announce their decision, I can send you on a mission. If you were to right the wrongs you have done—"

"You mean I have to kill the prince?"

Halia nodded.

"I—I can't do that," Celeste said, the hope withering within her. "I couldn't even sing the Song, let alone *kill* anything."

The queen squeezed her daughter's hands firmly. "Celeste, this is the only way I can think of. You made a grave mistake, and these are the consequences. If you are able to sing to the prince and return with his head, the council will have no choice but to reconsider their verdict."

Celeste pulled her hands away. "There are many others better trained—"

"It must be you, Celeste. You must prove to the council your loyalty is to the kingdom."

"I—I don't know if I can do this," the princess stammered.

"I'm sorry, little star. But this is the only way." Halia touched her hand to the place where Celeste had been stabbed, gently moving her thumb back and forth along the delicate new skin.

King Tidus appeared in the doorway.

"Helena is here," he said.

Halia pulled her daughter into her arms and squeezed tight. The touch brought a fresh wave of tears to Celeste's eyes. For it was the first time since she was a child that her mother had embraced her. "Please come home soon."

"I—" Celeste paused, then softened. "I will, Mother."

"Good," Halia said, releasing her daughter and collecting herself.

King Tidus rested his hand on his daughter's back and guided her gently down the hall and out of the dungeons, leaving the queen behind them.

"Good tides, Princess," Helena said softly when she saw them approach.

"They've been better," Celeste admitted with a watery smile. In her hands, Helena held Celeste's beloved spear, which had been taken upon her capture. The sight of it warmed Celeste, just a little. The guard returned it to her, and Celeste's father helped slide it back into place along her back. The siren king looked down at his daughter, dark circles lining his red-rimmed eyes.

"I'm sorry. I will return soon. I promise."

He nodded and pulled her into his arms, cradling her close. Another piece of Celeste fractured inside her chest. She couldn't recall being held by her father. She felt so small in his arms, and she wished desperately that she didn't have to leave.

"I love you," he told her.

"I love you too, Father," she answered, her composure slipping.

His arms released her, and he handed her a sack of rations. Then without another word, the King of Staria turned his back and swam away to return to his wife. Celeste watched him go, waiting until he disappeared from sight.

"Are you ready, Your Highness?" Helena asked.

"No," Celeste said. "But the sooner I leave, the sooner I may return."

Helena only nodded. She was quiet as she escorted Celeste away from her home. When they reached the border, she stopped and watched as Celeste swam on alone.

It was said only the most desperate and depraved sought answers from the Sea Witch. Which explained why Celeste found herself swimming like a current to find her. The water grew cooler as she descended, and the colorful ocean floor she knew disappeared. It was replaced by jagged dark clusters of bland rock. The light from the surface dimmed until it no longer felt like day. A shiver ran down her spine, and she wasn't sure if it was from the cold or from fear sliding its boney fingers down her spine. Everything around her screamed, *You don't belong here. Turn back now.* And if she'd believed she had any other option, she would have. But the prince had not responded to her Song, and she didn't have any way of finding him on land. So she set her jaw, the echo of her mother's voice ringing in her ears: *I'm sorry, little star. But this is the only way.*

Celeste had dreamed of adventure. Had yearned for escape. But now that she had it, she wasn't sure it's what she wanted after all. Not like this. She'd never felt so alone in her life. So afraid. All she had was her mission.

She had made this mess, and now she had to fix it.

No matter what she saw in the human prince's dark eyes—the feelings he stirred within her that she dared not look too closely at—it didn't change the fact he was a human. A threat. And his father killed her grandmother, a fact she conveniently hadn't put together until her mother had reminded her. Celeste had only ever wanted to make her parents proud, and now look what she'd done. How she wished she could go back to how things were. If she had to sell her soul to the Sea Witch to return to Staria, she would do it.

Or at least that's what she told herself.

A shadow passed, and Celeste whipped around to stare blindly after it. Was it a fish? A predator? The Sea Witch herself? She didn't know what she was looking for or where to go, beyond into the Wasting Waters. Some said the Sea Witch changed shape depending on who visited her, just to manipulate her visitors and get into their heads. Sephone had always said the Sea Witch was a monster. Celeste, ever the optimist, maintained the witch was misunderstood. But all the stories said she would help anyone achieve their wildest desires. At least, so long as they could pay her price.

Celeste's hand wandered to the strap of her spear, pulling the weapon across her torso. She let her fingers slide over the smooth leather. It was the only thing she could think to barter with. Having grown up a princess, Celeste hadn't had the opportunity to barter or trade very often. Whatever she wanted, she could ask for. *I suppose I could offer the color of my hair, or my eyes. Maybe even a precious memory*, she thought as she descended deeper into darkness.

The ocean felt so quiet and lonely down there. Nothing lived in the Wasting Waters. At least, nothing that she could see. There was only empty water around her and sharp rocks beneath. She paused, her certainty beginning to waver. For some reason, she expected there to be a sort of path or clue that would appear to help lead her toward the witch's grotto. How else could all the desperate souls find it? But for all Celeste knew, she was headed in the wrong direction entirely. Being a siren who prided herself on how well she knew the ocean, it was a disconcerting feeling. But she kept swimming deeper anyway, not ready to try a new direction just yet.

The tips of Celeste's fingers and tail grew cold. She balled her hands into fists and tucked them under her arms. Then, out of the corner of her eye, she saw movement. Something as thin as seaweed slithered through the water. She knew at once it was an eel, but she hadn't seen one like this before. Sensing her gaze, the eel opened its huge triangular jaw. Its head expanded, billowing into a large inflated sphere. Celeste jerked backward and watched as it writhed around, eerie and mesmerizing. It moved toward her, and her heart beat faster. The eels she knew weren't inherently dangerous. Like most animals, they attacked if they felt threatened. She wasn't sure how to proceed. Should she swim away? Fight? Stay frozen until it moved on?

She was in uncharted waters.

Something moved behind her. She glanced away from the eel and realized it had not reacted to her at all. Moving gracefully through the water toward them was a shark. Like the eel, this shark was a different species than those she knew, twice the length of her. The fin atop its back was down near its tail. It watched her with large green eyes on either side of its broad, flat head. The creature looked ancient, its closed mouth like an old wound pressed closed. As it moved closer, Celeste turned and saw the eel fleeing into the darkness.

The shark closed in, now only a tail's length away, and she readied her spear. But the shark only swam past her. Celeste's shoulders sagged in relief as she watched it continue for several feet, then pause. Strange—it didn't seem to be hunting. Did it sense a predator even worse than itself nearby? It began swimming again, slowly. Not a predator, then. Its movements almost reminded her of sirens on patrol. After another sweep, the shark moved on.

With no better idea about where to go, Celeste found herself following. The shark did not seem to mind her as it turned south, continuing along the slope of the ocean bottom further and further into darkness. There were no longer many rocks around them, only open ocean. Despite her excellent vision, she couldn't see anything farther than the shark's fin in front of her. Maybe this was a bad idea. Water pressed in around her, building in pressure. Her breathing became ragged as the amount of oxygen in the water changed. Sirens could exist in deep waters, but it certainly wasn't comfortable and took time to adjust. She swam blindly behind the shark for what felt like ages, until she finally saw something in the darkness. Some sort of blue-and-purple light. As she neared, she realized it was a cave with two more identical sharks prowling in front of its glowing entrance.

The shark she followed darted into the mouth of the cave, disappearing into its glowing depths and leaving her staring after it.

"Good tides?" Celeste called into the cave. It felt rude to simply swim in.

No response.

It can't possibly be worse than an execution, she assured herself as she began to swim forward. But this was a lie. She knew many stories of fates worse than death. As Celeste entered the cave, she prayed this wasn't the beginning of that sort of story.

CHAPTER 10

"Why are you here, Princess?" the Sea Witch asked. Or rather, *Nerissa* asked. Celeste had almost forgotten that the Sea Witch of lore had a name. Nerissa stared at Celeste with large, liquid-black, pupilless eyes. This, too, was a surprise. Celeste had always pictured her with glowing red eyes, pointed fingers that could tear skin, and shark teeth. The shark teeth had sort of been a common theme.

The siren before her was nothing like that.

Nerissa's skin was a dark, inky blue, like a perfect night sky. She would have blended into the darkness of the Wasting Waters perfectly, had she not been—somehow—glowing. The witch's skin gleamed a phosphorescent blue from uneven stripes that covered her body. Dark blue hair, so dark it was nearly black, hung in a sheet behind her, rippling gently as she moved. Two webbed ears protruded from the sides of her head; the webbing moved between four points that grew smaller as they curved down her ear. Her face was all angles: high cheekbones, a sharp chin and jawline. The only remotely soft thing about her was her lips, which were full, black, and bowed. Although Celeste had seen little to no food this deep in the ocean, Nerissa's body was full and curving all the way down to her tail, which also had the same glowing pattern as her torso.

She wore no embellishment or clothing, save for a necklace holding a large pearl. The effect was otherworldly and intimidating. If the Sea Witch did have the power to look however she liked, it was clear why she chose to present herself this way.

"I need help that only you can provide," Celeste said, trying an indirect approach.

Nerissa cocked an eyebrow at the princess, before returning to her busywork. It looked as though she was organizing hundreds of bottles that were stored on the walls of the cave. Each little jar and bottle varied in size and color. One bottle was green and sparkling, while another was purple and glowing so brightly that everything around was cast in a violet hue, and another held something red and thick as blood. Within them, the Sea Witch kept *parts*. Fish teeth. Scales. Jellyfish tentacles. And even what looked like siren fingers. This last one sent a shiver down Celeste's spine. It was rare for sirens to find and keep glass. Such delicate things couldn't last in the ocean and were often more trouble than they were worth. Celeste had never seen such a collection before. What did the witch use them for. Magic? The only magic Celeste was aware of was a siren's Song. Could the Sea Witch be using these things as ingredients? Or were they trophies? Celeste drew her eyes away. Perhaps she was allowing her imagination to run away with her. She needed to stay on task.

The witch remained silent as she carefully pulled a bottle from her shelf, checked its stopper, then placed it in a new location along the shelf. It was clear Nerissa wasn't a strong conversationalist. A characteristic Celeste was familiar with.

"What do you know about humans?" Celeste asked.

Nerissa turned and fixed the princess with her glossy black gaze. "I know many things," she said. After looking Celeste over, she added, "What do you want?" It wasn't a demand but a careful question. As though everything Celeste could ever hope for could be hers, and all she'd have to do was say the word.

Celeste swallowed. "Legs," she said. No point in drifting around the coral about it.

The witch laughed. It was a surprisingly normal sound. "Why?"

Celeste had imagined the Sea Witch would have all the answers. But Nerissa had only questions, and Celeste had plenty of her own questions to deal with.

"I—I want to find a human," Celeste said. Something in her gut told her that she shouldn't trust the Sea Witch with the entire story. But when Nerissa did nothing but stare at her for several long moments, the princess finally added, "On land."

This was going *swimmingly*.

Nerissa contemplated this for a moment, then swam forward. She took Celeste's chin in her hand, turning her head left and right to look at her face from every angle. Celeste balled her hands at her sides and attempted to keep her face neutral. *What was she looking for?*

"And so you ask me to give you legs," Nerissa said. It wasn't a question.

"I mean—" It felt like a trap, but Celeste wasn't sure she wanted to tell the Sea Witch any more about herself or her objectives than she had to. What if as soon as she said yes some sort of magic happened, and she was stuck in a terrible situation that she couldn't get out of? Maybe her fingers would end up in a jar. "Yes," she finished. She already *was* in a terrible situation she couldn't get out of.

The witch laughed again. "You are funny, Princess. I am not trying to trick you."

Sure you aren't.

Nerissa turned and swam across the room, stirring the bioluminescent seaweed that hung from the ceiling in waving tendrils and lit the grotto with a blue-and-purple glow. She lay languidly across the soft pink insides of a massive shining clamshell. One of her numerous sharks swam after her, circling her lazily. The sharks were everywhere. At least a dozen of them, from what the princess could see. Celeste remained where she was, waiting silently until Nerissa at last continued.

"I *can* manipulate the body," she said. "Change the fin into feet, remove your gills."

The princess's eyes widened. It was at this point that it dawned on her that she would essentially become a human. A fact she should have realized sooner, but in her defense, it had been a rather long few days.

"Will I still have my Song?"

Nerissa turned the question over in her mind. "Yes," she said at last. "So long as you have your voice, you will have your song. But humans do not have magic. You would have to hide it or risk discovery."

Celeste nodded, the cold reality of her situation settling in. She cleared her throat and charged forward. "Rumors say you require payment for your services."

"Of course. I do not simply help any unfortunate who wanders into this grotto."

"Name your price," Celeste said.

She expected the witch to take a moment, but her answer came right away.

"A favor," she said simply.

"A—a favor?" Celeste's voice came out an octave higher than normal.

Nerissa smiled. "Yes, Princess. Any favor I wish at any time I wish it."

Silence fell between them. Being in debt to the Sea Witch sounded both better and worse than what she'd imagined. A favor could be anything, and Celeste doubted it would be something simple. What if it was her firstborn? Not that she was considering reproducing anytime soon. Or what if the Sea Witch asked Celeste to murder someone? Countless questions ran through her mind, but she was unsure how to ask them. Still, she couldn't back down now. She was in too deep. Both literally and figuratively.

"A favor is rather broad," Celeste said.

"That is by design." Nerissa smirked.

Celeste fell silent again.

"I can agree to this price," she said at last. "But I would require boundaries."

Once more the Sea Witch laughed. Her black eyes crinkled with her smile, and Celeste saw not a monster—but not a friend either.

She almost wished Nerissa were a monster. Monsters seemed far more straightforward.

"Name them," the witch said.

"I will not kill myself or anything else."

"Done." She smiled.

"And"—Celeste paused—"I will not break any rules of my kingdom."

Nerissa's smile faded. "Done." The shark paused beside its master, and Nerissa stroked it gently upon the head. "Anything else?"

There really should be more, but Celeste had trouble thinking of anything. Eventually, she sighed and nodded.

"Then we are agreed?" Nerissa rose and extended a long-fingered hand toward Celeste.

The princess wavered for a moment. "And when I am finished, would you turn me back into a siren?"

Nerissa shrugged. "If you wish, I shall return your body to its current form. But after that, our deal is finished. If you ask to become human again, a new deal must be struck."

The Sea Witch's hand hung in the water between them, and Celeste stared at it, heart pounding. Unable to think of anything else to add to the agreement, she closed the distance between them. They clasped their hands at the wrist. The witch's grip was firm, and so Celeste squeezed a little harder to match it.

Then Nerissa began to sing. The Song sounded like a whispered lullaby, except in a minor key. Celeste had never heard it before. The witch's hand cooled against her skin. In fear, Celeste tried to pull away, but Nerissa's grip tightened, viselike around her wrist.

"Are you starting this right now?" Celeste asked.

The witch didn't answer. She remained concentrated, focusing on her hand, which was now growing colder and more painful by the second.

"A warning would have been nice," Celeste added. Her wrist felt as though it was burning with cold now, and Celeste hissed. At once, Nerissa finished the song and released her hand. Celeste snatched it away, cradling it against her. It was then that she noticed it. On the skin of her inner wrist, just where Nerissa's fingers had touched, was a black crescent.

"The moon," the witch explained in her rich, slow voice. "A symbol of promise. It will fade when the price is paid."

Celeste brushed her fingertips across the dark shape and met Nerissa's black eyes. "You could have said something before you branded me."

"I could have," she agreed.

The princess held her wrist up to the blue light. All pain had disappeared. What remained was a simple mark contrasting against Celeste's skin. She dropped her wrist to her side.

"How does the transformation work?" she asked, deciding she preferred her information in advance.

With a sweep of her arm, Nerissa gestured toward the large shell. "It is like your healings, except instead of manipulating your skin to be mended or your blood to fight sickness, I will be singing deeper and to all—bone and skin and blood alike—to form anew into human legs, feet, muscle. After, I shall sing to your gills in the same way, closing them so you breathe only air, as humans do."

Celeste scrunched her nose at that.

"You shall look exactly like them, except your hair—"

Although Celeste was not particularly fond of the color, her hand flew to her head. "I prefer to keep it."

"They may notice the color. Only older humans have such white hair." But seeing Celeste's insistence, she continued. "Now, are you ready to begin?"

She hesitated. A part of her wanted to go swimming home to her mother, to demand they find another way. Her mother never would have agreed to this plan, to her seeking out the Sea Witch. But another part of her had always wanted to know more about the humans. This was her chance. She could learn what there was to know, glean what information she could about why they had been in Staria's waters, kill the prince, and return home. But despite her training and capabilities, she couldn't imagine herself killing anyone.

If it was a question of his life or hers, she clearly had chosen him. But seeing her mother broken on the floor—she couldn't do that to her family. They didn't deserve it.

"Will it hurt?" Celeste asked, stalling.

"Yes." Nerissa smiled.

The Sea Witch took her hand and led her to the shell. Celeste lowered herself down onto it, marveling at how soft and comfortable the mouth of the clam was and wondering if it was in fact alive. She ran her hand along her tail. It was beautiful. The glowing light around her glittered against each shimmering silver-blue scale. She waved her fin back and forth, taking a moment to enjoy how it felt moving through the water one last time before it was taken from her. *Not for good*, she reminded herself. *Only until you can come home.*

Nerissa pulled something from a bag. What supplies would a healer need? They ordinarily used their Song and hands. Was this where her bottles came in? But Nerissa turned, and in her hands, Celeste saw *cooked* fish.

Celeste couldn't hide her surprise. Cooked food was incredibly hard to come by, due to the fact it required a heat source. Beneath the sea, it was a delicacy. Even the palace didn't receive cooked fish save for special occasions, like festivals. Celeste's heart twisted in her chest when she remembered one particular meal, where Sephone and Celeste had eaten their food so quickly they got stomachaches. Halia had taken her daughters, laughing, to a healer so they didn't have to miss the storytellers.

"How...?" she started to ask.

"There is a volcanic area nearby," Nerissa explained proudly as she pulled some meat off the bones and handed it to Celeste. "Eat. The process is hard on the body. You'll need energy."

"Oh, no need," Celeste said, pushing the offering away. "I have my own rations."

The witch scoffed. "Eat the fish, girl."

Celeste's eyes flicked to the sharks, several of which were still circling the room. But somehow the sharks did not look interested.

Odd. If it was a spell, Nerissa was certainly powerful, for she hadn't sung a note since Celeste arrived, and the sharks remained docile. But Celeste guessed these sharks had been raised by Nerissa and trained accordingly. Perhaps she kept them well-fed on food much more appealing to them than fish. A shiver ran down her spine at the thought of what or *who* that could be.

Dutifully, Celeste took the fish, thanked the witch, and ate it. It was cod and tasted delicious with its smoky flavor. It seemed Celeste hadn't realized until now how hungry she was. She couldn't remember when she'd last eaten. The food was gone quickly, and Nerissa handed Celeste a bit more, before finishing off the skin herself. Now full, Celeste lay on her side within the clam and rested her head upon her bicep.

"Hold still," Nerissa said, lowering beside her.

Celeste lifted her head, nervous. "Have you done this before?"

The witch ignored her and closed her eyes. The time for questions had passed. Celeste lowered her head, watching as Nerissa's breathing deepened, chest rising and falling. Then the Sea Witch began to hum. Vibrations started in her throat and poured out of her into the water. Celeste began to feel them. The tune she hummed was unfamiliar, and it didn't repeat. The notes rose and fell at intervals, weaving around each other until they rose again. Nerissa opened her eyes, reaching her hand to place it at the side of Celeste's tail, near the hip.

This time her hand grew warm. It heated quickly, and soon Celeste felt a burning sensation. But she felt vibrations too. It was as if every scale beneath the witch's hand trembled. Celeste sucked in a breath through her teeth. The pain felt like someone ripping the scales from her body, while at the same time, other scales were being pushed inside, tearing through her skin. A purple light radiated between Nerissa's fingers, pulsing with each hummed note. Nerissa remained still, focused as Celeste was pulled and pushed apart. It took everything she had not to move or cry out.

After what seemed like a lifetime, Nerissa moved her hand down Celeste's tail to a new location, revealing skin where there were once scales. Celeste sucked in a gasp.

"Be still," Nerissa snapped.

Celeste fell into silence, staring wide-eyed at the patch of fresh skin connecting her stomach to her hip. The excruciating process continued down the side of her fin, leaving a trail of soft pink skin in its wake. When Nerissa began to work her way back up, the process miraculously got worse. Not only were scales being pulled and pushed and melted and reformed into skin but her tail was being ripped apart, and deep within, new bones grew. Sharp pains shot up Celeste's tail again and again as the tip of her fin to her stomach were all remade. She turned her face away, trying to keep her composure. Her stomach rolled, threatening to be sick, but she breathed through it.

Long, agony-filled hours passed as Nerissa hummed her Song into Celeste's body, peeling her apart and reconstructing her. Celeste closed her eyes and lost track of how many times she wished she were unconscious. She was ready to beg for it to end when finally, mercifully, the humming stopped, and the pain with it. Celeste opened her eyes, looked down, and gasped. *Legs*. She had legs. Two of them. They were long, with bendy parts at the middle, and ended in the horrible second pair of hands. Celeste stared at them, a smile forming on her face. It was the first time she had really seen them. And the hands were just as horrifying as she'd pictured. Where the round palm should have been, it was long and thick. And where long fingers should have been were five stubby little finger things. Celeste wiggled them and watched in glee as they moved in a wave, one after the other.

With a trill of laughter, Celeste sat up, pulling one leg toward her and bending it this way and that. It was so much stiffer than a tail, and there were two to keep track of. No wonder humans were so awkward.

Nerissa eyed Celeste, waiting patiently for the princess to compose herself.

"I still have to remove your gills," she said, leaning back and appraising her handiwork. "But we'll find land first. *We wouldn't want you to drown now, would we?*"

Celeste did not laugh at the joke.

CHAPTER 11

Celeste sat upon the dry sand, staring at her useless legs. It had been a long time since the Sea Witch had deposited her upon the strange human beach, and she still hadn't managed to sort out walking despite her many attempts. This was frustrating. She so wanted to get up and explore the world around her. Instead, she remained seated against a large rock.

Thus far, everything was strange. And dry. Even her hair had dried. She couldn't stop reaching for it, marveling at how different it felt. Sand clung to every inch of her. She'd never thought about this; in the water, it just fell off. Behind her, further down the beach, Celeste saw rocks not wholly different from what they had in the ocean. Hard and tall. But these rocks were covered in green, like algae but different. And above the not-algae were the tallest plants she'd ever seen. Brown and thick on bottom and fragmenting into hundreds of little offshoots at the top. On each offshoot were leaves. But they weren't shaped like any she knew, and they didn't move the same way. Each time the wind blew, they rustled and fluttered. The sound of it was very pleasant.

Above her, she saw an animal sailing through the air, flapping two fins—but they weren't fins. Nor were they arms. Were these birds?

She had heard of them, even knew what feathers looked like from pictures she'd seen. But watching them soar with nothing holding them up took her breath away.

Below the birds sat a collection of squat buildings, none of which had more than two stories. The town was unfamiliar, and Celeste found it frustrating the witch had deposited her here. She only knew the names of a few human cities—Velluno, where she'd dropped the prince and his companions, being one. But she couldn't have said anything about it to Nerissa without revealing more about her motives.

Once the Sea Witch had finished the painful process of removing Celeste's gills from her neck, Celeste had only had time to ask if she needed to wear something more than her armor, which protected her upper body. All the humans she'd seen were almost completely covered in clothes. The witch blinked her inky eyes and said, *"I'm sure you'll make friends either way."* Which was hardly helpful. Then disappeared.

She was not looking forward to their next meeting.

Celeste's eyes fell onto the dark form of the crescent moon along her inner wrist. She'd made her choice, for better or worse. She could only hope she was doing the right thing. The transformation from siren to human had taken so much time; she didn't know how many days had passed. Who knew where the humans were now. A cool breeze blew, and Celeste shivered, tiny toes curling. After much asking, Nerissa had at least been kind enough to help her learn all about her new anatomy, pointing at each part and saying its name and function. One part in particular was terribly strange to talk about with the Sea Witch, not that Celeste considered herself a reserved siren.

After another cursory wiggle of the toes, Celeste planted both of her feet into the ground with the goal of trying to stand upright like a human. She curled her body into a ball with her hands flat beside her feet and pushed. Nothing happened. She tried again, this time straightening her legs as she did. When she felt steady enough, Celeste lifted her hands from the ground and tilted up her torso. The legs wobbled, but they were strong. Though having *two* of them to look after didn't help matters. She sort of had to move both at once, and yet separately. Some of it came naturally, but most didn't. Celeste shifted precariously, finally standing for the first time in her life. Her right knee began to bend and turn while her left remained steady. The world tilted, and she went down, slamming her right hip into the sand. She grunted.

Eventually, she decided to use the rock behind her and was able to pull herself to her feet. But once she managed to stay upright on her legs, she wasn't sure how to move. She'd not been paying attention to how the humans walked when she saw the ship. She'd been rather preoccupied with a certain prince's face, if she were honest. But she knew how sea creatures walked. So Celeste lowered herself to the sand and laid on her back, bending her legs and arms until she resembled a crab. She was certain humans did not walk like this, but it was the best she could sort out under the circumstances. Celeste pressed her hands and feet down while lifting her torso, then shifted one foot to move it forward. The other foot followed. Next came her hands. And soon Celeste was scuttling down the beach at an alarmingly slow pace.

Still, it was progress.

She traveled halfway toward the town, before turning back and heading for the rock. If she were ever to fit in as a human, she needed to try walking upright again. She used the rock to stand again. This process went remarkably better than the first time. But she wasn't able to move either foot without leaning heavily upon the rock to keep her shaking legs beneath her. The sinking sand threw her off-balance. No wonder humans were so uncoordinated and graceless. They had too many limbs. She wondered, frustration mounting, how in the Goddess's name she expected to *kill* the prince when she couldn't even manage walking.

Celeste continued to practice until at last she could complete one lap around the rock without falling over. She was considering attempting it without the rock in order to explore more of the beach when she heard a rough voice behind her.

"What are you doing out here? Where are your clothes?"

Ah... she *was* supposed to wear something.

Celeste turned her head to see a human man in a large hat striding toward her. His coat with many embellishments billowed behind him. In his hands, he carried a long object that reminded her of the weapons she had seen on the ship. Similar to cannons, but handheld, and much longer and narrower. A pistol? Was that what the Chorus had called them? The way his eyebrows pulled together told her he was upset.

"Explain yourself," he said stiffly.

Celeste froze. He expected her to speak common human to him. Her heart hammered. What if her accent was too thick, and he figured out what she was? What if when she spoke all the words came out wrong? She had little to no practice speaking his language, after all. Sirens learned it to listen to humans, not to speak to them. She hadn't prepared for this. And what would she say? She didn't have a good explanation for leaning against a rock on a beach or for not wearing clothes, which seemed very important to him for some reason.

The silence stretched long between them. The human tapped his foot. How was she expecting to live with humans if she couldn't speak with them? Her breathing quickened, and the man grew impatient.

"What's wrong with you, girl?" His voice grew louder. "Can't you speak?" He took another step toward her, and she let go of the rock, attempting to take a step backward. But her unstable legs buckled beneath her, and instead she fell into the sand.

The human's look of frustration morphed into one of disgust. "Listen, women of your *profession* are not permitted in this town, nor are public indecency and drunkenness," he sneered, showing a line of yellowing teeth. "You're coming with me."

Celeste might not have understood half of what he had said to her, but she understood that last bit. Her hands flew to her spear at her back, and she swung it around, pointing it at his neck. *Not one step closer*, her expression said. The human's eyes grew wide as he looked at the pointed blade. Then he laughed.

"A prostitute with a spear?" He grunted, looking down his nose at her. "Interesting."

The two remained still. Celeste didn't dare drop her weapon, but injuring him could cause more trouble for her. She had a feeling he was some sort of guard. She was already a fugitive from one kingdom; she didn't need to be making enemies on her first day here as well. Still, she couldn't very well let him lock her up either. Grabbing a handful of sand, Celeste threw it into his face. The human cried out, pawing at his eyes with his free hand. Taking advantage of the distraction, Celeste swung her spear, sweeping his legs from beneath him. He landed with a thud. Celeste tucked her weapon beneath her chin and began to crab-walk toward the water; surely she could outswim him. But she was not fast enough. The man regained his vision, and now, unfortunately, he was angry.

"Get back here, *whore*," he shouted.

In two long strides, he was upon her again. She rolled away, reaching for her spear, but his boot slammed down onto her, pinning her face into the ground. She cried out, pain shooting through her. In one movement, he pulled her spear from her grip. He attempted to snap it over his knee, but the spear was too strong. Celeste reached for it, but he flung it out of her reach with a snarl. While he was distracted, she crawled toward the water. He grabbed her ankle, dragging her back toward him through the rough sand. She kicked and flailed, but he clamped two metal bracelets around her wrists. They were cold and heavy, connected by a chain in the center. Celeste thrashed like a wild animal, but there was nothing more she could do. In the water, she was a siren. But on land, she was helpless.

The human dragged her to her feet and pushed her toward the port town. Her legs shook and stumbled. She fell. He watched, amused.

"Stupid drunk."

Drunk ... Celeste knew this word from her training. Humans drank certain substances that made them stupid and clumsy—it made them easier to attack. Why they would choose to become stupid or clumsy was beyond her. The man yanked on the cuffs, dragging her back to her feet. The process repeated itself. Each time the man pulled harder than the last, so she was dragged a little between each fall before she could find her feet again. Pieces of shell and branches scraped her, leaving small trails of blood running down her legs. Sand was everywhere. In her hair, her mouth. Eventually, they reached a series of wooden planks, each slightly higher than the one before. Celeste stopped.

"Get up them stairs. I'm not carrying you." The man grabbed her shoulders, holding her upright. His fingers gripped so hard she could feel bruises blossoming on her arms. She awkwardly tried to balance on one leg and bend and lift the other like he did. At least it was easier on a flat, hard surface.

As they reached the top and the dark human town, Celeste felt her body tremble, the cold of the ocean wind unrelenting. She had no idea where the human was taking her or what he planned to do with her when they arrived. Around them, the town was empty. Dark wooden buildings, like ships, crowded the streets. They leaned in as if to watch their horrible progress with their gleaming glass windows. She thought of how moments before she'd have given anything to walk through the town. Explore why the human buildings seemed to have no openings. How did they get inside? Now she was too scared to care. Beneath her feet, stones rose and fell at awkward angles, tripping her. But this time when she fell, the ground was harder than the sand. Celeste clenched her jaw shut, swallowing her cry as tears sprang to her eyes. Her body felt so heavy on land, as though she were bound to the ground beneath her.

"Get up," he said.

But she couldn't. She tried, but her bound hands made it impossible. With a grunt, the man lifted her to her feet. They continued down the road, turning a corner until they stopped before a building constructed with square stones.

"Move." He pushed her aside to open the door. Her eyes remained on her dirty feet as he nearly dragged her through the building. She didn't want this human to see her cry. *I should have stabbed him with my spear. Killed him when I had the chance*, she thought as he spun her body to face him. They were in a small dark room, lit by a single flame encased in glass mounted on the wall.

"Now let's get you looking *presentable*," he said, the last word dripping with poison. His hands gripped her armor on either side and pulled, as if to rip it down the front laces. The bodice, which was made of strong stingray leather, did not budge. Teeth bared, the human pulled a knife from his hip, the silver of it gleaming and deadly. It was as if Celeste woke from a dream. She cried out and kicked him, sending him leaping away. He spat at her, words she didn't understand. His red face made him look as though he were about to boil over. She lifted her leg to kick at him again, but the human caught hold of her ankle and pulled. Her back slammed into the cold stone floor, knocking the air from her lungs and leaving her gasping. His hands found her shoulders and held them down, wrestling her into submission. Then he sat upon her, straddling her with one knee on each side of her hips and trapping Celeste's arms beneath her. Sobs erupted from her as she writhed beneath him. But he didn't stop. He lowered his knife to the laces of her armor, and with a jerk, he began to cut them apart. Tears slid down her face as she watched the last thing she had of her home torn to pieces. The fight left her, and she laid still until he finished removing her bodice. He removed the metal things from her wrists and stood.

"Get dressed," he said, pointing with his knife toward a pile of human clothing. When she didn't move, he grabbed her arm and flung her toward it. "You're lucky I'm a decent man." He smiled. "Could've locked you up as you are. Bet a *lady* such as yourself wouldn't like giving it up for free now, would ya?"

Hands shaking, Celeste reached for the pile of dirty clothing. She didn't know what she was looking for. She picked up a piece of cloth and held it up in front of her. It was a sort of tube with two openings. Why was it so long? The humans clearly preferred to wear a lot of fabric. Although, given how cold she was, she could understand why.

Eventually, she found a shirt that reminded her of what the prince had worn. It was white and billowing, with a string on the front that laced up. She slid it on over her head and shoved her arms through the sleeves. But even with the added layer, the cold remained. Perhaps she should take more clothing? She recalled the prince wore a coat. A black one that brushed his legs. The one she found was black but had dirty brass buttons and a design on the right breast. She held it close, running her fingers along the intricate stitching. The long, writhing tentacles of a squid holding what resembled a star with long points at the top, bottom, left, and right. She stuck her arms through the sleeves and instantly felt warmer.

Next, she looked for some sort of leg covering. She found many, but they were too large, falling down her hips when she tried them on. Growing impatient, the human grabbed a large piece of red fabric and two hard leather boots and flung them into her arms.

"Stop wasting time and put these on."

It took her a moment to figure out the tube of fabric, but eventually she guessed the smaller end was for the waist and pulled it up over her hips. She hadn't seen anything like it before, but when she pushed herself to her feet, she could see the appeal. It swished pleasantly. Having been stepped on by them, she recognized quickly where the boots went and slipped those on as well. They were made of leather, but they weren't like any leather she was familiar with. This leather was dark brown and worn, the tops of them nearly reaching her knees before they folded over themselves.

Once she was dressed, the human walked her back out of the room. His horrible hands on her shoulders made her skin crawl. Each step they took echoed, a sound she had never heard. It sounded ominous, final. They continued down yet another dark stone hall and into a room. Or, to put it plainly, a cell. Celeste bristled, memories of her time in the palace dungeon all too fresh in her mind. But she was too tired, too upset, too overwhelmed to do anything but let herself be thrown inside like a rag doll. She fell into a heap on the stone floor and heard the door behind her clang closed.

Everything hurt. Bruises from his hands bloomed on her arms, tender and sore. Her new legs were covered in scratches and scrapes, and her poor knees were raw from landing on them over and over. She couldn't summon the strength to move from the hard surface beneath her. She missed floating. Moving in whatever direction she liked. Now it felt like there was only down. So she lay there, holding in her tears as best she could. *Humans do not deserve mercy*, she thought, pulling her knees into her chest and wrapping her arms around them. *Not if this is what they do to their own.* Footsteps retreated down the hallway, and a door slammed closed, signaling the human had gone.

Celeste squeezed her eyes shut and tried to focus on her breathing. She thought she was lonely at home, but she had been wrong. This was so much worse. A world away from everything she had ever known, she had never felt so alone in her life. She couldn't speak, couldn't move, couldn't protect herself. And now she had been imprisoned for being "drunk" and a "prostitute," two charges that she hardly understood. Eventually, she couldn't fight the tears any longer. She let them come. Because what was the point? The tears ran down her face, leaving trails in the sand and grime on her face.

"Looks like you've had a worse night than I have."

Celeste's eyes snapped open. She had thought she was alone. In an instant, she was sitting ramrod straight, hands held protectively in front of herself. Her eyes scanned the room, searching like startled prey. A human sat against the stone wall at the back of the cell. It was a *female*. Celeste had only seen human females in half-ruined paintings or as pictures in lockets. There hadn't been any women on the prince's ship. Celeste tried not to stare, but she failed. The human before her looked near her age, with dark hair that fell in waves around her shoulders, soft golden skin, and round dark eyes. She wore a leg covering like Celeste's, but her shirt had straight sleeves and wrapped around the torso, crossing over itself in the font and tying at her hip. And like her, this human was dirty. Celeste looked around and saw, to her relief, that there were no other humans in the cell. In fact, there was nothing in the stone room save for a bucket that sat in the corner and a small, barred window.

"I'm Kiyami," the human said. "What's your name?"

Celeste would have ignored her, if it were not for the woman's red-rimmed eyes and tear-soaked face. *So humans did cry.* Celeste opened her mouth and touched her hand to her throat, hoping to convey in some way that she couldn't speak. She didn't particularly want to talk with any human, let alone a criminal.

"Ah, not a talker?" Kiyami said, a subtle slur to her words.

Celeste nodded.

"Well, at least we're not alone, eh?" The human smiled.

The princess didn't return the gesture. Celeste did not trust this human. She did not trust any of them.

CHAPTER 12

A clang jolted Celeste awake. She hadn't been sleeping exactly. In fact, she hadn't slept at all that night. Not when the human who had attacked her paced through the room every hour or so, bringing in more criminals for incarceration. And certainly not when another human, girl or no, sat in the cell with her. While Kiyami slept like the dead, Celeste practiced walking, holding on to the walls of the cell and putting one foot before the other. She circled the room over and over until, after several hours, she hardly needed support. But somehow, just before dawn, Celeste's body had tired enough to doze off. When she woke, there was a new guard who looked unsettlingly similar to the other. As he opened the barred door, she pressed her body into the corner of the cell to get as far away from him as possible.

"All right, food and water." He dropped a metal bowl and cup on the floor.

Kiyami stirred as the man closed and locked the door. "Breakfast," she said.

The human food looked hard—a theme lately—and spongelike with a crust. Beside it was a cup filled with what looked like water, but not nearly enough to clean the grime from themselves. Kiyami ripped the food in half and offered some to Celeste.

Celeste jerked away, afraid the human would touch her.

Kiyami frowned. "It's only bread," she said. But when Celeste did not come forward to take it, she set the food in the bowl and slid it toward the center of the room. Despite her hunger, Celeste did not reach for it. Instead, she curled her body further in, wishing she could disappear. "Do you mind if I have some first? I'm awful dehydrated. It was a—long night. I normally am not much of a drinker."

Drink? Was this the substance that made people drunk? Why give them the same substance they'd just been punished for? Human logic was becoming more questionable by the second. Celeste shook her head, indicating she did not want it, and Kiyami shrugged. Celeste watched in horror as the human swallowed the stuff in strange gulps. She had never seen liquid being consumed before. Kiyami set down the cup, now half full, and slid it toward Celeste.

The siren ignored it. Instead, she stood to inspect the small, barred window above their heads. Outside, she could just glimpse the street. The town bustled with activity. Humans of all sorts went about their morning business. Some walked. Others ran. While some teetered back and forth. In fact, there were a surprising number of ways to move, given their restriction to the ground. A clopping noise sounded along the stone streets as many great four-legged creatures carried humans and goods. They reminded Celeste of the Sea Goddess's mythical Hippokamp. Why did they need help to get around? Was it because the air made everything so heavy? One animal drew close, and Celeste's eyes widened as she looked upon the beautiful fall of coarse black hair along its neck and soft puffing nose. She wished to reach out and touch its shining brown fur. But even if she could, she wouldn't have. The hard-learned lesson that she did not understand the rules of this strange new world still marked her with its purple-black bruises. And yet she couldn't help but marvel at the strangeness of it all.

No one would call the town beautiful. Half the windows were covered in rotting wooden boards, and the streets were narrow and winding. Everything was colored in shades of brown and gray.

There were a few plants, mainly green with only a few exceptions. But the exceptions were rather pretty. Little clumps of color among the monotony.

"New to town?"

Celeste jumped, her feet scrambling to catch her. She had forgotten Kiyami.

"Sorry! I couldn't help but notice. No one from here would give this place a second look. I'm new to Port Romsey too."

Port Romsey. How would she get to Port Velluno? Was the prince even still there, or was he already back at his castle? And where would that be? What was his kingdom called? She had been so worried about how she would bring herself to kill the prince that she hadn't considered how difficult it would be to find him. Any semblance of calm she had found in the busy town quickly turned sour.

Kiyami continued, as if sensing Celeste's discomfort. "One job led to another, and eventually I made port here. But since my last job, nothing's come up. I've been stuck here for a month now, and I really need to find work soon. I thought I had a job yesterday, but it fell through and..." Kiyami fell silent, staring at her hands.

Celeste's brow furrowed, and she lowered herself back to the floor. The idea that someone could be jobless, left behind by their own people without purpose, was startling. Worry clouded Kiyami's face, letting on a little more about the girl's situation than perhaps she had intended. Celeste's shoulders loosened. Apparently, they were both adrift. Kiyami must have noticed this too, for she offered Celeste a warm smile. And Celeste, in spite of herself, returned it.

"I must admit—I feel terrible not knowing your name," Kiyami said, taking a bite of her bread and chewing. "What if I tried to guess it?"

Celeste shrugged.

"All right," Kiyami said, turning to face her. "Is it a common Ethorian name? Like Jayne? Or Abagail? You are Ethorian, aren't you?"

The siren laughed.

"Right, sorry. One question at a time. Is it a common Ethorian name?"

Celeste shook her head.

"Ah, I see. That could make things more challenging. How long is your name? How many letters?"

Although Celeste had never learned to write, she had been taught the letters of her name. She counted each letter before lifting seven fingers.

Kiyami laughed. "Seven! Okay! We're getting somewhere. Is the first letter... *A*?"

Celeste shook her head.

"*B*?"

Another shake.

"*C*?"

At this, Celeste nodded, practically jumping up in excitement.

Kiyami beamed. "Yes! Seven letters and it begins with C. Hm..."

They continued this guessing game, Kiyami asking letter after letter and Celeste nodding or shaking her head for each. Celeste eventually brought herself to try the bread. It was rather hard and tasteless, but it was better than nothing. Once the food was finished, Celeste felt somewhat herself again, despite the circumstances. Kiyami guessed *T* for the sixth letter of Celeste's name, and the siren nodded again.

"Is the last letter *E*? Is your name Celeste?"

At once, all the air swept from Celeste's lungs. It didn't occur to her how it would feel to hear her name again, spoken to her by a human. It was as though, after days of drifting, she had at last made anchor. Someone in this world *knew* her. Celeste blinked back tears, and she nodded.

"Celeste," Kiyami said again, grinning. "It's nice to meet you."

Perhaps names had a special sort of magic. Because as the two looked at each other, something had changed between them. The shift was subtle, barely perceptible, but present all the same. Celeste didn't consider them friends, nor did she think letting her guard down around any humans was a good idea. But at least she wasn't afraid of this human. With careful fingers, she touched the painful bruises on her arms, as if to remind herself they could still be just as monstrous—a fact she had so brutally learned firsthand.

Shouting erupted somewhere within the jail, the echoes ringing through the cells. Kiyami turned and leaned toward the bars. They heard the unmistakable thud of a body hitting the floor. And... was that the growl of an animal? Celeste tensed, sliding further from the cell bars. Whatever was happening, she wanted no part in it.

"I think someone is coming," Kiyami said. "And it's not the guard."

Celeste tugged her coat around her shoulders. Whoever had overtaken the guards must be far worse.

Hurried footfalls and the jangle of metal signaled the intruder was entering the hall. Shouts of humans struggling continued. A bang silenced them, so loud it rang in Celeste's ears. She clutched her head, doubling over. A sound of death.

The cell door clanged open.

When Celeste looked up, Prince Raiden Sharp was framed in the doorway, staring down at her with fathomless dark eyes.

"Hello again." He smiled.

CHAPTER 13

"Rai? What are you doing here?" Kiyami picked herself up off the floor.

"I'm here to break you out of jail," he said with a crooked smile. "Obviously."

Panic rose like bile in Celeste's throat. She stood up, using the wall to aid her. But her legs were shaking. The human prince was here? Of all places?

Bastian joined them, chest heaving from exertion.

"Look who's here." Raiden's eyes flicked back to Celeste. "Aren't you full of surprises?"

"Do you two know each other?" Kiyami looked between them.

Celeste shook her head.

"She's—" The prince paused and looked from Celeste's feet to her face and back again. His eyes narrowed, his expression unreadable as he scrutinized her. Deep down, a part of her had wanted him to recognize her. To know it was her who had saved him. But this wasn't at all how she had pictured their reunion. She thought she'd have time to prepare.

The prince's face transformed into a cold smile. "She's the girl who saved my life."

All the blood drained from Celeste's face.

"What?" Bastian looked from his friend to Celeste as though trying to piece together a fading dream. Not with recognition, but confusion. *He doesn't remember me.* He had been seduced by the Song and knocked unconscious for the duration of their time together. The relief was short-lived, however, when her eyes glanced back toward the prince. Luckily, her legs would keep him from outing her as a siren. And sirens were a myth to humans anyway. She could just pretend she didn't know him, and maybe he'd think she *reminded* him of that siren.

The prince ran a hand through his dark hair and pushed into the cell. It was the first time Celeste realized how *tall* he was. He stood a head above her, at least. The left side of his mouth pulled into that now familiar smirk as he stalked toward her. Celeste couldn't move even if she wanted to. Hair stood up on her arms, a strange sensation.

"This is the girl who rescued Baz and me when our ship went down," he repeated. To Kiyami and Bastian, Celeste was certain he sounded friendly, perhaps even excited. But she could see in his eyes something else. Something that reminded her of a shark eyeing its prey. This was not the boy she rescued. The one who gave her space while she cried and would trade his life for his friend. This was the son of the king who killed sirens.

"Celeste, is this true?" Kiyami asked, a note of awe in her voice.

At the sound of her name, the prince cocked an eyebrow.

Celeste shook her head fervently. *No.* She wished she could scream it, but she didn't want Kiyami to know she had lied about not being able to speak. The humans needed to trust her.

The prince grinned, teeth bared. "No need to be modest," he said, ignoring Celeste's denial.

"I don't remember a girl," Bastian said.

"You hit your head pretty hard, my friend," Raiden admitted. "But I could never forget this face." His eyes moved from hers to her lips and back again. "And that hair... like starlight."

Celeste's hand flew to her hair of its own volition. Her face heated.

The prince's smile widened.

Anger boiled within her, white-hot. She had risked everything to save him, including her own life, her family's honor... and he was *toying with her*. The pompous human considered her nothing more than a fish caught in his net. *Good*, Celeste thought, bitterness on her tongue. *Let him believe that. It'll be that much easier to kill him when he underestimates me.*

A familiar pink nose and large eyes caught her attention. The Admiral beat his golden tail back and forth as it ambled toward her, nails tapping against the stone floor. Without thinking, Celeste smiled, reaching her hand down for it to nuzzle its soft head against her.

The prince's eyes lit in triumph. "See? Even my dog remembers her."

Damn him. She'd been caught by the animal.

"And I was afraid I'd never see you again," he went on. "How convenient that I came across you while trying to release my old friend Kiyami."

"Speaking of, to what do I owe the pleasure?" Kiyami asked, folding her arms across her chest. "Not that I mind."

The prince turned. "I'm putting together a crew, and—"

"I'm not interested," Kiyami interrupted, pushing past Raiden. "But thank you for the rescue."

Raiden's hand flew to her wrist. "Ito Kiyami has sworn off sailing?"

"Not sailing." She pulled her arm away. "I've sworn off working for people like *you and your father*."

Raiden flinched as though she had slapped him. His cocky expression slipped.

Kiyami turned her back to him and strode for the exit. But Bastian moved to block her path, casting Raiden an unsure glance.

"If you join us, I'll pay you so handsomely that you'll never have to work again," Raiden said.

She froze. "You can't promise that."

"I can."

She turned. "How much?"

"If we complete this job by the eclipse, we'll receive our weight in gold."

"And which *benefactor* is providing these riches?" she asked, her question as barbed as a sea urchin.

Raiden shrugged. "We're hunting lost treasure."

Celeste would have wondered what business a prince had searching for treasure, but she was a princess who had searched for treasure on numerous occasions. A commonality she resented at this point.

Kiyami let out a laugh. "A treasure hunt? You can't be serious."

The prince's eyes flashed. "If you're not interested, we can always leave you here."

She sighed, crossing her arms. "I get a captain's share."

"Of course."

"And passage to Oshiga," she added.

Raiden looked to Bastian, who sighed and rubbed his temples with the heels of his hands. "I suppose we can make it happen, if she's as good as you say she is," Bastian said.

"Welcome aboard." Raiden stuck out his hand. To Celeste's surprise, Kiyami wrapped her hand around his. What sort of relationship did they have? Kiyami's expression was anything but happy. She looked as though she had sold her soul to Death itself.

The prince turned his gaze to her. "And you, *Celeste* . . ." Her name on his lips sent an unexpected chill down her spine. She pulled the coat in her arms closer to her chest, trying to take up as little space as possible. "Why not come along? We know you're excellent in a crisis, given you saved Bastian, the Admiral, and myself from a watery grave."

Celeste's lips pressed into a thin line.

"What other skills do you have?"

It occurred to Celeste that up until now this pompous prince hadn't asked her a single question, let alone allowed her to get in a word. And Celeste was not about to start trying to speak now. She didn't want to give him any further proof of sirens.

"Celeste is mute, Rai," Kiyami offered.

"Ah," Raiden said, eyeing Celeste skeptically. For a moment, he was adrift, but soon his calculated demeanor returned. "The rest of the crew is too loud already anyway. You'll be the perfect addition."

Clearly, the prince wasn't about to take no for an answer. But why did he want her to join the crew so badly? What could he possibly want from her? He obviously recognized her, but for some reason he hadn't exposed her as a siren. Whatever game he was playing, it was only a matter of time until Celeste figured it out. But she needed time to plan—and to retrieve her spear.

She shook her head. *No.*

Raiden shrugged. "All right then, come along, Baz. Kiyami. I'm sure the guards will be excited to see Celeste is still here when they wake."

Celeste's eyes widened, and she reached out a hand, grabbing the front of his shirt. Raiden lowered his eyes to her hand and smiled.

"I knew you couldn't resist me," he purred.

Oh, how she wanted to slap him. But there was no way Celeste would let him leave her locked up here. Not if there was a chance of that first guard coming back. And as she thought about it, being aboard his ship meant she wouldn't have to track him down. It was the perfect excuse for her to learn why he had been in siren territory. Had he been going after this treasure there? Or had he been scared off, and this journey was something different? Although she hoped for the latter, she could easily believe this stubborn, egotistical human would attempt the journey into siren waters a second time.

What sort of monster led his crew to their deaths just to replace them? Her stomach rolled at the thought. Perhaps she'd push him overboard once she knew everything. She wouldn't even have to draw blood. At this moment, the idea sounded downright enjoyable. Once he drowned, she'd drag his lifeless body back to Staria and be welcomed home with open arms. *Easy.* She pulled on her coat, ready to go.

"We can't bring her on the ship, *Your Highness*," Bastian said, giving Celeste an apologetic look. "We hardly have money for supplies as it is. If she's joining the crew, she's got to fill a role."

Celeste wrung her hands. Her training was in combat and Song. She knew ships had a captain, but she knew little of other roles and didn't remember anything about them having warriors. Plus, she was still learning to use this new body and was completely unfamiliar with their weaponry. She glanced from Bastian to Raiden.

The prince searched her as if looking for some sign as to where her talents lay. His eyes snagged on her nervous fingers picking at the stitching of her coat.

"Is that—" His hand reached for the coat, and Celeste shrugged it off quickly, eager to avoid his touch. Raiden took it, examining the embroidered star with reverence. "This is the shield of the Guild of Wayfinders. Are you a member?"

Celeste had absolutely no idea what he was talking about. She nodded.

Bastian's face lit up in surprise, while Raiden's face clouded in confusion.

"What's the Guild of Wayfinders?" Kiyami asked.

"It's an Ethorian association that oversees the craft of mapmaking and the practice of navigating," Bastian explained. "Only the best navigators on the waters may join the esteemed members of the guild. They're—"

"Legendary," Raiden finished, staring at her. Whatever assumptions he had made about Celeste had been thoroughly shaken. He looked as though he was seeing her for the first time.

Celeste stuck out her chin and grinned. She didn't care that she had no idea what the Guild of Wayfinders was; nothing could take away the smug joy she felt finally getting the upper hand against the prince. She reached her hand out, flicking her eyes from his face to the coat. *Now give it back*. With a grunt, he returned the coat. Celeste made a show of dusting nonexistent sand from its sleeves, before reverently draping it back across her shoulders. When she looked up, she found Raiden's eyes still on her, dark and cold. She met his gaze steadily.

A moment passed between their heated looks.

"Well, we are in need of a navigator," Bastian said, breaking the tension between the two with an uncomfortable smile.

Raiden ran a hand through his dark hair and at last looked away. Celeste sneaked a look at Kiyami, who was grinning proudly at her. And to her surprise, Celeste found herself grinning back.

"Would you like to join our crew?" Bastian asked. "You'll have an equal share of the treasure we find, and there will be room for you to sleep with the other—"

She couldn't stop herself from grimacing at the mention of sharing a room with humans. It sounded horrifying, especially with memories of last night still on her mind. Plus, it would be much more challenging to sneak around the ship if she were constantly surrounded by humans.

"Don't like the sound of that, do you?" Raiden laughed.

Celeste ignored him.

"Quite the *negotiator*," he said. "But we should be able to find you a room of your own *if* you are as good as your guild's reputation suggests."

Bastian rubbed his temples again, less than pleased at this promise.

"So, are we agreed, Celeste?" The prince extended a large hand toward her.

Celeste flinched away, memories of the constable echoing in her head. But she swallowed the feeling and reached to clasp wrists as sirens did when greeting another siren or forming an agreement. When he grabbed her hand instead, a spark of electricity ran up her arm. Celeste's breath hitched. Sirens only held hands when they were intimate; it was a touch reserved for lovers. Raiden's hand was calloused and warm as it firmly gripped hers. She tightened her own grip in response, trying to match his actions as best she could. Maintaining eye contact, the prince lifted their clasped hands up and brought them back down. Once, then again. On the second shake, the white fabric of her sleeve fell open, revealing the dark black crescent on her wrist. Of the three deals she had made in the past three days, she wondered which she'd regret the most.

Raiden smiled.

Celeste considered returning his smile, attempting to play along, when he leaned into her, bringing his lips a breath away from her ear. Her heart hammered in her chest.

"I know what you are, *siren*," he said. His voice dropped so low that only she could hear. Celeste froze. "And I will find out why you've returned to me." His breath was warm against her cheek. "You may be my *savior*, but if you put any of this crew in danger, I will kill you."

Not if you're already dead. Celeste seethed.

A voice rang out from the front of the jail.

"I thought we took care of them." Raiden dropped Celeste's hand as he turned to Bastian.

"We might have missed one." His friend shrugged.

"Missed one?"

Several sets of voices shouted. They sounded angry.

"Or several," Bastian amended.

Raiden sighed, rubbing his temples before unsheathing his sword. Footsteps reverberated around the stone walls.

"Maybe there's a back way?" Bastian suggested.

"Good idea." The two left the cell, Bastian running away from the noise, with the Admiral barking at his heels, while Raiden held the cell door open.

"After you," he purred.

Kiyami rolled her eyes but grabbed her skirts in her hands and ran after Bastian. "What about my things? They have my favorite sword!"

"We'll get you a new sword," Raiden called back.

Celeste didn't move. She wasn't confident in walking, let alone running. And she refused to show weakness in front of the prince.

"Come on, love," Raiden pressed.

The commotion was just down the hall now. "They're here!" a voice shouted. "The prisoners are escaping!" It was the guard who'd cut her bodice from her.

Her body began to shake.

"Hurry!" Raiden put his hand on his sword.

Celeste set her jaw, released her hold on the cell wall, and stepped forward. Her legs promptly buckled. Raiden surged forward, catching her just before her shredded knees hit the stone ground.

"Sorry for this, but we're out of time," the prince said before scooping her into his arms and kicking the heavy cell door back open.

He had only taken two steps in the direction of the others when Bastian, Kiyami, and the Admiral came sprinting toward them.

"No back way," Bastian said as the trio ran past down the hall, a guard in pursuit.

Raiden cursed.

The too familiar guard stepped around the corner, blocking their escape. He smiled with his yellow teeth. "Nowhere to run."

Celeste, to her utter horror, wrapped her arms around Raiden's neck, curling into him as if to escape the man's gaze.

Raiden looked down at her, and a vein in his neck ticked.

"Now, put down the girl and get in the cell." The guard raised his sword. "We've got you surrounded."

The group huddled back-to-back in the center of the hall, two of them unarmed. The guards laughed, swords gleaming.

Raiden merely sighed, withdrew a pistol from his belt, and shot the guard in the leg.

"This is what we should have done the first time," he informed Bastian.

CHAPTER 14

The guard crumpled to the floor, crying out as blood poured from the wound in his leg. Celeste had to swallow her horror.

"I thought we agreed no bloodshed," Bastian argued before he fired his own weapon. The second guard went down screaming. "Now how are we to stay in town and get a crew?"

Raiden hefted Celeste in his arms, adjusting his grip. "I suppose we'll have to figure something out," he said, stepping over the guard and bolting down the hall. The others followed, ready for a fight.

But there was no need. As they sprinted through the front of the building, they found the other guard still unconscious on the floor. Kiyami tracked down her belt laden with weapons, checked her favorite sword, and the four of them—plus the Admiral—fled from the jail.

Outside the sun was bright, blindingly so compared to the dark cell they'd come from. Celeste squinted, taking in the city around her from a new perspective. Port Romsey felt like a different place than the one she was dragged through the night prior. Everywhere she looked there were humans going about their daily lives—shouting over each other, laughing, bartering, fighting. She saw a few animals similar to the Admiral poking around a pile of dirty crates, their matted fur far different from the prince's well-kept pet. The crates sat beside a couple of stands with what looked to be food—the scent of it was incredible. But before she could get a better look, the group turned onto a side street.

"We should go to the Broken Compass," Bastian gasped as they ducked into a darkened alcove to avoid a passing officer. "We can lie low there. Pick up more crew. I'd rather that than risk leading them back to my family."

"Worth a shot," Raiden agreed.

The Broken Compass, it turned out, was Port Romsey's most notorious pub and inn. It sagged on the corner of two streets that crossed at a narrow angle, looking as though it had been squeezed in order to fit. Its peeling red paint was faded to pink, and its windows were opaque with dirt. Even the doorway was crooked. The entrance was marked by a large wooden sign displaying a circle with four arrows painted on it, the downward one red. Celeste recognized the image immediately. It was just like the gold thing she had scavenged for her collection at home. *Compass*, she thought, but she wasn't sure how it was broken.

The group paused at the entrance.

"This the place?" Kiyami eyed the pub with distaste. "Doesn't look like much. The pub I went to last night was far nicer."

A cry came from down the street. "Stop! Criminals!" Apparently, a guard had woken up.

"I think it looks lovely," Raiden said, voice tight. "Shall we?"

Before anyone could respond, he shoved open the door with his foot and marched into the pub, Celeste still clutched in his arms.

"What are you doing kicking open my door?" a low voice called out.

Bastian and Kiyami hurried inside, ushering the Admiral in with them. Behind them, the guard was steps away.

Bastian took one look and closed the door in his face. He turned, pressing his back to the door, which trembled as the guard outside pounded on it. Raiden's shoulders relaxed, and he set Celeste down on her feet.

"My lady," he teased.

Celeste pushed away from him, rocking a little but able to remain upright. It took a moment for her eyes to adjust to the dimly lit interior of the pub. If the room was loud before, it was certainly quiet now. Only the clink of glasses and a few murmurs filled the room. A pair of men sat at the bar, nearly falling out of their seats as they leaned on one another. Looking around, Celeste could gather that a pub was a place where they served whatever made humans drunk. She still didn't understand the point. Why sell something that made humans act odd and then lock them up when they did? But considering Kiyami was unaffected this morning, she gathered water was harmless.

Celeste was distracted from her thoughts by the approach of a whale of a man, at least a head taller than Raiden, with a knit hat upon his head and a thick black beard. His muscular frame cast a shadow over their small group, reminding her of the guard who'd apprehended her. His tanned arms were thicker than one of Celeste's thighs.

"Who are you, and what trouble have you brought here?" the man asked.

"I'm Captain Raiden Sharp." Raiden dipped a little as if in a bow. "And this is my crew. We're looking for a place to stay." The banging on the door sounded again. "You don't happen to be the owner of this fine establishment?"

"I'm the cook," the man growled. "And the one who keeps trash like you from bringing us trouble. Looks like you have a friend outside who wants a word." He stepped toward the door.

Bastian and Raiden exchanged glances.

"Let's not get hasty, Mister . . . ?"

"Nasir," the man supplied.

"Nasir," Raiden repeated. "A *pleasure*. Well, Nasir, I'm sure there's something we could work out. You let us hide out in this wonderful establishment, and we'll owe you."

"*Captain* Raiden Sharp your name is?" Nasir asked, eyeing him.

Raiden cocked a brow. "Yes."

Nasir considered him for a moment. "I know a gunner from Yenri. He's been looking for work. Take him on, and I'll let you stay."

"It's a de—"

"Wait!" Bastian interrupted, frowning. "A gunner from Yenri? What's his name?"

"Torben Helvig." Nasir crossed his arms.

Raiden paled and glanced toward Bastian. "Name another price. Anything else."

"No," Nasir said. "Take it or leave."

"Let me in! By order of the guard!" a muffled voice called. The door rattled.

"All right," Raiden said quickly, "he can join us."

The two shook hands.

"Get upstairs," Nasir said. "I'll get rid of your friend."

"This calls for a toast!" Kiyami said, waving down the bartender.

The group had reconvened in the bar once they'd been alerted the guard had gone. Apparently, Nasir had convinced the guard they'd escaped and led the man on a wild chase heading clear across town. As soon as he returned, Nasir sent an errand boy to fetch Torben, an interaction that Raiden watched with obvious annoyance.

As the day drew on, many men entered the Compass to speak with the prince. News had spread that a captain was putting together a crew at the Compass. Raiden accepted them all, and it wasn't long before Celeste realized that him offering her a role on the ship wasn't a compliment. The man was desperate. This crew he was forming looked about as competent as a herd of sea slugs. Raiden was a prince, so why was he accepting any schmuck who wandered into the pub? Was he a prince of a different kingdom, with no pull here in Ethoria? Celeste knew Kiyami was not from here, and

Kiyami had told her she and Raiden knew each other as children, so it was likely he wasn't from here either. Or was it rumors of his last crew all dying at sea that kept any sane person away?

Over time, Raiden's posture began to slump, and Kiyami, bored, left the table to "chat" with the barmaid—although the chatting looked a lot more like flirting. Celeste, however, found everything fascinating. The very idea of sailing on a human ship was something she had fantasized about nearly her entire life.

Celeste learned that Bastian, as the quartermaster, was in charge of managing supplies and ensuring the crew followed the captain's orders. Between interviews, Raiden and Bastian almost exclusively conversed about which supplies they would need, where they would get them, how they would afford them. Typically, such dry talk would bore Celeste to tears. But everything Raiden and Bastian said was a new discovery. Humans apparently needed quite a bit to survive on the ocean. Food, water, livestock (whatever that was), feed for the livestock, ale, rum—the list went on and on.

"Do ya think you'd be able to get some chickens?" Nasir asked in his soft voice as he approached the table with four plates of food balanced on his forearms. "Always a treat to have fresh eggs." The food was completely different from what Celeste had seen in the jail. He called it chicken curry and rice, and it smelled of earthy spices and meat. Celeste nodded in thanks as Nasir placed a plate in front of her, and he gave her a warm smile in return. With his massive frame and quiet demeanor, Celeste would have thought him a warrior. But he positively lit up when talking about food.

Kiyami returned to the table just in time to eat, the barmaid watching her go with lovesick eyes as big as saucers.

"This looks delicious," Kiyami said, pulling up a stool and flicking her long, dark hair over her shoulder. She was right. The food was delicious. As warm and as comforting as a loved one's embrace. The complex, colorful flavors danced along Celeste's tongue, and before she knew it, she had finished. Nasir returned to take the cleaned plates away, and Celeste couldn't help but soften at his pleased smile when he thought no one was looking.

The door to the bar opened with a bang, and a short, broad man lumbered in, looking very much as though he didn't belong. For one thing, his blond hair was shaved on the sides, with the rest of his hair long and braided down his back. Silver rings adorned the braid, a style Celeste had not seen on any other men in town thus far. He was also shirtless and boasted a rather impressive amount of muscle beneath many black markings. Drawings perhaps? Across his hips he wore a heavy belt, upon which hung an ungodly number of weapons. Some of them she recognized, like daggers and swords, but many others she had never seen before. They jangled against each other as he stalked into the room, silver-blue eyes scanning.

"Oh no," Bastian breathed, shrinking in his seat.

"I've heard someone is hiring a crew," the blond man shouted above the din of the bar.

"Torben!" Nasir's eyes crinkled in the corners as he smiled, pushing through the doorway that led to the kitchens. Nasir looked upon the man as though there was no one else in the room.

"My heart," Torben said, closing the distance between them. "Where are the men who asked for me?"

Nasir nodded toward Raiden and Bastian, both of whom were looking determinedly in the opposite direction. Kiyami snorted.

"Gentlemen," grunted Torben, sauntering toward the table. "I have heard you requested my assistance on your crew."

Raiden turned first. "Ah! Torben! I didn't see you come in."

Do all humans know each other? Celeste wondered, looking between them.

At seeing Raiden, Torben straightened. His eyes grew as wide as saucers. And a smile lit his face, as if a vast treasure had been dropped directly into his lap. "If it isn't Captain Raiden Sharp!" Torben roared, his large hand smacking Raiden on the back. "I haven't seen you since you were no taller than me!"

Raiden's answering smile looked stiff. "Has it been that long?"

"Didn't your father send you off with your own crew?" Torben helped himself to a chair and Celeste's full tankard of ale. "Why are you lookin' for crew in this hellhole of all places?"

The prince's eyes narrowed. "If Romsey is such a wasteland, why are you here?" The way he said this led Celeste to believe Raiden already knew the answer. Torben's expression darkened.

"We actually came to speak with Kiyami," Bastian said, eyeing his captain. "We left Velluno, and Raiden heard she was last seen here. But it was our luck we ran into your husband, who told us you were"—he searched for the words—"between jobs," he finished delicately.

Torben downed the remainder of Celeste's ale and slammed the tankard on the table. "What's the job?"

Raiden looked toward Celeste and then leaned toward Torben, dropping his voice. "We're hunting treasure."

The man's eyes practically glittered, a devilish grin growing on his face. "Treasure?" His face sobered. "Where?" he asked, growing suspicious. "I haven't heard of anything."

The prince laughed, but there was no warmth in it. "You must believe me a fool if you think I would tell you the location."

Torben's face burned red. "Do you want to say that to me again, boy?" He spat. "Just like your father. Disloyal bunch of—"

"I'm not sure if an old-timer like you would be up for it anyway," Raiden interrupted.

Torben looked like a volcano, ready to erupt. "We'll just see about that, won't we?" he shouted, leaping to his feet. "Try to keep me away, boy! Which is your ship?"

"The *Red Revenge*," Raiden said, the picture of calm.

It was as if the prince had poured water over the man. One second he was a raging fire, and the next he was a wisp of smoke.

"The *Red Revenge*? Valencia's ship?"

"It's *my* ship now," Raiden said with an icy grin.

"You dare steal from the Queen of Pirates?"

An uncomfortable silence fell, not just on their table but over anyone within earshot.

"Commandeered. And she's no queen," the prince said, his voice as sharp as a blade.

From across the table, Kiyami's eyes locked with Celeste's. Her expression was as clear as day: *What exactly have we signed up for?*

"Like I said"—Raiden took a drink—"I'm not sure an old-timer like you would be up for it."

"You bastard," Torben said, sticking out his hand. "I'm in."

Celeste's mouth fell open as the two men shook hands, laughing.

"Good, I hope you have some men you can bring along. We still need plenty of bodies for our ship." Raiden removed his hand, stretching it as though pained.

Torben's eyes lit up. "What about my husband? He's an excellent chef, and he once trained as a surgeon."

Bastian's expression lifted. "*A surgeon?*"

Nasir, who had been watching the exchange, frowned. "I haven't practiced in years. Not since I've lived in Ethoria."

"Still," Bastian pressed, "a rare find."

Torben looked upon Nasir, beaming with pride. "He certainly is."

"It is true we are in need of a cook, and having a surgeon on board would certainly be an asset," Raiden said.

"I—would have to consider it," Nasir hesitated. "Who would run the Compass?"

"Viktoria can handle things," Torben insisted, taking up his husband's hands. "Come with me, my heart. This way we won't need to be separated for so long."

Nasir looked at Torben's face and softened. "All right," he said, then looked to Raiden. "I'll join your crew."

The captain clapped his hands. "Excellent. Now, what shall you both require?"

Once they finished discussing, Torben agreed to bring his men and meet them at the docks in the morning. He kissed his husband goodbye and left.

Nasir turned and smiled warmly at Raiden. "Thank you," he said, before disappearing into the kitchen.

As soon as the cook was gone, Bastian whirled on his prince. "What was *that*?"

"Whatever do you mean, Baz?" Raiden drew his dagger and began picking at his nails with its blade.

"I thought we were agreed! We weren't going to bring on Trigger Finger Torben!"

Raiden shrugged. "We had already promised Nasir. And now we have a surgeon."

A creeping unease settled into Celeste's stomach. She knew humans died on voyages like these all the time, even without siren interference. A competent crew could mean the difference between survival and death. Yet the prince was still accepting just about anyone. She was about to be stuck on a ship with the worst that Port Romsey had to offer.

What was making the prince so desperate? Was someone else after this treasure? Or was he running from this Valencia, the Pirate Queen? Celeste had never heard of her, but her very name had shaken every human at the table. Or was Raiden hiding something else? Perhaps there was something he needed this treasure for. A debt he owed?

A familiar itch rose up Celeste's neck, and she turned to see the prince's eyes on her.

"Don't worry," he said, with a wink. "I'll whip this crew into shape."

Celeste bristled. He hadn't correctly guessed everything she was thinking—but he knew what she was feeling. Straightening, Celeste ignored him. If he had hoped to ease her mind, he hadn't. In fact, he had only made her more nervous. This human was entirely too aware of her. How long before he found out something she didn't want him to know?

"Why didn't you want Torben on your crew?" Kiyami asked.

Raiden laughed. "Wherever did you get that idea?"

"He's got a bit of a reputation," Bastian said.

Kiyami arched a brow. "What sort of reputation?"

Bastian winced and looked to Raiden.

"You may have heard of him by a different name." The prince slid his dagger back onto his hip. "Most call him Ol' Trigger Finger."

Kiyami tensed. "You can't be serious." She looked between Bastian and Raiden, incredulous. "That's Trigger Finger Torben? You're hiring him to be on this crew? Do you have a death wish?"

Celeste seemed to be the only one who didn't already know about this "Trigger Finger," so she elbowed Raiden in the side.

"Haven't heard of him, have you?" he asked with a smirk.

Celeste shrugged.

"Torben 'Trigger Finger' Helvig is known for being a bit of a liability. He's worked as a master gunner all his life and is said to be brilliant when it comes to managing and building weapons—explosives in particular. But he's difficult to work with and volatile," Bastian said.

"He's a psychopath," Raiden corrected. "The last ship he was on, Torben went against direct orders from his captain and started firing on a passing ship without cause. It was Valencia's ship. Torben got most of his crew killed. And she nearly sank them."

"Wasn't he on your father's crew?" Kiyami asked.

Raiden paused, jaw tightening. It looked as though he was going to ignore her question, before he let out a breath and nodded. "Yes."

"The king pushed him overboard in the middle of the ocean," Bastian said. "Rumor was, he'd drowned, but it seems he managed to make his way here."

"It's not as though I'm much better," Raiden said, so quietly Celeste almost didn't hear him over the noise of the pub.

Bastian stiffened. "What happened to our crew wasn't your fault."

Raiden nodded and looked away.

A wave of nausea rose within Celeste at the memory of that night. The hundreds of writhing bodies. Her mother crying in a cell. She was tired—emotionally and physically. The more she learned about these humans, the more confused she became. It didn't help matters that she hadn't slept properly in days. She must have looked as horrible as she felt, because Kiyami glanced at her and laughed.

"You awake there, Celeste?" she teased.

The siren blinked, realizing her eyes had been drooping. A blush warmed her face, and she lifted her hands to hide it.

"It's getting late," Bastian said. "Why don't we all head off to bed? We'll want to set sail as soon as the ship is readied tomorrow."

And so their small crew dispersed. Kiyami and Celeste were given a room to share in the inn. The two of them walked up the winding staircase in the back of the pub to the second floor. Their room was number five, the farthest door to the right. Kiyami inserted the key the barmaid had given her into the lock and heard a satisfying click as she twisted. It took a couple of tries to open the door, as if it didn't want to admit them, but eventually it relented. The room was simple. There was no decoration upon the wooden walls, save for one portrait above the dresser that looked like a painting of the ocean from the docks. Two small beds with simple blue blankets faced the door, and between them was a window that faced another building.

It was the most perfect room Celeste had ever seen.

As soon as Kiyami had closed the door behind them, the exhaustion hit Celeste like a wave. The muscles at the back of her neck ached, as if she had been on high alert ever since she had become a human. She hadn't felt this fatigued since her early days of training for the Chorus.

Kiyami collapsed onto her small bed, removing her shoes, and Celeste did the same. The window showed the building next door was darkening, but as she looked up, she could see a small sliver of sky. A silver moon shined down upon the port town, the same crescent shape that darkened her wrist. Too tired to think anymore about the mess she found herself in, Celeste lay down on the bed, fully clothed and still clutching her Wayfinder coat. Sirens were perfectly comfortable floating as they slept. But many enjoyed having the option of lying upon something, so the concept of a bed wasn't entirely foreign. This bed, however, was far more comfortable than any surface she'd laid upon before. Springy and full of some sort of stuffing, it creaked as she moved. But she found her eyelids closing before she could inspect it further.

Despite her fatigue, every noise sent her bolt upright, heart racing. She noticed when Kiyami slipped out of the room sometime in the night, likely meeting with Viktoria, the barmaid. And when sleep at last found the little siren, it was wrapped in nightmares.

Celeste awoke to a loud banging. She gasped, feeling as though she couldn't breathe. There was no water around her. But as she sat upright, everything came flooding back. Her confusion was over in a moment, but it was a rather unpleasant way to wake up.

"Hurry, or we're leaving you on shore," Raiden called through the door.

Celeste turned and found Kiyami's bed empty. The sun shone brightly through the window behind her head. How long had she been asleep? She slipped off the bed, combed her hands through her hair, and opened the door.

"Did you sleep in that?" Raiden said, fixing her with an appraising look as he leaned against the wall near the stairway.

Celeste ignored him.

"If you ever need help changing, love, I'd be glad to be of ser—" Before he could finish his sentence, Celeste hurled her coat at his head.

He caught it easily, bursting into laughter. Indignant, Celeste marched past him, snatching the coat back before making her way down the stairs. The prince followed smoothly behind. Even the way he walked irritated her. Why did he insist on tormenting her every waking moment? As Celeste reached the bottom of the stairs, she noticed the pub was empty.

"The rest of them are already on the ship," Raiden said.

Why hadn't they woken her?

"You refused to wake up," Raiden said, as if he had read her mind. "You nearly strangled me to death when I tried."

Celeste sighed. It was a shame she hadn't succeeded.

CHAPTER 15

The spear was gone. In her heart, she'd known it would be, but it still didn't stop the pain she felt when she gazed upon the empty beach. Her heart squeezed within her chest. She had nothing left of her past. It was almost as if her life before had never existed. Or it would have been, if not for the very *alive* prince who watched her. He moved like her shadow, following in her wake as she combed the shore for her beloved weapon. He hadn't tried to stop her when she veered away from the docks and onto the beach, nor had he asked any questions. But it was clear he wanted to keep a very close eye on her. Celeste sighed. It wasn't as if Raiden would be giving her a weapon of her own anytime soon. And she needed something to protect herself around the nearly *fifty humans* that would be on the ship. Her stomach turned at the thought. Perhaps she'd have to steal something.

"Time to go," Raiden said.

She nodded, joining his side. The two of them walked along the beach in the sunshine, sounds of crashing waves filling the space between them. She may have felt as trapped today as she had that night she arrived on this beach, but at least she could walk this time. Even if it was slow and awkward. Her eyes roamed to Raiden:

His hair tousled in the sea breeze. His mole on his left cheek. The corner of his lip quirked up.

"You'll have plenty of time to stare at me during our voyage, *Wayfinder.*"

And just like that, her tentative ease with him splintered like thin ice. Oh, how she wished to cut out his tongue. Celeste didn't consider herself a particularly violent siren, but something about him made her so angry. She had risked her life for him, and he was nothing more than an egotistical, domineering princeling. Not to mention he stole the ship they were about to embark upon and planned to steal this treasure as well. And although his motives were yet to be determined, it was obvious they were selfish ones. With a huff, Celeste balled up the coat in her hands and stuck it beneath her arm, marching off alone toward the ship.

The *Red Revenge* towered above the other ships along the dock, its three huge masts standing proudly in the sunshine. The sides were freshly polished and gleaming, painted the deep red color of algae. Along the front and back of the ship, elaborate carved plants bloomed, wrapped in what looked like dark pointed teeth. Celeste drank in the splendor of it, her heart fluttering in her chest. Its deck was alive with activity. Crew members hefted large barrels of supplies down into the heart of the ship, while others ran about checking the ropes. She watched them with great interest, as she had schools of colorful fish. But these humans were not colorful. Their clothes were shades of gray and brown, and most of them wore multiple weapons on their hips. A mixture of excitement and dread swirled within her chest, pressing her forward. And behind, she heard the now familiar footsteps of their captain.

As they reached the gangway, the two were greeted by a happy bark. Celeste brightened, crouching down to meet the Admiral at eye level. The dog wriggled with joy, bouncing and barking like a seal before her. She let out a laugh as she combed her fingers through his soft fur. Raiden stood behind them, watching the interaction intently.

"Celeste!"

She lifted her chin to see Kiyami waving at her. The dark-haired girl stood out from the others. Because she was female, of course, but also from the black leather armor jutting out across her shoulders. It looked almost scaled the way the leather was layered, and similar pieces of leather fell in strips around her hips. Today she wore black pants and boots, a flat blade at her side. Beside Kiyami stood the pretty brunette barmaid from the night before, glaring daggers at Celeste. An expression she understood immediately. Perhaps humans and sirens weren't as different as she thought. They certainly had jealous lovers in common. Kiyami waved Celeste toward them. If she noticed the barmaid's expression, she hadn't let on.

Celeste's legs shook beneath her as she strode up the gangway. Partially because she was now balancing on a hunk of wood but also because she was setting foot *on a human ship*. Of all the times she had pictured a ship like this sailing across the ocean, she had never pictured herself upon it. The Admiral bounded off, tailing Nasir, who was carrying an armful of fat, feathered birds. Celeste wondered if those were the chickens he mentioned, and if their eggs were as delicious as the salmon ones from home. When she finally reached the deck, the ship swayed beneath her. Her feet stumbled as her body tilted off its axis, sending her falling backward toward the gangway. She braced for impact, curling her arms into herself, when a pair of strong arms wrapped around her. Celeste stilled, head turning back to see who caught her.

A pair of dark eyes stared down at her. It was Raiden, of course. He had been following close behind her. Her body froze, panic rising like bile in her throat. Although she'd been held by him before, being touched by any human still made her want to run away screaming. Celeste planted her feet and pulled away, and for a moment, she feared he wouldn't let go. But his arms loosened, and he placed his hands on her shoulders to steady her. A sharp pain shot through her arms at the touch, and Celeste winced.

"Did I hurt you?" he asked, pulling his hands from her as though she had burned him.

She shook her head, folding her arms protectively across her chest. Apparently, the bruises left from the constable were still tender, but she didn't want Raiden to know. Not to mention she was embarrassed. Raiden, she hated to admit, had helped her. Twice now. Why was she reacting this way?

The captain nodded, but his expression remained skeptical. He turned and made his way onto the deck, greeting crewmates and giving orders as he went. Celeste's gaze fell upon Kiyami, who was saying farewell to the Broken Compass's barmaid. As she brought the brunette's knuckles to her lips, the poor girl nearly dissolved. Celeste smiled at the sight and turned away to give them privacy.

"I'm happy to see you didn't sleep through our departure," Kiyami said, joining her. "Sorry I didn't stay last night. I had—other accommodations."

Celeste laughed but shrugged.

"Care for a tour?"

Celeste nodded, perhaps a bit *too* enthusiastically. With a smile, Kiyami beckoned Celeste toward the stairs that brought them down into the ship. On their way, they passed Raiden, who frowned.

"Don't wander too far," he called after them. "I wish to speak with our navigator to plan our course before we depart."

With a sinking feeling, Celeste nodded. But the time when she would have to pretend she was a Wayfinder—whatever that meant—was bound to happen eventually. She knew Raiden didn't actually believe her to be a Wayfinder. So what did he want to discuss with her? How much had his father told him about sirens anyway? How much did they know?

Kiyami pointed past Raiden toward a door below the quarterdeck.

"That's the captain's and superior officers' quarters," she said. "Raiden, Bastian, myself, Torben, and Nasir will be sleeping in there. I believe your room is in there as well." Kiyami pointed to a door that sat upon the quarterdeck. "Navigation room's there, as I'm sure you figured out. I expect that's where Raiden wants to speak with you."

Celeste nodded appreciatively, doing her best to keep a neutral, yet knowledgeable, countenance. Although the Chorus had taught her some parts of the ship, and she had seen many different shipwrecks, most of this was new to her. But she was fairly certain it wouldn't be new to an accomplished member of the Wayfinder guild.

Kiyami ushered Celeste below deck into a dimly lit, large wooden room. Sunlight peeked through narrow gaps where a window would be, if it weren't covered by a wooden flap. And before each of the windows was a large metal cannon. Humans bustled throughout the room, some hanging hammocks between the cannons, while others were rolling heavy barrels through a door at the back. The smell of salt air and human sweat sat thickly in the air.

"Bet you're glad you're not sleeping here in the berth," Kiyami said.

She was right about that.

"Through there is the gunport, and where they keep the rum and water casks," Kiyami said, pointing toward the bow. "And behind us is the infirmary, galley, and officers' mess. We *officers* will be having our meals there." She finished proudly, as if being an officer on this ship were a privilege and not something Celeste had been forced into. "Cargo access is here," Kiyami said, pointing toward a trapdoor in the floor. "And, of course, brig's down there too."

Celeste understood about half of what Kiyami had said. But she nodded along respectfully all the same. She did know the term *brig*. The Chorus had said that humans locked up others in there. Sometimes even sirens, although all of those had been rescued and those ships destroyed. Celeste hoped she would avoid having to see the brig at all, but considering her record thus far for being locked in cells, it wasn't out of the question.

"Now, let's get you upstairs before Raiden gets cross," Kiyami said with a smirk.

They made their way to the stairs as Raiden appeared at the top, blocking out the sun with his tall frame.

"Follow me," he said, before turning and walking away, leaving

Celeste no choice but to follow. As Kiyami had surmised, Raiden led her up onto the quarterdeck and toward a shining wooden door with a golden handle. He pulled it open to reveal a well-lit room, with a wall of curved windows at the back. Celeste stepped into the room upon a plush red rug and looked up at the iron chandelier rocking gently above her head. Whoever Valencia was, she had excellent taste in decor. And the room certainly looked fit for a queen.

Celeste's eyes caught on a large map that took up the entire wall to her left. She moved toward it. It was largely a map of the human kingdoms, along with the Southern Ocean and the Turquoise Sea to the south and east of it, respectively. Celeste had seen many maps before on sunken ships and from the Chorus's collection, but none so beautiful as this. Ethoria's large mass of land spread out in the center of the map like a handprint, and along the west coast sat Port Romsey. Or at least Celeste assumed as much, since she couldn't read a thing on the page.

An issue a real Wayfinder likely didn't have.

Raiden moved further into the room, coming to stand behind a large wooden desk at the center with one throne-like seat behind it. He gestured to a smaller chair before him.

"Join me," he said, the words just shy of a demand.

With a huff, Celeste did as he asked. Sitting upon the table was another map, this one specifically of Ethoria and a near-perfect depiction of the Southern Ocean. A small wooden object sat beside the map, looking very much like their ship. Celeste took the tiny boat and placed it atop the location she believed was Port Romsey. Although she couldn't read, Celeste knew her ocean. Every shallow and every shore. Every siren worth their salt did. It was a part of them. It was their birthright.

Raiden leaned over the map beside her.

"Our destination is here," he said, pointing to a small island far to the southwest of them. It was well past Ethoria's most southern island, upon which Port Velluno was located. In fact, it was past the siren Kingdom of Staria. So far south it would take them weeks to reach it at the slow speed ships sailed. Celeste blinked at the map. The island was so small she could have missed it. That made sense if someone were trying to hide treasure, she supposed. It hadn't been depicted on the map on the wall. The treasure must be great, given the prince was willing to spend so long sailing to an island in the middle of nowhere and back. And she doubted there was anything there. She had never heard of its existence. *Nothing* should have been out there.

"During our last journey..."

Celeste looked up. He blinked, and for a moment, she wondered if she saw a look of anguish cross his face. But it was gone before she could be certain. Then it hit her all at once.

He still mourned the lives of his former crew? Why would he choose to make this trip a second time? Anger flared within her, white-hot. This prince was *choosing* to put another fifty human lives at risk! For money. And despite the fact Celeste shouldn't have cared one way or another about any human lives, the idea of it made her sick.

"We followed this path," he continued, pushing the little wooden ship along a curved line, first moving west, then south through Staria's territory and to the island.

Celeste's nose wrinkled. Of course they would run into trouble going that way. Not only would they be sailing directly through her people's territory but they were taking *the longest route* through it. They would be traveling through Staria's boundaries for *days*. No wonder the Chorus put a stop to them. A shiver ran down Celeste's spine at the memory. If the Chorus found her on this ship before she managed to kill the prince, would they drag her back to Staria to face execution? Or had her mother been able to convince the council of their plan? Either way, she knew the others aboard this ship wouldn't survive such an encounter. But there was no way to reach the island without going through Staria. They could try to skirt around the perimeter, but that could add another week to the voyage.

"I take it you don't approve?" Raiden said.

She must have been making some sort of face again. Celeste looked up from the map, meeting his eyes. They were standing much closer together than she realized, his arm just a breath away from hers. She took a step back.

"We must arrive by the eclipse," he said, watching her closely. "What path do you suggest?"

Celeste stared at him. He was actually asking for her help. Asking her to navigate. Of all the reasons she'd suspected he had to bring her up here, this one hadn't been high on her list. If the prince were asking a siren he didn't trust for advice, he clearly was desperate. Celeste turned her gaze back to the map. Although she wanted the prince dead, it needed to be by her own hand in order to secure her pardon from the council and return home. She considered leading them to a different island. It would give her time to figure out more about the treasure. But Raiden would surely know if they veered too far off the path.

There was, of course, the powerful Lunastri Current that moved through the southern tip of Staria's territory and toward the island he had pointed to. Most sirens avoided it, afraid of being caught by its undertow and pushed miles away through the water. She wasn't even sure if a ship like this could withstand it. And as far as Celeste knew, no humans knew of this current. There was no way Celeste was going to show him *that*. It was more than likely she would kill him long before they made it anywhere near it.

With no better option, Celeste reached out her hand and moved the little wooden ship along a path that ran south, toward Port Velluno, before turning west, through the southeast side of her people's territory, but still remaining well away from the current. This way, she could avoid entering the siren territory for at least the first week at sea, giving herself plenty of time to uncover more about this treasure and to plan the prince's untimely death.

Raiden considered her proposal in silence.

"All right," he said at last, "but this better work."

CHAPTER 16

"I'm sure you'd like to settle in your quarters," Raiden said.

Celeste nodded.

Together they walked from the navigation room, down the stairs onto the deck, and into the officers' quarters. The hallway was short, with only five doors. She knew enough to know the captain's quarters would be the door at the end of the hall, but she wondered which door was Kiyami's. Celeste stiffened at the thought, surprised by it. Since when had she begun to care for the human? Raiden strode down the hallway, stopping abruptly in front of a door on the left.

"Your *room*." He swung open the door with great bravado.

The space was small, only big enough for a single person to lie down in one direction. And it was filled with human clothes. Dresses, pants, skirts, blouses, and belts hung along a rod running through the center. Celeste stepped inside, the smell of musty cloth overwhelming her. Upon the floor sat one flat pillow and a thin blanket. Raiden grinned proudly.

"You wanted your own room, and here it is." He looked at her frown and added, "I never promised it would be *nice*."

Celeste felt as though hot steam would come pouring out of her ears. She didn't expect a *nice* room per se, but this was downright fiendish. Especially after seeing the lavish navigation room. Surely the captain's quarters were as nice, if not nicer. Even the roof of the room was short! It sloped sadly as if sagging under the weight of the deck above. Celeste couldn't even walk fully into the room without ducking, and she was hardly what one would consider tall. The only benefit was a small circular window where she could look out and see the ocean and the sky. She turned her head to Raiden and fixed him with a glare.

This only made him laugh. "I'll let you get settled in," he said smugly, turning away and walking toward the door to his chambers. Which happened to be *right beside her room*. They even shared a wall! He reached the door before he turned back and added, "You could always sleep with the rest of the crew in the berth if this isn't to your liking."

Celeste narrowed her eyes at him, but Raiden merely continued into his quarters, whistling as if he hadn't a care in the world.

As much as she hated to admit it, she wished she knew what his room looked like. Celeste had encountered so many sunken ships, and on each one the captain's room was the most exciting. She heaved a sigh, and with the calm of a frenzied shark, she made herself at home. She kicked the pillow away from the door with a bit more aggression than needed and shut it firmly behind her. The room became significantly smaller with the door closed, but it was bright enough with the light from the window.

As she gazed upon the clothes above her, she wondered if perhaps she might borrow them. She hated wearing the clothes she had on. Not to mention she'd been wearing them for days, didn't like how they felt, and they reminded her of the guard who'd given them to her. It would be preferable to wear no clothes at all, but that didn't seem safe around humans. So, after shuffling through each item, she found a dress that looked rather pretty. It was a deep reddish purple with huge sleeves and black trim. Celeste happily shed her old clothing, but when she pulled the dress from its hanger, she realized she didn't know how to put it on. She recalled seeing many women in the jail in various states of undress as she'd practiced her walking, so she knew that women often wore short white pants beneath their dresses. And sometimes even several layers of skirts. So she found things similar and put them on first, followed by a sort of white armor that reminded Celeste of her stingray bodice. It circled her chest and laced up, with rigid boning holding her in place. Her hands tested the sides. Were they whale bones? She could feel the familiar shape of them. How strange that humans used bones in their clothing.

Celeste considered the bodice, wondering if she had in fact put it on correctly. It felt familiar yet terribly constricting. At least the clothing she had found at the jail was flowing. How was she supposed to sit in this? How was she supposed to fight? She felt ridiculous. But she soldiered onward, shuffling the red dress over the top of her head as she'd seen the other women in jail do. If she had put the clothing on incorrectly, she'd find out one way or another. Celeste pulled at the satin ribbons at her front, cinching herself into the dress. A small piece of the white underdress peeked out the front, and Celeste wondered if this was how the women wore them. It looked close enough to what she recalled, and yet was entirely different from what Kiyami wore.

The ship lurched beneath her, and she scampered to the window in time to see them pull away from the harbor. *They were leaving.* This was it. There was no going back now. A little thrill went through her as she gazed wide-eyed upon the waves moving beneath them, the tightness in her shoulders softening as she watched Port Romsey grow smaller. If everything went according to plan, she'd never see another human town again. This thought, although soothing, bore an unexpected sadness as well. It wasn't the adventure she'd have chosen for herself, yet it was more than likely this would be the one great adventure of her life. When she returned home to Staria, she doubted the council would let her do much of anything. And honestly, she could not blame them.

Smoothing down her skirts, Celeste opened the door to her room. In the hall, she saw Raiden and Bastian locked in what seemed to be a heated conversation, and she froze.

"We must act quickly if we have any chance of reaching the island before—" The sentence died in Raiden's throat as he saw Celeste. The princess dipped her head, trying to hide her intrigue as she stepped into the hall with them. If only she'd thought to listen at the door first.

"You—look much improved," Raiden said, staring.

Celeste flushed. What was that supposed to mean? Something in the way his dark eyes took her in made her feel uncomfortably warm, a feeling she disliked.

"Celeste, now that you're settled, why don't you join Kiyami at the helm?" Bastian said, looking between the two.

She nodded, thankful for any excuse to leave. Out on the deck, the ship was a flurry of activity. Everywhere she looked strange men scrambled around—releasing sails, adjusting rigging, and securing things on board. She thanked the Goddess for her good fortune that she had been assigned the role of navigator, for if she had been asked to do anything else, she would surely be found out. Kiyami stood behind the great wheel of the ship, her hair whipping behind her like a black flag. The ship was heading south, as Celeste had suggested. Pride swelled in her chest as she looked out over the roaring ocean. Despite her disdain for the prince and his obvious distrust of her, he hadn't questioned her. Hadn't ignored her advice or discounted her opinion. A smile formed on her lips. She was *navigating a ship*. She wanted to sing.

"A beautiful day to begin an adventure, wouldn't you say?" Kiyami shouted down to her.

Celeste grinned and walked up the stairs, pulling fistfuls of her skirt up to avoid tripping. When she reached the top of the quarterdeck, Kiyami raised her eyebrows.

"That dress becomes you," she said, then added with a cheeky grin, "I imagine our captain will be pleased."

Celeste grimaced.

"*Only teasing!*" she said through her laughter. "But it's hard not to notice how he can't—stop—looking—at you." Celeste continued to thwack her in between each word. Of course, she wouldn't have said such a thing if Kiyami knew the truth of *why* Raiden insisted on keeping such a close watch on Celeste. But she wouldn't correct her. She had no affection for the prince, though she *was* finding moments of excitement among these humans. Still, every day she spent here was another day her mother and father worried for her. And she couldn't bear the thought that she was hurting them. *Tonight you will work to find out more about this treasure*, she told herself. *The sooner I can get the information and kill him, the sooner I can go home.* Home. Celeste's heart ached in her chest. She was so close to it, and yet she couldn't feel farther away.

The day passed slowly. For the most part, they were following along Ethoria's coastline. But not too closely. Celeste watched with fascination as Port Romsey's flat, broken town gave way to vast golden fields, then to hills, then to rocky cliffs so high they seemed unreal. Occasionally, Celeste would direct Kiyami to avoid shallow waters or rocky terrain. They worked in companionable silence under the watchful eye of their captain, who was never far from view. He milled around the ship, shouting orders and breaking up disputes. There were an oddly large number of fights, most involving Torben.

"I brought a present for our first day," Nasir said, lumbering up the stairs.

Kiyami brightened. "Thank you, Nasir! What is it?"

The cook smiled and reached into his pocket, pulling out a folded cloth.

"They might be crumbled," he admitted, opening the top of the bag and revealing a pile of pale golden disks, smaller than Celeste's palm, with what looked to her like a little brown seed pushed into the center.

"Cookies?" Kiyami said, pulling one from the pile. "Oh, I love almonds. Nasir, you are too kind. Thank you." She took a bite of the edge and hummed happily, making the cook beam with pride. He offered them to Celeste, and she was suddenly hit with guilt for comparing him to the guard. She didn't know them well, but her gut told her Kiyami and Nasir were nice enough, at least compared to other humans. Stomach grumbling, Celeste brought a cookie to her nose and sniffed. The smell reminded her a little of the bread she had before, but much sweeter and softer. She tasted it. It was better than the bread.

"It's a popular treat where I'm from," Nasir said.

Celeste's eyes slid closed as she enjoyed the new sensation. The cookie was a little hard, so it crunched when she bit down. But as she chewed, it softened. She couldn't name the flavors, but it tasted like a warm memory. Sweet, and soft, and comforting. She chewed slowly, savoring every bite. What she thought was a seed in the center was hard, with a thin skin around the outside. An almond, Kiyami called it. When Celeste finished, she opened her eyes again and smiled at Nasir in thanks.

"I'm glad you like it," he said, his eyes crinkling in the corners.

Kiyami took another cookie as Bastian strode up the steps to join them.

Nasir offered them to him as well.

"I never could say no to a biscuit." The quartermaster laughed, helping himself. As Nasir left to continue handing out his cookies, Bastian and Kiyami fell into easy conversation. Although it seemed they hadn't known each other for long, it was clear they were already familiar. Perhaps seafaring was similar to her life in the palace that way. It was a small community, and if you lived there your whole life, eventually you began to know everyone. If only tangentially. The two attempted to include Celeste in the conversation as best they could, which meant sticking to simple yes-or-no questions.

"Do you have any family, Celeste?" Kiyami asked.

The warm sugar of the cookie turned in Celeste's stomach. Of course she had a family, a family who risked everything to save her life. But if she were being honest, it hadn't felt like a true family in a while. Shye was hardly interested in her on the best days, and she hadn't heard anything from Sephone in nearly a cycle. Tears threatened to form in her eyes, and she blinked them back, trying desperately to stop the emotion clawing its way up her throat. She couldn't cry, not in front of these humans. And why was she crying? She was a warrior! And she was fine a mere moment ago. Heroes in stories didn't cry.

A gentle touch landed on her shoulder, as warm as a ray of sun. Celeste looked up to see Kiyami's kind gaze.

"I'm sorry," Kiyami said. "I've lost family too. My mother died when I was ten, and my father"—she took in a breath—"he hasn't been the same since she passed. All the money I make I send back to them, to keep my father and siblings alive. I haven't seen them in years. But with a job like this, I can finally go home. Take care of them properly. One last job, and I'm free."

Celeste's eyes widened. She wasn't used to her family opening up to her, let alone humans she hardly knew. And although Kiyami didn't cry, Celeste could feel her sadness, like a river carving its way through stone. Deep and enduring.

Most sirens didn't show much emotion. In the lifetime that Celeste had known Maeve, she couldn't say she'd seen her friend cry once. Not even when Maeve was stung by that jellyfish when they were seven. Celeste had always admired how strong Maeve was. When bad things came her way, Maeve would carry on without skipping a beat, while Celeste found herself crying whenever she was overwhelmed, or angry, or sad. Her family had teased her for it growing up. Told her to calm down. Be less *human*. That no one would take her seriously if she cried. But no matter what they said, and no matter how hard she tried, she could never stop herself. For the thousandth time, Celeste wished she were normal. That she were strong and could control herself. Control her emotions. Even now, her feelings betrayed her and revealed too much.

"I lost my father too," Bastian said. "Left my mother and me alone with my baby sister. Do you have any siblings, Celeste?"

Celeste nodded, feeling the tears fall despite her best efforts. The only person in her life who she had lost had been her grandmother. And she'd been so young then. She couldn't imagine how she'd feel if she'd lost a parent, as Kiyami and Bastian had. Guilt washed over her. Here she was, making Bastian and Kiyami think she had lost her family, when in reality she had betrayed them. Her stomach squeezed. She felt sick. Suddenly, she wanted to run, to hide. But she was on a ship. There was nowhere to go save for her room.

"Is everything okay?" Raiden strode up the steps, his eyes firmly on her. It was perhaps the one time Celeste recalled being happy to see him. Thankful for the distraction, she wiped the tears from her cheek.

"Sorry, Captain, just getting to know one another," Bastian said hastily.

Raiden nodded, still not taking his eyes off Celeste. "Glad you all are getting along. You would be the first. The rest of the crew has been having"—he paused, considering—"*issues.*"

Bastian laughed. "Why don't I check on them." He made his way down the stairs, giving Celeste a soft smile as he went.

The rest of the day was spent in much the same way as the first half. All the while, Celeste could not shake her feelings. They rolled around inside her, thrashing like water in a storm. She was embarrassed for crying in front of Bastian and Kiyami; disgusted for daring to feel sorry for herself and the loss of her family, when she had been the traitor; and heartbroken for Kiyami's and Bastian's losses. Not to mention the loss of Raiden's previous crew. How many of them had families who would never see them again? Celeste hated that she had saved the prince, but a part of her hated that she hadn't saved more. Raiden may be selfish, but it was all too clear that not all humans were like that.

A large wave hit the side of the ship, sending Celeste stumbling over. She caught herself on the railing, relieved it was there to keep her from tumbling to the deck below.

"You okay?" Kiyami asked.

The siren nodded quickly, holding her hands up to show she was fine.

A crewman just below her said to another, "I heard the king was furious with Raiden after what happened the last time." He chuckled to himself. "Did you ever work on one of his ships?"

The king. This was the sort of information she needed to bring back to her mother. She certainly hadn't heard any of the other humans mentioning him like this before.

"I did," the other grunted. "I have seen the king's fury many times. It is not something one ordinarily walks away from."

The first man turned as green as the churning water below.

"Well, I'm sure he'd forgive his own blood." Something in the second man's face gave him pause. "Wouldn't he?"

"The king loves his son, but he is not a forgiving man. And with what happened to the *Sun*, not a man alive save Raiden and Bastian? Sounds like a curse to me. The way I see it, we're fools to join this crew. If I had any other choice, *I* wouldn't be here."

The Sun? Had that been the name of the prince's ship? It certainly sounded right. But the word *curse* sent a chill down her spine. Perhaps they *were* cursed. She certainly felt so lately.

The first man swallowed. "So this mysterious treasure we're hunting. It's for the king?"

That might explain why Raiden would risk this journey a second time. Each bit of information created more questions. *Why did Raiden never mention his father if they were doing this for him? Why risk more lives when Raiden knew better? Why did the king want this treasure? What was it?*

With a grave shake of his head, the second man answered the first. "Whatever the king has asked, we will succeed, or we will die."

CHAPTER 17

Celeste had never seen anything more beautiful than the sunset. As she gazed upon the burning red sun lowering upon the horizon, she knew it was a memory she would never forget. They sailed beside it, as if the two were companions, and belowdecks the crew became restless with energy. Night was falling fast. The sun dipped below the horizon, the sky turning the deep purple of a bruise as the first stars began to appear above them. The sea was calm, with just a gentle breeze pushing the ship along its way. She couldn't have pictured a more perfect night.

It had been a long day full of navigation and awkward conversations. Most of the crew had never worked together before, so it wasn't a surprise. The first dinner with the officers had been a little quiet, although delicious. There was creamy soup; fresh, crunchy vegetables; some sort of roasted meat; and berries for dessert. Celeste listened carefully as everyone spoke about the food so she could learn their names. Food was turning out to be her favorite part of being human. Desserts were a particular favorite.

"Can't eat like this most nights, but I thought we should celebrate," Nasir said.

Apparently, food was hard to keep fresh on a ship, so Nasir

used the fresh food first and later would move into the preserved foods: hard biscuits and cheeses, cured meats, pickled vegetables, and dried fruits. After the meal, they joined the rest of the crew on the decks. Bastian complained a little, insisting it had been a long day, but he couldn't say no when Raiden reminded him it was tradition to christen the first night, and it would be bad luck to break tradition. Evidently, humans were very anxious to avoid "bad luck."

"A toast!" called Raiden, emerging with a couple of crew members carrying wooden barrels. Bastian followed along with several others, cups haphazardly stacked in their arms.

The cups were quickly passed around among the crew, with Raiden following behind, filling each glass with dark red liquid. *Wine*, she heard him call it. Celeste wondered if this was one of those drinks that made humans stupid. What did it taste like? If it did make a human stupid, what did *that* feel like?

"Is our *hero* partaking in the libations this evening?" Raiden asked.

It was convenient that Raiden spoke to her in a way in which she could answer easily, but Celeste grew tired of head shakes. So she pointed to herself, shook her head, and pointed to the wine.

"You no wine?"

Celeste waved her hand back over her shoulder.

"Before?" Raiden said.

Celeste nodded.

"You haven't had wine before?"

She smiled unintentionally when he correctly guessed.

Raiden returned the smile, a celebration of this small victory shared between them. "Allow me to introduce you." He filled her cup generously. "Don't drink too fast," he said, meeting her eye. "Take it slowly and see how you feel."

Celeste scoffed. She was a warrior, after all. She could handle a *beverage*. If she chose to.

"Or, by all means, drink yourself into oblivion," he said cooly. "I'd love to watch you make a fool of yourself."

Celeste reached for the cup, but he pulled it from her grasp so that instead she grabbed his hand. She tensed, memories flooding her mind. Her body being dragged through the streets. Her clothes cut from her body. She had experienced an accidental touch before, but something about this was different.

In the ocean, water surrounded you, touching you always. But on land, the air felt like an absence. Every touch was uninhibited. There was nothing between you. When Raiden's hand met hers, it felt as though he was lightning, and she was water. His shock of energy went right through her. Celeste tore her hand away, squeezing her eyes shut. When she opened them, Raiden held the cup out, handle facing her. She gave him an awkward nod in thanks and then took it without having to touch him again. A flush creeped up her neck. He looked at her, his expression impassive. Perhaps he hadn't noticed her reaction after all.

But she did notice his left hand clench ever so slightly as he walked away.

A cold wind blew across her face, and she turned her face down toward her cup, watching the deep red liquid slide back and forth with the rocking of the ship. It looked too much like blood. Her stomach churned.

"I'd like to raise a glass to our first voyage together aboard the *Red Revenge*." As Raiden spoke, the rest of the crew fell silent. He lifted his glass into the air, and the others followed suit. Celeste lifted her own glass, mirroring their actions. "You're not the crew I would have chosen"—Torben growled angrily at this—"but you're the best crew for the job!" he finished with a knifelike grin.

"You mean the job where we could get killed if we don't succeed?" a man said.

"Killed? What do you mean?" another asked, large eyes widening.

Murmuring broke out among the crew as they all began shifting back and forth, their cups lowering. Raiden's expression grew murderous, and silence fell once more.

"When you sail with me, there will always be danger," he said, voice low. "Which makes you the most fearless crew on the Southern Ocean!"

This seemed to do the trick. Shouts of approval rang out as the crew knocked their cups against one another's before drinking deeply. With a mixture of excitement and nerves, Celeste followed their example, pretending to take her first sip of wine. The drink splashed against her lip, tasting bitter and strange. Before she set it back down, she took a deep inhale. It smelled vaguely like fruit, sweet and smooth, but it was also dark and deep. She waited a moment or two, expecting a loss of intelligence or really anything to happen from her almost-sip. But nothing did. Perhaps she needed to actually drink it to feel its effects. But instead she dumped half of it into the ocean when she was certain no one was looking.

The night wore on, and Celeste watched as the crew around her descended into drunkenness. It was fascinating, watching the wine take effect on the humans as they continued to drink. Some humans began to stumble, while others seemed to lose control of the volume of their voice. Some grew sad, while others became joyful. It seemed the effects of the drink were as varied as the drinkers. She wondered, as she listened to a large human tell two others a very tragic and personal tale, whether humans would be more pliable when drunk? It would make her job of getting information out of the captain much easier.

Scanning the deck to gauge Raiden's drunkenness, Celeste noticed all the members of the crew had begun to form into small groups. Torben and Nasir were together, Torben trying to fight anyone who got too close and Nasir gently pulling him back. Bastian said something, and Kiyami laughed while cradling the Admiral in her arms. Another crew member had taken her place at the helm for the night. Among them, Celeste suddenly felt a world apart. It reminded her of a story her mother once told her about the daughters of the Goddess.

"Before the creatures or this world existed, there were only the gods. As they built the earth, the two chose what they would reign. The Goddess chose the ocean, night, and Song for her kingdoms. She gifted the world with great rivers, lakes, and seas. When she finished, she placed each star in the heavens and hung the moon in the sky. Then she created every living creature that resided within her domain and gave them life and balance.

"After she made them, the creatures swam away and multiplied. With her job complete, she rested. She spent her days swimming in the waters of her oceans or bathing in her moonlight. She counted each star as she lay along the shores of the God of Land. But one day as she sat on the shore watching the moonrise and her creatures play together, she began to weep. For she had no one. As her tears mixed with the seafoam, she gathered it to herself and breathed life into four daughters: Isla the Protector, Suna the Wise, Klara the Strong, and Lyra the Beautiful. These were the first sirens. And as they celebrated their first day of life, they sang together."

"Queen Isla is our ancestor! She founded Staria!" Celeste exclaimed.

"Yes, my little star." Halia laughed.

"But how did Isla have children? She didn't have them with her sisters." The little princess pulled a face.

"No, no," Halia corrected. "The Goddess then made males so the sirens could fill the ocean with their kin. At that time, we sirens were a nomadic tribe. We wandered throughout the ocean among the creatures as great rulers. Until"—the queen paused for dramatic effect—"one day the youngest daughter, Lyra, was sunning herself on the shore. There she met Man. Much like the Goddess and her sirens, Man had been created by the God of Land. Lyra sang for Man, and he was so enraptured by her beauty that he dragged her from the ocean and took her back to his home.

"Lyra tried to escape, but after so much time away from the ocean, she dissolved into the seafoam that she came from. When the Goddess heard of this, she became vengeful. She demanded justice.

But the God of Land would not punish Man. Instead, he hid them from her, shielding them from her wrath. So the Goddess gifted sirens the Song so that we may protect ourselves against the humans."

Celeste looked out to sea, wishing she could speak to her mother again. To her own sisters.

"I'm glad it's not raining."

Celeste turned to see a crew member who she believed was a gunner named Oakes. His arms were roped in corded muscle, and his jaw was pronounced and square. The boy wasn't taller than Nasir; Celeste expected no one on the ship was, but she had to tilt her head quite a bit to look at him. He had the longest, darkest eyelashes she had ever seen on a man. They almost looked like a doll. She had seen a couple of dolls intact in shipwrecks, and they all had the same eyes as him.

Politely, Celeste nodded in agreement.

"Oh! You can't talk. Right. I did hear about that," he said. "I couldn't talk once. But it was because I had shouted too much the day before."

Celeste nodded again.

"But I got my voice back. Do you think you'll get your voice back?"

She shrugged, and Oakes nodded solemnly.

"I hope you do. It must be hard to talk to people when you can't talk. Once I had to talk to someone from Hinarso, but they didn't speak common... so I kind of used a lot of hand gestures like this!" Oakes waved his arms around wildly, gesturing to himself, then to her, and then to things around them. The more he spoke, the more he reminded Celeste of a fish. Pretty and without a lot going on inside his head. She wondered if this was from the drink, but she had a feeling it was not. Oakes flung out his arm to communicate how big something was, and Raiden, who had appeared behind him, caught it before it collided with his head.

"Oh! I didn't see you there, Captain." Oakes dropped his arm. "You should watch where you're going. I could have hurt you."

Raiden narrowed his eyes at the boy.

Celeste stifled a laugh, but not well enough, because Raiden's attention turned to her. He cocked an eyebrow, and she lifted the glass of wine toward him in a mock toast. She liked how quickly she was picking up these human habits. It made things much easier.

Raiden's lip quirked upward.

"Excuse me, Captain." Oakes suddenly looked about ten inches tall. He moved away, attempting conversation with a new target who seemed less than thrilled about the experience.

Raiden eyed Celeste's half-empty cup. "How do you like the wine?"

Celeste smiled what she hoped was the smile of a drunk person.

He eyed her, and she knew he saw through her act easily. "I'm glad it meets your approval." The captain rested against the railing beside her, but while Celeste gazed upon the crew, he looked out over the water. It was getting so dark that one could hardly see anything save the stars above them. He tipped his head back, running a large hand mindlessly through his hair.

"The three daughters are out tonight," he said.

Celeste followed his gaze. The sky was clear above them, each star shining brightly upon the inky velvet sky. Something inside her opened wide at the sight of them all. Awestruck. There were so many of them. Her eyes fell to the stars Raiden had pointed to, and she wrinkled her nose. The captain's arm dropped, and he raised an eyebrow at her. But before he could ask, Celeste held up four fingers.

There were four daughters, she corrected him, pointing from the first daughter, to the second, the third, and the fourth. Together they formed a jagged line. The fourth star wasn't as bright as the other three, and perhaps for this it had always been Celeste's favorite.

"Four daughters? Really? And why have I never heard of the fourth?"

Of course your people wouldn't mention the fourth sister. Not after a human stole her and killed her. But how was she to explain that to him without her voice? Celeste squared her shoulders toward him and rolled her head limply to one side. Her eyes closed dramatically.

"She died?"

Close, but not exactly what she meant. Thinking of a better action, Celeste curled her fingers into a fist, as if it held a knife, and plunged the invisible weapon deep into her heart.

"She killed herself?"

Celeste shook her head, reaching to grab Raiden's hand.

Before she made contact, her mind caught up with her action. She froze, hand raised and trembling in front of her. She had intended to use his hand as the "killer" but was too afraid to touch him. Too afraid to be touched. So instead she pointed to him and then to herself.

"Oh," he said, his voice a little gruff. "She was killed."

She dropped her arms to her sides and nodded.

"I can't believe I thought there were only three," he said, still looking at Celeste's face.

Celeste shrugged and jokingly tapped her fist against her temple twice. *You're too dense, I guess,* she informed him with a grin.

Raiden laughed, as if he understood her perfectly. She eyed him, hoping to find some sign as to whether or not he was drunk. He seemed to be in a good enough mood. Perhaps she could attempt to steer the conversation toward the treasure and see what details she could uncover. But he was already pointing to a different cluster of stars in the west that formed what looked like an empty cup that had been tipped over.

"All right, Wayfinder, who's that?"

That's the Goddess's Mouth, she thought as she gently touched her bottom lip with her finger and pointed above her toward the sky.

"Lips of Heaven?" His eyes lingered on her mouth.

It would have been funny, but Celeste couldn't laugh with him looking at her like that. Her body heated, and her head swam. Her left hand tightened around the wine cup. This wasn't Raiden's normal showy bravado. This was something burning. Perhaps he *was* drunk.

Her eyes traced his face, noticing how the flickering lamplight threw his sharp features into stark relief. They stood together, staring. The human prince and the siren princess. Their war was as old as time and written in the stars above them.

It would have been so much easier for her if she had stayed away from him.

Raiden's gaze climbed from her lips to her eyes, and she remembered he had asked her a question. Shaking her head, she pointed again to her lips and then the sky. Then, with every ounce of royal poise she possessed, Celeste held the cup of wine atop her head, lifting her chin as though she were a god.

"The Lips of God?" he asked, taking a step closer.

Celeste swallowed and shook her head. She wanted to take a step back, but she was already pressed against the railing of the ship. Again, she pointed to her mouth, but this time she parted her lips. *Mouth*, she repeated. *The Goddess's Mouth!*

"Is it the Voice—" Raiden stopped speaking, a sudden frostiness coming over his expression.

A shiver ran down Celeste's spine as she watched the change. What did she do? With a sinking feeling, she remembered how she had screamed in front of him. How he was the only one left standing. The wind suddenly felt sharper.

"Why are you here?" he said, eyes searing.

He only suspected something. If he knew why she was really here, he would have killed her already. But clearly he had not forgotten what had happened the night of the storm. She willed herself to keep her breathing even. Although she had never actually gone on any missions for the Chorus, they trained her. She knew how to remain calm in stressful situations. *Theoretically.*

Celeste knit her eyebrows together, twisting her face into a perfectly confused pout. Raiden watched her, glaring. It was no use. Whatever small headway she had made with him was gone. She had to get him to trust her to get the information she needed. If she could somehow show him a reason for her being here, perhaps he would stop searching for one. But she couldn't think of any reason a siren would end up on his ship. Unless... she had followed him there. *Perhaps she could convince him she was in love with him.* The thought almost made her laugh. Still, it wasn't entirely outside the realm of possibility. When Celeste did fall, she fell fast. And it wasn't as if he was unattractive.

But she had hesitated for too long. Although she had never seen the king, she could see the echo of him now in his son's expression. Afraid of causing a scene, she looked around, but the decks were bare. Only the night shift was awake, their eyes keeping watch at sea. The rest of the crew must have gone to bed.

Celeste turned to do the same, but Raiden cut in front of her path, causing her to halt so she didn't run into him.

"Take one step out of line, and I'll make you wish I had drowned that day."

I already do.

Celeste tried to stride past him, but he blocked her path once more. She tried again, and still he stopped her. So she grabbed his arm, turned, and flung him over her head. Or at least that's how it would have worked underwater. Instead, her legs locked together, throwing her off-balance, and he didn't so much fly through the air as tumble over her shoulder and onto his back. Still, it did the job.

Raiden's breath left him at once in an audible *whoosh*. He clutched his stomach, coughing. When he looked up, the hate in his gaze looked as though it could burn her.

Celeste stepped over him, refusing to meet his eye, and strode to her room.

CHAPTER 18

Celeste awoke to the sound of banging. Her heart pounded a furious rhythm against her chest as she sat upright, her head just missing the bottoms of an array of coats. The thin cover she wore was twisted up around her legs. It was dark, so she couldn't guess what time it was, but she knew it had been hours since she had gone to bed. She knew this because once again she had tossed and turned. Every time she felt herself falling into sleep's embrace, she began to feel the hands of the guard upon her body, the knife against her skin, and she would jolt awake, sweating. But she must have fallen asleep at some point, because she distinctly remembered having a nightmare in which Kiyami had grown fangs and tried to rip out her neck.

Bang. Bang. Bang. Bang.

The noise shook the little room. It sounded as if it came from the wall she shared with the captain's quarters. A wave of anger rolled through her, and she hammered her fist against the wall. One, two, three times. Silence. Then

Bang. Bang. Bang.

He was insufferable. Celeste let out a frustrated sound and slammed her palm against the wall three times.

Bang. Bang. Bang.

His muffled voice came through the wall. *"Stop making noise! You're waking me up!"*

She wished she could yell back. *You woke me up!* But instead she lay down and muffled her frustrated scream with a pillow. Soon, she reminded herself. *Soon it'll all be over, and I can go home.*

Raiden did not speak to Celeste the following day, nor the day after. Save for waking her up in the middle of the night to yell at her for being loud. Each night she wished she could scream that she couldn't help that she was having nightmares. And each day that passed without her learning anything new about the treasure made her more anxious. Should she just kill him to get it over with? Return to her siren form and visit the island herself? But in her gut, she knew there must be something else. Something that had to do with the king.

Countless times, Celeste felt Raiden's heated gaze on her back and would turn to see him glaring at her, suspicion rolling off his broad shoulders in waves. And every time she would meet his glare with one of her own. Whatever had caused his sudden attitude shift remained a mystery to her. Not that they were exactly friends before, but at least he spoke to her. And although part of her was relieved to no longer have him pestering her with his confident grin and cheeky jokes, it was hurting her chances to learn anything useful. Raiden was as temperamental as a flame. One moment his light was steady and warm, and the next he was a raging fire, burning down everything in his path.

And one small part of her, a part she did not wish to acknowledge, missed the attention.

Celeste really hated that part.

On day three, Raiden requested she look over the map again to see if they were making good progress. The conversation was stilted, and not because Celeste couldn't talk.

On the fourth day at sea, Bastian spotted another ship.

"It's a cargo ship," he reported. The crew gathered around to hear more, but Celeste was more interested in what Bastian was holding than what he was saying. Bastian peered down a beautiful golden tube that was larger on one end than the other. When he lowered the object from his face, Celeste reached out a hand, excitedly asking with her eyes if she could take a look. It had become a somewhat normal occurrence in the past couple of days. If anyone found it odd that their navigator was constantly excited over various tools and objects, no one said anything. With a smile, Bastian acquiesced, placing the shining golden tube gently into Celeste's waiting palm. It was surprisingly heavy. When she placed the small end in front of her eye, as Bastian had, she found the horizon as close as if she could reach out her hand and touch it. With a hum of excitement, Celeste turned and began to scan the seas around them, searching for the cargo ship.

"Must be coming from Port Warren," Raiden said.

Celeste had never seen Port Warren, but she knew it was south of Romsey. It was known for being a larger and wealthier town than Port Romsey, a destination for traders. She turned her head once more, and finally saw it. The cargo ship. Due southwest of them and heading north. Huge white sails puffed up like clouds around it, and a blue flag fluttered near the front. She wasn't sure how Bastian knew it was a cargo ship. Was the flag the indicator? Or perhaps the type of ship? After looking around a bit more, and seeing nothing of interest, Celeste handed the object back to Bastian.

"Kiyami, change course. I'd like to say hello," the prince said with a smile. The one that reminded Celeste of a shark.

"Yes, Captain," Kiyami said.

Bastian grinned. "Shall we prepare for boarding, Highness?"

"Oh yes, certainly."

Bastian shouted the signal, and the ship whipped into a flurry of energy.

"At last some action!" said Torben, practically skipping down to the berth. "And here I thought this be the dullest crew I ever had the misfortune to be stuck with." He slapped Oakes on the back at his own joke. Oakes laughed, if only to please his superior, as the two jogged lightly downstairs. As if they were chittering dolphins, ready to play.

Nasir, however, looked stricken. His usual calm exterior melting into a cool panic. "Boarding? I thought we were simply picking up treasure."

"If this was a simple voyage, why would we need a surgeon?" Kiyami said.

All at once, the crew descended into chaos, each of them shouting above the other and arguing. Nasir insisted he remain with his husband, despite Bastian's order that the surgeon stay behind to take care of the wounded. Others bickered over who should lead the charge. All the while, Torben's voice below deck could be heard shouting excited orders at Oakes to "grab more weapons" and "get the gunpowder."

Celeste stood in the center of it all, still as a stone against the tide. Whatever boarding meant, she didn't think she'd like it.

"Enough," Raiden said.

The crew quieted.

"My orders are not up for discussion."

With this, the humans dispersed, going about their duties to prepare the ship without another word. Celeste, unsure of what her role was in this situation, remained beside Kiyami, watching as she turned the great wheel. If Celeste had learned one thing in the last several days, it was if she remained by Kiyami, the humans assumed she was doing her job, and no one would bother her. For the most part, Kiyami didn't require much direction. The path was simple enough, which meant Celeste had plenty of time to relax and overthink harebrained plots for uncovering the prince's secrets.

Now Celeste's thoughts were busy trying to uncover what boarding meant. *Why are they preparing the weapons? If it's just a cargo ship, wouldn't that mean it's not a threat?* The minutes passed quickly and slowly at once. Each moment felt eternal, with the tension thick in the air, and yet the cargo ship grew rapidly closer. Although they were working, the crew continued to bicker as the hot afternoon sun beat down from above.

"We're gaining!" Raiden said, a feral excitement burning in his eyes.

"Do you have a weapon, girl?" came Torben's gravelly voice as he approached her.

Celeste shook her head.

"I thought not," Torben puffed out his chest. "I did you the favor of grabbing a few necessities." He handed over a thick leather belt, on which dangled several holsters. Celeste accepted and secured it around her waist using Torben's own belt as an example. "Here's your sword"—she sheathed it—"your pistol"—she tucked it into the front of her belt, as Torben had—"and a dagger." It was small and simple, with a pretty wooden handle and a sharp blade.

After nearly a week of seeing such weapons on the others, Celeste finally held them herself. Excitement filled her, mixed with a thick sense of foreboding. Sparring was her favorite part of training, but it was just that, training. Sparring was poised, calm, a game of wits. The real thing was brutal, like being caught in an undertow and fighting for breath. And in the end, you were left with wounds you didn't know how to heal.

"Make sure to hide the dagger," Torben instructed. "Somewhere that won't hurt you, and you can reach, but also where someone else won't find it. You never know when you might be captured and will need to cut someone's eye from their skull!" He looked particularly gleeful as he said this last part, as if recalling a fond memory.

Celeste's skin turned a shade green at the thought. She hadn't actually killed anyone before, and she had hoped that her first and only kill outside of the Chorus would be Raiden.

The *Red Revenge* closed in on the cargo ship, only a few lengths away.

"Man your stations!" came a shout.

"You do . . . know how to use these weapons, right?" Torben

asked, peering at Celeste's face. Celeste pushed her fears away and put on a confident smile.

"That a girl." Torben patted her shoulder. "Don't want you dying and all, since we don't have another navigator. Good luck!" And with that he strode away, barreling through the crowd forming near the starboard railing.

"Don't shoot until I give the orders, Torben!" Raiden shouted after him, but Celeste was certain he wasn't listening.

As the ships approached, Kiyami turned the great wheel in time to pull up against the cargo ship. The *Red Revenge* towered over its very sails, throwing a dark shadow upon the frantic crew as they shouted and passed around weapons. Torben and the others began to cheer, pounding their feet against the deck. The sounds rose into a terrible crescendo. As their captain approached, they parted and faced him, growing silent.

"Board the ship," said Raiden.

A guttural roar exploded in response. The metal sound of drawn swords rang. Then a large plank fell between the railings of the two ships. The crew of the *Red Revenge* surged toward it. But as they climbed on, a large man from the opposite crew put his hands on either side of the plank, pushing. The board was slipping sideways an inch, then another, when out of nowhere a great axe flew across the gap and sank with a wet thud into the man's face. He fell, dead before he hit the ground.

With a whoop of triumph, Torben sprinted over the plank. Nasir's intimidating frame closely followed his husband. Apparently, Bastian had lost that argument.

Celeste sprinted to the side of the ship where Raiden stood to get a better look, tucking her dagger safely into the folds of her skirt. But as she did, a bullet flew past her ear.

"Get down!" Raiden ordered, and for once she couldn't argue.

As Torben reached the end of the plank, he was met with three men, their swords drawn. Although they outnumbered him, the men hesitated, clearly nervous to engage him after seeing what he had done to the first man. Without hesitation, Torben jumped over them, rolled across the floor, and pulled his axe from the man's face. As they stared at Torben's dripping axe, Nasir picked one of them up from behind and flung him into the other two, knocking them all into a heap and clearing a path.

One by one the crew stormed across the plank, jumping into the fight. The color drained from Celeste's face as she watched. The humans were *killing* each other. But she didn't understand why.

Raiden joined them and was halfway across the plank before a member of the other crew disentangled himself from the battle and saw him. The two made eye contact, and Celeste could swear recognition dawned in the crew member's eyes. Panicked, the man ran to the plank and pushed. Raiden leaped backward as the plank gave a great lurch. As the crew member pushed again, Raiden heaved a great sigh, turned, and sprinted back toward the *Red Revenge*, leaping just as the plank slipped from the cargo ship's railing and fell into the water below. Raiden hit the deck, rolling to avoid the impact. Beside him he saw Celeste, who alternated between sticking her head over the railing to watch the action and ducking to avoid stray bullets.

"You," Raiden said, peeling himself off the ground and getting to his feet. He leaped upon the railing of the ship, pulling a rope into his hand. After a tug to make sure it was secure, he extended a hand toward her. "Come with me. Unless you have something better to do than help your crew."

It was the first time he had spoken to her all day. She scowled and looked at his hand. But thankfully she did not recoil. With a steadying breath, Celeste took his hand and allowed him to hoist her onto the banister beside him. Raiden wrapped his free arm around her waist, pulling her tightly into his chest. The feeling wasn't pleasant, but she did not tremble as she had before. Perhaps these days at sea had helped somewhat. Even the bruises had begun to fade.

"Hold on tight," he said, and Celeste begrudgingly wrapped her arms around his neck. She felt utterly ridiculous being carried into battle by a *human man*. The fabric of her dress, a light blue one she had borrowed from her room, flapped like a sail in the breeze.

"Jump," he said.

And together, they leaped.

The rope creaked as the two went careening through the air. If it weren't for Raiden's arms around her, she would have enjoyed the feeling. They passed over the gap between the two ships in an arc. But as they neared the farthest point the rope would reach, Celeste realized with a lurch that it was still shy of the other ship's deck.

"Jump!" he shouted.

There is nothing to jump off! She wanted to scream at him.

Raiden let go of the rope. He wrapped his now free arm around her as their bodies continued to move, sailing through the air toward the banister of the cargo ship. Celeste pulled her arms away from Raiden's neck, reaching them toward the ship as she fell. They wouldn't make it. They weren't close enough.

But at least I know how to swim.

Their bodies smacked against the side of the ship, but they didn't fall. Dazed, Celeste blinked up into the smiling face of Nasir. The tree of a man towered over them, holding Raiden by the back of his coat. Celeste let out a sigh of relief.

"I got us over here in one piece, didn't I?" Raiden grinned.

As the words left his lips, a sword raised over Nasir's shoulder. Celeste sucked in a breath, but before she could cry out, a familiar axe came sailing into view.

"You get away from my husband, ya lobcock!"

It hit its target handle first, sending the man and his sword stumbling backward. With one swift movement, Nasir hoisted Celeste and Raiden over the side of the ship, depositing them on the floor. He turned, pulling his cutlass from his hip, to join his husband. Together, the two made quick work of the man and his sword.

Celeste got to her feet. The clanging of metal rang out around her as swords collided again and again. It was barbaric. It was violent. It was—*exciting*. Unlike the last skirmish Celeste had found herself in, this seemed much more an even fight. Although the reason for their fight still remained a mystery.

"Look out!" Oakes cried from behind. Celeste unsheathed her sword and turned just in time. Her blade collided with another, interrupting a blow aimed for her back. She grinned. This sword was very different from her spear ... but at least *some* things remained the same.

"Aren't you pretty." The man's one beady eye roamed her body while the other remained hidden beneath a black patch. When he grinned, he bared rotting teeth, one of which was missing.

Celeste grunted and thrust the sword toward his heart. He knocked it out of the way.

"Why are all the pretty ones so angry?" He laughed.

Sailors like him were why she suspected many women weren't on ships. She swung her sword again, aiming for his neck, letting all her anger and pain roar to life within her.

He blocked it, but barely. The smile slid off his face, and he lunged. She tried to block, but the handle of the blade was strange in her hand. The sword flew from her hands. She tried to run after it but stopped when a blade touched her throat.

"Maybe I'll keep you as a pet," he said, his rancid breath hot against her face.

Celeste grimaced and kicked. She intended to hurt him, even throw him off-balance. What she hadn't expected was for him to double over, crying in pain and holding his crotch in his hands. Humans, apparently, had a weak spot.

Retrieving her sword, Celeste found Raiden before her. The wind tousled his dark hair and played with his billowing white shirt. He looked every inch the fearsome prince.

"You make a better pirate than I thought," he said.

CHAPTER 19

Pirate.

A pirate?

Raiden was—

Pieces started falling into place one after the other. How Kiyami didn't want to work for his father. Why Raiden seemed to have no support or authority. Raiden Sharp was a *pirate*. It all fit the stories she knew from home about the pirates who sailed the ocean, butchering each other and stealing. Was he even royalty at all? Was his father even a king? Celeste's mind reeled. She had been sailing for days upon a pirate ship and was now helping said pirates to ransack an innocent cargo ship. Which, in all probability, made her a pirate too.

In retrospect, Celeste should have put this together on her own. Should have seen the men Raiden had hired for his crew and known what they were. No kingdom sent Raiden aid when he was left without a crew or a ship at Port Velluno. And yet, in a matter of days, he had both. And he certainly didn't act like a royal prince. He had no shame and no apparent rules he had to obey. The boy hardly had manners, not that Celeste really expected most humans to have manners. He'd become angry when someone called Valencia the Queen of Pirates. Was she his mother? His father's lover? His father's rival? Those who called him "Your Highness" must have been doing so in jest.

She had not heroically saved a prince like something out of a heroic tale.

Celeste had saved a pirate. The Prince of Pirates.

They may have not had red eyes and fangs, but these humans who made their living by being violent and selfish were every bit as monstrous as the stories. Even Kiyami was striking down men one after the other. A pirate through and through.

"You may want to pay attention," grunted Raiden, dodging in front of her to block a sword that had been sweeping toward her head.

She nodded. There would be a time to mull over this rather upsetting turn of events later, but not if she let herself get killed. Stepping out from behind Raiden, Celeste raised her sword, taking a defensive stance. Two men from the other crew circled them. One was short and thin, while the other was tall and muscular, with a horrendously long mustache. Mustache moved first, his sword arcing downward toward Celeste's head. She spun away, as elegantly as if she had been underwater, and swung her sword at his side. It sliced him cleanly, drawing blood. He stumbled back, blinking in shock.

To her left, the short man exchanged strikes with Raiden. But it almost looked as though instead of a proper fight, Raiden was toying with the man. The so-called prince practically glowed with delight as he danced around, his sword parrying every blow, his jabs leaving little cuts all over his opponent's body. It was mesmerizing to watch. Each swing and step timed just so, calculated and smooth.

Again, Mustache swung at Celeste. She raised her sword to block, but her grip was wrong, and the sword went flying to the deck. *Why do swords have such small handles?* she thought bitterly. Mustache stepped back, his gaze falling to the sword on the floor and back up to her. His mouth formed a horrible smile. With a lunge, he jabbed the point of his sword toward Celeste's stomach. She jumped backward. He thrusted again. As she jumped back once more, her back collided with the railing of the ship. Hard. Celeste's toes curled in her shoes. She had nowhere to go. Mustache smiled wider. Swinging his arms up in a great show, he brought his sword down at a diagonal angle.

Celeste ducked under the blade, and with one step had moved around him. Crying out in anger, the man spun around to face her, sword raised once more. She was already dropping to the ground, holding herself up with her arms and kicking him square in the stomach with her legs held together. He staggered backward, catching himself against the ship's railing. She cast a look around for her sword, but it had slid too far out of reach. So she grabbed the first thing she saw nearby—a pole with a pile of rope on the end.

She could tell it wasn't a weapon, but it was much closer to a spear than the sword was. Before Mustache had time to right himself, Celeste hopped forward, the rounded top of the pole sinking into his throat. The wind swept from his lungs. He coughed and leaned forward, choking. Without hesitation, Celeste thrust the roped end of her makeshift weapon into the ground, using it as leverage to swing her body around and lift herself off the ground. As she spun, she kicked out her feet, as if they were a fin, and they collided squarely with his jaw, sending the man careening off the ship and into the waters below.

Celeste landed awkwardly but spun the pole with a flourish. She could get used to having extra limbs. They packed a better punch than her tail had.

Before her, Raiden stared, the smaller man he had been fighting lying unconscious and bleeding at his feet.

"That was oddly attractive," he said with a lopsided smile. "If that's what you do with a mop, imagine what you could do if you learned to keep hold of a sword."

Celeste fixed him with an unamused stare before turning to look for her sword. The rest of the crew seemed to have a handle on things—sort of. It was rather chaotic, and no one looked as though they were working together. If anything, the crew of the *Red Revenge* only got in each other's way. Torben moved with the grace of a boulder, throwing his axe at anything that moved, while Nasir followed along after him, pushing men out of their way. At one point, Torben raised his axe and aimed, before realizing at the last second the man he was aiming at was Oakes. But the pause in his rhythm was enough to give the real enemy an advantage. A man sent a kick into Torben's stomach, knocking both him and Oakes to the ground.

Celeste took a step toward them, hoping to be of some help, but Nasir was quicker. He lowered his head and charged toward them. Anyone unfortunate enough to be in his way, he knocked to the side with a simple thrust of his great shoulder or elbow. Unfortunately for Nasir, one of those people happened to be Torben. In the heat of battle, Nasir did not see him stand back up. Celeste winced as Torben sailed like a flying fish over the heads of the others, a string of obscenities trailing after him.

"Learn to stay out of my way, ya idiot!" Torben cried at Oakes, picking himself up from the ground. Furious, he closed the distance between them and leaped upon a barrel to be eye level with the boy. He reared back and attempted to whack Oakes with the pommel of his sword. But just as the pommel was about to collide with Oakes's jaw, the boy took a step back, stumbling over his own feet, and the pommel continued its arc straight into Nasir's face. Nasir cried out, hands flying to his face as blood streamed from his nose.

"What were you thinking? Why did you get in the way?" Torben barked as he leaped down and rushed to his husband's side.

"What are you saying? You hit me!" Nasir shot back, his voice muffled by his own hands.

"I wasn't trying to hit you," Torben said, then softened. "Is your nose all right?"

It was then that Celeste noticed the ship around them had gone quiet. Eerily quiet. She turned, dread pouring over her like cold water. The crew of the *Red Revenge* were grouped together, fighting each other, and surrounding them with pistols raised was the crew of the cargo ship. What was left of them, anyway. Celeste searched for Bastian and Raiden in the crowd and found them behind her, staring daggers at someone. She followed their gaze and saw a man standing on the quarterdeck above them. From his large hat and air of importance, she assumed it was the other captain. And to add insult to injury, he was holding her sword.

"So this is the infamous crew of Captain Raiden Sharp, son of the Pirate King?" He tilted the sword back and forth as the hot sun glistened on the blade. "I must admit. You're even more pathetic than I expected."

"I've been called worse by better," Raiden said. He lowered his sword and strode toward the captain. One of the cargo crew shoved a sword in his face when he reached the base of the stairs. Raiden halted, looking unperturbed.

The other captain made a face, one that looked very much as though he smelled something awful and offensive. "Surrender now, Raiden," he said, speaking louder than before. "And I will graciously allow you and your pathetic crew to crawl back to whatever hole you climbed out of."

"You can surrender to my arse!" Torben cried.

The other captain bristled.

"You heard him." Raiden smiled. "Torben's arse is ready when you are."

Celeste swallowed. They were surrounded. This man had given them the option to leave. And Raiden was insulting him. Typical. But if Raiden was going to die, it was going to be by her hand and when she was good and ready.

She could make quick work of them if she used her Song, but she couldn't reveal herself. Not if she wanted to learn what Raiden's goal was—what the king wanted this treasure for.

"I'll give you one more chance. Surrender or perish," the captain shouted.

"I don't think your threat is the deterrent you think it is," Raiden said. "You haven't even been in this fight, not until we were surrounded."

The cargo ship's crew shifted their feet. Torben, nearly a head shorter than all the others, seemed to disappear in the crowd.

"But you are surrounded," the captain said, growing irritated.

"A temporary setback." Raiden shrugged.

"Why don't we just accept his gracious offer and be on our way," one crew member said, his hands raised above his head in surrender.

"Shut up, Edmund," Raiden said without looking at him. "The captains are talking."

Edmund turned a brilliant shade of red and lowered his hands.

"He does make an excellent point. Why offer us our freedom? Why not kill us if you're so confident you can do so?"

"Because unlike you, I actually make an effort to keep my crew alive."

Raiden's confident smirk slipped for a second. But it reformed as he turned to Bastian, who stood at his shoulder. "I think this old man is scared."

"Oh, most certainly," agreed Bastian.

"In fact, I bet I could beat him with my right arm tied behind my back," Raiden said.

"Both arms, surely." Bastian nodded solemnly.

"Quiet!" the captain shouted, the feather on his hat shaking.

"And blindfolded," Raiden added.

"Enough!" The captain swept from the quarterdeck toward Raiden, each footstep beating a foreboding drum as he drew closer. Raiden's eyes danced. He had planned this. He wanted to face off against the captain one-on-one. Perhaps if he could best him, there would be no need for further bloodshed.

Celeste hated to admit it, but she was impressed. Until the captain grabbed her instead of Raiden, placing her sword at her throat. "Surrender, or I cut her pretty neck," he said.

Celeste stiffened. Her skin crawled where he touched her, just below the green bruising on her upper arms. The blade pressed into her skin, and she drew in a sharp breath. Her mind searched for something, anything, she could do to fight back. But she wasn't used to fighting where swords were involved. One wrong move, and she'd be killed.

Raiden held his hands up. "Okay, perhaps we got off on the wrong foot, Captain... what was your name?" His eyes met Celeste's, and she saw behind his act that he was afraid.

"Clarke," the captain growled.

"Captain Clarke! Of course. You're a reasonable man. Let's not be hasty."

"I am perfectly reasonable. I have given you your choice. Her death, or your surrender. I grow tired of your silly games, Sharp. Choose now, or I shall choose for you." The blade pressed harder, its steel cold against her throat. A thin line of blood bloomed along her neck, and she hissed at the sting.

No one spoke. The moment was as delicate as coral—one wrong move, and it all could snap.

Raiden's brows formed a hard line. "That's hardly a reasonable request."

Celeste's eyes widened. What was he doing? Was he trying to get her killed?

"Raiden, let's go," Bastian whispered beside his friend, growing anxious.

Raiden's gaze remained on Celeste. His eyes narrowed. He looked about as likely to surrender as the world was to stop turning. She wasn't surprised. He had threatened to kill her multiple times now. She was certainly not the bargaining chip Captain Clarke thought she was.

"Fire!" Raiden yelled.

A loud bang echoed. It sounded almost as though it came from somewhere far away.

Crack! The deck beneath them shook, sending both crews tumbling. Splintered wood flew through the air like ocean spray. Celeste looked across at the *Red Revenge* to see Torben standing behind a smoking cannon. How had he gotten over there?

Shouts of panic rose as the cargo crew recognized the ship was taking on water. In the chaos, Celeste threw her head back, her skull colliding with Captain Clarke's nose. He grunted, the sword at her neck dropping a couple of inches. This was her chance. She grabbed the hand holding the sword with hers and yanked down. The movement was easy and familiar, her body following the familiar motions that had been drilled into her. In one fluid motion, Celeste twirled, twisting his hand up behind his back. The grip on her sword loosened, and she pulled it free while keeping his hand secured.

"Men, to your stations!" cried Clarke as he struggled against her hold. "Prepare the cannons! Don't let them get away!"

Celeste sheathed her sword and chanced a look around. The battle had reignited. But upon hearing their captain's orders, the cargo crew attempted to disengage and run downstairs. Celeste's stomach dropped. They were going to try to sink the *Red Revenge*. Three of the members of the cargo crew managed to reach the door to the lower decks. One reached to pull it open. His body was sent flying backward. The two others turned to find Nasir, baring his teeth. Celeste nearly laughed. She had never seen Nasir try to look scary before, and it was somehow endearing.

"Good work, hero," said Raiden as he joined her. He nodded toward Clarke, who she still had in a hold. "And here I thought I was rescuing you."

Celeste smiled, quite pleased with herself.

"All right," he said, eyes darkening as he looked at Clarke, "I'll take this from here."

CHAPTER 20

The cargo ship shook as another cannonball sank into its side. Celeste raised her arm to shield her eyes as splintered wood rained down. It gave another lurch, and she scrambled to keep her legs beneath her.

"Stop blowing holes in the ship while we're on it!" Raiden roared, but it was unlikely Torben could hear him. With a sigh, he turned back to Captain Clarke and raised his sword high above the captain's head, prepared to swing.

Clarke stood still beneath the blade. Defeated. The few surviving members of his crew had abandoned ship in the rowboat. The rest were strewn across the floor. There was no one belowdecks to return fire.

Was Raiden really going to kill this man in front of her? She hated him, but she didn't want to watch Raiden cut his throat. This realization was like salt water in a wound. She already feared she was unfit for her task. If she couldn't bear watching someone else end a man who wanted to hurt them, how could she kill Raiden when the time came? But that was different, right? Raiden had invaded this man's ship. Raiden had killed his crew. Raiden was the villain here.

Raiden looked up, as if to check that Celeste had a good hold on Clarke. As usual, he managed to see everything she was thinking plain on her face.

"Lucky for you, Captain, I'm feeling generous," the pirate said. "We'll see how you fare with the sharks." He brought the pommel down into Captain Clarke's skull.

The man fell limp, a puppet with his strings cut, sinking into a heap on the floor. Raiden crouched beside Clarke's unconscious body and relieved him of a small purse. He held it up and shook it, smiling when he heard the chatter of coins. A stray bottle rolled past their feet toward the bow of the ship. Raiden and Celeste watched it. Their eyes grew wide, and they looked up at each other, realization dawning.

The floor wasn't level anymore. The ship was sinking.

"Grab what you can and get off the ship!" Raiden commanded his crew.

Bastian and Kiyami, both nearby, called back in reply and disappeared belowdecks to grab what they could and inform the others. Motioning for Celeste to follow, Raiden ran to the captain's quarters.

"Grab anything that looks valuable and put it in here," he ordered, rushing over to the bed to strip the top two blankets. He tied the corners to make a sort of bag—one he slung over his shoulders and the other he tossed to Celeste. She caught it easily and looped it over her head. There was no going back now. Not if she pillaged this ship with him. She'd be a pirate. But since the ship was going down anyway, and she had grown up scavenging ships, Celeste's pesky moral compass didn't stop her for long. Heart hammering and cheeks flushed, she joined the search, heading first for the desk in the back. Pickings were slim underwater. Most things in a shipwreck were damaged.

Scavenging this room was a dream of hers made real.

Celeste tried her best to hurry, but she couldn't help but become consumed by each object she encountered. On the desk, she found a glass bottle, thin at the top with a wide base and filled with golden liquid. Two matching glasses sat beside it. Something like this was normally broken on shipwrecks. She held it up toward Raiden to see if it was valuable, and he groaned.

"Not anything glass! Look for gold things! Coins or jewels!"

She dropped it back onto the table and picked up a heavy silver object. This one had an ornate base, with three arms. Two elegantly stuck out at the sides, turning their heads upward, while the middle stayed straight and resolute. Each arm held a white candle. This she decided to place in the sack, as she'd heard candles were fairly precious upon the ship. A golden compass was next, which she inspected for a long moment, watching as the hands inside moved as she turned it. She reached for the next item on the desk. An open piece of parchment. It probably wasn't valuable, but she hadn't seen a human letter before, and Celeste wanted to take a closer look at the glistening gold wax seal at the top.

Crack! A cannonball blew through the far wall of the captain's quarters at an angle, ripping a hole as it sunk into the floor beneath. The ship tilted again, and a wave crashed against the side of the ship, spilling water into the room.

"All right, time to go," Raiden said.

He walked toward the door, bag at his hip jangling, paused, and returned for a couple of half-full liquor bottles. With nimble fingers, Celeste folded up the parchment, tucking it into the front of her dress. She hadn't taken nearly as much as she could have. But there was no time to rectify this. The floor was now under a couple of inches of water, and each second it rose higher. Together they ran for the door. Raiden ripped it open and found, looming in the doorframe with his sword raised, Captain Clarke.

Raiden shut the door in his face.

"Perhaps there's another way out?"

There wasn't. The two looked around the room. The only other exit was through the hole the cannon had made in the wall. Celeste doubted either of them could avoid losing some of the treasure in the water if they chose to swim. A loud hammering shook the door on its hinges.

Raiden groaned and opened the door again. "Clarke! Good to see you're up. We were just leaving."

The prince made to dash around Clarke, but the disgruntled captain brandished his sword like a madman. He sliced at Raiden's head, causing the prince to jump backward into Celeste. The blade lodged into the thick wood of the doorframe. Clarke pulled at the sword, but it remained in place. The water climbed higher. It was up to their ankles now. Shouts echoed down from the decks. Their crew was leaving. They were trapped between their freedom and a ship that was rapidly filling with water.

"You have made a huge mistake," spat Clarke. "You will regret this day."

"I'm sure your parents felt the same way after conceiving you," Raiden said.

Clarke lunged at Raiden, hands grasping for his neck. Raiden spun out of the way, grabbing Celeste as he moved to clear her from Clarke's grip as well. They landed hard on the wall behind them, Raiden pressing her against it. The air flew from Celeste's lungs, and she felt something fall from her into the water beneath them. The silver candleholder perhaps? She didn't have time to fetch it.

Having expected to collide with them, Clarke went tumbling forward, landing face-first. Celeste's eyes rose to meet Raiden's, her heart pounding against his chest.

"Don't you go falling for me too," Raiden said.

I hope you drown, Celeste thought, pushing him off her with a huff. Raiden smirked.

While Clarke floundered in the rising waters, the two raced through the door. The deck was empty. Even most of the bodies had slid off the angled deck and into the ocean.

The ship lurched, tilting starboard as it sank lower and lower. Celeste's feet slipped from beneath her, and she went tumbling.

"Celeste!" Raiden clung to the railing of the quarterdeck and reached one arm out to her, but she was already too far away. Her hands scrambled and clawed against the floorboards to find purchase.

There was nothing to break her fall, and her body crashed down the quarterdeck stairs. At last her hands caught the handle of a hatch, and her body jerked to a halt.

The ship's masts creaked. Celeste looked up and saw Captain Clarke appear behind Raiden in the doorway of the captain's quarters. He lifted a pistol. *Her pistol*. That's what fell when they collided with the wall. Celeste opened her mouth to scream a warning.

There was a deafening crack.

Raiden's body flew sideways, landing on the floor with a terrible thud. Lifeless, he slid down the quarterdeck stairs, leaving a trail of blood in his wake. She cried out, reaching, but he slipped past, directly into the churning water.

Clarke turned the shaking pistol toward her, his free hand in a white-knuckle grip on the doorframe to remain standing. Before he could fire, Celeste let go, sliding down the deck and into the water after Raiden's body.

Icy, frothing water enveloped her. *Had the ocean always been this cold?* The blue dress grew heavy, dragging her body down. Breath caught in her throat. She blinked and looked around the green waters. There was no sign of him. Her feet kicked, tangling in her skirts. Everything felt wrong. This human body didn't work right in the water.

Her lungs burned. Her shoes fell from her feet. She was sinking. The heavy belt at her waist was like deadweight. Kicking as hard as she could, she managed to rise through the surface of the ocean. The wind whipped against her damp skin. She pushed her wet hair from her face and twisted around. Where was he? She wanted to scream. To cry out for him. She cursed herself for her stupid choice to hide her voice. But something in her wouldn't use it. She was still afraid of what would happen. Could she sing? Try to lure him to her? She doubted it. He'd have to be conscious for it to work. *He'd have to be alive*, a small voice said. A voice that made her search grow more desperate.

He couldn't be dead. She didn't know enough yet.

She took in a gasp of air and plunged back under the water toward the sinking ship. And that's when she saw him. He looked eerily green as he floated beneath her. His white shirt was now see-through. He wasn't moving. Or at least that's what it looked like at first. He looked almost blissful. But as she watched him, she realized she was wrong. He *was* moving. As the ship behind him was swallowed by the ocean, Raiden was being dragged down along in its wake. She dove after him, kicking her feet as hard as she could manage. She may not have the body she was born with, a body built to cut through the water with ease, but she was still a siren.

Down she swam. When the bag of stolen items hit against her thigh, reminding her of its presence, she threw it off. Immediately the swim was easier, straighter. It would have been even easier if she removed her dress, but there wasn't time. Celeste didn't know how long most humans could survive underwater, but based on how her own lungs burned for air, she knew they were running out of time.

At last she reached him. She wrapped her arms around his waist, pulling him close. A trail of red floated behind his back. *Blood.* Celeste stiffened. The siren part of her could taste it in the water around them. Heart hammering, lungs screaming, she turned and kicked toward the surface, but his heavy body slowed their progress. The sinking ship's pull was too strong. She wasn't going to make it. If he wasn't already dead, he would be soon.

Somewhere behind her something in the water moved.

A shark, its body nearly twice the length of Raiden's, writhing back and forth. With teeth as long as a finger and soulless black eyes, it followed the scent of Raiden's blood. Her arms clutched him tighter. With a newfound sense of urgency, Celeste kicked toward the surface. But it was no use. Although she was strong, she wasn't going to be fast enough with this human body to reach the surface in time.

The beast opened its great jaw, only feet away.

Sing! her instincts shouted. *Why don't you sing!* But she was too afraid.

Instead, Celeste kicked out, her heel colliding with the shark's left eye. It recoiled, and she used the momentum to push them toward the surface. They were close. Perhaps five feet below.

The shark charged toward them once more. With all her strength, Celeste pushed Raiden above her. The shark opened its great jaws. She pulled her dagger from her hip, and with both hands, she plunged it through the roof of its mouth and into its head.

A sharp pain lanced through her left arm, above the elbow. Blood filled the water. She couldn't tell what was hers and what was the shark's. With a grunt, she pulled the dagger free. Agony burned up her arm, sending her reeling. She kicked the shark's body away from her and swam to the surface, her head about to explode from the lack of oxygen. Sweet, salty air rushed into her lungs as she crashed through the water, sputtering. But all she could think about was Raiden. It took her two seconds to find him, floating belly-up in the water to her right. She swam to him and placed her hand on his neck, searching for a pulse.

It was there.

But they were both losing blood.

Idiot. Why did he attack that ship? Why did he humiliate its captain? What if he didn't wake up? What if she never found out why the king wanted this treasure in the middle of the ocean? What if she could never go home? And it was all his fault. She got to decide when he died. And today was not that day. So Celeste slapped him. Hard. Across the face.

Raiden sputtered awake, coughing. His eyes cracked open, and he winced.

"What was that for?" he croaked between wet coughs.

Celeste gave him a particularly rude gesture she'd seen Torben use.

"If you dislike me so much, why are you saving me?"

She threw her hands into the air. *I don't know!*

The waves roared in her ears. Above them, she heard shouting.

"Here! They're here! Thank God. I see them!"

"Throw down the ladder!"

A rope ladder came sailing down through the air, landing with a splash in front of them. Celeste nearly cried with relief. She shoved her bare feet into the bottom rung, and when she turned back for Raiden, she saw he wasn't moving. *No.* She grabbed his arm, pulling him into her, and positioned his back to the ladder. He looked terrible. He was still bleeding.

Stop trying to die, you coward.

The crew confirmed the two were secure and heaved the ladder up. The process was agonizingly slow. Each passing second felt like a lifetime. But at last, with one final heave, they were pulled to the banister. Nasir and Bastian wrapped their arms around Raiden's chest and dragged him up and over the railing. They laid him down on the floor, Nasir setting to work examining him. Bastian returned to help Celeste, but she had already swung her leg up and over the railing. She reached the deck, but with the adrenaline fading, her legs gave out beneath her. Celeste crumbled unceremoniously into a pile on the floor, blood dripping down her arm.

"Celeste!" Kiyami crouched down beside her, pressing a piece of cloth against the wound. Celeste shrugged her off, crawling over to where Raiden lay unconscious. She wanted to shake him for all the trouble he'd put them through. What was he thinking? The bullet wound, she could now see, was on his right upper arm near his shoulder. Nasir placed fabric into it to stop the bleeding. The captain's head tilted to the side, letting a small amount of water fall from his mouth. More water dripped from his black hair and into his closed eyes.

"Rai, wake up," Bastian pleaded.

But the prince did not wake.

With a rough hand, Bastian turned Raiden's head back up and began to hammer on his chest. He leaned down and plugged Raiden's nose, breathing into his mouth.

"Come on, Rai. Come on . . ." Bastian muttered over and over again, like a prayer.

Celeste knelt next to them, trying not to get in the way. At some point, Kiyami got ahold of Celeste's arm, cleaned it, and wrapped it in cloth.

Horrible moments passed. Tears sprang to Celeste's eyes, and she did not have the energy to try to stop them. Her chance to go home dying in front of her. *But it wasn't that, was it?*

"Please, Rai... *Please*..."

The crew stood in silence around them. Kiyami rested her hand against Celeste's back. The only sound was the hollow *thump, thump, thump* of Bastian's hands against Raiden's chest.

Raiden coughed. At last, mercifully.

Water sputtered from his lips, and his long, dark lashes fluttered. He opened his eyes and turned to see Celeste sitting over him, tears mixing with the seawater dripping from her chin.

A weak smirk crossed his lips.

"My hero," he said.

CHAPTER 21

Human wounds, as it happened, couldn't be healed in a day. Or even two. Apparently, all a human healer could do was clean the wound, stitch it closed, and wait until the body did the healing itself. The process could even take cycles, depending on the severity of the injury. Celeste was baffled. No wonder humans didn't live very long.

"You're both lucky," Nasir said as he set about cleaning Raiden's wound. The bullet had gone clean through his arm, avoiding anything too important. Raiden should be healed enough to function in a couple of months, Nasir informed them, but to regain the full strength of his arm—only time would tell. "Don't lift anything heavy," Nasir added. But there was no chance of that. At least not yet. Raiden couldn't even lift his arm without breaking into a cold sweat.

Celeste's wound was far less troublesome. Because she thrust her arm up into the shark's teeth and hadn't actually been bitten, the punctures were shallow. "You'll probably be healed up in a couple of weeks. Although you'll probably have scarring." The teeth had left a curved line across her inner bicep. A siren healer could remove it later, if she wanted. But she had a feeling she'd like to keep it. It went rather nicely with the black crescent on her other arm. And it could serve as a reminder not to go about rescuing stupid humans.

She couldn't believe she had done so *again*.

If only she hadn't lost her gun, and her sword, it was possible neither of them would have been injured at all. Guilt washed over her. She always seemed to make a mess of situations. Perhaps she should practice with the sword and gun to avoid being such a deadweight. She had seen plenty of the other crew members conducting target practice on the deck or dueling each other to hone their skills. She could join them, though it made her nervous to even think about being around a group of men. Despite being on this ship for days, she'd gone out of her way to avoid meeting any more of them. Kiyami and she were the only women on the ship, a fact Celeste couldn't avoid noticing.

Nasir ordered her to bed. She refused.

"Cuts and bruises aren't the only things that need time to heal, love," Nasir said.

She ignored him. Today was a wake-up call. Yes, she was shaken from how close both she and Raiden had come to death. And the discovery that she was among pirates didn't help her feel any safer upon the *Red Revenge*. But as she moved through her routine, helping Kiyami to avoid the debris of the sunken ship before getting them back on course, she couldn't stop running through the battle again and again. As loath as she was to admit it, as much as it felt like a betrayal of her family, Celeste couldn't ignore the fact she had never felt so alive.

The waxing moon rose before the sun had set, hanging above as if it were watching her. She wondered what it saw. A girl? A siren? A loyal princess? A deceitful pirate?

When she joined the crew for dinner, she stared at her plate. Nasir had outdone himself, perhaps in an attempt to give everyone a good end to an otherwise wearisome day. The remainder of the pork he had brought from Romsey was cooked and served with potatoes, crisp bread, and hard cheese.

Ordinarily, the officers drank wine with dinner, but tonight the group passed around a bottle of rum. When Kiyami passed the bottle to Celeste, the siren took the bottle and stared at it. She still hadn't tried a drop of alcohol since coming aboard. Perhaps she would like to feel dumb tonight, if only to give her brain some rest. But Celeste still didn't feel comfortable enough to lose any sort of control, so she passed it across to Bastian, trying not to look at Raiden's empty chair at the head of the table. She closed her eyes and saw Raiden sliding down the stairs in a trail of blood.

The other crew members must have felt similarly, because the atmosphere of the ship was off. It was a considerably disastrous event, even for a group of pirates. They had been surrounded, nearly forced into surrender, all because they were unable to work together for more than twenty minutes without dissolving into discord. If they had been captured, they would have surely been killed. After all, pirates didn't leave survivors. Raiden's crew certainly hadn't. Another thing that weighed on Celeste heavily. What was worse, she didn't feel that bad about it.

What was happening to her?

And, to top it all off, the cargo ship had been transporting what looked like someone's personal items. Nothing particularly valuable, like treasure or tradable goods. When the crew had gone to loot, they had found a huge wooden bedframe, books, tables, and the like. Not a lot worth stealing besides some weaponry and trinkets.

At the table, Kiyami perched in her chair, moving her potatoes around in circles. Nasir, who albeit was *normally* quiet, didn't speak a word save for answering a question or two with a grunt. Even Torben, who should have been overjoyed after a good fight, jabbed at his food using much more force than necessary. Each stab made loud scraping noises that rang through the small room. Bastian flinched at every scrape. And the Admiral, who usually sat below the table waiting for scraps, was absent. The dog had refused to leave Raiden's side since the wounded captain had boarded the ship.

"Torben! For the love of God, would you please stop slamming your knife into the table?" Bastian snapped, leaning back in his chair.

Torben's face burned red. He threw his knife, blade down, into the wood of the table.

"All right, twatface!" Torben shoved the table away from him as he stood. "You have a problem with how I eat? Why don't I show you where you can put your kni—"

Nasir reached out a hand and placed it on Torben's shoulder. The Yenrian stopped shouting and let out a breath. He placed his hand on top of his husband's. Nasir smiled softly as their fingers interlaced. Taking his time, Torben sat back down. But he still shot Bastian a dirty look before pulling his knife up from the table and returning to his meal. For a moment, the only sound was the squeak of the swaying lantern's rusted chain above their heads and the roar of the ocean outside.

"Did you get anything interesting?" Kiyami asked, turning to Celeste. Her attempt at steering the conversation didn't go unnoticed by the others, but it was welcomed.

Celeste shook her head. What little she had taken was lost, but none of it was useful anyway. Then Celeste remembered the parchment tucked into her dress. It was probably nothing, but she did still wish to inspect the gold seal closer. Perhaps it would give some clue as to whose furniture had been on the ship and why. Not valuable information, but at least it would be something to talk about. So Celeste fished it from her bodice. The wax was gold, and jutting forth from it was the image of a blazing sun. Celeste offered it to Kiyami, but the girl's fingers had hardly touched the parchment before Bastian pulled it from her grasp.

"What's wrong?" Kiyami asked.

"This is the king's seal," he said, frowning.

The crew stopped eating.

"Why would a cargo ship captain have a letter from the king?" Kiyami said. "They were transporting furniture."

"We're all talking about the *Pirate* King, right? King Leonidas?" Torben asked.

"Yes, what other king would I be talking about?" said Bastian.

"There are other kings!" Torben crossed his arms.

Kiyami leaned forward across the table, straining to look. "What does it say?"

Bastian frowned deeper. "There's too much water damage. I can't make out anything."

"A cargo ship filled with furniture and weapons and a letter from the king." Kiyami grabbed the rum and took a long drink. "Is the king... *moving*?"

"Did Raiden see this?" Bastian said, looking to Celeste.

She shook her head.

"Do you think he knows anything?" Kiyami asked.

Bastian thought for a moment and then shrugged. "If he does, he hasn't told me."

"That boy certainly loves to keep secrets." Kiyami sighed.

Bastian grimaced but didn't disagree. The group fell once more into silence. Nasir asked if anyone would like dessert, but no one wanted any. They passed the bottle around again.

"Whose night is it to wash the dishes?" Kiyami asked at last. It was something of a Captain Sharp rule that the officers did their own dishes. He said it made the meals feel more like one big happy family. Celeste had thought it a joke when he first told them, but now she wasn't so sure. They certainly squabbled over it like a family.

"Celeste did them yesterday," Nasir noted. Thankful, Celeste reached out, placing a hand on top of his and squeezed. He smiled, eyes crinkling at the corners, and squeezed back. Her heart pinched in her chest. The swirling emotions from the day rose up inside her at once. She tried to press them back, but they were a whorl of color, painting her from the inside out. The bright orange of stress, a bruised purple homesickness, and queasy yellow fear—her constant companion. She took her hand away. If Nasir had noted her change, he didn't show it.

Meanwhile, Torben, Bastian, and Kiyami looked among themselves. It was the same song and dance every night. Bastian and

Torben hated doing dishes. They had been avoiding it since the voyage began. This normally left Kiyami and Celeste to volunteer.

"Oh no," Kiyami said, staring down Bastian and Torben in turn. "I've already washed dishes twice! And we've only been at sea less than a week. You two grow up and sort it out among yourselves."

"All right, let's arm-wrestle for it," said Torben.

"I'm—I'm not going to *arm-wrestle for it*," said Bastian, avoiding the man's gaze.

"Why not?"

"Be—because . . ." Bastian sputtered. Anyone with eyes could see why he wouldn't want to wrestle. Torben's one arm was bigger than both of Bastian's. And although Bastian was much taller than Torben, the gunner was built like a cannon. Short and compact. "I'll do the dishes."

Torben, who clearly wanted to wrestle Bastian for it, looked rather put out.

Bastian stood from the table and held up the parchment. "Would someone check on Rai and show him this?"

Celeste had been wanting an excuse to see Raiden's room ever since she arrived. She reached for the parchment.

Bastian hesitated. The pause was brief, but strange. Did he not trust her? Bastian had been more than kind to her up until now. And as far as she knew, Raiden hadn't told Bastian she was a siren. Did he blame her for what had happened to Raiden? Indigo guilt dropped like a stone in her stomach. She tried to push this away too, but it was getting harder to do so. Bastian was right not to trust her. No one on this ship should.

He placed the parchment in her hand. "Thank you," he said. "But if he's asleep, leave him be for tonight."

The group dispersed. But as Celeste pushed open the door to the officers' quarters, Kiyami followed.

"Are you okay?" she asked.

Celeste stopped walking and turned. With a look of concern, Kiyami reached out a hand toward Celeste but must have remembered the last time Celeste had flinched from her in the jail. Kiyami let it drop to her side. It was too much. She didn't want Kiyami digging through her feelings, bringing them up. But the feelings surfaced anyway. Purple, indigo, yellow, and orange mixed until she couldn't separate them. They turned black. Confused. She couldn't hold them down. She couldn't breathe. Why was this happening to her? Why was she like this? She had been fine a moment ago.

Falling apart in front of Kiyami was the last thing Celeste wanted to do. She'd look weak. Unreliable. These humans weren't her friends. Or her family. And if they were, they'd only push her away. Because these feelings were too big. And she couldn't control them. Why couldn't she control them? Why did she feel so much? Kiyami was strong and sturdy. Celeste wished to be like that.

And so she swallowed and gave Kiyami what she hoped was a reassuring smile.

"All right." Kiyami looked unconvinced. "You know where to find me if you need me." Then she turned and headed back to the deck.

The siren clenched and released her fists at her sides. Kiyami hadn't asked anyone else if they were okay. Even now, so far away from home, she couldn't escape it. It took mere days for Kiyami to discover how weak Celeste was. How fragile. How easily overwhelmed. Her feelings felt like water. She tried to hold them in her hands, to carry them as everyone else seemed to, but the feelings kept coming. Pouring over. Finding every crack between her fingers and slipping through. Spilling out. The only thing she'd found that helped was escaping to the surface. Or crying about it, apparently. Although usually that made everything feel worse. It was shameful to cry, especially in front of others. But Celeste couldn't count how many times she'd cried in front of Maeve. Maeve had never cried in front of her.

No one did.

She was simply weaker than them. And no amount of training or drills or lessons ever helped. Perhaps *she* was the problem. Her stupid bleeding heart was the whole reason she was in this mess in the first place. All because she couldn't stomach watching a human die. And now she had saved him again. Betrayed her people, again. All for the sake of a murderous pirate.

The tears came. They always did. And she couldn't hold them either.

Maybe she would go to bed. She didn't want Raiden to see her like this, and he was probably asleep anyway. Nasir had ordered him to rest, after all. Raiden could see the parchment tomorrow. Then she would have fresh eyes to search his room for clues as to what sort of secret treasure he was risking their lives for. She slipped inside her room, hoping the space would calm her. It didn't. The walls were too thin, and he could hear her. *Be strong*, she demanded. A strangled sob escaped her lips.

She wasn't strong.

Another sob.

She was out of control.

Another.

And at this rate, she was never going home.

Through the wall beside her, Celeste heard a soft knock. She stilled, her hand clamping over her mouth. The knock came again. She pressed her hand against the wall.

Another sob.

Another knock.

She sighed and, at last, knocked back.

Silence.

Then—

Two knocks.

She sniffed, a ghost of a smile appearing in the darkness. She knocked twice.

Three knocks.

Shouldn't he be resting? She returned the pattern.

Four.

With a sigh, Celeste realized she couldn't avoid Raiden after all. There was no privacy on this ridiculous ship. So she wiped her face on her sleeve. And before he could knock again, Celeste slipped from her room and took the two steps to his door.

She knocked. Four times.

He opened the door.

"My hero." He smiled.

CHAPTER 22

"Don't look at me in that tone of voice," Raiden said.

Celeste laughed despite herself. He looked wretched. Absolutely wretched. And yet this, too, became him. As though the deep circles beneath his eyes and the large bandage around his arm made him appear all the more interesting. His dark curling hair was mussed as if he had just woken up. His smooth skin, although a shade paler than usual, still glowed in the light from the flickering candles around his room. He stood in the door, dressed in nothing but a pair of soft pants. The shirtless male form did not faze Celeste. Siren males often didn't wear bodices. Many females didn't either, for that matter. And yet she averted her gaze. Her eyes landed upon the Admiral sitting upon his bed, alert and protective. *Clever animal*, she thought.

"I'm perfectly fine. Except for being shot."

Celeste placed her hand to her neck and mimicked being unable to breathe.

"All right, *and the drowning*," he added with a smirk.

He took a step back, opening the door wider to welcome her inside. The room behind him was filled with polished wooden furniture. At the back sat a large desk, similar to the navigation room, with scrolls and quills upon it. Beyond that was a wall of windows from which Celeste could see the twilight. Elaborate paintings of ships at sea lined the walls. And at her left was a bed nearly three times the size of her "room," covered in rich red fabric. All four wooden posts of the bed rose high, carved with depictions of sea creatures. The effect was rather impressive. But none of it gave her any clues to the treasure. Still, she maintained hope as she strode past him into the room. Something had to be here.

As she clutched the wet parchment in her fist, part of her wondered if he did know what his father was planning. *That man certainly loves to keep secrets.* Raiden wouldn't risk all their lives for a pile of gold. Would he? Perhaps he was just the selfish, cutthroat human her people believed him to be. She couldn't tell. Every time she thought she had him figured out, he'd do something to make her question it. He was maddening. And yet he seemed to read *her* thoughts with a single glance.

"What's on your mind?" He closed the door behind her with a soft snap.

Celeste crossed to the bed, reaching out a hand to scratch behind the Admiral's ears. The dog stretched and rolled, offering her his soft belly. She smiled, perching on the edge of the bed beside the silly creature. Raiden waited, his eyes scanning her face. So Celeste handed him the parchment, and he took it without a word. He turned it over in his hands, taking in the blurred text. When his eyes caught on the seal at the top of the page, his jaw clenched.

"Where did you get this?"

She gestured toward his wound.

"Captain Clarke?" He frowned. "Did anyone else see this?"

Celeste nodded and gestured broadly toward the rest of the officers' rooms.

"I see. I'd imagine Bastian recognized my father's seal."

She didn't need to give him confirmation. He already knew.

Raiden fell quiet, examining the piece of parchment again for any indication of what had once been written on it. He looked angry, and

Celeste couldn't decide if it was because the crew knew about the letter, because he couldn't read it, or if there was something else. Silence fell as he ran his eyes over the wet parchment again and again. Finally, he set it down on the bedside table. He sank down into the mattress, running his hand through his hair. Whatever he was thinking about, he did not share it with her.

Ocean waves thumped against the side of the ship. The Admiral breathed deeply, perhaps snoring. She reached her hand out toward the animal and affectionately rubbed her thumb along the bridge of his nose.

"Thank you," Raiden said at last.

Celeste looked up at him, brows furrowed.

"For saving my life again," he added.

I shouldn't have.

Another silence.

With her duty now fulfilled, there was no reason for her to stay. But perhaps she could search a bit before he asked her to take her leave. It was the first time she was in his chamber, after all—maybe she could pass it off as idle curiosity. Rising from the bed, Celeste saw the Admiral stir. His large brown eyes watched her as she walked in a great curve around the room, taking in each painting, each little treasure in the room that was not Raiden's. And some she guessed might have been. But she froze when she found his gun, sitting upon the top of his dresser. In an instant, she was there again. Watching in horror as the bullet went through him. How he crumpled. The bloody trail he left.

Soft footsteps sounded upon the carpet. She turned to see Raiden standing behind her, *looking* at her. It was unnerving, being seen like this. It was as though he looked into her very soul. Saw the beating heart inside her. A heart she did not wish for him to know. Celeste made to step past him, when a gentle hand circled her wrist.

"Are you okay?"

The touch sent a shock through her. But for once it did not make her shake like a battered sail. Her eyes fell to his hand, so loose she could pull away. She didn't. It took a moment to remember what he had said. Her eyes found his face, so open in the candlelight. So unlike the hardened, cocky pirate she knew. Was he only searching for more information? A bat of the eye or a curve of her lip that would betray her?

Of course she wasn't okay. But it wasn't his business. And who was he to check on her? This man who had threatened her after she saved his life, and in doing so, ruined hers. Why did everyone think she was this weak thing that needed to be checked on?

And what's worse... *Why did she wish she could tell him everything?* This prince who somehow knew everything she was feeling and told her so little. This man who was an enemy to her people. A killer. A pirate. Even if he was sincere. Even if he cared about her... wasn't that worse? She was sent here to kill him.

She should do it now.

The dagger hidden at her side suddenly felt uncomfortable. Celeste pulled her hand away from him, trying to break their connection. But it remained. They stood so close together. Close enough to stab him. And yet too close to breathe. Heart hammering, Celeste slid her hand to her hip. Beneath her fingers, she felt the hilt of her dagger. *It could all be over.* She only needed to be quick.

"I thought I heard a noise coming from your room," he said.

Celeste's hand curled around the dagger's hilt.

"I've been shot before. It's a sort of occupational risk." He paused and took a breath as if he wanted to share more but thought better of it. Instead, he continued. "But today scared me. I've never been with people this inexperienced. When we were surrounded, I was afraid of my crew getting hurt. *Again.*" The way he said that last word left her ruined.

Why was he telling her these things? To gain her sympathy? Her grip on the dagger tightened. In silence, she watched him step away and sink back onto the bed. His shoulders sagged, and he stared at the floor. It wasn't the son of her enemy before her. It was a captain who was haunted by those he had lost. Without meaning to, her hand fell to her side.

"I knocked because—" He lifted his eyes to meet hers, and he sighed. "Honestly, I don't know why I knocked." Celeste walked to the bed and sat down between him and his dog. In response, the Admiral snuggled a bit closer, his head against her thigh. "I suppose I wanted to see if you were all right. If you needed some company..." Raiden let the sentence trickle off at the end, a question. The dagger against her hip burned.

A part of her wanted to accept this peace offering. To dive into it headfirst and see how deep it was and where it went. To share every color of these feelings inside her with him. But she was sent here to kill him, and she was beginning to realize that being around him made it too hard. This path did not lead anywhere good. In fact, she was sure it would lead to her own ruin, in one way or the other. And so, despite every part of her wishing to stay, to lean into this warmth and let herself be seen, she lifted her stubborn chin and rose from the bed.

Perhaps today she was not strong enough to kill him. But she had to be strong enough to leave.

If Raiden was unconvinced by her performance, he didn't say anything. He merely nodded. She could tell there was something else he wanted to say. Something hanging in the air between them. And yet he turned his gaze away, to the darkness beyond the windows.

"Goodnight, then," he said.

She closed the door behind her.

Alone in her room, Celeste lay on her back, staring blankly at the ceiling. What had possibly been the third-worst day of her life was now over. The second and first being the day she betrayed the Chorus and the day she arrived in Port Romsey.

How unfortunate that all of them happened to her within a week.

Her body still felt the echoes of waves crashing and rolling against her from earlier in the day. Sleep remained fickle, evading her. So she lay in the dark, letting the minutes pass with only her thoughts for company. A part of her wished she had stayed with Raiden in his room. A part of her wished she had stabbed him. And a part of her wished she had never gone into his room at all. It took a night like tonight for Celeste to wish she had a hammock with everyone else. At least there she could be listening to Oakes's snores that the others loved to complain about, instead of her thoughts swimming around. They circled like predators, ready to devour her whole.

Every night as a human felt like this. She'd get in bed, bone-tired, and then spend her night slipping between torturous thoughts and horrible nightmares. Sometimes she avoided sleep, as if she were afraid of it. And every time she closed her eyes and began to drift off, she'd remember her mother's face, or the fight with the Chorus, and her mind was off again, racing down familiar paths.

She missed home.

The tears came quickly, overwhelming her until she was shaking with them. She was trapped in a body that wasn't her own, upon a ship that was sailing toward its doom, surrounded by the very creatures her kingdom feared most. She couldn't even protect herself! At least in the water she was a competent fighter, if not the best. Now she was voiceless. Hopeless. It was a miracle she survived the fight today given how many times that sword fell from her hands.

It was a miracle Raiden survived.

He shouldn't have.

It would have been so easy. To let him drown. She wished she knew why she had done it. Why she continued to stay her hand. She only had to *let him die*. And even at this she managed to fail. They had been aboard this vessel for days, and she had very little to show for it. There wasn't anything more to find. She knew this in her gut. These were pirates working for a king who desired untold riches found on a remote island. This feigned investigation was a ruse. A flimsy attempt to delay the inevitable. She didn't want to kill him. Not really. But if she refused, she'd never be able to return home. Could never return to the sea for fear of being tracked down and killed for her crimes.

A sob escaped her throat. She missed her family. She missed being a siren and knowing with certainty what her future held. She missed following orders she understood and trusting someone else to tell her what to do. She missed Maeve. She even missed Shye. But what she missed most was herself. In Staria, she was a princess. A siren. A daughter. A sister. A soldier. She had a future. But her stars were no longer aligned. And it was all her fault.

If she had been more like Kiyami, she'd never be in this situation. Kiyami was every bit the hero in those stories Celeste had been told her entire life. Strong, but not only in the physical sense. A girl who was straightforward and knew why she was here, what she wanted. A girl who would do anything for her family. Everything Celeste was not. And Kiyami being thoughtful enough to ask if Celeste was okay was salt in the wound. As if Celeste needed the reminder of what she was. *Betrayer… weakling…* Her sobs grew louder. She shoved her face into her pillow to muffle the noise. The life she had was gone. Nothing remained of the siren she once was.

A scratching sound came from the bottom of the door, near Celeste's head. It was late, well past midnight. No one would be up except the night crew. The scratch came again, more insistent this time. Celeste rubbed her eyes with her fists, a half-hearted attempt to hide all evidence of her emotional state. She stretched her arm above her head, cracking open the door without getting up. A wet nose pressed its way into her room.

"Hello," Celeste whispered in common with a watery smile. The very act of speaking felt like a soothing balm. Even if it was to an animal. Her voice cracked from lack of use, but she felt herself beaming. The first word she had ever spoken in the human tongue.

The Admiral wagged his tail.

"Inside?" she whispered, cracking the door open wider.

The dog's tail beat back and forth as it trotted into the room, which felt smaller with the added presence. Even so, it found a place between Celeste's hip and the wall to curl up. Its head rested once more against her thigh. She closed the door with a soft click and rested her hand on its back, stroking down its curling fur. It was funny to think that last week she watched this dog yip and dance around the deck of a different ship. The creature looked so strange to her then. Now it pressed against her, belly rising and falling in even breaths.

"You did not find me on your own, did you?" she asked.

The dog's back leg twitched.

Celeste remembered shutting the door behind her as she left. And Raiden always locked his door. The Admiral was a clever boy, but he couldn't work a doorknob. Raiden clearly hadn't believed she didn't want company. But she wasn't annoyed. Her hand found the wall between their rooms, her fingers brushing the grooved wood. She considered knocking on the wall. A little signal to let him know she knew what he had done. But instead she let it rest there.

After a moment, she took her hand away. She laid her head back onto the pillow. The Admiral adjusted to fit the curve of her hip. And for the first time since she had become human, Celeste fell into an easy sleep.

CHAPTER 23

Celeste awoke to the Admiral staring down at her, wet tongue lolling out of his mouth.

"Good morning," she whispered with a sleepy smile.

The Admiral bounced up and down. Light poured over everything in the room. She wondered why Bastian had not come to knock on her door and tell her to get up as he normally did. But she guessed he had let her sleep in after the events of yesterday. *Great*, she thought. Growing up as a princess in the palace, everyone treated her as this fragile little thing. Being on this ship was the first time she was simply Celeste and nothing more. But apparently, after her performance the night before, that had ended.

She cracked open the door for the Admiral. He bounded out, barking to let everyone on the ship know he was coming. She got ready quickly. Today she chose black pants, a white blouse with a black corset, and boots that rose over her knees. Across her hips, she wore the belt that Torben had given her, the sword tapping at her side. He had yet to ask for it back, and she had a feeling he wouldn't. Torben had plenty of new toys from their raid of the cargo ship to occupy himself with. Next, she braided her hair away from her face, as her sister Sephone had taught her when she was young.

The sun was not as high as she had expected, but it was clear the rest of the crew had been up for an hour or two. Their captain was nowhere to be seen. The fact came as a surprise, although she knew full well he'd be resting. It was as if she'd grown accustomed to seeing him each day, and his absence felt like taking an extra step when there wasn't a stair.

Kiyami waved from her place at the wheel.

"Good morning, Celeste! You look well," she said with a warm smile. Kiyami wore her long, dark hair slicked back and secured at the base of her neck. She, too, wore pants, although hers were made of black fabric with a subtle floral pattern on it. Her top was dark blue, with one side wrapped over the other and secured at her hip. It was trimmed in gray, and it, too, bore a subtle but intricate pattern. The golden hilt of her shining cutlass bobbed against her hip.

Celeste returned the wave and strode up the stairs to meet her. When they were close, she pointed toward the sword at her own hip and to Kiyami.

"Your sword and me?"

She tried again, pointing to Kiyami's sword, then to Kiyami, and then to her own sword and herself.

"You ... want us to fight?" Kiyami tried, although clearly opposed to the idea.

She shook her head. With resolute posture, Celeste wagged a finger at an invisible student, correcting some mistake.

"You want me to scold ... no ..." Kiyami's face folded in on itself in confusion before understanding dawned. "Teach! Teach you! You'd like me to teach you to use a sword."

A laugh trilled from Celeste's lips, and she nodded.

"Of course I can teach you. Would you like to start after lunch today?"

Celeste nodded again and reached out to clasp Kiyami's wrist. It was a gut reaction—something she was so used to doing when she thanked a mentor in her kingdom. Kiyami looked down at Celeste's hand, eyebrows knitting together. But as Celeste pulled her hand back, Kiyami closed her own hand around Celeste's wrist and squeezed gently. The gesture was small, but it felt like home.

"Let's begin with footwork," Kiyami said.

The late-afternoon sun washed the deck in a warm, golden light. Celeste shifted back and forth on her feet, hands clenching and unclenching at her sides. They had quite the audience, with the crew having little better to do than watch this lesson. And of course Raiden, who had been in bed resting all day, chose this moment to get a breath of fresh air. Celeste's lips pressed into a hard line. She knew well how the first lesson of any new training went. The idea of landing on her back in front of Raiden was nearly enough to make her call the whole thing off.

He had more color in his face than the night before, but not much. And his dark eyes hadn't left her for the past ten minutes. Celeste hoped the others assumed the flush on her cheeks was from exertion and heat rather than embarrassment. Each day had begun to feel warmer than the last.

"It's the southern heat," Nasir had said at lunch.

"It's going to be the death of me," grunted Torben. Apparently, summers in Yenri weren't nearly as punishing.

Celeste took a deep breath, centering herself. She let the distractions around her drift away, like water down a river. Torben's laugh, Raiden's gaze, and the other crew members fell away until there was nothing but Celeste and the rhythm of her breath.

"Begin with your right foot forward and left behind," Kiyami said, demonstrating. "Try to keep your heels in line with each other. The goal is to make your body a smaller target."

Celeste did as she was told, moving her feet so they matched Kiyami's. Or at least she thought they had. Kiyami was quick to point out that Celeste's feet didn't point in the right way. Or her legs weren't far enough apart. Or her weight was too much on one foot or the other. Kiyami made corrections bluntly. Her sharp eyes saw every mistake. When Celeste's foot turned out again, Kiyami kicked it back into place with her toe. If Celeste hadn't already been blushing, she was now. Of course sword work began with the *feet*. The one thing Celeste had no training in. Although she was used to walking by now, she still tripped often.

"Bend your knees."

Knees... Celeste's heart dropped. She knew this word. She *knew* it. Nerissa had told her where they were the day she got them. And yet every time she got close to remembering, it would slip through her fingers like water.

Mercifully, Kiyami didn't wait long. She gently tapped the back of Celeste's leg with the tip of her boot, and the leg bent. *Ugh, of course*, Celeste thought. *The knees are the bendy part. Which was why she said "bend."*

"Now advance."

The girls drilled each step again and again, until sweat dripped down Celeste's face, and her thighs burned. Her legs were not yet as strong as her upper body. But her stamina was still quite high, so they were able to continue for a couple of hours. In time, Celeste began building better awareness of her legs. She noticed which direction her feet pointed, where her weight was held. Soon she stepped backward and forward in tandem with Kiyami. It became like a dance. They drilled forward movement, backward movement, and even began turning before Kiyami stopped them.

"You're a quick study!" she said, grinning.

It was a joy to watch Kiyami work. She was a natural teacher, and Celeste was grateful for how patient she was. Celeste did her best to communicate as much, but the miming fell short. Still, Kiyami gathered the gist.

"I taught my siblings how to fight," she said proudly, and laughed. "There's five of them, so I've had a lot of practice." Something crossed over her face as she spoke of them. It was a look that

Celeste could relate to all too well. Homesickness. "Let's end things here for today. Tomorrow we will review today's movements and begin attacks and parries."

Inexplicably, it was Celeste's turn to wash dishes. Again. Raiden hadn't come to dinner, choosing instead to stay in bed. Kiyami, who had done dishes several times already, had returned to man the wheel. And Torben and Bastian were, as usual, missing once the meal had concluded. Nasir insisted he'd hunt them down, but Celeste waved his offer away. So the two cleaned the table together and set about their chores, using the usual small ration of water and whale soap to wash the remnants of food from each plate.

The two worked in silence, side by side. Nasir cleaned the dishes, and Celeste dried them with a towel and put them away. It was a comfortable routine. Nasir was not much for conversation, which made things easy for Celeste. But when he did speak, he enjoyed getting to know the others. So it didn't come entirely as a surprise when he introduced a topic of conversation.

"You have a family back home?"

Celeste nodded and held up five fingers.

"Ah... five of you? This includes parents and yourself?"

She nodded again.

"I always wanted siblings."

Celeste looked up from her work and tilted her head, listening.

"My parents died when I was a young man." He kept his eyes on his work. "We were staying in Port Warren at the time, when my baba passed. We moved there for me to attend school to be a doctor, like him. But we couldn't afford for me to finish after he went."

He finished cleaning a dish and handed it to Celeste. It felt as though she were intruding, even though he was speaking to her directly.

"My muta died soon after . . . so I traveled around looking for work. Not many in Ethoria would hire a Sumredan boy who hadn't finished his schooling."

Celeste finished drying and gently placed the plate with the others. She glanced up at Nasir's face. He looked back at her. There was no sadness there, only a straightforward openness. This happened to him long ago. It was a part of him, but it didn't hurt him to share it.

"I traveled around and picked up odd jobs. I was good in the kitchen. My muta taught me everything she knew. Eventually, I found my way to the Broken Compass, and that's where I met Torben." A private smile Celeste had seen many times pulled at the corner of his lips. A smile only for Torben.

"Most of the time, I find life doesn't go the way you want it to," Nasir said, his dark brown eyes creasing at the corners. "But most of the time, things turn out the way they should."

Celeste let his words settle within her. After so many days set adrift, she wasn't sure she'd ever find solid ground again.

Nasir turned his face back to his work. "Can you hand me the vanilla? The bottle's sticky, and I want to clean it. It's in the cupboard."

She nodded and went to the cupboard, retrieving a sticky bottle. The cook took one glance at the bottle and frowned.

"That's olive oil, dear," he said, taking the bottle from her hands. She flushed red as he set down his things to go retrieve the vanilla himself. When he returned, he fixed her with an unreadable expression. "Do you not know how to read?"

She lowered her gaze to the floor.

"Don't be embarrassed. I've always disliked the fact most women aren't allowed an education." He set the bottle down on the table. "Would you like to learn? It might make communicating easier."

Celeste's eyes grew wide. She could actually learn to *read*? To *write*? Her heart skipped a beat as she thought of how she could finally have conversations with her crewmates.

She nodded and pointed to the floor.

"You'd like to start now?"

Celeste nodded again, and he laughed.

The first writing lesson went as well as expected. Nasir sat down with Celeste in the empty dining room, the lantern above lighting the table before them. He provided two quills and parchment. Celeste couldn't help running her hands all over them, enjoying the way the feather tickled her fingers and how soft the parchment felt. First, they went over the numbers and letters of the common language. The quill felt awkward in her hand, much the same way a fork had the first time she used one. He wrote them one at a time, and she mimicked them. But while his numbers and letters were neat and straight, hers were blotchy and crooked. Some were so awful it looked as though a squid had projected its ink onto the page.

Nasir was an encouraging, if quiet, teacher. He was straightforward and would gently correct her when she made an error. They practiced for the better part of an hour, and even tried a few simple words before they moved on to reading. But because Celeste didn't speak, this provided a challenge.

"I know there is a language of hands, but I'm afraid I don't know it," Nasir confessed. "I was taught to read by sounding out the words and letters. Perhaps we'll try association?"

And so Nasir carefully wrote out the letters and read them all aloud to Celeste so she could hear how they sounded. Then he carefully wrote out words of things that were in the room: *Chair* and *light*, *table* and *book*, *you* and *I*. He slowly sounded out each word a few times, then ripped the parchment with each word and shuffled them around. Celeste picked up a word, tried to read it, and pointed to where it was in the room. The process worked well enough, and eventually she memorized what the words looked like.

The two practiced for another hour, until Celeste let out a yawn.

"Keep those and practice. We can continue tomorrow."

She nodded, eyes drooping, and gathered the parchment, quill, and ink from the table. As she stood, she could feel her muscles protest with each movement. It had been a long time since she had felt this sore and mentally drained, but she also felt satisfied. She waved goodbye to Nasir and began her stiff journey toward her room. Each step was awkward, and she almost laughed at herself. It took her cycles to learn to understand the human language and to fight. She wasn't sure how long she'd be on the *Red Revenge*, but she doubted it would be long enough for her to become proficient with the sword, reading, and writing. Still, how could she not use this opportunity for as long as she had it?

"Why are we doing this?" Bastian's voice echoed around the corner. Something in his hushed tone made her stop.

"You know why." Raiden's voice was hard and pointed, like the steel of a blade. "The king asked me to retrieve it. We do this, and we're back in his good graces."

"But we're leading this crew into the same waters where we were last attacked." It sounded like an old argument, the words worn and practiced.

"What happened then will not happen again."

"What *did* happen, Rai?" They were moving down the hall in her direction. Celeste took a step back.

Raiden sighed. "*I told you*—we were attacked by a passing ship. You fell overboard, I dove to save you, and the ship went down. We were adrift until Celeste found us and rowed us to shore."

"And I told you I know when you're lying," Bastian hissed. "Why would a girl be in the middle of the ocean in a rowboat? Why didn't a single crew member survive?"

"I don't know. I don't remember everything. And we can't exactly ask her, can we?"

Their footsteps stopped. "You're keeping something from me. Something to do with her."

A silence descended. The silence that came between lightning and thunder.

"At least tell me what it is he wants. What's out there? Where exactly are we going?"

Celeste pressed herself into the wall, her heart pounding in her chest. This was it. What she had been waiting for.

"Lunapesce," Raiden said, like the roll of thunder.

Lunapesce. Celeste's breath hitched. The sacred island of the Goddess of Moon and Sea. She slipped back to hide in the galley, waiting for them to pass before returning to her room. As she did, Celeste searched her memories for what she knew of Lunapesce, which was very little. Treasure and power beyond imagination awaited those who could find the mythical island, which only appeared during a solar eclipse, when the moon and sun met in the sky.

How could this *human* possibly believe he knew where to find it, when it had been lost to sirens for generations? There wasn't a siren alive who believed the place was *real*. And humans didn't believe in the Goddess. From what Celeste was taught, humans believed in the God of Sun and Land, their creator, but saw him as the only god. They did not recognize the duality of God and Goddess as the sirens did.

But at least she now knew why the humans had been near Staria, what they were searching for.

Which meant the time had come to kill Raiden and go home.

CHAPTER 24

"We need to make port," Bastian said at breakfast, his voice lacking its usual warmth. "Our water supply was damaged in the firefight, among other things, and I doubt we'll make it to our destination and back without replenishing our supplies."

"No," Raiden said, surprising them as he entered the room. It was the first meal he'd joined since his injury.

The table went quiet as he took his usual seat beside Bastian.

"It's not a suggestion, Captain," Bastian said, his tone even.

"And I said *no*," Raiden repeated, lifting his eyes to his friend as he heaped food on his plate.

Either Bastian did not know enough about Lunapesce to know that he was dooming them to failure, or he didn't care. If they stopped, they would not make it in time for the eclipse. This journey would be in vain.

Of course, this crew would never make it to Lunapesce anyway. Not after Celeste killed their captain and left them all without a navigator. She'd burn the map too, of course. Bastian and Kiyami knew the sea but not well enough to manage such uncharted waters. With Raiden gone, they wouldn't risk the journey. A knot formed in her stomach. What would happen to them after she left them stranded without a captain? Without their bounty, the money they needed to survive? She thought of Kiyami. Of the family who relied on her. Celeste curled her hands into fists. These pirates didn't deserve the sacred treasure of her people.

Anyway, they were not yet so far from land that they couldn't make it back without a captain or navigator. She could not delay. The closer they sailed to Lunapesce, the more likely the crew would be stranded in Staria's waters. As much as she didn't want any more humans wandering into her kingdom's territory, she also wished to avoid as much bloodshed as possible.

Tense glances were exchanged around the table. Nasir's lips pressed into a line.

"Let me be clear: We will not survive without stopping," Bastian said.

Raiden set his fork down to rub his temple with his hand. "Fine," he relented, then turned his dark gaze on Celeste. "Come. We should look over the maps to choose a port."

Port. They were going to go to another human town. Celeste kept her face neutral, but inside fear bloomed. Not only did this complicate her plan but she'd rather drown than step on land again. The memory of her bodice being cut apart unfolded in her mind's eye. Perhaps she could ask to remain on the ship.

"After you," Raiden said, opening the door wide.

She avoided his eye, walking ahead. This human was too observant, and she couldn't lose what little trust she had gained with him. Not now that the end was finally within reach. And so she tried not to think about what she had heard in that very hall the night before. She tried not to wonder why Raiden and Bastian, who were like brothers, now acted like strangers. Night after night, she watched them drink together, swapping stories of their countless foolish adventures growing up aboard the Pirate King's ship. The two had even stayed with Bastian's family when they were at Port Romsey. And although Celeste was thankful Raiden hadn't told Bastian the truth of who she was—about the siren attack on the ship—it didn't make any sense that he wouldn't. There had to be something else she didn't know. Some reason why he would hide the truth from the person he loved most.

Not that she had any legs to stand on in that regard.

They entered the navigation room, the Admiral trotting along in their wake. She bent down and stroked his head, as she had seen Raiden do. The dog leaned into her hand, wiggling around as if trying to help her reach the best spot.

"The Admiral has a soft spot for beautiful women."

Celeste stilled. *Women.* It was such a human word. Images of all the women she had seen in paintings on so many broken ships flew through her mind. Their soft faces and round, reddened cheeks. Curling hair and small, rounded ears. He knew what she was, and yet he called her a *woman*. Was he mocking her? Trying to convince her that she was one of them? Or perhaps... it was what it seemed. A compliment. A far more dangerous thing.

In a few long strides, he moved to the desk beside the window, pulling a map from one of its drawers. He used only his right hand, his injured arm tucked into his side.

"Let's see," he said, dropping the map onto the table. His fingers fumbled, unable to open the curled map one-handed. Celeste reached out, smoothing the paper and placing the weights at each corner as she saw him do countless times. He didn't say a word, only watched as she placed the little wooden ship where she knew them to be on the map.

"My first thought was Port Velluno."

At the name, Celeste's eyes flew to his, and she saw his mouth quirk up at her reaction. That night she had left him along the cliffside beach felt so long ago. Of course they would stop there. It was the closest human port to the siren waters. Regaining her composure, Celeste turned back to the map, leaning into her hands on the table. As she peered down, she noticed with pleasure that she recognized a few of the letters now. They were jumbled into unrecognizable combinations, but even so. Her fingers brushed against the swooping letters along the southern tip of Ethoria, where she knew Velluno was. It wasn't far. They could be there by tomorrow morning. Perhaps she could borrow the map for this evening's lesson with Nasir. *Probably her last lesson*, she reminded herself.

"How many days will we lose?"

Celeste pulled a piece of empty parchment that sat atop his desk toward her and picked up his quill. Raiden's eyebrows raised in surprise as he watched the little siren slowly form the number *three* in her shaky hand.

"You know how to write now?" he asked, a warm smile cracking through his frustration.

Celeste beamed and wrote an *N*, but she couldn't remember the rest. Still, he understood.

"*Nasir* is teaching you? He hardly talks with anyone."

A bubbling laugh ripped through her, and her eyebrows knit together. Nasir had never given her that impression. If he had meant to avoid her, he would have been wise to have never offered her that cookie on their first day.

"I'm glad to see you're getting along with the crew. You fit right in."

By his tone, she discerned that this came as a surprise to him, but not an unwelcome one. It came as a surprise to her too. She hadn't thought of it. Hadn't allowed herself to notice how comfortable she felt around the others lately. In fact, she'd begun to like her life on the ship. Even without a voice, she felt listened to. Valued. But the realization was a horrible one, given what she had to do.

"I'm proud of you," he said. "Learning the sword and now writing as well."

No… Why today of all days did this infuriating man choose to be nice to her? She couldn't remember the last time anyone had been proud of her. This was a distraction. It did not matter how he felt.

"So, seems we have no choice." He ran a hand through his hair. "We're going to have to take this detour. Do you think we might be able to make up the time?" He spoke as if his words before hadn't mattered. As if this were just another conversation between them.

Celeste's hand shook as she wrote the word *Yes* on the page. But it was not due to her lack of skill. The lie hurt. How she wished it could all be over. That she could be home, and all this would be but a distant memory.

"What's wrong?" His fingers met her chin, raising his knuckle beneath it until she met his eye. It was like looking into the sun. His gaze burned. And she could not hide from the light.

"We'll figure something out," he assured her.

And Celeste nodded.

If she didn't kill him tonight, she would have to wait days for another opportunity on the ship. She couldn't very well manage it in a human town. Even if she was able to get him alone, she'd be stuck on land. And who knew what the guards were like in this port. And each passing day made what she had to do that much harder. Her mother's tearstained face swam in her vision, and she turned to leave, jaw clenched, before he could read her face.

Celeste waited for the dead of the night, emerging from her quarters dressed in black, dagger pressed to her side. The siren princess carried nothing else, for she had nothing worth keeping. She hadn't slept. Couldn't sleep. Not with Port Velluno drawing closer with each passing moment. The longer she sat in the darkness, the surer she became. It ended tonight. What else could she do? Stay with the humans? Live the rest of her life in silent servitude to the son of her enemy? She couldn't let them reach Lunapesce to ransack a sacred island like they had that cargo ship.

The ship swayed beneath her feet as she scanned the darkened hallway, listening for any sign of life. When none came, she crept toward the captain's quarters on silent feet. One step. Then another. Her hand closed around the golden doorknob. She did not hesitate. The door slid open, creaking on its hinges. She tensed, searching the room for a sign of the Admiral, but found none. The dog wasn't in the room. Her shoulders dropped a fraction, and she slipped inside, leaving the door ajar for her escape. Pulse pounding, she unsheathed her dagger and approached the bed.

It lay empty.

She cursed, spinning around the room to see if she had missed him in some darkened corner. When she found he wasn't there, her shoulders slumped. Sliding the dagger back into its place along her hip, Celeste crept from the room, closing the door gently behind her. Raiden was on strict orders from Nasir to rest. He should have been there. But she refused to give up that easily. It needed to be over. *Had* to be over.

She swept down the hall, opening the door out onto the deck to go in search of the Pirate Prince. It didn't take long. She found him on the ship's bow, drinking from a bottle of wine and staring blankly out into the dark night. He was alone, but the night crew still walked the ship's deck. She considered stabbing him through the back in his ribs and jumping off ship before anyone was alarmed, but all the sailors had guns on their hips. One mistake, and she could be killed. No, it would be much better to wait for Raiden to be asleep in his room. Alone. And though she'd be loath to admit it, Celeste felt relief to avoid the task once more.

As she approached, Raiden turned his head toward her and smiled, lowering his half-empty bottle of wine. "Can't sleep either?"

She nodded, joining him along the banister. He held the bottle to her, but she declined with a wave of her hand. Raiden nodded and took another long drink. In the moonlight, he looked every inch the tragic prince. His shoulders slumped, and his hair was mussed, likely from his nervous habit of running his hands through it. All the usual confidence he wore like armor was discarded. She hated that she wondered why.

"Would you like to play a game?" he asked.

Celeste tilted her head to the side, questioning.

"War and Bones? Have you played before?"

She shook her head, unable to contain a smirk. Of course

humans had a game called "war." When her eyes fell back onto him, her breath caught. The soft light of the lamps shadowed the contours of his face, emphasizing the cut of his cheekbones and his jaw. Raiden wore an unreadable expression as he looked down at her. He was unavoidably beautiful. Dangerously so.

"It's a simple enough game. Best hand wins. I normally play with a wager, but since you're new, I'll spare you the humiliation for the time being," he said with a grin.

She scoffed, crossing her arms over her chest.

"Oh, feeling confident, hero?" He lifted an eyebrow. "Why don't I teach you, and we'll make a wager."

Appeased, the two sat down on the deck as he shuffled the cards. Celeste was rather good at games from playing with her sisters when they were children and confined to the palace, although they played with shells or other tokens. Still, despite Raiden's warnings, she liked her chances. He carefully explained the rules as he shuffled, but most of the words fell through her as she focused on his hands. They flexed and moved with the cards, shifting them deftly, splitting them, then sliding them back together again. Finished, he placed ten cards down, alternating between them so that each had five.

Raiden took another sip of wine.

"Any questions?" he asked, his eyes boring into hers.

She shook her head, but it was a lie. Celeste always had questions. Just none about the game. She recalled he said something about matching the colors. A groan escaped her lips as she looked at the cards. They were either red or black, but there were also little symbols and numbers on them. Some even had pictures. At least she knew some of the numbers now. But what was she supposed to do?

Celeste's brow furrowed as she rearranged her cards, placing ones with similarities together and discarding ones she couldn't match. Once both were finished, Raiden dealt new cards to replace the old ones. These, too, were organized based on her invented system.

"Still wish to continue?" he asked with a smirk. "You don't look confident in your hand."

Celeste stuck out her chin and nodded.

"Fine, show me your cards," he said.

Running her left hand down her skirt, she placed the cards from her right hand upon the table. Raiden appraised them and let out a low whistle.

"And you said you never played." He chuckled. "Now let's make things interesting."

CHAPTER 25

It may have been the exuberance of victory, but she smiled at him. A true, honest smile. Raiden's expression slid off his face as he looked at her, and Celeste's grin faltered. Had she done something wrong? He looked to the cards, sweeping them back into his hands.

"What shall we wager?"

Celeste stilled. She had nothing to bet. Even the clothes on her back were borrowed.

"It can be anything. A truth—"

Celeste's lips pressed into a hard line.

"A cookie—"

She narrowed her eyes at him, and he laughed. Although she had nothing to offer, she wasn't about to play this game for cookies like a *fry*.

"All right. How about whoever loses must grant the winner one wish. Anything that is within their power to give."

A wish? It sounded a lot like her deal with the Sea Witch. But this wasn't a siren deal. It wasn't bound in blood and magic. It was only a game. What exactly could he ask her for anyway? Surely he knew she had little to give. Perhaps he would ask her for her share of the treasure. Whatever it was, he likely wouldn't live long enough to receive it—although she didn't much want to think about that right now, not when she was enjoying his company. Anyway, she *had* won last time. Even if he was going easy on her before, she felt confident in her cleverness. So Celeste reached out her hand toward him, in the human way she now knew. When Raiden took it, his touch made her heart hammer.

"Deal," he said, eyes flashing.

And somehow she wondered if she'd come to regret this. She took her five cards, her assurance growing with each move she made. Although the cards did not form as many patterns as they had before, Raiden's expression looked downright murderous. He moved the cards back and forth through his hand, a wrinkle forming between his brows. It was terribly amusing watching him squirm. The prince clearly wanted to win. Raiden dealt more cards, and his mood only worsened. With a smirk, Celeste tapped him on his foot with her shoe. Teasing.

"Stop," he grunted, not looking up from his cards.

She tapped him again. Two knocks. A knowing smile pulled at the corners of his lips.

"You're incorrigible."

Celeste shrugged and placed her hand on the deck face down.

"Fine," he said, looking up and fixing her with a penetrating stare. "Show me."

With a flourish, Celeste flipped over her cards, holding them out to him. Three cards with the same woman stared back at them, with two outliers. And that's when a wolfish smile appeared on Raiden's lips.

"I'd say I hate to do this, but I'd be lying." He turned his cards over. All five had little red hearts on them and counted up perfectly.

Celeste's face fell. The whole thing had been an act. A pang of betrayal came first, followed by a boiling anger. She tossed the cards onto the deck, and Raiden barked with laughter.

"I'm sorry I deceived you, love, but you were entirely too fun to play with," he said with a grin. "And I wasn't about to go easy on you when there was such an interesting prize to be won."

Celeste folded her arms across her chest and waited, expecting him to announce whatever wish he wanted from her. A kiss perhaps. That sounded like him. Or perhaps something more sinister. *The truth.* But he did not ask. Instead, he gathered the cards, shuffling them neatly back together and returning them into his pocket. He took another long drink of wine, and this time, Celeste reached her hand out for it.

A look of surprise crossed the pirate's face as he handed it to her, liquid sloshing. Celeste merely shrugged. After weeks of watching humans drink wine every day, her curiosity had finally outweighed her fear. She lifted the bottle to her lips and took a sip. The drink tasted more bitter than she expected. It was smooth, with a hint of fruit, but the flavor was dark and deep. She was surprised to realize that she rather liked it. With bated breath, Celeste waited, expecting a loss of intelligence or really anything to happen. But nothing did. She risked another sip.

"Hold on there, hero," he warned. "Take it slowly and see how you feel."

Celeste scoffed at his concern, lifting the bottle to her lips a third time to prove her point.

"Fine, go ahead." Then his voice dropped low. "I just don't want to be stuck *taking care of you all night.*"

She sputtered and coughed, caught off guard by his words. Raiden laughed, drawing closer to pat her on the back until her fit subsided. But when she finally finished, his hand remained warm on her upper back. She did not move away. They both remained still, like two duelists waiting to see who'd draw first. Silence enveloped them, and Celeste risked a glance at the stars hanging above. Something about them looked different somehow. Brighter. And as Raiden's hand slid from her back across her shoulders, a star fell.

They passed the bottle between them until Celeste began to feel the drink's effects. It started in her head. A faint buzzy feeling at the crown, as if someone had filled it with wonderful, swirling clouds. She didn't feel stupid, but how was she supposed to tell?

The Admiral made an appearance, trotting over to them and curling up against Celeste's hip. Her hand fell upon his head, and she stroked her hand through his curls.

"The four daughters look especially bright tonight," Raiden remarked.

Celeste couldn't help but smile, pleased he remembered her correction from their first night on the ship. Much had changed since then. She recalled how horrible she felt in her body. But somewhere along the way, she had grown to love her odd legs. How strong they had become. She loved learning new things about the humans and spending time with Kiyami and Nasir. Even Torben, with his endlessly loud nature, had found his way into her heart. She would miss them when she went home.

A cold wind cut through the fabric of her shirt, sending a chill through her. Raiden pulled her closer, tucking her against the warmth of his side. It was a perfect fit, and she did not stop herself when her head drooped against his shoulder.

I'll kill him later. What are a few more days? And then I'll be home, she reminded herself, hoping it wasn't a lie. But for the moment, she couldn't picture a place she'd rather be. And with that traitorous thought, Celeste slipped into a blissful and dreamless sleep.

When Celeste woke in the morning, she was in her room. A thick red blanket was tucked around her, one she recalled seeing on the captain's bed. It had been the best sleep she'd had since the Admiral visited her. Of course, she'd slept through her chance to kill the prince, but she couldn't bring herself to feel anything but relief about that.

When she joined the crew for breakfast, she found one more reason to be thankful she hadn't left just yet.

"Doesn't Velluno's summer festival begin today?" Bastian asked.

"It does," Nasir said.

To Celeste's relief, Raiden had not mentioned their night together. Ordinarily, he sat beside Bastian, the two joking and chattering through most meals. But today he had chosen to sit beside her. With every move Raiden made, his sleeve brushed her own.

"What's the summer festival?" Kiyami asked.

"Ah, I forget you haven't been in Ethoria long," Bastian said. "For two weeks in the summer, Ethorians celebrate the season."

Torben grinned. "They party for days on end! It's almost as fun as celebrations in Yenri."

Kiyami considered this as she took a bite of dried meat. The supplies were limited lately, so breakfast consisted of a small amount of dried fruits, nuts, and meats. And if you were Torben, it also included ale. "So what happens during this celebration? Is it going to be a problem for us when we port?"

"A *problem*?" Torben laughed, "It's a gift! We shall drink, eat, dance, watch parades, and in the evening, there are bonfires and fireworks! Your Ethorian god must be smiling on us." The last part he directed toward Bastian, Raiden, and Celeste. Perhaps they all assumed she was Ethorian. It made her itch. Another lie added to the endless pile separating her from them. But she couldn't help but feel a thrill of excitement when hearing about this festival.

"The port will be busy, but it shouldn't impact us too much. Shops will still be open. It just might take a little more time. We'll be able to grab some men and gather the supplies quickly. We won't have to lose more than a day if we're quick," Bastian said.

The group fell into conversation, planning who should go where to get what. All the while, Bastian and Raiden made very little eye contact.

After breakfast, Celeste dove straight into her work. She went over the new course with Raiden and helped Kiyami navigate toward Port Velluno. After lunch, she trained with Kiyami, who decided to introduce sparring. Celeste beamed at the news. Because Kiyami felt it best to watch to give Celeste feedback, she suggested Celeste partner with someone else.

Raiden volunteered.

"I'm not sure you should be sparring, Rai." Kiyami crossed her arms. "If I recall, you were just shot days ago."

"I was shot in my left arm. My sword arm is fine." He grinned.

Even with his assurance, Kiyami ran belowdecks to check with Nasir. Nasir agreed Raiden shouldn't be fighting while injured, but given he would only be practicing at a rather slow pace, he saw no harm in it.

Celeste could see *some* harm in it, just not for *him*. Everything about Raiden was distracting to her today. From the way his dark hair clung to his forehead to the way his muscles moved beneath his shirt as he got in his fighting stance before her. Turning her gaze away, she tied her hair back at the nape and drew her own sword. Much to her surprise, he did not smirk or open his mouth to tease her as she lowered into her fighting posture.

"Wider stance, Celeste, and check your balance," Kiyami said.

Celeste did her best not to flush as she made the proper adjustments. She could feel Raiden's steady gaze burning into her skin.

"Raiden, I want you to react to her and keep her moving. Don't put pressure on her yet."

He nodded, and Celeste lifted a brow in surprise. She hadn't expected him to take this seriously, but she was rather thankful he was.

"Begin," Kiyami said.

Raiden advanced but did not strike. In response, Celeste retreated a step, keeping the same distance between her feet as she was taught. She took a step to the side. He followed. With a swing, Celeste swiped toward the side of his torso. But it was easily met, the swords colliding with a clang. He took a step to the side, and she followed. Everything on the ship died away until there was only the two of them, circling each other. There was no leader in the dance and no follower.

Raiden jabbed his sword toward her, and she twirled out of its path, swinging her own sword in retaliation. He met it at the last second with his own, and the steel of the swords slid against each other with a satisfying hiss.

"Maintain distance," Kiyami's voice drifted to her.

Celeste hadn't realized it, but they'd been drawing closer to each other. As if he were the moon and she were the helpless tide. Raiden lowered his sword, waiting for Celeste to make the correction. Shaking out her arms, Celeste drew back and lifted her sword to his throat to check they were once again far enough apart not to injure each other. A knifelike smile appeared on Raiden's face as his eyes slid down the length of her sword to rest on her face.

"Your move," he said.

She lunged, hoping to catch him by surprise, but with one swipe of his sword, he knocked her attack away. She stepped toward him again, careful to maintain their distance, first slashing from the right side, and then the left. Each blow he met easily as she backed him toward the side of the ship. Celeste jabbed once more, and he sliced his sword down in a twirling arc, knocking her sword back to her side. But as he did so, his heel knocked against the side of the ship.

"You're improving," he said, taking a step toward her and away from the ship's banister. Celeste raised her sword back to his throat with a grin, warning him not to step closer. His dark brows raised an inch in surprise. He took a look around himself. Before she could react, he leaped onto the ship's banister and took off. Celeste's mouth fell open, and she looked over at Kiyami for assistance.

"I thought you were helping her train, Captain." Kiyami laughed.

"I am." He stopped to look back at Celeste with a smirk. "The first lesson is to never trust a pirate to fight fair."

With a roll of her eyes, Celeste raced after him, but he was faster. He grabbed a rope and swung across the deck, landing behind her. She spun to face him, and he swiped at her, his sword passing so close she had to jump out of its path. They fell into a new dance. The movements were invigorating. Her eyes shone bright with excitement. Every step, and every slash, they matched each other. Celeste almost forgot about the lesson. All her attention was on her opponent, and he looked at her as though there was no one else. He never pushed too much or tried to corner her. But he challenged her. He would begin a pattern only to break it, to test if she were paying attention.

Eventually, her arms grew tired, and the muscles in her thighs sang. Raiden must have noticed, for his tactics changed. He started to make his movements more erratic and difficult to keep up with. Multiple times he would switch directions quickly, making her almost lose her footing. But Celeste was familiar with training like this. It was always when she started reaching her limit that she needed to push further. That's when the real work began. They continued, moving across the ship until Celeste began making foolish mistakes. When she missed an easy parry, Kiyami at last interrupted them.

"That's enough for today."

Celeste couldn't tell if they had been sparring for minutes or hours. With a blink, she stepped away from Raiden, breaking herself from the spell.

"Good work," he said, chest rising and falling slightly.

Celeste sheathed her sword and bowed her head in thanks. He had been the perfect partner. She felt guilty for assuming the worst of him earlier.

"You're welcome," he said with a dazzling smile.

Mere hours passed before the shadow of Port Velluno appeared on the horizon. Even with the sea breeze, the air was oppressively hot. The shrill sound of seagulls rang out as they approached. Many of the crew pressed against the ship's banister, cheering as the cliffs of Velluno drew closer. Kiyami manned the wheel as usual, with Celeste close beside. Soon she could see tiny humans running about the town, preparing for the festivities. There also looked to be a gaggle of giggling girls clustered beside the port, waving at sailors as they docked. One of them blew a kiss to Raiden, who mimed catching it and clutching it to his chest before throwing a look at Celeste. She rolled her eyes.

"Velluno has the best wine in Ethoria," Torben told anyone who would listen.

"My mother told me stories of Velluno," Kiyami told Celeste, her eyes shining. "She said they had the most wonderful food, and the people kissed each other hello."

"That much is true," Raiden said from Celeste's other side, a coy smile playing on his lips. "The locals are very *friendly*."

Celeste pulled her eyes away from the town to give him a disgusted look, but his smile only widened as he leaned casually against the ship's banister. Her scowl deepened, and she could not explain why. But she was certain it was his fault. With a sigh, Celeste raised her hand to playfully push him, or perhaps not so playfully. But he caught her wrist.

"Oh, don't worry, love," he said, his voice a caress. "I'm all yours for today."

She tore her arm from his grip and turned to look at Kiyami, who tried to hold in a laugh.

"Baz and Rai split the crew into groups so we could grab supplies quickly. Nasir and Torben are obviously together, and I need to go with Bastian because he wants my help getting the right wood for repairs." She tried and failed to hide her smile as she finished. "So that leaves you and our captain here."

It was a setup, and Celeste knew it. Much to her dismay, the growing tension between her and the captain hadn't gone unnoticed by the rest of the crew. So now she was stuck with him for the entire day. *Incredible*. Her decision to not kill him on land remained steadfast. She would not be giving local law enforcement any reason to lock her up again. But she dearly wished to wring his neck.

"Don't worry. We'll all meet up before it gets dark to celebrate together." Kiyami squeezed Celeste's arm in reassurance.

A ghost of a smile appeared on Celeste's lips. The gesture reminded her a lot of her sister Sephone, and how she comforted her when their parents would make a hurtful comment. Celeste wondered if Sephone knew what had happened to her.

Velluno quickly came into focus. The town looked so different from Port Romsey, vibrant and pulsing with life. Buildings painted in brilliant colors that reminded Celeste of sunrise crowded along the lush green cliffs, nearly stacked on top of each other in a way that reminded her of Staria. Their flaming reds, burning oranges, and bright yellows contrasted with the white beach and turquoise sea. The water was so clear here that Celeste could look through to the bottom and see the colorful fish that swam there.

And music.

It was faint, but Celeste could hear music coming from the town. Weaving and hopping from note to note in a happy tune. A song so different from the ones she knew.

When she was able to see the people better, her heart stilled. Everything looked beautiful, but it still was home to humans. A few looked likely to prey on the weak and vulnerable, just like in Port Romsey. Her breathing grew ragged, and her hands shook.

This will be different. I'm not defenseless now, she tried to tell herself. Her sword training should have made her feel a little more confident in herself, like Kiyami—at least now it didn't fly from her hands every time someone hit her—but apparently not much had changed.

A small tugboat approached their vessel, and a man waved from it. Kiyami threw him rope, which he secured before he began pulling the ship behind him toward the docks.

"Our escort has arrived!" cried Raiden. "Velluno awaits."

CHAPTER 26

"All right, Admiral, you keep these men in line," Raiden said, bending low to the ground so he could be eye level with his dog. He put his hands on either side of the animal's head and brushed across the tops of the ears with his thumbs. Although Raiden had said he was keeping a group of men aboard the ship at all times for security reasons, Celeste guessed a large part was due to the fact Bastian had managed to convince Raiden that bringing the Admiral along to get supplies was a bad idea. The captain stood, brushed himself off, and squared his shoulders. It was like watching him transform from one person to another. The transition from Raiden the animal lover to Captain Raiden Sharp the pirate.

"Make sure to get our supplies first," he told the crew surrounding him. "Then you're free to spend the rest of the time as you please."

"I still need money for supplies," Torben said, jutting out a hand toward Raiden.

Raiden scoffed. "I know I gave everyone their portion of the raid money and more for supplies, Torben. You're not fooling me."

Celeste's hand fell to her side, feeling the weight of her own raid money in her pocket. She almost had refused it, then considered giving it to Kiyami. She wouldn't be needing it. But she didn't want to rouse suspicion.

Torben grinned and shrugged. "Wanted to make sure you're paying attention, Captain!"

Nasir chuckled under his breath and took his partner's hand, steering him away from the group. The gunner Oakes stalked after them, getting quickly distracted by the sights of the festival. Bastian and Kiyami peeled off next, heading toward the lumberyard. Kiyami held her map aloft, which she and Bastian had used to plan their route around the city. Soon they disappeared, swallowed by the thick crowd.

The town was overwhelming in its activity. Small humans—children, Celeste corrected herself—chased each other about and shouted joyfully. Humans argued at stalls while others walked in pairs, holding hands. One couple in particular, Celeste noticed, pressed their lips together in a kiss. A sign of love. A soft smile reached her lips. At least humans and sirens had some things in common.

The people of Velluno shone as brightly as their buildings. Among the red, orange, and yellow, some stuck out in shades of blue like the sky and sea. Celeste's simple blue dress seemed pale in comparison. The clothes were the same in style and silhouette to those in Port Romsey, but here the women often wore woven brown hats on their heads, tied with ribbons to keep the sun off their faces. Others wore crowns woven of ribbons and flowers. Celeste pulled her attention away from the town long enough to see Raiden trotting off down the dock. Her feet clipped along the floorboards as she dashed after him, but as she drew closer to the city, she found more to distract her. Men climbed on ladders, hanging lanterns and ribbons all along the main street. Flowers decorated every doorway and window, drooping with the weight of the blooms. Vendors fanned themselves with colorful papers, sitting beneath fabrics stretched above them to block the punishing sun. Carriages passed, drawn by what she now knew were horses, and she saw people riding horses as well. She wondered what that would be like. She had ridden on a dolphin, but only a couple of times.

As she caught up to Raiden on the cobblestone street, the smells of Velluno filled Celeste's nose. Beyond the salt spray of the ocean and the fresh fish being sold by vendors along the dock was the sweet scent of the white blossoms on the trees that wove through the town. And, of course, there was the food. Some of it was now familiar. The warm butter of fresh bread, the sharpness of pungent cheese, but others were new. Different. There was something that smelled acidic and sweet.

"This area is known for its citrus," Raiden commented, smiling as he watched her eyes devour the sights of the food stalls around them. "Have you ever eaten an orange?"

The siren princess raised an eyebrow at him, as if to say, *What do you think?* Without another word, Raiden took her hand in his, guiding her toward the stalls further down the main street. Celeste stared at his large hand, curled around hers. His grip wasn't tight, and she knew she could slide her hand free if she chose to. But she let him lead her. Nothing about it felt real. Soon she would wake to find she was still in the water looking at shore and watching a human girl hold a human boy's hand.

Raiden weaved through the crowd, his hand the tether that kept her from being swept away in their current. She should have been afraid among all these humans. Or even nervous. But those feelings did not come. Instead, she took in the sights around her, enjoying the energy of the crowd. It reminded her of holidays in Staria. In the spring, they held the celebration of the Mother, honoring the Mother Goddess and all the siren mothers. They would crown the women in delicate corals, raised for sacred days such as those, and sing songs. With a pang, she realized she had missed this cycle's celebration. That her mother was left without two of her children. Her heart squeezed in her chest. But Staria did not celebrate the summer like this. Sirens did not honor the sun as humans did. They were children of the moon.

Raiden came to a stop in line for a vendor with a purple awning. On the table beneath sat piles of fruit, round as pearls but far larger. Some were as big as her palm and colored orange, while others were smaller and yellow or green. With a gentle tug, Raiden pulled Celeste into his side and out of the way of those passing. She had been too preoccupied to notice them.

"It's tradition to eat citrus fruits during the summer festival. That's when they're in season, and they're hard to come by... so it's sort of a delicacy," he explained, his hand still holding hers. She stilled when she felt his rough thumb brush idly against the back of her hand. It was such a small touch, and yet she noticed every movement of his hand in hers. The sweet and tart smell she had encountered earlier was stronger now and the music louder. It mixed with the hum of the crowd into a perfect melody. She took in a long breath, tilting her head back to let the sun warm her face as she listened. It was a feeling unlike any she had ever experienced. To be surrounded by sound and smell and... *people*. A smile pulled at the corner of her lips as she let herself soak it all in.

"One orange, please," Raiden's familiar baritone sounded from beside her.

She opened her eyes when Raiden's hand pulled free from hers and watched as he pulled out coins and handed them to the vendor. She pulled out coins of her own and tried to offer them to him, but Raiden ignored her. With their single orange fruit in tow—an aptly named thing, she noted—the captain took her hand back into his and pulled Celeste behind him up into the crowd. She nudged him in the ribs with her elbow, an eyebrow raised.

"I wanted to take you to a nice spot to enjoy our festival treat," he said in answer.

The two made their way down the busy street, passing vendors selling food, clothes, jewelry, paintings, and knickknacks. Unable to help herself, Celeste pulled Raiden to a stop so she could admire some of the paintings up close. Most of them depicted the city around her through blurry, dreamlike strokes. After she had her fill,

Celeste turned from the booth and walked straight into the back of a passing guard.

She froze, every muscle tightening. Her hand left Raiden's and instinctively went to the knife hidden in her waistband. The sound of her bodice ripping echoed in her ears. But before she could pull the knife free, Raiden's hand caught her wrist and held it.

"Stop," he breathed, his lips pressed against her ear.

But it was too late. The guard turned toward them.

"Good afternoon, miss," the man said, his voice firm. "Is this man bothering you?" He eyed Raiden's hand around her wrist.

"No, Constable. We were just on our way to enjoy our fruit in the square," Raiden said.

The guard—constable—narrowed his eyes.

"I was speaking to the lady."

Celeste pulled her wrist from Raiden's grasp and hid the knife from view behind her back. She tried her best to keep from shaking.

"She doesn't speak, sir."

"Sounds to me like you won't let her." The constable's hand moved to the hilt of his sword. Raiden's body became tense, ready for a fight.

The constable turned to her. "Is this true? You can't speak?"

She nodded, but his skeptical expression did not change.

"Was this *foreigner* bothering you?" he asked again.

She shook her head, but he could tell she was afraid. Of course, this man wouldn't know it was *him* she was afraid of. It was jarring to hear him speak to her as if he wished to *protect* her, even respected her, when just weeks ago a man wearing a similar uniform stripped her naked. She wondered why this situation was so different. Why would this man wish to protect her now when she did not want or need protection? And why did he call Raiden a foreigner, as if it had been a dirty word? She knew Raiden was born in Hinarso, but he had grown up in Ethoria, as far as she was aware.

"Why don't you come with me, and we can get you sorted," the constable said, taking a step toward Celeste as if to pull her from Raiden's side. She took a step back.

"You'd separate a wife from her husband on this sacred day?" Raiden said.

Both the constable and Celeste stopped cold.

Wife? She turned to look up at Raiden, and he gave her a smile. He was *lying* to this human. And he did it so well. Celeste wanted to argue, but to deny him would just make things worse. So she decided, against her better judgment, to play along. She wrapped her free arm around his waist, pulling his body closer to hers and trying not to show how her pulse jumped at the feeling. Then she fixed the constable with her best pleading expression.

The constable frowned. She couldn't blame him. Her acting *was* atrocious. And she clearly wasn't behaving like a human wife.

"Come along," he grunted, reaching for her.

Panicked, she mimicked that other human couple she'd seen. She lifted herself up onto her toes and pressed her lips to Raiden's. At first it felt as though she were kissing a wall. Her captain stood stock-still, as if he had stopped breathing. Then his lips softened against hers, and his hands were on her back, pulling her closer. It felt real. Too real. And in that moment, she knew she had made a terrible mistake. Celeste broke away, heart pounding.

What had she done?

"I'm sorry for disturbing you, sir," the constable said, flushed in embarrassment, though Celeste wasn't sure why *he'd* be embarrassed. "And, miss, you can never be too careful. People get a little rowdy during the festival."

Celeste stepped backward out of Raiden's arms, leaving his hands to fall to his sides.

"I understand, Constable," he said, his voice huskier than before, and his eyes still on Celeste. "Thank you for your service." He pulled his gaze away and stuck out his hand to the officer, who shook it. The two made a little more idle conversation, but Celeste didn't hear it. She could only hear her heartbeat pounding in her ears, and the ghost of his lips on hers.

"Aren't you a clever one," Raiden said, when the constable had disappeared. His words were teasing, but the look on his face was anything but. His jaw was tight as his eyes roamed across her face. She wasn't sure what he was looking for. And so she shrugged, avoiding his eyes as she set about folding her knife back into the waist of her skirt. "But you're a terrible liar," he said, leaning down so that his face was inches from hers. She swallowed, trying to meet his gaze with an equally even look. Inside, her heart beat out its own rhythm. A frantic staccato. The corner of his right lip curled up in response, as if he had found whatever he had been looking for.

He turned and began walking again, forcing Celeste to follow. After a step or two, he turned and took her hand back in his to make sure she didn't get lost in the crowd. The touch of his rough hand sent another wave of heat rushing through her.

She didn't want to think about what had just happened, but it was undeniable. There was a sort of gravity between them now. And although she was desperately trying to resist it, it pulled at her. She tried to distract herself with the many things going on around them. But it didn't work. All she could think about were his soft lips when he kissed her back. His hands on her back. The hungry look in his eyes when she pulled away.

Sure, she had always been painfully aware of how attractive she found Raiden. Annoyingly so. Every look from his big, dark eyes had made her stomach churn since the day they met. He was funny and charismatic and entirely too easy to like. But his pretty face and sparkling personality weren't enough to distract her from her goal. It was a passing fascination. Something to be brushed aside and ignored, like plenty of other crushes before him.

Only this didn't feel like that anymore.

And it was ruining everything.

The street opened up into a large square, where people gathered, talking and chattering around a great fountain. It depicted a triumphant scene filled with creatures Celeste had never seen before. There were small, childlike creatures with hairy bottom halves that ended in hooves. These creatures rode on small horses and lifted instruments into the air from which the water poured, rushing down in arcs into the pool beneath. In the center, raised high by a large clamshell, was a beautiful young siren. Celeste's eyes widened in shock as she beheld her, dropping Raiden's hand. The statue was crowned with a wreath of pearls and flowers, her long hair artfully covering each breast. An intricately carved tail curled up beneath her, adorned with eight oysters, four on each side of her fin. Despite the girl being carved of white stone, she looked soft and wistful. As if she desperately wanted to come to life and walk among the people who filled the square.

Celeste's heart filled with sorrow for the statue before her. It reminded her of a statue she had in her room in the palace of a young human boy. As if they were somehow cut by the same hand. And yet if that were true, they would never be together. He lay at the bottom of the ocean, and she was trapped in this shell on land.

"She looks like you," Raiden said, offering her half of the orange. He had removed the outer layer of the fruit in one circling strip, revealing the gorgeous heart. The many segments clung together, forming a half circle. Celeste hadn't seen anything like it before.

She pulled off one section like he did, and when she bit down on it, juice burst from the skin unexpectedly. It dripped down her chin and fingers. The fruit tasted like sunshine, bright and sweet. Raiden's eyes crinkled at the corners as he watched her cautious curiosity turn to utter delight. Eagerly, she pulled another section apart and popped it in her mouth. Raiden guided her to the ledge of the fountain, and the two sat together in silence as they ate. They licked the juices from their fingers and watched the passersby.

Celeste knew she shouldn't be enjoying this. That every second she spent with the humans was one more second of pain for her mother and father as they waited for her return. Every moment she spent with Raiden made it harder to kill him. And what did that make her? Enjoying his company, letting him speak to her in soft words as she plotted to cut his throat.

And yet she was quite possibly the happiest she had been in

quite a long time. The orange was delicious, and as she took in the city around her, she realized that humans *made* all this. If she could just show her mother these things, maybe she, too, would see that humans couldn't all be bad.

The smell of the citrus still lingered on her hands after she polished off the final bite.

"I admit I'm disappointed," Raiden said.

Celeste turned her head to raise an eyebrow at him, wondering how he could possibly be disappointed with anything in that moment.

"That was not how I pictured our first kiss."

Her heart skipped a beat, and she blinked in surprise. She didn't know how to respond.

Luckily, she did not have to. For at that moment, a woman with shining brown hair and sea glass–green eyes strode through the crowd toward them, her long maroon coat billowing. People parted around her like an ocean. Her hand reached up to her hat, dipping it just below one eye.

"Raiden Sharp." Her voice was a blade that could draw blood.

He stiffened like an animal sensing a predator. Then his hand was in Celeste's, tightening protectively. "Hello, Valencia," he seethed, standing to use his full height, dragging Celeste with him.

Valencia's bloodred lips curled into a sinister smile. "Don't look so surprised. You knew I'd come for you after you *stole my ship*."

CHAPTER 27

"Nice dress." Valencia's eyes flicked over Celeste.

The siren flinched. Suddenly, the lacing felt too tight. She wished more than anything that she could take it all off.

The Pirate Queen smiled at her discomfort. She looked exactly as Celeste had imagined her. Elegant and predatory. She looked perhaps near her twenty-fourth cycle. Too young to be Raiden's mother, as she'd once wondered. Plus, they looked nothing alike. Violence radiated from the woman, despite carrying no visible weapons. Perhaps Valencia *was* the weapon. Her eyes looked as if they could cut much deeper than steel.

Raiden angled his body to tuck Celeste behind him, pulling Valencia's attention away from the siren girl. The fact Celeste had ever believed Raiden a human prince was laughable to her now. She should have known the moment she heard him speak of how he had "commandeered" a ship for their crew.

"Did you think you'd seen the last of me?" the Pirate Queen asked, smirking.

"Of course not," Raiden said. "Vermin are terribly hard to get rid of, after all."

Valencia's smile disappeared. "Don't push me, boy." She

glowered. "Or I might become better acquainted with your little clothing thief here." Her kohl-lined eyes raked over Celeste's body, as if looking for a weak point to sink her teeth into. "I bet she'd *love* to hear all I know about *you*."

"I'd stop talking if you'd like to keep your tongue," he replied.

Valencia laughed. "I would love to see you try, but I'm afraid I don't have the time. Why don't you give me my ship back, and I'll promise to not send you to your father in pieces."

A movement in the square snagged Celeste's attention, and she looked up to see two humans staring at them. One was a tall and muscular woman with golden hair and skin, the other was slender and pale, with curling dark hair that fell around their angular shoulders. A glint of silver flashed in the slender human's hand. Celeste glanced back to Raiden and saw that he, too, had noticed them.

"I'd say it was fun catching up, but I'd be lying," Raiden said. "See you in hell, Valencia."

And he bolted, dragging Celeste in his wake.

At first Celeste could not keep up as they tore out of the square. She'd never run before and did not know how it worked. She began by walking quickly, Raiden practically pulling her along. But soon her legs began to move differently. Knees bending more. Her steps lengthening. Shouts rang out as Raiden shouldered through the crowd. Only as they left the square did Celeste risk a look behind.

Valencia had not moved. The pirate stared after them, smiling, the two humans now joining her. She spoke to them, but her eyes didn't leave Celeste's until Raiden pulled her down a side street and out of sight. They continued running, putting more distance between them and the woman, until Raiden pulled Celeste into a secluded doorway, out of sight from the main street.

"I'm afraid we haven't seen the last of her."

Celeste pulled her hand free from his grip and fixed him with a glare. In the small doorway, there was less than a foot of space between them.

"I suppose I do owe you an explanation, seeing as she threatened you." He let out a long sigh. "That was Valencia, my father's rival." His hand swept through his hair, and he leaned out of the doorway, scanning the street before retreating into the safety of the doorway. "All pirates who sail the ocean bend the knee to my father. It's why they call him the king. All... except for *her*." Celeste heard a bit of venom behind this last word.

"My father and she were close. She was once his quartermaster. He trusted her with his life. Until one day, without warning, she led a mutiny. It failed, and to punish her, my father marooned her on an island. He wanted to humiliate her, leave her to die. But she somehow escaped. She formed her own crew and has been gathering followers and working to dethrone him for the past five years. Thus far, she has remained unsuccessful. No one wishes to anger the Pirate King, and those who do—they don't live long. But Valencia is just as cruel and just as dangerous. She—" He looked as if he wanted to say more, but stopped.

And so he stole her ship. No wonder the woman hated him so much. Perhaps Celeste should have been working with Valencia this whole time.

"The fact she hasn't followed can't be good. Come, we must find the crew."

"Valencia is here?" Bastian practically yelled. "And you *ran from her*?"

"I wouldn't put it like *that*," Raiden grunted, patting the Admiral on the head. The dog's body could not hold the joy it felt at seeing Raiden's return, and it wiggled all over the place.

Torben burst into a fit of laughter. "You saw Valencia—and you *ran away*—like a *child*!" he spoke in between thundering cackles. Then he doubled over, tears springing to his eyes. Celeste wasn't sure if his laughter was even genuine. He guffawed so loudly that people along the docks turned to stare. Even Nasir looked as though he were doing his best to keep a straight face while watching his partner howl. Raiden glared at Torben with a murderous glint in his eyes, and Bastian patted the captain's shoulder.

"What did she want?" Kiyami asked over Torben's roars.

"She wants the *Red Revenge* back," Raiden answered, his voice like ice.

"And what did you tell her?" Bastian said.

"I told her I'd see her in hell," he replied.

Bastian sighed.

"So we don't know where she is or what she's planning," Bastian said.

"Well... yes," Raiden admitted. "But we did see two of her crew with her."

"We should leave, then, right?" Kiyami looked between Bastian and Raiden. "We've gotten our most necessary supplies. If we leave now, we can put plenty of space between them and us."

Raiden laughed, but there was no humor in it. "That's what she wants. For us to set sail right now while her crew is ready to attack us as soon as we're away from port. And I'm not about to let Valencia scare me off. We'll just *hide* the *Red Revenge* for a couple of hours, enjoy the festival, and slip away in a different direction under cover of night."

Torben, who had almost calmed down at this point, burst into a new peal of laughter.

A muscle in Raiden's neck twitched, which made Celeste giggle.

"You two better watch it, or I'll leave you here," the captain growled, looking first at Torben and then Celeste. But there was no real threat in his eyes. If anything, he looked amused. It was a sharp contrast to Bastian, who did not.

"Captain, with all due respect... I think that is a very bad idea," he said.

"Bad ideas tend to work out in my favor," Raiden countered.

Bastian heaved a sigh. He could only question Raiden in front of the others so much. They may be like brothers, but

Raiden was still the captain. And he wouldn't back down, not now that his mind was set. Still, it struck Celeste as odd that Raiden didn't agree to leave immediately when he was the one who had been worried about missing the eclipse.

"So we hide the ship and station a few extra crew as guards?" Kiyami suggested.

Bastian and Nasir looked as though they agreed, but no one offered to guard the ship. The entire crew wanted this chance to celebrate. Celeste didn't blame them. Port Velluno's energy was infectious. But after Raiden offered a bigger cut to those who stayed behind, it was not hard to find some willing volunteers. Together, the crew boarded the ship and moved it to a more secluded place away from the docks. And thankfully, there was no sign of Valencia.

By the time the crew returned to town, the sun had begun to set. The sky looked as though a street painter brushed it with broad strokes of burning reds, glowing yellows, and soft purples. As the sun slid lower and lower into the water, the city began to change. In the streets, lanterns were lit. Hundreds of them. They glowed a soft, beautiful yellow. And each home was lit from within as well. It was as though the town was only now waking up, its bright eyes blinking into the night. There was something magical about it.

The crew agreed to meet at the *Red Revenge* at midnight, then broke into small groups. Celeste remained with the officers as they wove through the town toward the main square. As they neared, she heard music playing. The tune began with a single instrument, playing a melody that leaped and danced like the ocean. A tinny noise sounded, like metal coins clattering against each other to the beat. Kiyami looped an arm through Celeste's. The weight of it was comforting. Even with all these strangers surrounding her, she felt safe with her crew. The air was thick with so many bodies pressed in around them, and although the sun had gone down, the heat of the day remained. Shouts and songs poured from every open door and window as humans lifted overflowing cups in celebration.

Kiyami pointed out a man selling colored glass, each delicate piece curved into intricate designs. They were interrupted by a woman calling after them, promising to tell their fortunes. Kiyami scoffed at this, dragging Celeste away before she could discern what tools the woman used. The next stall held exquisite dresses of colorful silks. Celeste reached out and let the delicate fabric slide through her fingers like water, wondering what it would feel like to wear something so vibrant. The siren hadn't noticed Raiden had disappeared until she felt a tap on her shoulder.

When she turned, she found him holding a circlet of thick, braided ribbons of cerulean blue woven with flowers of purple. He smiled, the corner of his lip near that mole of his curling up. Inside her chest, her heart faltered. He drew close, lifting the little circlet and placing it gently atop her head.

"I thought it'd look nice with your hair," he said, grazing against the silver strands as he pulled his hand away. The statement was so matter-of-fact, as though it had been but a passing thought. And yet she felt her cheeks flush, nearly glowing. It was a treasure unlike any she had collected. The delicate weight of the simple human crown made her feel more like herself than any Starian tiara.

"Where's *mine*?" Kiyami smirked, crossing her arms over her chest.

Raiden snorted and pulled a second circlet of scarlet flowers from behind his back. "I knew you'd say something like that."

"Aw, Captain! You shouldn't have!" she said as she snatched the crown and placed it on her dark hair. Then she turned. "Cel! They're starting the dance."

It took a moment for Celeste to realize Kiyami was speaking to her. *Cel*. Nicknames weren't common for sirens, and Celeste had never had someone shorten her name before. If anything, sirens would lengthen it and use her full title. *Cel*. She liked it immediately.

"Let's go watch."

The two made their way to the outer circle, where people had gathered to watch the dance, Raiden following close behind. It was fascinating. The only time Celeste had seen a human dance was aboard the *Red Revenge*, when the pirates' moves were bold and loud, with lots of stomping feet and clapping hands. But the festival dance was synchronized. Each human moving through the same steps at the same time. They looked like a school of fish, the many moving as one. As the music played, the humans clasped hands, drawing close together, then far apart. They spun and wove around each other, partners separating and reuniting. As Celeste watched, she began to see the variation. The little imperfections. Individualities. A step offbeat. A turn missed. Laughter.

Behind the dancers, the musicians played. Celeste rose up on her toes, straining to get a proper look at them. The music came from objects. One was curved with a long, narrow neck and a thick base with strings on top. The human playing it nodded to the rhythm, fingers flying over each string. One instrument sat beneath a player's chin, played with a stick, while another was held in hand, a circlet of coins clinking together. The last instrument was perhaps the most curious of all. It stretched and squeezed between the player's hands.

"You two look radiant!"

The voice was Torben's, and Celeste turned to see the rest of the crew had joined them, carrying drinks. Kiyami and Torben fell into easy conversation, discussing various weapons they saw in town, while the others watched the dance. As Celeste drank her cup, she found her attention drawn to Nasir. His face went soft as he watched his husband, little crinkles at the corners of his eyes, as though Torben hung the stars in the heavens. It was the same look Celeste's mother gave her father. The same look she saw in the faces of some of the dancing couples. And for a moment, Celeste let herself wonder if anyone would ever look at her that way. The thought came unbidden, unwanted into her mind. And she could not shake it. She had never considered it before. Somehow Celeste always imagined she'd remain alone. But now she wondered if that would be true. Surely, when she returned to Staria, they would not allow her to join the Chorus. What would become of her? Would she remain a royal figurehead? Or, like Sephone, would they marry her off to a foreign prince or princess?

"The next dance is starting!" Kiyami said, eyes shining as she grabbed Celeste. "Come on. If we're bad, we'll be bad together." She pulled her onto the dance floor, squeezing between the other pairs. Neither of the girls knew what they were doing. They stared blatantly at the other couples, doing their best to mirror the movements. Step. Twirl. Step. Twirl. Celeste's arm nearly smacked Kiyami in the face, and they giggled their way through the first refrain. Step forward, step back, spin around your partner, kick your right leg, then left, and clap your hands. The movement began to feel like sword practice, and yet there was a life to dancing that Celeste had never experienced. It was as though the music was a current, and her body had no choice but to be pulled along. The strings played in a tumbling trot, and by the third refrain, Celeste had memorized the dance.

It was as if she were in the water again, her body gliding and graceful. Celeste had been so focused on how wobbly her legs had been those first few days that she hadn't really noticed how much that had changed until now. She could feel the eyes of the crowd watching her as she swept by them, weaving through the other dancers to find Kiyami again.

"I should have known you were a dancer," Kiyami said as they linked arms. "You always have this unnerving elegance."

Celeste laughed.

"My sister is a dancer," Kiyami said, her gaze turning wistful. "I want to write to her before we leave tonight about how talented my friend is."

Celeste's ears snagged on the word as soon as it was uttered. *Friend.* How that word felt as sweet as a gift and as bitter as loss. Everything about Celeste was a lie. How could a friendship be built on such a rotting foundation? And even if Celeste did stay, the Chorus would begin looking for Raiden. Hunting him until this final loose end was eliminated. He would not be able to sail safely ever again. Nor would any crew with him.

"You might have to teach her a thing or two when you meet her," Kiyami said as the music soared and ended in a triumphant final note. Cheers burst from the crowd. Celeste clapped her hands with them, turning her face away from Kiyami. And through the crowd, her eyes met Raiden's. He stood beside Bastian, a cup of wine in his hand, and he was smiling. It wasn't like the smiles he had given her before. Arrogant. Proud. Teasing. This smile was soft. Unassuming. As if it had happened without him noticing it. And she found herself smiling back.

Then he was moving toward her, parting the crowd before him with each long stride. The band strummed the first chords of the next song—something different, dreamy and slow. When Celeste turned, looking for her dance partner, she found Kiyami was no longer there. The girl was backing away with a knowing smile.

A hand looped its way around Celeste's waist and pulled.

And suddenly she felt her body tip, falling into the arms of a stranger, who dragged her backward over the cobblestones before she could scream.

CHAPTER 28

A wad of fabric forced its way into her mouth. A bag was thrown over her head. Celeste kicked and pulled, but it was no use.

"Celeste!" Raiden's voice called out, but it already sounded far away.

Her hand reached for her knife, but she quickly thought better of it.

Without her sight, it was likely she'd be disarmed before she could do much with it. Better to wait and have something up her sleeve when an opportunity presented itself. Celeste sent one more wild kick into the darkness and felt one make contact.

"*Ugh!*" came the response. The voice feminine.

Celeste pulled her foot back, rearing to kick again, when a hand wrapped around her ankle. She felt the rough weight of rope being wrapped around her at the wrists and ankles. But she would not go down without a fight. Perhaps if she could delay them long enough, Raiden and the others could find her. But her hopes were not high. The city was crowded and vast. It would be too easy for someone to go missing. Celeste wriggled, throwing elbows and knees where she could, but soon the rope tightened, and the fight was lost.

As they half carried and half dragged her bound body, the clamor of the city died away. It was soon replaced by echoing drips and cold, humid air. Eventually, her body was dropped onto a stone floor. Hands touched her, searched her, and she felt her body begin to tremble. They took the heavy bag of coin at her hip but, praise the Goddess, did not find her knife. She hadn't known what she'd use the coins for . . . or even if she would ever use them. But she had hoped to keep them. To add them to her collection in her room at the palace. Something to look upon and remember the journey she'd had. And now that, too, was taken from her.

This felt all too similar to the last time she was on land. Painful memories flooded her mind, nearly drowning her. Her heartbeat quickened. Sweat pooled on her brow. She forced herself to take deep breaths. It was all she could do to keep calm.

At last they drew the bag from her head and the gag from her mouth.

Valencia stood above her, holding a sword to her throat.

"I thought you and I could have a little chat," she said.

A laugh bubbled up in Celeste's throat. She couldn't help it. This woman kidnapped the only person on their crew who wouldn't tell her anything. But Celeste sobered when she felt the steel of the sword press into her neck, the blade so sharp she almost didn't feel it when it cut her. Blood trickled down her chest.

"You're brave." Valencia smiled. "I like that."

Celeste risked a look around. Wherever they were, it was dark. The only light came from a lantern held by Valencia's massive, golden-haired crony, who Celeste recognized from earlier that day. The skinny, dark-haired human was there too, standing beside the taller one with a scowl. Behind them, in the shadows, were what Celeste assumed was Valencia's crew. She couldn't help but wonder why the crew was noticeably lacking males, when in her experience, sailors were usually men.

The walls were wet and round, as if she were inside a tube. Before her, the tube continued, curving past her line of sight. She would have called it a cave, had she not known for certain that the structure was human made.

Valencia moved the sword to Celeste's chin, and the siren had no choice but to lift her head until their eyes met once again.

"I would threaten you," Valencia said, "tell you that if you make any sudden moves I'll cut you so deep your pretty face will never look the same..." The woman's eyes crinkled at the corners. A chill crept down Celeste's spine. "But given your *association* with the infamously reckless Raiden Sharp, I fear I'd be wasting my breath."

Despite Celeste largely *agreeing* with this assessment of the captain, her face fell into a scowl at the words.

"So I'll make this simple: Tell me where the *Red Revenge* is, and I'll let you live."

Celeste didn't have to stop herself from laughing this time. There was nothing funny about the look in Valencia's eyes. The cut at Celeste's neck continued to bleed, a red stain blooming at the top of her dress. She didn't like her chances. Valencia wouldn't believe her if she insisted she couldn't speak. And even if she did, she would still find a way to force Celeste to show her where the ship was.

Celeste could lie. Lure them all to a false location. But then what? How would she escape? What if she couldn't? Her crew was probably out looking for her. Unless... *unless they were on the ship getting ready to depart.*

Celeste slowly nodded.

"Good girl." Valencia grinned, lowering her sword.

Moving carefully to not alarm her captors, Celeste reached her bound hands toward the mud and drew a circle with an arrow inside with careful strokes of her finger. A compass. She understood them now from all her work as a navigator. How they worked with the maps to show where things were. She had learned so much. The very idea helped ground her. Steady her.

Valencia hummed to herself. "So, you're the one I heard about. The silent one."

Now it was Celeste's turn to be surprised.

"Oh, child"—she laughed—"you think my ship was taken from me by the son of my sworn enemy, and I didn't inquire about where he went and with whom?"

Celeste supposed the group hadn't exactly been subtle when they were in Port Romsey. Still, a chill ran down her spine at the thought. The human world felt endless compared to the siren world. In the ocean, there were perhaps a few hundred thousand sirens. But there were *millions* of humans spread out across lands so vast that not only did they have countries and even towns but they also had villages and districts and whatever else they had to differentiate one from the other. But perhaps pirates were more like sirens. A community where it seemed little remained secret.

Valencia turned to her companions with a grin. "Looks like we're going for a little walk."

"Captain, forgive me, but what if she's lying? Or trying to trick us?" asked the thin human, stepping out of the shadows to their leader's side.

"She could be," agreed Valencia. She closed the distance between herself and Celeste in one long-legged stride, taking the siren's chin in her hand. Her grip was unnecessarily firm, fingernails biting into the skin. "But this is likely all she'll give us." She sighed. "And a warm hostage is better leverage than a cold one."

Celeste jerked her chin, but the Pirate Queen's grip remained strong, a coy smile playing upon her bloodred lips. "I would hate to waste a perfectly good Wayfinder. They're so *hard* to come by these days." Valencia tipped Celeste's head up so that their eyes met.

Celeste kept her face neutral, but inside she burned with annoyance. She hated how much this woman knew of her, even if most of it was a lie. She hated the way she spoke of her as if Celeste wasn't even there or was too stupid to understand. And she hated that this woman reminded her of how small and helpless she was. A fish struggling in a net.

With a grunt, Celeste kicked, her foot landing just between

Valencia's legs in the spot she knew to be sensitive to humans. But the Pirate Queen did not double over, crying out in pain. She jerked away, dropping Celeste's chin with a surprised look on her face, before laughing.

"Do I look like a man to you?"

Did it only work on males?

Valencia turned to the human at her side. "Hex, get the rest of the crew." Her bloodred lips pulled into a smile. "We've got a ship to catch."

Leading Valencia and her crew to the ship might've been a bad idea. But Celeste did not have any good ones. She had considered leading them somewhere else; however, the town was a labyrinth to her. If she got lost, they'd know what she was doing and kill her on the spot. Plus, if she led them far away, the chances of her crew finding her would be lower, though it was likely most of the crew had returned to the ship by now.

What if they already left? The thought came unprompted, a poison rotting her from the inside out. Pirates weren't known to be particularly loyal. But they couldn't hope to get to the island in time for the eclipse without her. *Right?* She'd already proven herself as a navigator. And even if Raiden could navigate the ship there himself, a captain like him took his responsibility to his crew very seriously. He would not abandon a member of his crew if he could do something about it.

And something happened between them today. A feeling she wouldn't dare to name.

The bite of cold metal pressed against Celeste's back. A silent reminder. The group trekked through the city, an odd little parade that kept to side streets to avoid the large crowds. They weren't going to give Celeste the opportunity to slip away into the festival, it seemed. Dirt and mud coated the streets, and a rancid stink filled the air, a noticeable departure from the cleaner streets Celeste and Raiden had trod mere hours earlier. They didn't run into many people, but when they did, they didn't appear friendly and turned a blind eye to the girl at gunpoint. It seemed even this prosperous and beautiful city had a darker side if you ended up on the wrong street. There were many dangers to sirens in the ocean, but the citizens of her own kingdom were never one of them.

Celeste led them on and found that despite the twisting streets she could use the darkening sky to lead her back to shore. The familiar sound of the waves called to her above the noise of the festival, pulling her home. Behind her, the Pirate Queen's boots clipped on the sidewalk, her stride casual and swaggering. But the others in the party were tense, like strings pulled tight. Beside Valencia walked the thin, dark-haired human called Hex and the larger blond woman. The rest of the crew followed behind in silence.

As they neared the edge of town, Celeste's hands grew slick with moisture, a sensation she hadn't felt before. Was this a human thing? Where was the moisture even coming from?

Bang!

The sound cracked against the stone walls of the city. Celeste dropped to the ground. But the sound hadn't come from the gun in Valencia's hand. It had come from above.

Bang!

A shower of glittering red light exploded in the sky above. Sparks rained down. Far away, a crowd erupted with awe. Celeste steadied herself as another burst of light exploded above them, washing them all in its sparkling blue light. The explosions were beautiful, now that she gathered they weren't a threat.

"Get up, girl," Valencia said, pistol now pointed at Celeste's heart. She looked over Celeste as if she were nothing more than a wounded creature. Pathetic.

The siren pushed herself to her feet, and the party was off again. Celeste wished she could be back with the crowd now, watching the lights in the sky. She wondered what she'd be doing if she hadn't been captured. Would she be dancing with Raiden? Laughing with

Kiyami? Drinking honeyed wine? Instead, she was leading a crew twice the size of her own toward her ship. *Goddess help her.*

But if the Goddess was listening, there was no answer.

A gleam of dark water beneath anchored ships appeared at the end of the street. And soon a stretch of beach and a cliff was all that separated them from the *Red Revenge*. *Please let me be right. Let the crew be there and ready to fight.* Each step felt like an eternity.

Bang! Bang!

Two new colors burst in the sky, gold and purple. Celeste watched the reflections of them dance across the shimmering waves. Her feet sunk into the sand with every step. They turned around the last bend into the cliffside. Celeste's heart shuddered in her chest.

There was nothing there. An empty ocean ebbed and flowed against the beach before them. There wasn't so much as a footprint to show that anyone had been there.

Celeste was certain this was the right place. The pirates had *abandoned her.* She clenched her shaking hands into fists. Humans couldn't be trusted. She knew that. So why did it feel as though the air had been knocked from her lungs? Why was she so surprised?

The cold barrel of the gun pressed into her temple. "I believe I made myself perfectly clear, love," Valencia said. All the swagger had left her voice. Now she only sounded cold.

A clicking noise came from the back of the gun, priming the weapon to fire.

Tears sprung to Celeste's eyes. Her mind raced, trying to quell the rising panic and grief. She still had one weapon she could use. One that could possibly wipe out every last member of Valencia's gang. But it was too risky. There was no way she could sing by herself to such a big crew and keep them all under her control. Even if she could, what then? She'd be stranded alone in this human town, far from her home and her people. And what would that constable do to her if she was found among hundreds of bodies?

Bang.

Celeste flinched as sparks rained again over the city. Tears trailed down her cheeks as joyful cries rang out.

Valencia circled, dragging the tip of the gun from Celeste's temple to below her chin. "They left you." It wasn't a question.

Celeste's heart felt as though it were splitting apart. She hadn't expected this pain. She had let her guard down and had started to trust these humans. Hells, she had even started to *like* them. They were pirates and villains, but they were warm and kind. They had treated her like one of them. Or at least they had when they *needed her.*

All this time she had believed she had so few friends, that sirens didn't want her around because of what she was—a princess who couldn't control her power. But these humans hadn't known any of that about her. And they *still* rejected her.

"I suppose you must not be a very good navigator." Valencia laughed, letting the gun drop to her side. The words were worse than if she had shot her.

"I don't know... she did an *excellent* job steering you here."

At the sound, Celeste's heart faltered. Her eyes scanned the darkening shoreline.

And there he was, emerging from the shadows, sweeping the strands of his dark hair from his eyes. Captain Raiden Sharp. All the fear and tension released from her at once, and she felt herself smile as she blinked back her tears. The captain's eyes met hers, and he gave her a wink.

And then he was running.

Running in the opposite direction.

CHAPTER 29

Celeste blinked in shock. Raiden had not sailed off without her. But he was now *running away*?

Beside her, the Pirate Queen let out a shriek of frustration. "Get him!"

Her large crew ran like rabid dogs, unsheathing swords and pulling out their pistols as they followed the path where Raiden had disappeared seconds before.

Celeste remained rooted to the spot, bound and bewildered. Something moved behind her. She turned in time to see Kiyami's foot connect with the back of Valencia's knees, sending the woman sprawling to the ground. The dark-haired pirate spared Celeste a grin before bringing down the hilt of her sword into the crown of Valencia's head, knocking her unconscious. With a flourish, Kiyami sheathed her sword and turned to Celeste, but her face crumpled when she beheld the siren.

"Are—were you crying?"

Celeste shook her head, trying and failing to use her hands to wipe at her tears.

Boom.

This time there were no colorful sparks. Instead, a ball of fire erupted into the side of the cliffs where Raiden's and Valencia's crews had been. Rock and ash rained down around them.

Kiyami took Celeste's wrist and yanked her sideways as a boulder fell with a thud in the place where she had stood seconds before. The cliff was crumbling. Falling into the sand below. Smoke surrounded them, filling their lungs. Celeste let out a strangled gasp, lurching for the place where Raiden had disappeared, nearly crying out his name. But Kiyami pulled her back.

"Rai's fine! That explosion was Torben. He blocked the path so that Valencia's crew couldn't circle back and come looking for us. Rai knows a shortcut and is going to meet us at the ship. He'll lose Valencia's crew in the crowd of the festival. But we need to go now!"

Celeste tore her eyes away from the crumbling cliffs and found Kiyami's steady gaze. Then the two took off down the beach.

"When Raiden saw you taken, we knew it was Valencia. We didn't have a lot of time, which might explain why everyone agreed to Torben's plan," Kiyami said between breaths, pointing upward.

Celeste laughed, spotting Torben running atop the cliffs with several explosives cradled in his arms like a child with its favorite toy. His eyes met hers, and he grinned. Or at least he smiled as much as a man could with a knife held between his teeth. He lifted a hand and waved at her. She waved back with both arms. Then he lit the end of one stick and threw it over his shoulder.

Boom!

Ash and rock exploded behind them, pushing the girls forward. But the sand beneath their feet kept moving. Celeste would have fallen if not for Kiyami, who reached an arm out to steady her. But when Celeste righted herself and looked back up for Torben, he was gone. *He's probably heading down to the docks to meet us*, she told herself, tucking away her worry for the master gunner.

Kiyami and Celeste reached the stairs to the boardwalk. They took them two at a time, the old wood groaning beneath their feet. Despite the late hour, the festival had not died down. If anything, the party had only grown more uproarious. Humans, drunk on wine and music, stumbled through the streets. They filled the night with noise. The fleeing girls dove into their midst, weaving and dodging as they tried to keep track of each other.

"We're almost there!" Kiyami shouted above the crowd. Before them, a group of males shouted a song while one consumed ale without stopping to breathe. "Do you see it?"

The *Red Revenge* waited, tucked in a shadow just beyond the dock. Celeste couldn't help but smile at the sight. It was easy to overlook, as the crew had placed it behind a larger, flashier ship. Because Valencia and Celeste had been looking for the ship in the opposite direction, they had missed it completely.

"We took a risk," Kiyami panted, weaving around one human to draw closer to Celeste on her right. As the crowd thickened, their pace was forced to slow. "Let's just hope Valencia and her crew are still—" Her gaze slid to something behind Celeste. Eyes widening, Kiyami uttered a word in a language Celeste did not know. But it certainly wasn't a *good word*.

The siren turned to see Torben and Raiden running down a side street toward them. But they were not alone.

"Stop! Thieves!" Valencia pointed a finger at the two men. The outcry started a commotion. Raiden and Torben zigzagged through the thick crowd, shouldering people out of their way. But their progress was slow. Torben risked a glance behind and saw that Valencia's crew gained as people leaped from their path. In one smooth motion, he pulled his gun from his hip and fired into the sky.

"Move!" he bellowed.

The crowd erupted in chaos, screaming and fleeing in every direction. A passing constable began pushing his way toward the source of the disturbance.

"Run faster!" Raiden cried.

Torben trailed not far behind, his face red with effort. "I am running faster, ya prick!"

A hard yank drew Celeste's attention away from the chase.

"Hurry! Your lover boy will be fine," Kiyami said with a smirk before taking off in the direction of the *Red Revenge*. Celeste flushed pink but followed without protest.

Thankfully, the crowd thinned near the dock. Their feet hammered faster against the wooden boards. Wind whipped at their faces, as if the sea itself urged them on. Upon the *Red Revenge*, the lanterns lit one by one. Time for concealment had passed. If she squinted, Celeste could just make out the tall, broad figure of Nasir and the narrower figure of Bastian beside him on the deck. The two ducked down and reappeared, carrying what looked to be the rope ladder. Kiyami tore down the last walkway, legs flying. But the ship wasn't close enough to the dock to be boarded. They would have to swim. Or—

"Stop! You there!"

The constable had joined in the chase. Celeste threw a look over her shoulder in time to see Raiden and Torben nearing the docks. But the law enforcer pursued, hot on their heels. With a grunt, Raiden grabbed the nearest barrel and hurled it back at their pursuers. It collided with the constable's chest, sending him flying backward into Valencia and her crew. The group collapsed into a heap of angry shouts. But as Raiden turned and let out a whooping cheer, a second constable tackled him. The very one who had accosted him earlier in the day.

Celeste's legs stilled beneath her as she watched the constable wrestle Raiden to the ground, the two disappearing from sight into the crowd.

"Celeste! Come on!" Kiyami pleaded.

Celeste's feet were moving before her mind knew what she was doing. Fireworks exploded in the sky above her, but her steps did not falter. She dove back into the crowd headfirst, eyes scanning for any sign of Torben or Raiden. But the throng was too thick. Her heart pounded against her chest. She neared the spot where she had last seen him and found nothing. Without thinking, she opened her mouth to cry out his name.

"What are you doing here, lass?" It was Torben.

Celeste tried to push past him, but he stepped into her path.

"Get on the bloody ship!" he shouted.

A cry rang out, and Celeste turned to find Raiden bursting through the crowd with a bag of coins clutched in his hand and a constable's hat on his head. Celeste nearly sagged in relief. But Raiden was staring at her in disbelief.

"Why aren't you on the ship?" He turned to Torben. "Why isn't she on the ship?"

"Bloody search me!" Torben shot back.

"She's supposed to be on the ship," Raiden said, a note of anger in his tone.

"Well, I expect she came running here after you, ya fool!"

Raiden's eyes slid to Celeste's, a smile pulling at the corner of his mouth. Something about the look he gave her made her heart stumble.

"I'll kill you, Raiden Sharp!" came the Pirate Queen's alto. Valencia was running toward them like a nightmare made real.

"Time to go," Raiden said, grabbing Celeste's bound hands and bolting.

They reached the dock, where Kiyami was waiting, a look of concern etched into her face. But upon catching sight of them, she dove into the water without hesitation. Torben reached the end of the dock second, entering the dark water with a loud splash. They were close. Just a few feet away. And then the sharp crack of gunfire split the night. Raiden threw his arms around Celeste, covering her body as if on instinct.

"Change of plans," he said into her ear, before zigzagging them away from Kiyami and Torben, who would have been easy targets as they swam through the water, and toward the grand ship that sat in front of the *Red Revenge*. Bullets whizzed by their heads as they scrambled up the gangplank.

The two hit the deck of the ship, and Raiden turned, kicking the plank to the side so it sank into the water beneath them, forcing Valencia's crew to find a different way of boarding. A bullet whizzed by Celeste's ear, and she dropped to the ground, covering her head with her bound hands. Raiden pulled his gun from his hip and fired back, hitting one of the pursuers in the knee and downing them. Celeste wanted to help, but with nothing but a dagger on her, she was useless in the fight. Still, she grabbed a nearby bucket and flung it with all her strength toward Valencia's crew. The bucket hit Valencia square in the face with a satisfying *thunk*.

"Captain! Shall we set sail?" Bastian shouted across the gap between the two ships.

Celeste and Raiden turned to see Nasir pulling a soaked Torben onto the deck of the ship with Kiyami just behind him.

Raiden hopped up onto the banister of the ship, then offered a hand to Celeste. "All right, hero, that's enough adventure for today." He tugged on a piece of rope before wrapping it around his wrist. "What do you say we get out of here?"

With a smirk, Celeste placed a hand in his, and he pulled her onto the railing beside him. She could hear the clambering of Valencia's crew against the ship as they began to climb the sides. Raiden wound his free arm around Celeste's waist, pulling her into his chest. She looped her bound hands around his neck. Their eyes met. Celeste's pulse jumped.

"Don't let go," he said.

And then they were in free fall, stomachs flipping before the rope pulled taut and the two jerked together. Raiden's fingers dug into her back, and her arms wound tighter, their bodies flush against each other as they sailed through the air above the darkened ocean. They crashed onto the deck of the *Red Revenge* in a tangle of limbs. The impact left Celeste gasping.

Beside her, Raiden coughed. "Get us the hell out of here, Baz!" he wheezed.

"Way ahead of you, Captain!" Bastian replied. "Release the sails!"

At his order, the crew sprang to life, lowering the sails until they filled with wind. The ship lurched. *They did it. They actually did it.* Celeste let her body fall limp, her heart still pounding in her chest.

"Nasir!" said Raiden.

"Aye, Captain?"

"Grab some men and shoot anyone who tries to board this ship, would you?" he said.

"Aye, Captain."

Behind them, Valencia and her crew stood upon the other ship, glaring daggers as the space between the ships grew. Nasir and several others trained their pistols on them, firing warning shots at their feet, though none of them moved.

"You'll pay for this, you bastard!" Valencia cried.

Raiden lifted his head, watching as the Pirate Queen's crew began to retreat. The *Red Revenge* was already picking up speed. They knew a lost cause when they saw one.

"A pleasure as always, Valencia!" Raiden called back, throwing her a rude hand gesture as they sailed into the night. A firework lit the sky above their heads with a celebratory *bang*. And as the golden sparks fell from the sky, Raiden appeared above Celeste, the light reflecting off his dark hair. His eyes were unreadable as he scanned her face.

"Are you okay?"

Celeste smiled weakly and nodded, sitting up. She could still feel the press of his fingers in her lower back, as if he had burned her. A knife appeared in his hands, and he set to work cutting the rope that bound her, taking care not to touch the raw skin along her wrists. Now freed, Celeste made to push to her feet, but Raiden stopped her with a hand at her neck.

"Did *she* do this to you?" he asked, his voice tight. They may have just managed to get enough distance between them and Valencia's crew to be safe, but the look in his eyes gave Celeste the impression that the looming eclipse was the only thing keeping him from turning the ship around to exact vengeance. The Admiral padded over to them, whining as if he, too, were worried about the siren's well-being. Celeste tried to cover the cut at her neck with her hands and push him away, but the touch sent a sharp sting through her. She winced.

"Well, don't go touching it!" Raiden huffed. "Let me see..."

He was achingly gentle as he leaned into her, taking her shoulders in his hands and turning her toward the lanterns above. The light press of his calloused fingers on her skin sent shivers down her spine. His dark eyes searched her neck for any sign of infection or further injury. Celeste was so close she could see the light lines between his brows where he had them furrowed. The salty breeze played with his dark hair, tossing it in pieces across his forehead. It was all she could do to not reach out and brush them with her fingers.

Eventually, his gaze rose to meet hers, and Celeste swallowed.

"We should have blown them all up," he said, voice low and angry.

"That's what I said!" Torben shouted.

Celeste couldn't help but roll her eyes and gesture toward Raiden. *You couldn't have blown them up. You were too close to them.*

"She's right. You would have gotten *yourself* blown up, Your Highness," Kiyami called from her place at the wheel. "And then who would worry over poor Celeste's cut?"

"I believe that is my job." Nasir chuckled.

Raiden did not respond. He reached up, taking Celeste's chin in his hand, and gently drew her closer to him. His thumb slid across her jawline as he tilted her head to the side to get another look at the cut, as if it would've magically become infected in the seconds since he last looked at it. It was amusing to see him this way. The infamous Captain Raiden Sharp, son of the Pirate King, huffing over a *cut*. His jaw clenched and unclenched, and it looked... *incredible*. All sharp angles and tension. Celeste had to admit—she was enjoying every second of him fussing over her.

"It doesn't look deep," he said finally, letting his hand drop from her chin. "Nasir, clean this and get it covered. See to her wrists as well."

"Yes, Captain." Nasir nodded.

The captain stood and broke away from her, striding toward the quarterdeck. "Kiyami, turn due west," he said, expression hard.

Bastian frowned. "West? But we need to head south if—"

"We don't have a choice," the captain interrupted. "We can't risk Valencia following us there. If we head west, we can be sure she's not behind us before changing course. It will mean l-losing time, but—" His face fell as the reality of the situation landed upon his shoulders. *They weren't going to make it in time.*

Somehow this fact made Celeste feel incredibly guilty. The crew would have to waste precious hours evading Valencia *because of her.* They'd all gotten away unharmed this time. Would they be so lucky again if Valencia and her crew caught up to them? Raiden could have taken off and gotten a head start. The crew didn't have to come back to save her. Not to mention sailing due west would lead them directly into Starian waters. Into the very heart of her territory.

A sharp sting brought Celeste back to Nasir, who had opened his small medical pack on his lap and was now applying some sort of burning liquid to her cut.

"I'm sure I'll figure something out," Raiden said, his familiar mask of confidence and bravado firmly in place. "And then we can all go our separate ways with riches and renown. Like I promised." But as he turned for the navigation room, Celeste saw his face fall. And she knew as surely as the tide rose and fell that he was lying.

CHAPTER 30

"Hello, Wayfinder," Raiden said, his voice a caress. He didn't so much as look up as Celeste entered the navigation room. He stood at the back of the room. Head bent over a map as a solitary candle burned low on the desk beside him. "A little late. To what do I owe the pleasure?"

It *was* late. As usual, Celeste hadn't been able to sleep. All but the night crew had gone to bed, and she sat awake, staring out at sea for hours as her mind grappled with what to do next. Until at last her legs brought her here. To him. For she couldn't leave him alone in here to wallow any longer. She knew he didn't have a plan for getting them to Lunapesce in time.

But she did.

Still, she hesitated. *Can you trust him?*

Nothing was stopping her from leaving him now. She had all she needed. She could return to Staria and be welcomed back. All she had to do was put her dagger in his heart and finish the job. Yet she knew she couldn't—wouldn't do it. Not now that he'd thrown everything away to save her.

And even if she did end his life herself, his ship was sailing straight toward Staria. She couldn't leave the crew to that fate.

How she wished she knew more words to write on the parchment. *Turn around,* she'd write. *You'll doom them all to your former crew's fate.* He had said in the hallway to Bastian that what had happened before wouldn't happen again, but he didn't know what she knew. He obviously didn't know that the run-in with sirens was not an accident. It would happen again unless she stopped it. All these people on the ship—Bastian, Torben, Kiyami, and Nasir—would surely perish if she didn't find a way to help them cross the siren waters safely. Something had to be done.

But can you betray your people again? That was the real question.

Although she trusted the captain not to hurt her, he was still his father's son. The King of Pirates had murdered her grandmother. The siren she was named after. *But I want to trust him.*

Raiden looked up after her long moment of silence, so she shrugged and pointed to her mouth.

"Ah, words evading you?" he asked, reading her perfectly as usual.

But this time it grated on her. She felt heavy, as if a weight dropped into her stomach. If she trusted the humans and something happened to the sirens, she could never forgive herself. She could practically hear her sister Sephone's voice in her head. The voice of reason. *This is a bad idea, little star. Just make up a lie and send them off in another direction.*

"My *father* sent us on this trip ... I'm sure you've already gathered that much." He sighed. The way he said the word *father* was curious. It didn't sound resentful. More *weighty.* As if the word itself were the tip of an iceberg, and the mass of it could not be seen. "He told me I had to bring him the treasure on that island. But after stopping for supplies and having to lead Valencia astray"—he ran his hand through his hair—"we're not going to make it in time."

She, too, yearned to know what lay upon that sacred island. What secrets she could uncover. Even if she did as her mother wanted and killed Raiden, it wouldn't change anything. The Pirate King knew of the siren's existence and where Lunapesce was. She wasn't fool enough to believe that his son's death would stop him.

The king would continue to send humans until he got what he wanted. But if *she* led their crew there—a crew who proved to her just how much they cared—perhaps she could protect the most sacred of the treasures from the king. Perhaps everyone could get what they wanted, and no one had to die. Maybe there was a way she didn't have to pick a side. It was probably naive to think so. But if she could have everything she wanted, wouldn't it be foolish not to try? Could she live with herself if she didn't?

Approaching the desk, Celeste let her eyes roam over his face, taking in his creased brow and downcast eyes.

"Perhaps it's time to admit I've failed again." His voice was like the sound of a door being closed in the dead of night, low and quiet. The echoes of the crew he lost filled the room, suffocating them. She could see his desire to make his father proud plain on his face. It was the same feeling she had when she promised her mother to return to Staria.

Celeste stepped around the desk, coming to a stop at his side. Their bodies were so close she was certain he could hear her heart beating. She wanted to reach out a hand, to place it atop his and squeeze in some semblance of comfort. Anything to reassure him. To bring them closer. But the moment felt too delicate. And she was too afraid to ruin it. Raiden's shoulders slumped. "He's"—his voice wavered—"he's all I have left."

A crack emerged in his dark armor, giving her a glimpse of the man beneath. She'd glimpsed behind the confident and cool exterior he often wore, but this was different. As she looked at him, Celeste felt a piece of her own armor fall away. Their eyes met, and it was as if she could finally read him as easily as he did her. They weren't so different. Not really. He may be human and she a siren, but they both just wanted to belong. She understood how it felt to not fit into the role you were given. Her hand found his upon the map. Then his fingers entwined with hers, squeezing them as though she were a lifeline.

And her heart broke. Because she knew she could take this pain away.

If she were only brave enough to trust him.

To reveal the pattern of the currents would be to hand the humans a powerful weapon against the sirens. No human had encountered it and lived. And even among sirens, only Chorus members knew it. If she told this man about the way through the siren waters... what would he do with that information? *Would he use it against them?* And it would be dangerous. Not only would they still be crossing through Staria but the ships were not built to withstand such currents.

But if she planned it right, by the time the Chorus discovered their ship, they'd already be gone.

Raiden drew closer, her shoulder pressing into his arm. The smell of him—salt and rum and leather—surrounded her. In all her wildest dreams, she wouldn't have pictured this. How beautiful he was. Not just his dashing good looks, which were obvious to anyone. But *him*. His sense of humor, his loyalty, the way he took the time to really see her, like no one ever had. He was violent, arrogant, infuriating, and guarded. But tonight the things that separated them felt less important than the things that made them the same.

"He'll kill us all if we don't succeed," he admitted, his eyes far away. "My father never gives second chances. The only reason he allowed me this one was because of how dangerous it was. How likely it would end in disaster. Maybe he figured if I died in the pursuit, he wouldn't have to do the job himself."

Her stomach turned like churning water. What kind of monster would do that to his own son? To these people? In her anger, she felt tears prick her eyes. Then she took her hand from his and faced the map beneath them. With one long finger, she charted a new course. Starting from where their ship was, then west and south to the Lunastri Current. Raiden raised a brow.

"I thought it wise to avoid that area," he said, his voice a low murmur that made the hair on the back of her neck stand up. She'd never felt such a sensation before. Glorious and unnerving. But she returned her focus to the map, noting the symbols that marked the other ocean currents. Her hands trembled a little as she picked up the quill. And with a steadying breath, she drew the symbol for a current on the parchment below her.

"A *current*," he breathed. There was a note of hope in his voice that wasn't there before. Her heart squeezed in her chest. He did not question her or ask her how she knew of it when these mapmakers had not. Raiden simply smiled. "My God, you're brilliant."

And Celeste glowed like a moonbeam.

"We'll be on the current in two days," Raiden told the others at breakfast.

"We're—using a *current*?" Kiyami said, a tremor of fear in her voice. "There isn't any current large enough this far south."

"There is," he replied simply.

Nasir and Bastian exchanged a look.

"Isn't that rather dangerous, Captain?" Bastian hedged. "We don't know anything about this current. It could lead us miles off course. Or topple our ship from its strength alone."

"It was our navigator's call, and I trust her judgment." Raiden fixed his friend with a look. "It's the only way to arrive by the eclipse. If we arrive late, we won't get paid."

Kiyami's worried gaze slid over to Celeste, but she said nothing. *I'll get you home to your family*, Celeste thought, wishing her friend could somehow read her mind. *This will be your last voyage, just like you planned.*

And that was that.

Throughout the day, Celeste monitored their progress, and in the afternoon, she had sword training with Kiyami and her now permanent sparring partner, Raiden.

"I love that little crease in your forehead when you focus," the captain said as she thrust toward him. The comment made her steps falter, and he leaped away easily, laughing.

And I love when you hold still, Celeste thought with a huff, getting her feet back under her. But the pirate was too practiced, easily evading her every strike. He backed her into the mast without her realizing, pinning her between his sword and the wood.

"You know, I've pictured us here before," he growled, so low that only she could hear. His warm brown eyes fell to her lips. "But it wasn't with an audience."

Celeste's heart skipped a beat. That gaze was like a powerful undertow, pulling her beneath the waves. She didn't want to fight it. And yet, just as he leaned forward, Celeste took her free hand and punched him in the side. With a gasp, Raiden dropped his weapon.

"Excellent job, Celeste!" Kiyami laughed. "Way to see an opening."

After dinner, her writing and reading lesson with Nasir felt long. When Celeste's attention began to wander, Nasir mercifully told her she had done enough. The two walked up to the decks, where the rest of the crew were drinking and passing the time. Now that their stores were replenished, the crew enjoyed fresh meals and plenty of wine. Raiden even surprised Celeste with a stash of the honeyed wine she had loved so much from the festival, a gesture that left her smiling like a fool for hours. The crew sat together under the stars, singing songs when the wine caught up to them. Nasir, it turned out, had a beautiful voice.

"Remember when we had to pretend to be bards to avoid walking the plank on that ship we stowed away on?" Bastian asked. The night had grown so late that even the quartermaster managed to unwind.

Raiden threw his head back and laughed. "Remember? How could I forget! We had a famous song! 'The Admiral's Tail'!"

"I believe you mean infamous," Bastian corrected, grinning.

"Baz can sing?" Kiyami asked, a look of confusion on her face.

"No." Raiden chuckled. "He was the reason we still ended up on that plank."

The crew burst into laughter, insisting Bastian sing a few bars. But Raiden was quick to recount another misadventure, saving his friend the embarrassment.

There was a special sort of magic about the long summer days on the ship. The calm before the storm. No one spoke of the current or the time slipping away toward the solstice. But it was always there. Like their own shadows, their futures silently followed them around, always at their heels.

At one point, Torben convinced Bastian and Raiden to join a game of cards. It was a different game than the one Celeste had played with Raiden. After a few rounds, Celeste joined them and won a fair bit of money off Torben, enough that the Yenrian had been bitter all the next day, grumbling about Raiden helping her cheat, which he most certainly hadn't. It wasn't until the following evening, when Torben won the pants off Raiden, that his mood improved.

Raiden excused himself to go find new pants, causing raucous laughter to erupt among the crew.

"But, Highness!" Bastian protested, his tankard spilling over one side, "why deny us the simple pleasure of a fine pair of legs?"

Another round of laughter sprung up, which grew tenfold when Raiden took off his shirt and threw it in Bastian's face. Celeste wished she could say she had averted her eyes. But she had not. She drank in his lean, muscled body as he swaggered away, rewarding her with a light smack from Kiyami.

"Keep your eyes in your head, Cel!" her friend snorted.

A blush burned her cheeks as she trained her eyes on her cup of honeyed wine, absently patting the Admiral on the head.

The night passed by until one by one the crew started drifting to their bunks. A yawn escaped Celeste's lips, her lids growing heavy. And when even Raiden's reappearance did nothing to rouse her, she finally decided to drag her body to bed.

She was halfway to the officers' quarters when something in the water caught her attention.

Not entirely trusting her eyes after a night of drinking, Celeste moved to the railing. That's when she saw her. *Nerissa*. Glowing faintly with her bioluminescence. The Sea Witch bobbed in the wake of the ship, staring with a white-toothed smile. Celeste started, then threw a look behind her to see if anyone else had noticed. But the few remaining crew were preoccupied with a new game. Apparently, Torben wanted this new pair of pants too, even if they were entirely too long for him.

Sucking in a breath through her teeth, Celeste crept around the back of the ship, positioning herself as far from the others as she could. When she was certain no one was there to overhear her, she turned to the Sea Witch.

"What do you want?" Her hushed voice sounded strange, even to her own ears. Hoarse from underuse. The crescent upon her wrist prickled faintly, and Celeste rubbed it with her thumb. Had she really almost forgotten about her bargain? Was that why the witch was here?

Nerissa drew closer, ink-black eyes unblinking. "You have not called upon me. Are you not finished with your task?"

Celeste swallowed, throwing another look over her shoulder before answering. "I—I do not need to change back yet." Guilt washed over her as she said it. She wished she could ask about her family, but she knew better than to seek information from the Sea Witch without expecting to pay a price.

"Really? How interesting." The witch's smile was knifelike, as if with one look she could read all of Celeste's guilt. Every betrayal of her heart.

"Is that why you're here?" *Please let that be all*, she prayed, rubbing her hands against her hips. *Please do not ask for your favor. Not yet.*

The Sea Witch waved a hand. "I like to check on my investments."

A cry rang out. Celeste's head snapped around in time to see Torben seize Raiden's second pair of pants. Her shoulders dropped. False alarm.

When she turned back to the water, there was nothing but seafoam. Nerissa was gone. Uneasiness settled in Celeste's stomach as she scanned the night, looking for any sign of disturbance. When she found nothing, she drifted back to her room, hoping that the next time she saw Nerissa, it would be the last.

When the day arrived that they were to reach the current's mouth, it began to rain. The wind, which had been so fair throughout their trip, turned punishing. They had to take down the sails for fear of them being shredded. And with the wind and rain came rough, choppy waters. The great ship tossed back and forth, at the mercy of the waves. It was all Celeste and Kiyami could do to keep the ship on course to enter the current.

"It's only a storm!" Raiden shouted over the roar of the wind, attempting to reassure his shivering crew. "It'll pass eventually!"

But as the day dragged on, the crew had to take turns going belowdecks to warm up and change clothes. This far from shore, any sickness could mean death. The Admiral was kept downstairs in Raiden's quarters, much to his dislike, and was only let out a couple of times to relieve himself. It was a miserable day. The *Red Revenge* moved so slowly that they weren't able to reach the current as planned. Celeste considered it a blessing. Navigating the strength of a powerful current with a ship this size would have been difficult enough, let alone during a storm.

The next day, Celeste awoke to a soft knock at her door. She groaned. Between the ship tossing her about all night and her continued nightmares, she'd hardly had a moment of sleep. Beside her, the Admiral yawned and stretched, sticking his paws in her face. Then, with a cute little flop, the dog curled belly-up beside her. Since Port Velluno, the Admiral slept with her every night. Although she wanted to believe it was because the dog liked her best, she had a sneaking suspicion that Raiden was purposefully sending the animal to her in an attempt to help her feel safe. And although she would ordinarily find the gesture embarrassing, she couldn't deny that the dog's presence helped. Each time she woke sweating after another dream of being abandoned on the shore or cut apart by a human guard, the warmth of the dog steadied her.

Another knock rattled the door.

"Celeste," Raiden hissed, "knock twice if you're awake."

Heaving a sigh, she obliged.

"Good. Get dressed." A pause. "Something warm."

It was then that Celeste heard the patter of rain against the window. With a sigh, she rose to her feet and pulled off her nightshirt. With fumbling fingers, she slipped on her underclothes and her white dress, deciding against adding the corset. Even though it was stylish, she'd likely have to change out of this outfit and into another one to keep from catching a cold. She ran her fingers through her long hair, carefully detangling it before she braided. With the winds as they were, it'd be easier to have it kept away from her face. She wove the braids into a knot at the base of her neck and secured it to her head using some pins she had found in Valencia's things. It didn't feel strange using them anymore. Perhaps it was a sort of payment for what the Pirate Queen had done to her.

That night felt so far away already.

At last she opened the door, the Admiral leaping upon his owner with a joyful bark.

"Quiet," Raiden ordered. The dog obeyed, dropping to all fours and sitting stoically.

Raiden's head of thick dark hair looked uncommonly disheveled, some of it sticking up at odd angles in the back. He gazed at Celeste, his eyes dipping down to her dress and lack of corset, before blinking and looking away. She flushed, realizing her mistake and pulling a long coat from the closet behind her.

"I wanted to meet with you before we entered the current," he said.

Celeste nodded, part of her still wrapped in the soft, hazy

embrace of sleep as she followed him down the hall into his quarters. Upon entering, she plopped with a thud into his chair behind the desk. Raiden's lips pulled at the corner in a half smile. She supposed it was rather insubordinate of her to sit in the captain's chair. But he said nothing and pulled up the smaller chair to sit beside her.

Once more the two pored over the map. Celeste corrected him when he mistakenly marked the current's mouth too far south. If they stayed on course, they would enter siren waters in a couple of hours. A knot formed in her stomach at the thought. But the journey should only take them three days, with them arriving on the day of the eclipse.

"The current bends here and here?" Raiden clarified, reaching across her to point along the line she had drawn. "We'll hit the first near the end of today and one midday on the second?"

Celeste shook her head. Without thinking, she placed her hand atop his and moved it gently so it was closer to the end of the current. But she dropped it when his eyes met hers.

"Ah, so it bends right as we're exiting the current?"

She nodded.

"That's not great."

It wasn't. Any bend in a current was difficult for a ship of this size to manage. It was why most ships avoided currents so close to the ocean's surface. If the *Revenge* was not pointed in the right direction as the current bent, the ship would capsize. But a bend at the end of a current meant the water would be turning, so the ship would have to turn with it as it was trying to navigate moving between a current and open water. One wrong turn and the ship would go down, the crew with it. But they had no other options.

"You think we can do this?" he asked.

Celeste turned her head to look him in the eye. It wasn't like him to seek validation from anyone. If anything, Raiden thought a bit *too much* of himself. But she took his hand in hers and squeezed, this time not pulling away.

Yes. I think we can.

His worried gaze softened.

CHAPTER 31

Any sane crew would stop and wait it out. As the hours wore on, the rain and winds worsened. It was clear none of the crew liked the idea of pushing forward into a current in this weather, but they had no choice. If they stopped now, all would be for nothing. So they soldiered on through the battering wind and rain, doing their best to keep the masts from being blown over and using a push broom to sweep the water from the decks.

Every minute or so, Celeste found herself scanning the rough seas. She couldn't help herself, even though siren territory was still hours away. They needed to be moving as quickly as possible. If they ran into the Chorus ... there was no hope of her protecting all of them. She had barely managed to rescue Bastian, Raiden, and the Admiral last time. But the storm made spotting anything impossible. Rain dripped down from her hair into her eyes, blurring her vision. She wiped them furiously, scanning the same place again. *Scouts don't swim this close to the current*, she reminded herself. The risk of being dragged into the rushing water and displaced far away from Staria was too great. And a long journey alone for a siren could often be a death sentence, with so many ocean predators. Although the Song would help fend off the occasional shark or jellyfish, a siren's voice tired after strenuous use. Not to mention any loss of focus would result in the Song being undone.

The ship swayed dangerously in the wind as Kiyami fought to keep them on course. Celeste began to pace beside her.

As if hearing her thoughts, Raiden appeared to check on her, his brow creased with worry. She pulled a face, sticking her tongue out at him just to see him smile. A rough wind sent the ship toppling sideways, knocking them to the floor. Beneath, Celeste heard shouts from Torben and his men. They shifted cannons to try to help balance the weight of the *Red Revenge*. Eventually, the ship straightened. The crew regained their footing. But it was a harsh reminder that there was only so much they could do. The Goddess of the Sea decided their fates.

"We're entering the current!" cried Kiyami at the helm, waving her hands in the air to get Bastian's attention. The winds were too loud for them to hear each other. Bastian waved back, signifying he had understood her, and began running between crew members, spreading the word. Raiden drew closer to Celeste beside the wheel, his rain-slick hand finding hers. She sent up a prayer, asking for protection.

The ship groaned as it lurched forward, picking up speed. While they entered the current straight on, the rough winds blowing against the starboard side made the entrance clumsy. The ship tilted to the left as it surged them forward at twice the speed they had been moving seconds before.

"Hang on!" Kiyami cried, pulling at the wheel with all her strength. The ship adjusted, only to fall in the opposite direction. A flash of light flared in the distance, illuminating the dark clouds.

"Kiyami!" cried Raiden.

"I've got this," Kiyami grunted, gripping the wheel with white knuckles.

As the great ship dipped further, Celeste's feet slipped beneath her. She lurched, grasping desperately to catch ahold of something to steady her. A strong arm looped around her waist. Raiden pulled her into his chest, his grip tight.

"Hang on," he said in her ear.

Nodding, she laced her arms around his torso, pressing close to his warmth. Her thick jacket sagged with water, the white dress beneath now clinging to her shivering body.

With a grunt of effort, Kiyami turned the wheel further left and held it in place. Another flash of lightning cracked through the clouds above.

Then, mercifully, the bow began to turn left.

The ship righted. Barrels settled back onto the deck. Celeste's grip on Raiden loosened.

"That was close, Highness," shouted Bastian.

Raiden grinned. "I like to keep things interesting." He turned to Kiyami, clapping her on the back. "Excellent job."

The latch at the center of the ship popped open, and Nasir emerged. "Everything below is secure, Captain," he reported, his dry clothes soon soaking wet as he walked toward them.

For days, Celeste had dreaded this moment, but they'd survived the first test. She really had done it. They all had. A giggle slipped past her lips, tension releasing all at once. Raiden looked over at her, lifting a brow as she continued to laugh. But soon a smile broke out across his face. He looked so unlike the loathsome prince she had once believed him to be. If she didn't know better, he could have been just another young siren in Staria. His body shook with laughter, arm still warm against her back. Neither of them noticed they were still holding each other.

With a firm pull, Raiden tugged Celeste into his chest, resting his chin on her sopping-wet hair. Then he thrust his free arm into the air and let out a whoop of victory. The crew cheered in response, the sound rising above the storm. Nasir began to sing, a boisterous song of victory. Bastian clapped his hands. Kiyami stomped her feet. And Torben's head popped up from belowdecks just as the *Red Revenge* was slammed by a colossal wave.

The ship jerked sideways.

Celeste's body sailed backward into the mizzenmast like a rag doll. Water poured across the deck. Thunder clapped. Then a horrible cry cut through the sound of the wind. Two words that no sailor ever wanted to hear.

"Man overboard!"

"Nasir!" Torben roared.

Celeste sputtered, coughing up salt water as her eyes blinked open. *Nasir was overboard.* The world shifted sideways, becoming a blur of sea and rain and the sound of Torben shouting. Screaming. *No.* It couldn't be happening. Not Nasir. Hissing through her teeth, Celeste lifted her throbbing head from the deck. And that's when she saw Raiden leap to his feet and run.

"Kiyami! Keep the ship steady." He threw commands over his shoulder as he moved. Nothing of the laughing boy remained. He was her captain again. "Torben, don't you dare leave this ship. You aren't a strong enough swimmer. That's an order from your captain."

Torben roared with anger. "Try and stop me!"

But his men were on him in a moment, restraining him. The Yenrian bellowed, punching and kicking in an effort to get free. Still, the men held.

"I don't see him!" Bastian cried as he and Raiden scanned the churning waters.

The wheel spun wildly out of control, the ship turning quickly left. Too quickly. And Kiyami hadn't gotten up from her place on the ship's deck.

Heart hammering, Celeste pushed herself to her feet. Pain shot down her back from where she had collided with the mast. She stumbled, surprised, but limped to the wheel. With inhuman strength, Celeste caught the spinning wheel in her hands. The ship jerked to a stop, the weight of it straining against her muscles. A grunt escaped her lips. Then slowly, laboriously, Celeste began to right the ship.

The wheel was more difficult to move than she expected. Celeste repositioned herself, using her legs to help push the wheel back and back and back. Raiden discarded his heavy belt to the deck, his sword and pistol with it. Next went his boots.

"Raiden! Wait!" cried Bastian, but it was too late.

Without a look back, Raiden dove. His arms reached above his head, pointed as a blade, before he disappeared into the black water.

And suddenly she was right back where she started. Except she couldn't see if he reemerged. Because this time she was on the ship. This time she watched from the other side. Her throat went dry as paper. Try as she might, she couldn't see what was happening below, not without leaving the wheel. *They could be drowning.* She knew she shouldn't think such things. Raiden had swam well enough that night. But Nasir was so heavy, and the water was so rough.

A hand rested on her shoulder. Celeste turned to see Kiyami, expression solemn as she rubbed a bump forming on her head.

"I can take it from here."

Celeste nodded numbly, backing away from the wheel as her friend took control. Then she was running down the stairs, stopping only when she reached the ship's side.

"Nasir!" Torben cried, searching the waves as his body sagged beneath the weight of his men. His voice was hoarse from screaming the name again and again over the howling winds. Tears rolled down his cheeks. He looked so helpless and small. It was unnerving to see this hardened man fall to pieces before her. His normally red face, full of passion, shone pale and white as the rain dripped down from his braided hair into his eyes. Celeste peered down into the violent waters. She waited. One minute. Then two. But no one emerged.

"Celeste! Help me!"

It was Bastian. His free arm waved frantically from the main deck as he struggled to pull free the waterlogged rope ladder. Glad to be useful, Celeste ran to him. The ladder itself was curled tightly, secured by intricate knots to the side of the ship. While Bastian's wet fingers worked on one of the knots, Celeste fumbled with the other. The knot did not yield.

Over and over, her fingers slid against the fibers of the rope. What little composure she had began to slip away. Bastian moved to the next knot, but she couldn't get past her first. Tears gathered in her eyes. She felt her magic building in her stomach. Pulsing. *No... please no... not now.* Beside her, Bastian unraveled his third knot. But Raiden and Nasir were nowhere to be found.

Crying doesn't help.

The voice was her mother's.

I can't talk to you when you're like this.

Calm down.

Then a new voice.

She's a danger to herself and others.

And suddenly she was nine cycles old again, pressed flat against the wall outside her father's study. Tears sliding down her face as her teacher, the most recent in a line of many, informed her parents that they could not train her. That she should never sing. That her voice was dangerous. That she was too uncontrollable. Too unstable. Too... *human*. But after days at sea surrounded by them, being human held new meaning.

I can't lose them. Not after everything. I can't lose anyone else. She thought of Sephone, the only one who ever was able to withstand her moods, sent away just as she needed her. Of Maeve and her look of disappointment as she watched Celeste throw everything away for a *human* she didn't know. And even though it ruined her life, she'd do it again in a heartbeat. Again and again and again.

At last the knot loosened in her hands. Her fingers flew to the next knot, and the next. And as she finished, Bastian unfurled the rope ladder onto the sodden deck beneath them.

"I found him!"

It was Raiden. Celeste's shoulders sagged in relief. The Pirate Prince splashed clumsily in the waves as they crashed over him, using all his effort to keep his head above water. But he was *alive*. And beside him, a large, limp body floated, supported by his arm. *Nasir.* From this far away, she couldn't tell if he was breathing or not.

With newfound speed, Bastian gathered the rope ladder and flung it overboard. It landed with a wet slap against the side of the ship.

Raiden pulled Nasir forward, swimming for the ladder. Lightning flashed against a wave gathering behind them, growing in size every second.

"Look out!" cried Torben, but his warning was swallowed by the wind.

The great wave slammed against the ship, swallowing the two men in its path.

No... no... please no.

Celeste's fingers pulled at her belt buckle.

"Stop! It's too dangerous," Bastian said, rushing forward. She didn't care. The belt fell to the floor at her feet. "Celeste, stop!" Bastian tried again, but Celeste ignored him. She tore her heavy coat from her shoulders and had one foot upon the railing when Bastian's hands closed around her wrist.

"Enough!" he bellowed. This time his eyes blazed. "Don't act like you're the only one who cares about him!" Bastian's usual calm demeanor cracked. "We can't sail this ship safely through this current without you. If you drown, we'll *all* die."

Celeste stilled. The thought hadn't crossed her mind. No one had ever relied on her before. Not like this. All her life she had been the little princess. No one needed her for anything. She was a liability. *A danger to herself and others.*

All she'd ever *wanted* was to be needed. To be useful. It hadn't occurred to her until now. She'd always thought it was some great adventure she was chasing. Some sort of *glory*. But it was so much simpler than that.

Celeste let her foot fall back to the floor.

"Oh, thank God," Bastian said, his anger dissolving. Celeste watched in shock as his shoulders shook and his eyes watered. "I have to get home," he said through his tears. "I can't leave them."

His family. Celeste remembered. Unlike the rest of them, Bastian and Kiyami actually had loved ones to go home to. How could she have forgotten? Only thinking of herself. Of Raiden. She had forgotten about the others. *Selfish.* Celeste wrapped her arms around Bastian's shoulders. *We'll get back to them,* Celeste told her friend in the way she tightened her grip.

As if he understood, Bastian squeezed back. "Thank you," he whispered.

"I hate to break up what I'm sure is a wonderful moment..." came a shout from below, breaking the two apart. "But I could use some assistance!"

Raiden.

Celeste's heart swelled as she looked down and saw him clinging to the rope ladder with Nasir under his arm. Nasir was coughing but awake. *Alive.* Torben's men released him, and he leaped into action, racing to the ladder and dragging it up over the deck one rung at a time. Bastian and Celeste joined him, and inch by inch the ladder rose until the two men fell upon the deck of the ship.

Torben swept Nasir into his arms in an instant, pressing his forehead to his husband's.

"I thought I'd lost you," the Yenrian whispered.

"They'd have to kill me first," Nasir replied thickly, still coughing.

Tears gathered in Celeste's eyes as she watched them. Her instinct told her to stop, as it always did, but it was interrupted by a new thought. *To feel is human.* The word was no longer an insult. The once barbed weapon she used against herself to punish her frailty had finally lost its teeth. *To feel is human.* It was—a fact? A *truth.* And beautiful.

And then Celeste felt a pair of eyes on her.

She turned and met Raiden's gaze steadily. He stood at the banister, chest heaving as his white shirt clung to his muscled chest. The same familiar crooked smile hung on his lips as he gazed at her. And the raging world fell away. She stepped forward. Slowly at first, then faster. His smile widened. He opened his arms. And she flew into them. He pulled her close, warm despite the cold ocean water.

"I'm sorry I kept you waiting, love," he said into her wet hair.

She squeezed him tighter in reply.

The ship beneath them rocked. The wind howled. And Celeste held Raiden.

And it was okay.

She was okay.

And she felt the last shred of resistance fall away. Celeste cared for him. She couldn't pretend otherwise anymore. And maybe—just maybe—it was okay that she did. Because although he made her angry and afraid and sad and happy and every stupid little feeling all at once, it was all worth it. She'd rather live with the fear of losing him than live without letting herself feel *this*—whatever this was—for as long as she had it. And whatever happened, she knew she could weather the storm.

CHAPTER 32

The hours passed in a blur, and the storm raged on. But, praise the Goddess, things went smoothly. Or as smoothly as they could while sailing a dangerous current during a horrible storm. But no one complained. Not even Torben, who ordinarily enjoyed complaining often about a range of topics. Celeste kept her eyes trained on the churning waters, watching for any sign of a scout—the splash of a fin or the crown of a head. But she saw nothing. Which was good, given she wasn't certain what she'd do if she did see one. Reason with them? She doubted anyone from the Chorus would trust her, even if she was technically on a mission from the queen. Would she tell the crew? Capture the siren temporarily until they were safe? She hoped she never had to figure it out.

When she wasn't on the quarterdeck with Kiyami, Celeste was in the navigation room with Raiden, going over directions and giving him guidance. And although she felt the grueling stress weighing on her, she was invigorated. The work was hard but rewarding. She was useful for once. More than useful. *Indispensable*. And Raiden followed her instructions with ease. Every moment between them was easy. When they reached the first bend of the current, the crew was more than prepared. The turn was smooth compared to the horrors of the entrance. And after they completed the turn, Raiden took one look at Celeste and ordered her belowdecks.

"Get some rest," he said.

Celeste ignored him. She didn't feel tired, and it was only afternoon, despite the storm making it appear otherwise. But as she helped Nasir mop some of the water off the deck, she found herself nodding off.

"Go rest, Celeste," Raiden repeated, snatching the mop from her hands and glaring at her. "I won't tell you again. We need you well rested for the next leg of the journey."

She gave him a look of annoyance but turned to head toward her room.

"I'm *still* your captain," he called after her. "You seem to forget that on a regular basis."

Celeste offered him a rude hand gesture she had learned from Torben, before ducking out of the rain and into the hallway to the officers' quarters. But she did not stop at her closet. Instead, she strolled to the captain's door. When she checked the handle, she found it unlocked. With a little smirk, she entered, allowing herself to drip all over the lovely rugs. A stir-crazy Admiral leaped upon her, tail wagging so furiously that his entire body shook.

"Hello there," she whispered after closing the door behind her. With a smile, she crouched down to the dog's height, scratching his head and back. Once the Admiral settled, Celeste peeled off her wet clothes and used a towel she found on the dresser to wring out her hair. She tossed the wet things into a heap on the floor. Payback for making her sleep in a closet for weeks. It wasn't as though he was using the room anyway. And the plush bed was practically begging for someone to sleep in it.

She opened a drawer in his dresser to find one of Raiden's many billowing black shirts. *Thank you, Captain, for your generosity!* the siren thought with a smirk as she pulled one over her head. She padded to the bed, sinking wearily into the silken sheets and fluffy pillows. It was heavenly. Like lying in a cloud. Celeste stretched her legs and arms, savoring how much *space* she had compared to her tiny closet. A part of her raged, knowing Raiden slept in such luxury while she slept in a cramped closet with a dog.

On cue, the Admiral leaped upon the bed, curling against her hip. The dog's body was familiar and warm. In seconds, she was asleep.

Celeste awoke to the feeling of someone watching her.

She bolted upright, pushing her white hair from her face. But it was only the captain. He leaned against the door, arms crossed over his muscled chest. His brown eyes danced with amusement as he took in her unkempt appearance. The surprise on her face.

Night had fallen. The only light in the room came from a flickering oil lamp held beside the bed. Celeste looked around for the Admiral, but he had gone. Raiden must have let him out.

"Did I interrupt?"

Celeste made a show of yawning and stretching. *Yes, you did,* it seemed to say, as she threw him a sleepy grin.

"Please, don't get up on my account," Raiden said. His eyes snagged on what she was wearing. His shirt was only long enough to cover the tops of her thighs. She tugged at the hem, avoiding his gaze. *When did I start worrying about nudity?* Apparently, after several months of being around humans, she had somehow picked up some of their ridiculous modesty. Or perhaps it was the expression on Raiden's face. The humor had disappeared from his eyes, and his lips parted slightly. They looked soft.

Her heart hammered. But she didn't move to cover herself. Instead, she let him look. Watched him as his darkening eyes ran up her legs to his shirt. It hung off her shoulder, baring the column of her neck. When his eyes at last met hers, she suddenly felt wide-awake.

"If you wanted to stay in my bed, you only had to ask." He smirked.

In response, Celeste leaned back into the pillows and made herself very comfortable. *Oh, he'll regret saying that.*

Raiden watched her and laughed. "I'll inform the Admiral he's getting a roommate."

A chuckle escaped Celeste at the joke, and Raiden's face softened.

"Thank you," he said, an almost pained expression crossing his face, "for helping us get to the island. Without you, we wouldn't have made it."

Celeste shrugged, unsure how else to respond. She didn't regret telling him about the current, but it still sat like an uncomfortable weight upon her. *Better you and this crew find Lunapesce than someone else the Pirate King sends*, she reminded herself firmly.

The captain walked around the bed and sank down onto the foot of it. He leaned upon the tall wooden bedpost, running a hand through his hair. It was a tell of his she had become familiar with now. Something was on his mind. Silence stretched between them. Not uncomfortable, but expectant.

"I haven't been entirely honest with you," he said at last.

Celeste straightened.

"I—" He paused, thinking carefully about his next words. Something tightened in her chest. *What are you not telling me?* Heart hammering, Celeste tucked her legs beneath her. She hated the way his confession made her feel. As though she were bracing for something terrible.

"When I got my first ship a year ago, I got cocky and led my crew into a trap, and—well, you've met Valencia." His voice grew taut, and his eyes hardened.

Pieces fell into place in Celeste's mind one after the other. Why he would go out of his way to steal Valencia's ship. Valencia's mockery of him in Port Velluno. And what's worse, Celeste realized with a pang, he hadn't only failed one crew. He'd failed *two*.

"We managed to escape, but she sank the ship. That was when my father gave me one chance to make it up to him." He did not meet her eyes; he gazed blankly at the oil lamp on the bedside table. The light flickered upon his haunted expression. "That's the real reason we're on this treasure hunt. Not for money. Or glory. Because I was overconfident and ignored my crew's warnings. When my father found out, I honestly thought he was going to execute me." At last he turned to look at her, his eyes searching her face. She could see how nervous this confession made him. How the muscles in his back were tense, as if ready for a blow. She knew that feeling. Knew how it felt to lay yourself bare and vulnerable to someone, hoping they would accept you anyway. Even if they saw the worst of yourself.

Leaning forward, she took his hand and gave it a squeeze. *It's okay. We all make mistakes*, she tried to tell him. Raiden's shoulders fell. His hand was so warm, unusually so for a human or siren. Did he have a fever from the storm? He opened his mouth to say more.

A knock sounded at the door. "Captain, you're needed on deck." Bastian stood in the doorway, his face stern. Raiden sighed heavily and released Celeste's hand. The moment between them dissolved like seafoam.

"I'll be up shortly," the captain replied, his eyes remaining on hers. Ever so gently, he leaned forward and tucked a stray piece of her silvery hair behind her ear. "As you were," he said with a teasing wink, before rising from the bed and leaving the room.

Celeste walked dutifully from barrel to barrel, tugging on the ropes that held them in place to check that they were secure. The winds were fairer today, so they had been able to lower the sails. As she finished with the final barrel, Raiden approached her. Shadows circled his eyes, betraying how much this past week weighed on him.

"You look terrible," he said by way of greeting.

Celeste gave him a withering look.

"Cheer up, love. We're almost out of the storm," he said, grinning and pointing.

And sure enough, at the edge of the horizon, she saw a sliver of clear skies. A bit of the waxing moon alighting the sky early. She almost wept with joy.

"Captain, we're approaching the final turn," Kiyami called from the wheel, dark hair sticking to her neck from the rain. If Raiden looked worse for wear, Kiyami looked like a dead girl walking.

"Kiyami, you haven't slept in over twenty-four hours. I'll take over. Go get some sleep," Raiden said.

She frowned. "Captain, this is the end of the current. Shouldn't it be all hands on deck?"

"Not if the hands in question haven't rested in days," Raiden insisted. "It's not a risk I'm willing to take. Besides, this used to be my job before I became a captain. The *Red Revenge* is in good hands. Go. That's an order."

Kiyami nodded. Her shoulders relaxed, as if a great weight had been lifted.

"Wake me if you need anything," Kiyami called over her shoulder before she dragged her soaked body below deck. The rest of the crew remained, securing themselves to the masts of the ship with rope. No one would fall overboard this time.

Celeste and Raiden looped their ropes around the mizzenmast, each with enough length for them to walk a little around the upper deck, but no more.

Celeste cast one final glance around, searching for any sign of the Chorus. She saw nothing but churning ocean. *We might just pull this off yet*, she thought with a swell of pride. Then the current appeared in the sea before them, water bending abruptly. She placed a hand on Raiden's shoulder to get his attention and pointed to the knot of waves.

"We're approaching the bend!" he called. "Brace yourselves!"

The crew pulled the ropes tight around their waists. Some offered prayers. Others did nothing but stare blankly out to sea.

The ship jerked sideways as it hit the bend. Raiden's hands flew over the wheel. It was a hairpin turn, almost impossible to do even with their reasonably sized ship. Barrels strained against their supports. The ship tilted. Bastian slipped, falling upon the deck. Hard. He slid for a horrible moment, before catching ahold of his rope.

She looked to Raiden, realizing her hand hadn't left his shoulder. She loosened her white-knuckle grip on him. His eyes remained trained on the wheel. But his hands struggled to keep the ship steady. Waves hit against the bow, tossing the vessel up and down. The end of the current was just a few lengths ahead.

"Almost there!" Bastian cried.

But the ship was not righting itself. It tilted further left, its port side dipping lower with each passing moment. Raiden's jaw clenched, and he grunted, using all his weight to turn the wheel. Still nothing. Waves slapped the side of the ship, washing over the side and onto the deck.

Celeste's feet began to slip. The floor beneath them was tilting. Its angle grew with each second. Her free hand found Raiden's arm as she attempted to steady herself. But he was sliding too.

His eyes went wide. "We're capsizing!"

Another wave hit the side of the ship, knocking them both to the deck. They tried to find their feet again, but the ship was now slanted at a forty-five-degree angle. Crew members screamed. The cries of doomed men. Celeste and Raiden plunged down toward the roaring black ocean below. Raiden's arms wrapped around her waist. They jerked to a stop, the ropes that bound them to the ship pulled taut.

"Celeste? Are you okay?" Raiden's voice was in her ear.

She nodded. But it was a lie. With no one at the wheel, the ship had no chance to right itself. It tilted further. Sinking. Celeste looked around her for the crew and saw them clinging to the ship, fear in their eyes. Nasir gripped Torben's arm in one hand, the other wrapped around the railing. Bastian was nowhere to be found.

"Baz!" Raiden cried out. "Where is Bastian?"

Torben pointed to a rope. The end of it sank into the waves below.

Raiden cursed. "And Kiyami? Kiyami's below!" It was too late. No one could do anything to help her.

Setting his jaw, Raiden looked toward the spinning wheel above them. "Hang on, love," he whispered into her ear.

Celeste wrapped her arms around his neck tightly as his arms released her. Raiden gripped the rope holding them in place and hauled them upward, fist over fist. A wave crashed over them, leaving them gasping. Raiden's arms shook. Beneath them, water poured over the deck and into the hold. Half the ship was already submerged. They inched toward the wheel, Raiden grunting with the effort.

"It's too late, Captain!" Nasir cried. "We can't right it! The ship's going down!"

"I can fix it," Raiden insisted, releasing one hand to reach for the rope above. They were only a body's length from the wheel now. But his grip slipped. The two went sliding several feet. Raiden cried out as his hand burned against the rope, stopping them short and sending them swinging.

"No!" he grunted, but Celeste could see the fight leave his eyes as he gazed at what was left of his crew. They looked back to him, waiting for orders. For him to save them from what was surely a watery grave.

"Abandon ship!" Raiden called.

Celeste's stomach twisted painfully at the words. Surely he couldn't be serious. They would die. Be swept into the current and drowned.

Around them the crew began to move, to untie themselves. Celeste shook her head.

"Celeste, there is no other way," Raiden said, his voice unnervingly gentle. "The ship is too far gone. If we stay any longer, we risk being dragged down with it."

Still, she resisted. There had to be another way. This couldn't be the end. He couldn't just give up like this. They had almost made it to the wheel.

"Take your rope off," Raiden ordered.

Fine. With one arm still wrapped around Raiden, Celeste reached for the rope at his hips.

"No," he said, eyes hard. "I'm going down with my ship."

All the air left her lungs. *No...*

"I won't abandon my ship again," he said. "I'll hold you while you get the knot undone. You need to hurry. The next wave will—"

Celeste cupped his cheek in her hand, and tears sprang to her eyes. Her captain, who lived with the knowledge of all the people he'd led to their deaths. Cursed with a doomed mission from his father. She pressed her forehead against his. Rain slid down their faces. The ship lurched. *Would any of the others make it? Was Kiyami already lost?* Raiden's arms pulled her closer against his warm chest, fingers pressing into her skin. Holding her. Saying goodbye.

"Please, Celeste. You need to get away."

His hands reached for her rope, and he began to pull apart the knot. Tears fell down her cheeks in streams. She wrapped both arms around his neck. *I can't let him go,* she thought, anger weaving into her grief. *Not after everything we've done. Everything we've sacrificed.* But her power as a siren was useless here. She couldn't sing the sea into submission. Only the Goddess could do that.

Could she sing to him? Convince him to remove his rope and let them both take their chances in the sea together? But even as she thought it, she knew Raiden would never forgive her. He wished to go down with his ship. He'd hate her for taking this final stand from him. And she couldn't live in a world where he hated her.

She couldn't live in a world without him either.

"You have to let me go," he said in her ear, her rope falling from his hands.

The truth came unbidden, the thought appearing in her mind as she clung to him. A thought as delicate as coral, and just as sharp.

I'm falling in love with him.

And suddenly she was undone. Her hands twisted into the fabric of his shirt, and she turned her face to the sky. *It cannot end this way.*

Raiden pulled at her arms, trying to release her into the water beneath them. The moon hung low, golden and growing larger. As if it, too, were caught in her pull. And that's when she saw it. Something looming above them. Forming in the corner of her eye. A colossal wave. It appeared as if pulled from the sea by an unseen hand, gathering water into itself until it stood as tall as the *Red Revenge*. Celeste froze, her body bracing for the impact as it rushed toward them. With a crash, the great wave slammed against the side of the ship.

The port side.

CHAPTER 33

Raiden's hand found her head, shielding her as the *Red Revenge* heaved, swinging them wildly. With a dull thud, they hit the deck. Beneath them, the ship groaned, rocking, rolling. *Righting itself.*

The *Red Revenge* careened out from the end of the current with a splash.

For a moment, neither Celeste nor Raiden moved.

They were safe. The ship was sailing.

"Did—did you do that?" Raiden lifted his head and stared at Celeste, eyes wide.

Her look of confusion dissolved into amusement. She shook her head. Clearly, his father had told him little truth about siren abilities.

"Ah," he said, using his thumb to push a strand of silver hair from her cheek. "Well, I suppose that was lucky."

A laugh bubbled up through her throat. And then she was crying, pulling Raiden into a fierce hug as her body shook. All the tension within her released at once. And soon Raiden was laughing too.

"That was *terrible*!"

Kiyami! The pirate appeared at the stairs, her legs shaking. "I thought we were goners."

"Unquestionably!" replied Torben, in a suspiciously gleeful tone. "It's been ages since I really thought I was about to die."

"Is everyone accounted for?" Bastian called out as he unfastened his rope. Raiden looked on his friend with relief.

The crew took stock of each other, and strangely, everyone was unharmed. Physically, at least. Some were still in the water, but they were quickly found and pulled aboard.

For the first time, Celeste found herself all too ready to be on dry land once more. The crew moved about, checking the ship for harm. There was still quite a bit of water belowdecks; otherwise, nothing was amiss. Even the Admiral, although shaken up, was perfectly fine. Apparently, Kiyami had been with him when they started to capsize and was able to strap them both down in time.

Goddess be praised—the strange little crew had made it out alive.

Celeste joined Torben and some of the other crew to gather water in buckets and throw it overboard. They'd made a dent in the knee-deep water when they heard a call from above.

"The rain! It's stopped!"

The bucket in Celeste's hands landed with a splash. She took the stairs two at a time. And sure enough, when she reached the deck, she saw the sky had cleared. Stars glittered. The moon, nearly full and bright, appeared larger than usual over their heads. Strange. But Celeste smiled at the sight all the same. It felt as if they had been stuck inside a cave for the past week, and now they found their way out to freedom. Her shoulders sagged in relief.

Torben whooped with joy and ran to Nasir. They spun around together on the still-glistening deck, shouting joyfully. Beneath their feet, the slick surface reflected the stars above, as though they danced in the heavens. Kiyami struck up a rhythm with a stomp of her foot, and even Bastian let out a whistle and began to clap his hands. Without meaning to, Celeste felt her body begin to sway in time with the unusual music. There were no instruments. No singers. There was nothing controlled or even beautiful about it. It was wild and ugly and—fun. Raiden appeared before her, reaching out his hand.

"I believe I owe you a dance," he said, his smile wide and unbound.

Celeste's cheeks heated as she placed her hand upon his. The simple touch of his warm, rough fingers sent shivers down her spine. With a jerk, he twirled her into his chest and slid his free arm around her waist. She let out a laugh, surprise and pleasure blooming within her chest. The warmth of him pressed close, and beneath their wet clothes she could feel every place they touched. Where before the merest brush would have sent her running, Celeste realized she felt safe within his arms. With another twist of his wrist, Celeste was spinning away, whirling across the deck until the tether of their arms pulled taut. When sparring, Raiden was brazen, each strike and thrust executed with strength and determination. There was a ferocity to him. A passion. It was present in everything he did. Everything he was. And she could feel it in the way he moved with her. But while Raiden was a burning sun, consuming and bright, Celeste was an icy moon. Smooth and practiced. Giving. Following each step.

All the while, his gaze never left her face. He watched in delight as she let out a surprised gasp as he dipped her backward.

"Don't worry, love. I've got you," he whispered against her ear, his arms tightening around her. Suddenly, her stomach felt as though it'd filled with bubbles.

He lifted her slowly, smile widening until he was blazing with it. The joy and relief and victory. *They'd done it. They'd made it through. Together.* And Celeste found she was beaming back.

"*Oh, have you ever met such a fearless crew? Who fight the good fight on the ocean blue?*" Nasir began to sing, a song Celeste had heard once before. And yet she felt as though she'd heard it a hundred times in her head. It was the song Raiden had sung on his birthday, the first time she'd seen him. That seemed like a lifetime ago now. After a verse, the captain joined:

> *Drink, drink 'fore we run dry!*
> *We'll dance till the sun falls from the sky.*
> *Take what you can and never say die,*
> *until our final bell tolls.*

Next came Bastian and Kiyami, until the entire crew sang together. Their song was—not *good*—but wonderfully imperfect. One voice would miss a note, and another, blending in a way that wasn't necessarily dulcet. But it was loud and shouting and full. And Celeste wished so dearly she could join. With few exceptions, music was a weapon for sirens. But this was self-expression. It was community and passion, two things that Celeste was learning she held dearly.

> *Soon enough our tides will turn!*
> *Treasure, glory, and fame we'll earn.*
> *We'll tell our tale, and they will learn,*
> *When we all return.*

Celeste soaked it all in. Every sharp note and each pounding beat of their feet. The sound of the crew singing together off-key. The feeling of Raiden's rough hand gripping hers. His other hand pressing against her back. How her captain's eyes crinkled at the corners when he gazed at her. The fluttering feeling in her chest. And then that thought again.

I'm falling in love with him.

A thought that perhaps didn't seem so dangerous anymore. It whispered itself to her as if it blew in on the light breeze. Although she had no experience with love, she knew it was true. The feeling felt inevitable. Like night yielding to the day.

Raiden leaned in close, bowing his head so his mouth was beside her ear. "Your smile outshines the stars tonight."

Her heart stammered.

Drink, drink 'fore we run dry!
We'll dance till the sun falls from the sky.
Take what you can and never say die,
until our final bell tolls.

The song ended with a rather long and shouty crescendo. Raiden spun Celeste away from him and gave her a little bow, a smirk on his lips. Celeste repeated the gesture back to him, and the action made Raiden burst into laughter. Although Celeste did not know the reason for it, she was pleased knowing she made him laugh.

Torben appeared beside them, pushing cups overflowing with strong-smelling liquid into everyone's hands. He waved off questions as to *what exactly was in the cups* and instead thrust his tankard into the air.

"To the toughest bunch of idiots on the sea!"

"And to the gods who keep us," Nasir added, thrusting his own cup into the air as well.

The crew gathered into a circle and one by one raised their cups, crashed them together, then drank heavily. The mystery drink was one of Torben's own making.

"It's not jus' alcohol!" he insisted, but the taste was bitter and burned all the way down. After one sip, Celeste dumped it overboard when she believed no one was looking.

But with the rest of the crew, the drink went quickly. They passed around more bottles and raised glasses to all sorts of things. "To clear skies and fair seas."

"To treasures untold."

"To bonds that can never be broken."

"To one hell of a story to tell."

Celeste declined as Torben offered her more "libations."

"All right! More for me," he grunted, taking the bottle back and pouring the remainder into his own tankard. Seeing this as an opportunity to seek out her own libations, Celeste grabbed the empty bottle from his hands, wiggled it, and pointed toward the stairs.

"Ah! That's a girl! Get the ale next!" Torben said, clapping her on the back.

Celeste nodded and slipped away below deck to the galley. Behind her, she left the door ajar so she could still hear the festivities above. The ebb and flow of sound soothed her. Around her, the room was dark, but she knew it well.

Her hands found the matches left on the table, and soon the oil lamps were burning bright. She had learned how to light a candle from watching the others. More and more, she noticed little human things that she'd accidentally picked up. A gesture hello. The way she used utensils. Celeste placed the empty bottle on the table. Although she had developed a taste for alcohol, whatever Torben had given them was, in a word, terrible. She hadn't the faintest idea why anyone would willingly consume more of it.

Picking up the lamp, she ducked into the back room where Nasir stored the food and drink. The light shone upon bottle after bottle, and Celeste marveled over how many words she recognized on the labels. They were still too few to read them in entirety, but a trill of excitement ran through her all the same. Her hand found the familiar bottle of honeyed wine and plucked it from the shelf, before looking for the bottle Torben wanted. He drank ale plenty of times at dinner, so she knew what it looked like. Eventually, she discovered it on the floor in the back right corner. She passed the lamp from one hand to another, considering how to carry it all.

"Need a hand?" The voice startled her. Sirens were used to feeling a presence before it was seen.

Celeste straightened and turned to see Raiden leaning with his hand atop the door frame, watching her with an amused expression. Putting his stealth aside, Celeste passed Raiden the lamp.

"Good choice," he said, pointing to the wine in her hand. "I saw you weren't a fan of Torben's Yenrian drink."

A look of surprise crossed her face. She'd been certain no one noticed her discarding it. She shrugged and nodded, earning a chuckle from the captain. He set the lamp on the table, then reached to help her with the bottles. But Celeste held up a hand to stop him.

"I know you can handle yourself," he scoffed. "I was attempting to be chivalrous."

She huffed but handed him the bottle of wine. Then she pulled two mismatched glasses and a corkscrew from a cabinet and set them down on the counter.

"Why don't we open this now," Raiden said with a grin. He removed the cork with a satisfying pop and poured them each a glass. "To you," he said, lifting his wine, "the best Wayfinder I've ever met."

Celeste beamed with pride.

Raiden amended, "And the only Wayfinder I've ever met."

This earned a light laugh from her as she touched her glass to his. The title felt good, even if they both knew it wasn't true. Celeste sipped, and the liquid tasted as lovely and sweet as she remembered. In an instant, she was back at the festival, enjoying her orange.

"What are you thinking about?" he asked.

Celeste shrugged and pointed at the wine.

"Wine?"

She shook her head.

"Port Velluno?" he tried again.

Close enough. She smiled and nodded.

"You know—you never fail to surprise me. Trying to *pull a knife on a guard*," he teased.

Her free hand flew to his shoulder, giving it a playful push. But in one swift movement, he caught her, pressing her palm gently into his chest. Her lips parted in a soft gasp. He pulled her close. So close. The lamp on the table cast a golden glow upon Raiden's face. His mole was only a breath away. And before she knew what was happening, he dipped his head and brushed his lips against hers. The touch was tentative, questioning, as if waiting for her to pull away. But she felt it everywhere. Every part of her body lit on fire. Burning. And she wanted more.

When she didn't draw back, he stepped forward, pressing his lips more firmly against hers. Her heart stuttered in her chest. Her mind went blank. The kiss was a question. An answer. A call-and-response. It was the single greatest kiss she'd ever had. A kiss that felt, in a way, like magic. All too soon, he pulled away, and suddenly there was entirely too much space between them.

"That's how I wanted our first kiss to—"

"You kiss me," she breathed, accent thick.

Raiden blinked. "What?"

"You *kissed* me," she corrected herself, still dizzy.

"You can *talk*!"

Oh. Shit.

Celeste froze. Her heart dropped. What had she done? Blind panic seized her. The game was up, and all it took was one foolish kiss. Celeste's hands rubbed against her hips, and her breathing hitched. *And why did she speak in the human language?* But she knew why. Even her dreams lately were in the human language. And if she were to be honest, half of her thoughts were too. These humans were *infecting* her with their *humanity*. Was there anything siren left within her?

"Would you mind explaining why you can suddenly *speak*?"

Celeste considered her words carefully. "I did not want you to"—Celeste searched for the word, avoiding eye contact—"hear my accent."

Raiden stared at her.

"You didn't... *you didn't*..." He ran a hand through his dark hair, incredulous. "I'm sorry, love, but that's just about the worst explanation I've ever heard."

"Don't call me *love*," she snapped.

"She finds her voice and somehow becomes a larger pain in my ass."

Celeste glared at him.

"You *kissed* me," she repeated, words dripping in venom.

"I did," he said, eyes flaring. "And I'd do it again, if you weren't so infuriatingly—"

The words stopped short as Celeste grabbed a fistful of his shirt and dragged his lips to hers. He smirked against her mouth, sliding his hands around her lower back to pull her closer. And Celeste was lost.

Her hands loosened on his shirt, and she slid them beneath the fabric, enjoying the feel of him beneath her fingers. The heat of him. He was always so much warmer than she was.

Raiden pulled away for just a moment to murmur, "I just want to point out, for the record, that you kissed me first. Days ago."

Before she could reply, his mouth was trailing down her jaw, drawing a gasp from her lips. She tilted her head, giving him more of the column of her neck. His kisses were hungry. His hands daring.

A shout sounded from above.

Celeste stiffened. *What if Raiden tells them I can speak? Would they ever trust me again?*

Sensing a shift, Raiden pulled away, shirt delightfully rumpled and hair mussed. Celeste had to stop herself from kissing him again.

"Please don't tell others I speak," she said, voice husky. "I promise I—"

"It's not my secret to share," he said, tucking a strand of her hair behind her ear.

But somehow his words didn't calm her nerves. The captain appeared surprisingly unbothered by her deception, but Celeste doubted Kiyami would feel the same. *What if they never forgive me?*

Raiden took her chin in his hand and lifted her worried gaze to his. "Would it make you feel better if I shared something with you? A secret for a secret?"

"Yes."

He released her and took a long sip of his wine.

"I blame my father for my mother's death."

CHAPTER 34

Celeste blinked. It felt as though the air had left the room. But before she could say anything, Raiden continued.

"My mother and father met on the docks. He was a pirate captain of a fleet, and she was a young girl who lived by the sea. When my mother told him she was pregnant, my father left. He never wanted a family, let alone a child. When my mother's family found out—they threw her out." His voice hardened. "It's not common practice in Hinarso, but there are still those who look down upon unmarried women having children. So when my mother had me, she was all alone. She named me Raiden. Her little thunderstorm."

Celeste's hand reached for his of its own accord. He laced his fingers within hers and squeezed in thanks.

"She struggled to keep a job. I was five when a fever broke out in our city. My mother, like many, took ill and died within two weeks." He paused, and Celeste hadn't noticed the tears in her eyes. "When my father was informed she'd died and left his son—well, I suppose he figured he'd bring me on and raise me to be his heir.

"I've never told anyone, but I've always believed if he'd only taken my mother with him, if he hadn't cast her aside, she'd still be alive. He's the reason she died alone and poor in the street." Raiden finally met Celeste's gaze. "So I'll keep your secret if you keep mine."

Celeste nodded but remained quiet. She wondered why he hadn't told anyone this before. Bastian was his closest friend—practically his brother. Why would Raiden hide this? Was it because Bastian had worked for his father? And why did Raiden still wish to win his father's approval after everything he'd done? But a different question slipped out instead.

"Why tell me?"

Raiden moved their entwined hands to his chest.

"Because it was easy," he answered.

Celeste stiffened. A secret that was easy to tell wasn't a good trade. But he continued. "Talking with you is the easiest thing I've ever done. We could talk for hours, days, years, and I would never tire of it. And now that I've heard your voice, I confess it's my favorite sound." There was such an earnestness in his face.

Her eyes widened, and her heart pounded in her chest.

"So, do we have a deal?" he asked.

Celeste pulled her hand free from his and offered it back to him, palm up. A human's agreement. He smiled and took her hand, but before she could shake, he tugged her forward, meeting her lips with his.

She melted into the kiss. It was much better than a handshake.

"So this is why the drinks were taking so long."

Celeste sprung away from Raiden as though she'd been burned. In the doorway stood Kiyami, grinning.

"Were they swapping spit?" Torben called from above.

"Yep," Kiyami shouted back.

Cheers and groans erupted from above.

"You owe me five silver, Baz! I told you it'd happen after the festival!" Kiyami said, wiggling her eyebrows at Celeste. The siren wrapped her arms around herself and groaned. She wished she could turn into seafoam and dissolve into the floor.

"Took 'em long enough," grumbled Torben. "If Valencia hadn't interrupted, I would've won!"

Raiden stood before her grinning from ear to ear. His muscled arms were crossed across his wide chest, the picture of smug confidence. It made Celeste want to smack the expression from his face. Or kiss it away. But instead she took her wineglass from the table, downed it in one swig, then picked up the bottle and marched upstairs.

"If you break her heart, I will help her kill you," Kiyami said smoothly to Raiden as she gathered up the remaining bottles and followed Celeste up the stairs.

"Two on one? Sounds thrilling!" Raiden called after them.

Thankfully, the appearance of more alcohol provided enough distraction to the crew for Celeste to avoid any awkward questions. After a time, Raiden joined the party too. She worried it would be uncomfortable. Not only between her and Raiden but between him and the rest of the crew. Noticing Celeste's discomfort, Kiyami looped an arm around Celeste's shoulders and squeezed. The gesture was so human it made her smile.

"Seeing you two together . . . it makes sense," Kiyami said. "And the way he looks at you—I've never seen him look at anyone that way."

The words made her nervous, her stomach feeling like fizzing bubbles. It wasn't unpleasant. Celeste squeezed her friend back, glad she did not need to respond. When her gaze lifted, she saw Raiden staring at her from across the ship. He stood with Bastian, sharing a drink and a laugh. And suddenly, despite the crowded deck, it felt as though they were the only two. Bastian, noticing Raiden's attention shifting, followed his friend's gaze. But when his eyes met Celeste's, the smile on his face vanished. Suddenly, she felt cold. Was he angry with her? Why?

"You missed it! There was a shower of stars earlier," Nasir told Celeste, mercifully blocking Bastian from view.

"I think she saw sparks flying," Kiyami blurted.

Celeste snorted, sending Kiyami into a fit of laughter. As the two descended into a fit of giggles, Nasir chuckled a little, watching them with amusement. The interaction was strangely familial. And suddenly Celeste was smiling for an entirely different reason. Blessedly, once they regained composure, Kiyami chose to change the subject.

"Did you and Torben fall in love at sea?" she asked.

"You know, this is our first voyage together," Nasir said. "I've never sailed before this."

Celeste and Kiyami exchanged a look of surprise.

"Torben was the pirate. But he ended up at Port Romsey for a time, looking for work, and he came into my pub. He told me stories of his adventures, of his family, of how he ended up marooned by the Pirate King, and more than once he would fight customers who tried to start something with me," he said with a fond laugh.

"And you fell in love," Kiyami said.

"And I fell in love," Nasir repeated, eyes drifting toward his husband. The gruff Yenrian was now with Raiden and Bastian, gesturing wildly with his drink as he spoke.

"I didn't realize this was your first time at sea," Kiyami said.

"Didn't tell any of ya," Nasir said simply.

The conversation continued, but as they talked, guilt settled heavily on Celeste's chest. Even now, they made an effort to include her in the conversation in spite of her silence. She hadn't wanted to get close to these humans. But now she couldn't imagine her life without them. *I'll tell them*, she decided, *when the time is right*. Maybe her accent would betray her as a siren, and maybe it wouldn't. Either way, she was tired of the charade. Still, what if they never forgave her for deceiving them? What if they found out she was a siren and cast her out? *Then they wouldn't be the people I believe they are.*

"Do you think it'll storm again, Celeste?" Kiyami asked, shaking her from her thoughts.

Celeste shook her head. *No, I think the sun's finally here to stay.*

The party began to fade. With the strong drink and such little sleep, one by one each crew member staggered off for bed until it was only Torben, Celeste, and Raiden sitting around a flickering lantern.

"I want to... thank you, Raiden," Torben said, rocking a little as he gripped his bottle. "After my—erm, *incident*—no one would offer me a job. Not *anyone*! Till you came along. After this, I think I'll finally be back in your dad's good graces and can sail the seas once more..." He trailed off, tears pooling in his eyes. He hastily wiped them on his sleeve as Raiden reached out and clapped him upon his shoulder.

"You were the right man for the job."

Celeste tried her best to keep her face neutral. She hadn't forgotten how Raiden resisted Torben joining the crew. But there was some truth in the captain's words. Torben, despite all his flaws, was the best man for the job. He had helped rescue her in Port Velluno, after all, even if it did feel like a thinly veiled excuse to use explosives.

"Are you heading to bed soon?" Nasir asked, appearing at the stairs.

"Yeah, comin'." Torben stood and shook Raiden's hand vigorously. "You're a good man, Captain," he said, before stumbling after his husband below deck, leaving Celeste and Raiden alone for the first time since their kiss.

A moment of quiet passed between them. Celeste tilted her head back to see the four daughters shining, just as they had the first night. The stars glittered above her like jewels in a crown. Memories of Raiden and how coldly he acted toward her played in her mind. She almost didn't recognize the man before her as the same person.

"Do you have any siblings?" he asked, breaking the silence.

The question was so surprisingly normal that Celeste laughed.

"What? I'm curious." He grinned.

"I have two siblings," she said. "Shye, my eldest sister, and Sephone, our middle sister."

"What's Shye like?"

"Difficult." Celeste sighed.

Raiden nodded, listening.

"Sephone is the favorite." Although it stung to talk of her family, there was relief in it, as if the very act of being known was something she'd been craving for some time. "She's gifted and kind. When we were young, and Shye and I would fight, Sephone would be the one to calm the waters. After Sephone went away, Shye and I never really stopped fighting."

"Where did she go?"

"To another kingdom. I guess my parents convinced her she'd be more valuable as a bride to some prince." Her eyes fell to the floor.

"Are you meant to marry some prince in another kingdom?" Raiden asked, tone serious as he stared at her with that familiar burning gaze.

She swallowed the wine in her mouth and set the glass down with a sigh.

"Probably," Celeste admitted, "if I ever learn to *control* myself." A second later, she realized what she'd let slip.

"So you're a princess?" He smirked.

Celeste narrowed her eyes at him, her annoyance with his tone somehow outweighing her fear of where this conversation was leading.

"Yes," she replied, lifting her chin.

"Somehow this doesn't surprise me," he drawled.

"And why is that?" she snapped.

Raiden's eyes lit with mischief. "Well—for one, you're clearly used to getting your way." He leaned back against the ship's railing.

Celeste let out a bitter laugh. "Hardly. My life was decided for me."

Raiden's snarky manner softened at this. He let his leg fall and press against hers, a steadying presence.

"What would you want to do if you could decide?" he asked.

Celeste paused, considering. "I—I've never thought about it."

An anxious feeling rose in her stomach. She pushed to her feet, moving away, giving herself some space. They were wandering too close to the great unsaid thing. The truth she would never be able to take back. She'd already failed her people so many times. If she told him and anyone found out, she wouldn't be the one who suffered.

In some ways, the treaty between kingdoms had been broken the day she walked into the Broken Compass. Still, it was one thing for Raiden to guess who she was. It was quite another for her to admit it. To speak it aloud. But she trusted him. As foolish as that might be. She knew that if she told him, it would stay between them. Because Raiden knew already and hadn't told a soul. And she knew she could never go back to her family, her people, after failing to kill him.

Worst of all, she loved him. She loved him so much it stole her breath and left her reeling. Loved him so much she hated him for it. And more than anything, she hoped he loved her back. But how could he possibly love her back if he didn't know her? All of her?

Breathing in the warm night air, Celeste leaned against the railing of the ship and looked out over the water. A leap of faith stood before her.

And she jumped.

"It wasn't until I"—she took a breath, steeling her nerves—"until I saw you dancing on your ship that I even dreamed of anything more than what I knew." She thought she had finished speaking, until the next words slipped out, so quiet she wasn't sure if he could hear it. "Sirens don't dance like that."

She did not turn. Did not dare to look at him. But behind her, she heard him stand. Felt his eyes on her back, as if his gaze could burn through her and see her beating heart. Her throat was dry. The secret was out. The moment she had feared had come at last. And she had chosen to do it.

Silence fell between them. A breeze brushed across her skin, sending a shiver down her spine. She felt naked, despite her layers.

And then—

"I never thanked you. For saving Baz and I."

"No," she said softly, "you didn't."

She turned, unable to bear it a moment longer. And Raiden was there. Striding the few steps toward her. Slowly. Deliberately. The same warm expression he always wore on his face. Nothing had changed. And everything had. It was almost anticlimactic. *Had she been worrying over nothing?* Probably. It sounded very much like something she'd do. And yet the knots in her stomach loosened as she looked into his face and saw they had weathered this storm too.

"Thank you," he said with a smile, stepping so close she could reach out and touch him. "May I ask—why you did?"

"Because—because you jumped overboard to save your friend. Because you weren't the villain I was told you were."

A pained look crossed his face.

"What if I am?" he asked, voice low. "What if I'm *worse*?"

Celeste's hand found his cheek, and he turned his face into her touch. In his eyes, she saw regret and sorrow, drowning him from the inside. How many of his drowned crew had families like Kiyami or Bastian? Or dreams like Torben? Things left unsaid or undone. She could see how it haunted him. How he tortured himself. Could see it in how protective he was of his crew. Such horrible things he'd done in the king's name.

"You're not your father," she said.

Raiden took a step back, irritation flickering in his eyes. "You don't know him."

And suddenly Raiden was slipping away from her, replaced by Captain Raiden Sharp, son of the Pirate King. She let her hand fall limply to her side. Had she somehow misread his feelings?

"I didn't think—"

"No," he said, "you didn't."

Frustration flared, cold and bright in her stomach. "You know, Raiden, I'm trying to see things from your point of view, but I can't get my head that far up my arse!" she snapped.

He froze.

"Say that again."

Celeste's anger faltered. "I—I'm trying to see your point of view, but—"

"No," he said. "The part where you said *my name*."

"Raiden," she said, heart hammering. It was the first time she'd spoken his name in her voice. "*Raiden*, I'm trying—"

He crashed into her like gravity. Inevitable. And when his mouth met hers, she felt the stars fall from her skies. All her secrets were laid bare to him, and he'd accepted her as she was. His hands tangled in her silver hair and hers slid around his neck, pressing close. The kiss was passionate, hungry. There was no control. Kisses had never felt like this. This was passionate and wild and beautiful. This was *human*.

Above, stars streaked across the sky in great glittering arcs. It was as if the heavens themselves were timed with the sparks bursting within her chest as Raiden placed kisses along her jaw. He pinned her against the side of the ship, moved his arms around her. She knew he wouldn't let her fall. And if she did, they would fall together.

CHAPTER 35

When Celeste woke, she was smiling. The night had passed in seemingly endless kisses and conversation until Celeste's eyelids had drooped, and Raiden carried her to bed. Now she found herself in the captain's quarters, tucked between creamy pillows and soft blankets. No captain or dog in sight. With a happy sigh, Celeste stretched her arms above her head, wiggling her toes and soaking in the pleasure of a good night's rest. She felt lighter. As if her secrets had been weighing her down all this time. Across the room, she saw morning light, soft and pale, falling through the windows. How long had she been asleep? Sliding from the bed, she noticed her clothes were from the night before. She'd been so taken with sleep that her corset was still on. But it seemed Raiden had the kindness of removing her shoes. Those were placed neatly on a stool by the door. She padded over to them, shuffling them on before walking from the room to go look for her captain.

But he was not in the officers' dining room with the others. Nor was he on the deck or the navigation room. And so she headed down into the belly of the ship, excited to simply tell him good morning. Words that, until now, she hadn't been able to say. It was funny how such a simple thing sparked so much joy in her. And it was funnier how her heart fluttered at the memory of his lips against hers. His hands on her hips. His teeth on her neck.

A flush rose to her cheeks, and she picked up her pace.

Perhaps she would surprise him with a kiss.

Or a hundred.

Celeste took the stairs two at a time until she reached the cargo hold. She hadn't been here since her first week, when she was given a tour. Spare sails and rigging lined the walls, perfectly organized by Bastian, but no Raiden. She continued through the rooms, searching until she reached the tall and heavy door to the brig. When Kiyami had given the tour, she hadn't gone inside, but she figured she'd at least take a glance, as she was running out of places to look.

Memories of her time in the human prison filled her mind as she stepped inside, but for once they did not topple her. And the brig wasn't as she expected. A long hallway with four small barred rooms, two on each side, reeked of stale, wet air. She knew without a doubt that Valencia, that witch of a woman, had probably kept loads of prisoners here. On the wall, a ring of thick keys hung, old and black, the metal matching the bars on the cells. She continued down the hall, each step echoing dully through the room. *He wasn't here either*, she thought with a sigh as she reached the final cell.

And then Celeste screamed. The unearthly sound poured out of her, but it felt as if it came from someone else. When it stopped, she was left with nothing but emptiness.

"Maeve," she gasped, falling to her knees before the motionless cecaelia with cerulean hair. Celeste reached through the bars for her friend. A net twisted across her body, wound too tight and pressing into her once beautiful magenta skin, which was now tinted green. It was as if Maeve had been left to writhe within it.

"No..." Celeste said. "Please, no." This couldn't be real.

On unsteady legs, she rushed to get the keys. When she returned, Maeve hadn't moved. *No... no, no, no.* Fingers trembling, she tried each one in the lock. This couldn't be happening. This couldn't be real.

At last the lock opened with a click, and Celeste flung open the door, rushing to Maeve's side. The siren's body was ice-cold and unmoving. Little impressions from the net were left on her once firm and strong tentacles like bruises. And the gills along her throat lay still.

This was real.

And Raiden knew. *He knew she was a siren.* How long had Maeve been down here? Had she been sent as a Chorus scout? If so, where was her second? And when had this happened? Why hadn't Celeste heard about it? The ship was so small. Someone would have mentioned it.

Unless their captain told them not to.

And with that thought, she was undone. She had begun to think of this crew as *family*.

Celeste pulled her knife from her belt and began cutting the net away one rope at a time. Her movements were wild, unhinged.

Heavy footsteps sounded on the floorboards in the hall.

"Celeste!" an achingly familiar voice called out. "Celeste, where are you?"

Raiden.

The way he said her name sounded like a song, as it always did. But now it filled her with rage. It was only then that Celeste noticed she was sobbing. And then he was there in the doorway, his tall frame casting a shadow over her. She watched him as his expression turned from one of concern to one of horror and then... fear.

He was *afraid* of her.

And that hit her like a dagger to the heart.

"*Why...*" It was the only thing she could say.

"She would have told the sirens we were here," he said slowly. "I couldn't let that happen."

Celeste's sorrow sharpened to a point. "When."

"A couple of days ago. You went to bed early."

Her eyes squeezed shut. *A couple of days.* That meant... she was just upstairs. When they were dancing... drinking... celebrating... *kissing...* Maeve was here. Alone, scared, and imprisoned.

Celeste's felt as though she might be sick.

Raiden crossed the threshold, reaching for her, but she pushed him away. Hard. His back collided with the doorway with a thud.

"How could you?" Tears rolled down her face. "How *could* you!"

Memories flashed across her mind. Maeve and her sneaking out to train. Sharing secrets. Complaining about Madam Auralia. How Maeve began to drift away. How it hurt. How it pained her to watch the last person she felt she could be at least *most* of herself with slip away. Of course, Maeve never understood why Celeste was so sensitive. But there were still the late nights talking about what life would be like when they were members of the Chorus.

They will sing songs of us for generations! The day the human prince was lured to his doom by the Chorus and their princess.

"You knew..." She was shouting now. "You *knew* what I am, and you did this!"

"I did what I had to do to protect us," the captain insisted.

Footsteps sounded in the hall. But Celeste didn't care. She couldn't think.

"She is my *friend!*" Celeste bellowed, pulling Maeve's limp body into her arms.

Raiden's eyes went wide, just as Bastian rounded the corner, Kiyami, Torben, and Nasir following close behind.

"Is everything okay, Captain? We heard shouting..." Bastian started, then stopped when he took in the scene. His eyes went from Maeve's half-squid body in Celeste's arms to Raiden in the doorway. But he didn't look surprised.

"You told *him*," Celeste's voice broke.

Kiyami's mouth fell open, and Celeste realized what she'd done. But she didn't have time to explain herself.

"Of course he did," Bastian spat, venom Celeste could have never expected rising to the surface. "But not until after we captured this one. Raiden knew I wouldn't let you on the ship if I knew. I figured it out. How you knew about the current. Why I didn't remember anything from that night."

"But I saved you," she said.

"And left our crew to drown!"

"Then why didn't you just kill me too?" Celeste said, tears spilling down her cheeks.

"Because we *needed* you," Bastian said. "We can't get to the island without the help of a siren. Without you, we would have died like the others."

It was as if he had slapped her.

"You used me," she said, her eyes turning to Raiden. "You—"

"My father gave me a suicide mission," Raiden said, his expression unreadable. "A mission I couldn't refuse. It was a punishment for letting Valencia get the better of me. Succeed or die. And I failed. Failed and didn't even have the decency to die with my crew. You saved me. A siren. And then, just when I was losing hope... there you were again in that cell—"

"You brought us on a *suicide mission*?" Kiyami cut in, fury on her face. "What about us, Rai? *What about my family?*"

He turned to look at her but said nothing.

"You told me this job would set me up for life! That I could retire after this. If I die, my family... they'll be left with *nothing*!" She looked as though she was about to spring at him, but she stopped when Torben put a hand on her arm.

"You kept this from us. Fed us lies," Nasir said, his gaze holding none of the warmth Celeste had come to know in it. Her heart cracked at the sound.

They stared at their captain, but his eyes were only on Celeste. Jaw tight. "I didn't have a choice," was all he said.

"So everything was a lie," Celeste said, her voice cold.

"Not everything," Raiden said, although his voice did not soften. It was as if he always knew this was coming, "I didn't *intend* for anything to happen between us."

Her chest hurt. "But you certainly used it to your advantage," Celeste said.

Once more, he said nothing.

A crack formed within Celeste, her trust fracturing. She was foolish. Foolish for trusting a human. Foolish for thinking she could stop this silent war between their kinds. Sirens may be cold and emotionless, but they were *honest*. They didn't toy with feelings like some sick game, using them like pieces. How could she have been so naive? To fall in love with this man. And he had played his part beautifully. The tragic Prince of Pirates. How much of what he told her was just to get her to feel for him? To help him?

And she'd fallen for it. *Fallen for him.*

Pain ripped through her, greater than any wound. She tilted her head back, releasing a horrible keening sound. She couldn't control anything anymore. All the rage and fear and horror came flooding out all at once, darkening the air around them.

And suddenly she was a child again.

A child learning that her grandmother had been killed by humans. The one after whom she'd been named. Celeste. Child of the stars. She had wailed then too.

The sound of her cries filled the cell, echoing off metal and wood and water. It vibrated, shifted, grew. Until one by one the crew crumpled to the floor, their bodies falling like stones. Just like before. Just like every other time she'd lost control.

But Raiden remained upright. He did not so much as flinch as he watched her, pain painted on his beautiful face. The cry died in her throat as she looked down at Maeve and saw the darkness pooling around her on the floor. This, too, had happened before... but... not like this. She had always been in the water before, assumed it was the water's color changing. It'd never been like this. *Like... shadow?*

"You've always been full of surprises," Raiden said.

She ignored him, placing a hand atop Maeve's heart. Beneath her fingers, she felt it.

A weak heartbeat.

She lifted her chin and met his eyes, hatred burning in her gaze.

"Get out of my way," she said, her voice low.

"No."

She did not ask a second time. Celeste pulled Torben's knife from her waist and launched herself from the floor.

He saw her coming. With one smooth motion, his hand caught her wrist and twisted, pinning the knife against her back. Celeste swore and struggled, but his grip tightened. He shook her, trying to get her hand to drop the weapon. *Once again your emotions got the better of you, Celeste*, she thought bitterly. *They made you weak. Sloppy.*

But then a new voice spoke.

No... I'm not.

It was quiet at first but spoke again. Louder.

I'm not weak.

She gazed upon the unconscious bodies of her friends around her. *I'm sorry*, she thought. *I'm sorry. I'm sorry.*

Then she curled her free hand into a fist and swung it backward.

Right into his manhood.

Raiden crumpled to the floor with a groan. It would only distract him momentarily, but it was enough. She ran to Maeve, scooping her limp body into her arms. Her thighs screamed as she stood, trying to adjust the weight of her friend in her arms. But Celeste was strong enough. She had to be. Long tentacles dragged against the floor as Celeste sprinted from the brig, slamming the door behind her with her foot. She raced to the stairs, taking them two at a time. Each step was clumsy, slow. Celeste had just reached the top of the deck when she heard the door below slam open.

"Celeste! Wait!"

The captain was coming.

"Maeve, wake up," Celeste whimpered.

She heaved the cecaelia onto her shoulder, staggering to the side of the ship. The same place where she had stood just last night. The place where his body pressed her into the railing.

"Maeve, *please*. Please wake up. Please, Maeve," she repeated, her voice raw.

She couldn't throw Maeve overboard like this. Anything could happen to her in the ocean. But despite her pleas, her friend did not wake. Did not move in her arms. Footsteps pounded against the stairs.

They were out of time.

With a cry, Celeste bent her knees, and with all the strength she could muster, she flung Maeve's body overboard.

"No!" Raiden cried.

For a moment, the cecaelia looked serene. Her purple tentacles waved gently as she plummeted through the air. And then her body hit the waves with a deafening crash. Celeste swung a leg over the banister as a pair of hands clamped down on her shoulders, dragging her backward.

"Let me go!" Celeste cried, thrashing like a caged animal.

Raiden said nothing as he struggled with her, pulling her away from the side of the ship. Away from Maeve.

Shouts sounded on the stairs. The others had awoken. Bastian reached the decks first, his face contorted with rage. Behind him, the others blinked warily in the daylight, groggy and concerned. Celeste twisted in Raiden's grip until she could face him. She wanted to see him. See the look in his eyes. But he refused to meet her gaze.

"Please," she sobbed, hope withering inside her. "Raiden, please let me go."

"Put her in the brig," Raiden said to Bastian, voice tight. "We still need her in case there's any surprises waiting for us on the island. I'm not taking any chances. Torben, help him."

Torben didn't move.

"That's an order," Raiden snapped.

With a shake of his head, Torben obeyed.

The last shred of hope in these humans shattered within her as they pulled her farther and farther from the banister. From Maeve. Of course it ended like this. Why did she ever believe they could really care about her? A siren?

The men walked her toward the stairs, Nasir and Kiyami watching with quiet horror. *They must think I'm a monster*, she thought, fresh tears filling her eyes. Each step was agony as they retraced her journey back to the brig. They walked her into the very cell she had found Maeve in just moments before. It felt like a dream. A nightmare. And when she awoke, she'd be back in the captain's bed, waking from what she had thought was the best night of her life.

When they let go, she didn't move. It was as if the light had died from within her.

And when they gagged and bound her, she let them.

CHAPTER 36

Celeste sank to the dirty cell floor.

There was no way out. She had betrayed her people at every turn.

She leaned her back against the cold metal bars, trying to find a comfortable position with her rope-bound hands behind her back. The bars surrounded her on three sides, while the fourth was the wooden side of the ship. What little light there was came from a small window at the far end of the hall, which grew brighter and dimmer as the day wore on. Time slipped through her fingers as she sat alone. Her mind felt as though it were stuck in a whirlpool, spinning around and around. Coming up with nothing new. At some point, the tears stopped, and when they did, she laid down on the floor, curling in on herself. Lonely didn't seem to capture what she was feeling. Nor did the word *lost* ... but the two combined came close. There was an ache inside her that grew and grew with each memory that arose, each treasured moment upon the *Red Revenge* that turned acrid now.

She wasn't sure how much time had passed when she heard footfalls in the hall.

Captain Raiden Sharp appeared in the doorway, a shadow

blotting out the light in his long black coat and leather gloves. A sword gleamed at his hip. His mouth was a hard line as he opened her cell door and entered, gaze falling upon the crumpled siren on the floor. Celeste's body tensed as if waiting for another blow.

"I never meant for this to happen," he said, removing her gag.

She squeezed her eyes shut as another wave of pain hit her in the chest. *Don't cry. Don't let him see you cry.* But she never had been able to stop herself, and today was not the day she would start. Hot tears pooled in her eyes and slipped down her face, dripping onto the floor.

"If you didn't help us, we would have died. All of us. Even if the sirens didn't kill us . . . my father would have. For failing him."

"You could have told me," Celeste said, voice faltering. She finally turned to look at him, but it was a mistake. His hair was tousled, the way it always was when he was running his hands through it over and over. A habit that had once been dear to her.

"You wouldn't have helped if you knew."

"I would have," she said.

And it was true.

Another piece of her heart broke at the realization. She would have done anything for him. *And she had.* She'd revealed herself as a siren to a human, breaking the treaty between siren kingdoms. She spared him and doomed herself to never return home to Staria. And last, she revealed siren secrets to lead him straight to a sacred island.

Raiden went silent. For a moment, the only sound in the room was the soft hiss of the ocean waves hitting the side of the ship. Her thoughts strayed once again to Maeve. If she survived, would she come back for her? Did she even know Celeste was on this ship? *Did anyone even care?* It wasn't as if a siren would be able to board the ship and rescue her. If the Chorus returned to this ship, it would be to sink it. No, Celeste was trapped. And even if she were able to escape, where would she go? She had no one. Belonged nowhere. She wasn't even a siren anymore. She had sold that part of herself to the Sea Witch.

Raiden looked as though he wished to say something else, but instead he turned and exited the cell, closing the door behind him with a clang. But just before he left the hall, he paused.

"We only need you a little longer," he said. "Once we reach the island and get what we need, you will be free to go."

Celeste awoke to the sound of soft voices.

After Raiden had gone, the day had passed sluggishly. No one else visited her. Pitiful sobbing gave way to white-hot anger, first at Raiden and then herself. Eventually, she fell asleep. But she slept horribly. Tossing and turning, despite how weary she was from the past week of little to no sleep. And the cycle would begin again, fresh tears. Fresh hatred. Like a scab that she'd pick off again and again as it healed. It wasn't until night had fallen that she had finally settled into some semblance of rest.

But it hadn't lasted long.

Raiden's voice drifted to her, low and stern. "We will do no such thing."

"Why not? She's a siren, Rai. Would you rather go in there blind?" Bastian replied. "What if there are traps? Enchantments? It can't hurt to question her. We don't even know what it looks like."

Raiden, as was his new habit, fell silent. She could picture him, his dark eyes hard and his full lips flattened into a line. "We can't risk her knowing," he said at last.

Bastian's voice grew louder, more frustrated. "Why?" Then he paused, the sound of shifting feet. "You know we can't let her go after this, Raiden. She's too dangerous."

"Fine," Raiden said through his teeth. "You go right ahead. Ask her about the Voice of the Ocean. See what happens."

Bastian fell silent. And Celeste's world tilted on its axis.

The Voice of the Ocean.

The legendary power of the Goddess herself.

That was what they were searching for? All this time she thought it was treasure the Pirate King wanted. But no. Of course not. *He wanted control over the ocean itself.* But the Voice of the Ocean had been lost for centuries. It was practically legend.

Much like the island of Lunapesce.

Celeste racked her brain for any knowledge of the Voice of the Ocean, but she knew so little. It was said that the Voice was the final gift passed from the Goddess to one of her daughters. Any who possessed the Voice of the Ocean would have the power to control the sea. The Voice could sink cities.

She couldn't let them find it.

The sound of two pairs of retreating footsteps sounded upon the stairs, signaling the departure of the two men.

Once she was certain they had gone, Celeste sat up and took stock of her surroundings. As Bastian had said, it wasn't as if they were planning to let her go when things were finished, despite what Raiden said to the contrary. As if she'd believe a single word out of his mouth now. No, they'd surely kill her when she was no longer useful. They'd be fools not to.

A darkened, empty room greeted her. There was not even a chair or chamber pot. The only thing she found was a piece of bread, set just outside the bars where she could reach. She took it, suddenly hungry, and devoured it in seconds.

But she found no means of escape.

They still hadn't reached the island. It was more than likely they'd need her at some point to help. She'd just have to bide her time until an opportunity presented itself.

Feeling a small semblance of herself returning, Celeste laid down upon the floor to try to let sleep take her once again.

It was still night when a clanging sound sent her bolt upright on the dirty floor. Her eyes, still more siren than human, saw what it was right away.

Or, more accurately, *who.*

Kiyami stood before her, holding keys. The door was open.

"Celeste," she said, voice cracking. "Oh, Celeste, I'm so sorry. Are you okay?" Tears streamed down her face as she fell to her knees. "I should have stood up for you. Everything happened so fast. I had no idea you were a—I saw them capture the siren—your—*friend*, and I thought they t-told you." Her body shook in Celeste's arms as it all came pouring out of her. "I didn't even *believe* in sirens until I saw her, and she was writhing and looked so very monstrous. But when I saw you with her—everything felt so *wr-wrong*." Her hands shook as they unbound Celeste. "Raiden said we still need you, to be sure there's nothing on the island that we're not prepared for but—but I *couldn't*—I couldn't l-leave you here."

"It's okay," Celeste said, pulling Kiyami into her arms. "It's okay."

She had never seen Kiyami cry before. Not like this. In fact, she had never seen *anyone* cry like this before. And although it broke her heart to see Kiyami hurting, there was something wonderful in it too. In some ways, Kiyami had given her a gift. A gift of her vulnerability. And for the first time, Celeste got to see from the other side.

And the tears did not make Kiyami weak, in her eyes.

The human girl pulled away, cheeks shining softly in the moonlit room. "I waited until the captain was asleep, and I stole the keys," she said quickly, gripping Celeste's hands. "We don't have much time. I need to get back to the wheel before anyone notices I've gone."

In a moment, Kiyami was on her feet, pulling Celeste with her.

"What if he finds out you did it?" the siren protested, taking a step back. "You could risk your chance to help your family."

Kiyami smiled, if a bit sadly. "I'll figure something else out," she said, shrugging. "If I left you here, I—I'd never forgive myself. You're my family too, Cel."

Celeste gave her a watery smile. "And you're mine."

Hand in hand, the two crept swiftly through the belly of the ship, avoiding every creaky floorboard on their way up the stairs and past the room of sleeping crew. It was a special sort of bittersweet to know this would be the last time she would see the *Red Revenge*. Despite everything, it was a place she had just started to consider home. With a pang, she realized she wouldn't get the chance to say goodbye to the Admiral.

As they stepped out onto the deck, Celeste once more felt the soothing touch of salty wind against her face. She would miss this. Miss the ship rocking beneath her feet and the wind in her hair. The sun on her face. The feeling of rope in her hands. It was the last night before the eclipse, the moon full in the sky. Dawn would come too soon.

Kiyami drew her into a fierce hug.

"May our God keep you until we meet again," she whispered into her hair.

"No siren swims alone who has family," Celeste replied. "Until the tides turn."

They parted, and Celeste laughed lightly, seeing Kiyami's eyes glistening with tears, for there were tears in her own eyes as well.

"We should hurry," Kiyami said, squeezing Celeste's hand and pushing her toward the lifeboat. Celeste nodded, realizing with a twist in her gut that she'd still need to see the Sea Witch to get her fins back. Perhaps then she'd be able to swim home and warn her mother about the king's plan to steal the Voice of the Ocean.

Kiyami pulled at the ropes that lowered the lifeboat toward the dark waters below. It dropped slowly. Inch by inch.

"Wait."

The word did not come from Kiyami.

Celeste turned her head to see the captain, frozen at the top of the ship's stairs. His chest was heaving up and down, and there was panic in his eyes, as if he had been running. Perhaps he had gone to check on her and found the cell empty.

"Go, Celeste!" Kiyami said, her hand finding the hilt of her sword.

But the lifeboat was nowhere near the water. She'd have to cut it free. Celeste's hand went to her hip, but her knife was gone.

How could she have forgotten? They'd taken it from her when they bound her.

Just like they'd taken everything.

"I want to call in the favor I won from you," Raiden said.

Celeste met the captain's fierce gaze. But he didn't look like Captain Raiden Sharp. He was just Raiden. A cloud passed over the stars, blotting them from the sky.

"Name it," she said.

"Stay." His face was open, vulnerable. It wasn't a demand, but a request. A hope. "Please," he added, his voice breaking.

Strong winds blew. The sails flapped. Celeste stared, unable to move beneath the gaze of the one who betrayed her. The man she loved.

"I told you," she said, her heart breaking, "it has to be something in my power."

And then she dove overboard.

Raiden's face appeared at the banister, watching from above as she dove. With an inhuman grace, Celeste arched her back, bringing her hands up over her head into a perfect line. The waves grew closer and closer, as if rushing to welcome her. And then her body sliced through the water, as it had a thousand times before. And suddenly her time on the ship felt like a dream. A dream from which she was finally waking up.

But her lungs were human lungs. Her legs were human legs. When she surfaced, she couldn't make out his expression. Couldn't tell if his cries were in sorrow or rage. She held her breath as she put as much distance between her and the ship as possible.

Celeste swam quickly. Much quicker than any human, but not even a quarter of the speed of the siren she once was. To keep out of sight, she swam beneath the water as much as possible. Even so, she had to surface every few minutes for air, risking one gasping breath before diving back down beneath the safety of the waves. If they could capture Maeve, they could surely catch her.

But no nets were cast nor harpoons shot.

He let me go. The thought came unbidden, and at once she cast it aside. *It doesn't matter if he did.* Soon she was far enough from the ship that she felt safe to surface. And so she did, white hair clinging to the sides of her face as she bobbed with the waves. Through the darkness, she could still make out the ship, sailing toward the horizon.

Now what?

It wasn't as if she could go looking for Maeve. If her friend were alive, she'd be on her way to Staria right now, and if she wasn't—well, there was nothing Celeste could do to help her. They were nearly a day's journey from where Maeve went overboard.

There were too many wrongs Celeste wished she could make right. Too many mistakes. Too many failures. She had trusted a human and now paid the price. And soon, so would all sirens. The King of Pirates was planning something. She didn't know what, but she knew if he had the power of the ocean at his fingertips . . . there was no telling what he could do. And she had guided him straight to it.

But there was still hope. They didn't know how to get on the island. It was a legendary place of the gods. It wasn't as though one could simply dock their ship on it. There would be magic protecting that island. Ancient magic.

Still, it was possible the king already knew a way in. She couldn't assume the island was safe. *I shouldn't have jumped off the ship*, Celeste thought bitterly. *I should have just thrown Raiden overboard.*

But she couldn't change what she'd done. Now she had to focus on finding a way to stop the humans from getting the Voice of the Ocean. Trying to stop the ship itself was out of the question. Her voice was not strong enough alone to lure the entire crew into the water. And Raiden was somehow impervious. *I should go back to Staria*, she told herself, turning in the direction of home. But would they even listen to her? And Staria was so far. She'd never get there in time.

I am too human, she thought angrily, kicking her legs. *I can't do this.* At her best, she wasn't the best soldier. At her strongest, she wasn't the strongest singer. She wasn't wise and calm like Sephone or strong and decisive like Shye. Even in those few moments when her powers had been remarkable she couldn't *control* them. She didn't even *understand* them.

But she *was* the only one who knew what the humans had planned.

And right now that had to be enough.

If I could just beat them to the island... maybe I could grab the Voice and leave before they arrive. The thought energized her, even if it was only a half-baked plan. Celeste looked above her to the stars. The thin clouds that had been covering them slid by to reveal the four daughters watching over her. She oriented herself, turning to face the direction she knew the island to be. And then she dove into the water. She scanned the sea below, hoping to find some passing creature to help tow her, but saw nothing. Unfortunately, a siren couldn't sing and have an animal come running. A Song was intended for a specific target, a bond between the singer and listener. It was not a net to be cast.

And so she began to swim.

CHAPTER 37

I will make things right.

The words formed a rhythm in her head as she swam. One stroke, then the next. *I will make things right. I will make things right.* She cut through the water smoothly, her legs pounding behind her as one. For the first time in weeks, she missed her tail. Missed its shimmering ice-blue scales and delicate translucent fins. And, of course, she missed the speed. If only she had found a way to call the Sea Witch to her. How foolish she had been when striking that deal. How was she to ever to find the Sea Witch again? Swim back to the Wasting Waters? As a human? She'd never be able to swim that deep.

But she could only deal with one mistake at a time.

The sun rose over the water, washing the sky in gold as it made its way toward the full moon. She could still see the ship, a tiny speck just on the horizon. *Come on . . .* she told herself as the day slipped by.

You have to swim faster.

There is no one else.

But her human body was sluggish, and she began to slow. Her breath came in heaving gasps. She would never reach the island first. She probably wouldn't reach the island at all.

The water no longer felt like home. Its salty waves did not feel safe or welcoming. They pushed against her, fighting her every stroke. She dove yet again, scanning to see if there were any animals she could sing to her side. All that she found was an endless expanse of clear turquoise water.

She pressed on, but her body was fading quickly. Each stroke was a battle now. If she kept pushing, she would drown.

Celeste was out of options.

Even if there was nothing to hear her, she had to try.

Celeste slowed to a stop. With a deep breath, she filled her burning lungs. The voice that came out of her was ethereal, haunting. She sang the Song the Chorus had taught her: the Song for controlling the mind.

From deep within the ocean, we sisters rise in song.

Her voice slid from note to note, circling her in a wave of sound. But there was something wrong in the noise. Like a hand that reached out for someone and found only air. Celeste sang louder, turning slowly in a circle and beckoning with her arms.

Come closer. Hear us calling. In our arms you belong.

The Song came out strained as her frustration grew. *Perhaps singing underwater would help?* She continued, diving beneath the waves.

Come rest your weary bones, love. Come join us in the sea.

Let the gentle waves consume you, for your heart belongs to me.

Singing underwater felt uncomfortable, unnatural, in a way it never had before. The vibrations did not move through the water, but instead felt as though it stopped short mere inches from her face. The realization stung—another part of herself she sacrificed to the Sea Witch. She continued in vain, the breath in her lungs diminishing quickly.

I'll fulfill your every longing.
I am everything you crave.

And still, she saw nothing. No creatures came to her. And when the need for air became too great, she surfaced with a gasp.

Let me kiss away your sorrows as I lay you in your grave.

She blinked the water from her eyes. The ship was no longer in sight.

No...

Celeste let out a cry of anger. *No... no... no... no...*

She thought of her family in Staria. Of her promise to her mother. Of Maeve. Of her grandmother, slain by King Leonidas. Of Kiyami, who risked her family's well-being to set Celeste free. Angry tears filled her eyes, blurring her vision. She slammed her fist into the water, sending up a splash.

This can't be it. It can't be over.

Tears fell in waves down her cheeks. She let them fall. She did not turn the anger on herself, molding it once more into a weapon meant to punish. No, instead Celeste allowed herself this moment. For once she let herself release the fury and sadness and frustration that she kept bottled up within her. She embraced the fear, the brokenheartedness, the disappointment. Everything she had pressed back for so long. Everything that, despite her best efforts, she'd never been able to control like others seemed to do. She let herself feel. Everything. And the emotions rolled through her like a storm, rumbling, clapping, shifting into shaking sobs.

I'm not strong enough alone... but I've come so far.

With every tear that rolled down her face, she let go a little more. She mourned for herself. The death of the siren she had wanted to be. The soldier. The princess. The daughter. The pirate. As much as she had wished she didn't feel this way, that she did not feel overwhelmed and helpless and afraid, these feelings were a part of her. No matter how hard she tried to ignore them, they were still there, shouting to be heard.

So, for the first time, she listened.

Listened to the feelings as they passed through her one after another. Listened to the betrayal and the sorrow and the shame. Listened until only a few remained, like stones in her throat.

Her mother's voice: *I can't talk to you when you're like this.*

Madam Auralia: *You're overreacting, girl! Get up and do the exercise.*

She was thirteen again, tears filling her eyes as she began to hyperventilate. It was just another drill. It shouldn't have been hard. But for some reason, her body felt weak, and she wanted a break. And initiates did not get breaks. Celeste hadn't known how to form the words to ask for what she needed. She didn't believe she would have received it if she had tried. And so instead... she'd cried.

Why don't you calm down a bit, dear?

This last one was a surprise. A memory eroded with time, like a portrait beneath the sea. Celeste was six and had been singing at the top of her lungs at their dining table. Not magic, just a melody she'd heard from a storyteller. Until her father told her she was too loud. Her song stopped in her throat, shame heating the back of her neck.

Celeste saw herself, small and shushed, and her heart broke. She was often chided for being too loud. Even in joy, there were limits to how sirens were allowed to celebrate.

But the song. The song she'd been singing. She hadn't heard it in *so long*. Another memory floated to her mind: Her grandmother Celeste singing to Sephone and her. A simple melody. A lullaby. Otherworldly, yet familiar as the moon.

Celeste's tears stopped.

She closed her eyes and began to sing along.

Once there was darkness
before there was light.
The world lay embraced by shadows.

The song moved through her as water, filling every part until it came spilling out, taking her feelings with it.

She who ruled darkness
would sing through the night.
Till one day another listened.

The melody was as old as time. It thrummed through her. Pulsing.

For him, she gifted
the moon in the sky,
so its pale face could reflect him.

The sea around her shook and rose, higher and higher. Celeste's eyes blinked open in surprise, but she did not stop singing. Her insatiable curiosity felt too strong.

As one they counted
each bright star up high,
lighting their way to each other.

Something moved far beneath in the sea. Then a huge wave rose before her, higher and higher, until she was certain it would crash, pulling her under. And yet she continued the song. This fear, too, she poured into it, letting it wash from her.

Daughter above us,
protect those we love.

Welcome us into your shadows.
She who rules darkness,
we sing to you still.
In starlight, we find our way home.

With a roar, the wave split apart, and a great, dripping creature emerged. Deep blue scales on its sides glittered in the early light of dawn. It tossed its majestic head, crowned with one long fin extending down its neck. Its nostrils flared. With large, soft eyes, the midnight blue of the purest ocean, the creature blinked at her under long, thick lashes. Celeste gasped in awe as she recognized it. A creature of myth that she thought only existed in statues with the Goddess or carved into the walls of buildings.

Girl and beast stared at each other in silence. It was said the Hippokamp was as old as the sea itself, created by the Goddess to pull her starlit chariot. Towering above her, it was certainly big enough. The Hippokamp pawed at the water impatiently with one long, muscled leg that ended in a fin. Everything about the creature was breathtaking. Celeste marveled at how much it reminded her of the human horses she'd seen on land, with its long neck and two front legs. In place of back legs, it had a long, curling tail, like a siren. She reached out her hand to it, and the beast lowered its nose to her touch, nuzzling.

A smile pulled at the corners of her lips as she stroked along its muzzle. The scales along its face were surprisingly soft, still slick with water. It pulled back, pawing at the water again, as if chiding her.

"You're right," she said, already wishing she had more time to unravel this mysterious creature. "Let's go."

Celeste swam around to the side of the great sea creature and prepared to mount, like she'd seen the humans do. But the Hippokamp did not have a flat back. Its hips connected in one elegant line to its tail, leaving no easy spot for her to sit upon.

"You didn't think to bring the chariot too?" she asked, only half joking.

The Hippokamp gave an annoyed snort.

"Sorry . . ." She sighed, throwing both legs over the creature's back. She looped her arms around its neck and squeezed her legs together.

"Take me to the island," she said.

With a booming neigh, the great beast took off across the water.

Celeste had used animals for transport before. Dolphins, whales, and even the occasional shark, when sung into submission, could help sirens traverse great distances. But nothing compared to this. The Hippokamp beat its tail through the water at an alarming pace. Wind whipped through her silver hair, drowning out all sound. She'd expected such a beautiful creature to have a smooth gait, like glass, but it wasn't. It rode wildly. Untamed. But they joined into a rhythm together. And above them, the summer sun burned punishingly as it slid across the sky toward the rising moon.

Before long she saw the *Red Revenge*, a black mark on the horizon. She leaned forward, pressing her body against the Hippokamp's neck so she could be heard over the howl of the winds.

"Don't let them see us," she warned.

The Hippokamp let out a sudden force of breath through its nose, as if in understanding. As they drew closer, it reared back and dove beneath the clear blue water. Celeste hardly had time to suck in a breath before they were submerged. Her eyes squeezed shut against the rush of water. She tightened her grip on the Hippokamp. After a somewhat excruciating minute, when she could hold her breath no longer, Celeste tapped on the side of the Hippokamp's neck. At once the beast rose, but only enough for the siren to stick her head above water and gasp before they plunged again.

The journey continued like this. The sensation of racing through the water was so overwhelming she could think of little else. It was hard to gauge how long they swam, how far they'd gone, or even if they'd passed the ship.

At last the Hippokamp broke through the surface and did not submerge again. Celeste blinked open her eyes, disoriented. The *Red Revenge* was nowhere to be seen. Above, the moon slid forward, darkening the edge of the sun. On they swam, until for no discernible reason the Hippokamp slowed to a stop.

Arms loosening, Celeste looked around.

And found nothing.

No island or land broke the endless blue.

"Do you need a break?" Celeste asked, stroking the creature's neck with her hand as she scanned the sea around them. But the Hippokamp did not seem tired or out of breath, despite the long ride. If anything, it looked annoyed. Celeste rubbed her hands against her hips. "I don't think this is the place—unless—"

She fell silent, listening. The sound of the Hippokamp's breath, low and steady, came first. Then the gentle sound of the wind, sweeping along the water around her. But after—after there was something else. A third sound. A melody so quiet one could almost believe it was an invention of the mind. A trick of the sea.

Lunapesce. It was there, calling to her. And yet she saw nothing.

Of course, she thought, remembering. *The island can only be accessed during a solar eclipse. When the sun and moon meet in the sky.*

"Don't suppose you know the way in?" Celeste asked the beast beneath her.

The Hippokamp turned its head to look at her with one withering eye.

"Right." She sighed, watching the sun's reflection in the water. With the moon covering half of it, it was crescent-shaped. And each moment brought the full eclipse closer. Time was running out.

Perhaps she should have listened better during lessons about the Goddess and her history. Maybe then she would know what to do. But after a moment, an idea came to her. Perhaps her grandmother's song would work here as well? It was better than nothing. She took in a deep breath and let the music pour from her.

Once there was darkness
before there was light.
The world lay embraced by shadows.

She scanned the waters around her and saw no change. But something in her urged her to keep going, and without any better ideas, she continued.

She who ruled darkness
would sing through the night.
Till one day another listened.

The Hippokamp let out a snort of frustration. Celeste sighed and stopped singing.

"Well? I'm singing the song! Why isn't it working?"

As expected, the great beast had no insight.

What was different last time? What did I do to call the Hippokamp? I was crying... I don't think tears are going to help. But as she thought those words, she stopped. The tears *had* helped. They helped her feel better, even if only a little. But it wasn't as though she could cry on command. Not to mention she found it highly unlikely the Goddess, creator of sea and night, would make crying a requirement to enter the sacred island. So if it wasn't the crying, perhaps it was... the feeling? Right now all Celeste felt was afraid. She was wasting time. Her thoughts went to her kingdom. The sirens living there. What would happen to them if the king got ahold of the Goddess's power?

So she tried once more, pouring emotion into it. The raw beating heart of herself.

Once there was darkness
before there was light.
The world lay embraced by shadows.

The song built within her, gathering up yellow fear swirling in her gut like poison. She filled with song and feeling until she overflowed.

Suddenly, the water grew frenzied, thrashing and churning. Beneath her, the Hippokamp remained strangely calm. The sun slid behind the moon, and the world plunged into darkness. A great swirling hole opened in front of her as she continued the song, using all the remaining power within her.

She who ruled darkness
would sing through the night.
Till one day another listened.

The music echoed around her as though the very ocean itself had joined her in song. The spinning water faltered, dropping several feet. Far below, the earth shook.

Then, up through the eye of the whirlpool, the sacred island of Lunapesce emerged.

CHAPTER 38

Earth pressed upward, pushing apart the sea. Soft white beaches encircled a lush forest of perfect green. And in the center of it all, the tops of white stone arches extended from the treetops. A temple, perhaps? If it was, it looked as though it'd been built for giants. But what truly captured Celeste's attention were the specks of light floating among the trees, glittering like stars on earth.

Celeste gasped in awe as she beheld the island. Magic hummed in the air, old as night and as wild as the sea. She slipped from the back of the Hippokamp and swam around to face it.

"Thank you," she said, head bowed in respect.

The beast mirrored her, gently pressing its soft head to hers. Then it reared back and disappeared into the depths of the ocean. Celeste watched the frothing water before her, the only sign it'd been there at all—a stolen moment of reverence for the beautiful creature that saved her. The sky brightened, the moon sliding away from the sun as she turned back to face Lunapesce.

She dove into the water, swimming until her lungs burned and her feet touched the sandy bottom of the shore. The sand between her toes was the softest her feet had ever touched, each grain so perfectly fine and warmed from the sun. As she drew closer, she saw deep streams cutting through the island, intertwining with the land. *What did the Goddess of the Ocean need an island for anyway?* Celeste wondered, taking it all in. But Celeste could feel her here. Could picture the Goddess sunning herself upon the soft beach and playing with her daughters in the bubbling streams.

At last Celeste's feet sank into dry sand.

The sound came again. The song from before. Still faint, but unquestionably there. It called to her, beckoning from deep within the heart of the forest.

The Voice of the Ocean.

She knew at once what it was. The sound was heartbreaking in its beauty. Haunting and ethereal. And—familiar. As if she remembered it from a dream. But she was certain she had never heard this melody before. The song pulled with each note. And soon the sand beneath her feet turned to soft, mossy earth. This, too, was perfect. Everything about the island was. Achingly so. In all her life, she'd never see a place more beautiful. The late-afternoon sun shone through the forest canopy, shadow mixing with the glittering flecks of light floating within the trees around her. Flowers Celeste had never seen before bloomed white along the streambeds. She followed beside, winding through the forest toward the Voice. The trees were so dense, and she soon lost sight of the white shore. But the song grew louder with each step.

A clearing appeared through the trees. Within it, an ancient temple of elegant white columns stood, glistening in the sunlight. The stream she followed disappeared under the temple. In fact, it seemed every stream on the island disappeared there. Green vines curled around the columns' bottoms, and flowers bloomed through the cracks in the stone steps leading to the entrance, which she climbed one at a time, listening.

The song came from within.

Sending up a silent prayer, Celeste pushed against the colossal white doors. They opened easily under her touch. She stepped inside.

At the far side of the massive temple stood a statue of the Goddess. She was beautiful. Her chin tilted up in triumph toward the light pouring in from the open ceiling, covered in vines. She was crowned in stars, with her hair falling in waves down her naked back. Her powerful tail was coiled beneath her, and in her stone hands, she held her legendary golden trident, carved with swirling stars and inlaid with pearls. At the base of the statue, as if they were her guardians, were her two Hippokamps. Their bodies sat on either side of a waterfall, which cascaded down into a wide, deep pool that filled the center of the room.

The place where every stream on the island met.

And within the pool were two sirens, their voices rising together in perfect harmony.

One was old. Older than any siren Celeste had ever seen. Her skin and hair and tail were the pale green of seawater. But her eyes were as black as the darkest depths of the ocean. She had the scaled bodice of a siren from Staria, but she was so thin that Celeste could count each protruding rib. Hands like worn leather reached out and gripped the other siren at the wrists. That siren was young, her back to Celeste. Her long, slender fingers encircled the old siren's wrists, completing the bond between them. Long rose-colored hair cascaded down her back, falling into the water.

"No," Celeste breathed.

The noise startled the singers, who did not hear her enter. With a swish of her beautiful hair, the young siren turned around to gaze upon the intruder, leaving the song to echo half finished. And Celeste's gaze was met with the wide, stunned eyes of her sister, Sephone.

"What are you doing?" Sephone hissed. "You shouldn't be here."

Five cycles. It had been five cycles since she'd seen her. And now here of all places.

"*I* shouldn't be here?" Celeste said, voice echoing. "You're supposed to be in Ayakashi flirting with some prince!"

"You need to leave."

"Who is that?" Celeste asked, pointing toward the ancient siren.

"Who are you?" But the siren acted as though she didn't hear her, as if her mind was elsewhere.

"Why—why do you have *legs*?" Sephone said, a look of disgust plain on her face.

Celeste shifted from foot to foot, suddenly self-conscious. "It's a long story."

"How did you even get here with *those*?" Her sister gestured to Celeste's legs, wet pantaloons clinging to them.

"I—rode here," Celeste said, adding, "on a Hippokamp."

"You *what*?"

"We do not have much longer, Princess," the ancient siren said, pulling at Sephone's hands. "We must continue."

"Celeste, you must leave. I will explain later." Sephone's voice sounded so much like their mother that Celeste flinched. This wasn't the sister she remembered. The gentle one who listened when no one else would.

"I'm not leaving. Not without the Voice of the Ocean."

Sephone froze. "Why are you *really* here, little star?" she asked, voice soft.

Celeste sucked in a breath. "Humans are coming. King Leonidas wants the Voice for himself. They will be here any second. We need to get the Voice and leave before—"

"*Humans?*" Sephone's once glowing face went pale. "It's not possible."

"We can't leave before the ritual is complete," the ancient siren said.

"They just want the Voice," Celeste insisted. "If I can just leave with it, maybe—"

Sephone's eyes met Celeste's, and the rest of her sentence died in her throat.

No... It can't be...

"The Voice of the Ocean isn't a thing, Celeste," Sephone said. "It's a *siren*. It's me."

"No..." Celeste breathed.

It felt as though the ground beneath her was crumbling.

"I wanted to tell you! But Mother thought it would be safer if we kept it secret. No one could know." Sephone drew closer to Celeste at the edge of the pool. "She sent me away to train with Gala when they found out I was blessed with the Goddess's gifts. To protect me. And for me to learn to protect our people." She gestured toward the siren behind her. "Gala, our great-aunt, is the current Voice, but it's time for me to accept my full powers. And the only way is to complete the ritual that passes the full power of the Voice of the Ocean to me. The same ritual the Goddess performed when she first gifted her powers to her daughter, Queen Isla."

Queen Isla was the Voice of the Ocean? The founder of Staria? And this siren was their grandmother's sister? Celeste's head spun. Of course Sephone was blessed. Her magic was always extraordinary. And all this time... All this time Celeste thought she was hunting treasure. But it had been her sister all along.

And Celeste had led the humans straight to her.

Guilt twisted like a knife in her gut. "We *can't* stay here." Celeste's voice quavered. "The humans are on their way. They'll be here any moment."

"There is no way for humans to find this island, Celeste," Sephone said in that same reassuring tone she always used when Celeste was upset. "They wouldn't even make it through the siren waters undetected. The Chorus—"

"They did." Celeste looked down at her hands. "Because I showed them how."

The temple fell silent.

"You did what?" Sephone's voice was cold.

"I thought they were only after *treasure*. By the time I figured it out—it was too late." Celeste walked to pool's edge and knelt, reaching for her sister. But Sephone backed away, face stricken.

"*Humans*," spat Gala. "Greedy, horrible creatures."

"They're not all like that," Celeste snapped, unable to stop herself.

Sephone's face turned from shock to anger in a flash. "You're defending them? After what they did to our grandmother?"

"We've killed them too! Murdered them one by one!"

"Mother was right." Sephone sighed. "You're too softhearted. I'd hoped with time you would grow out of it, but..."

It felt as though she had been slapped. Celeste stood, angry tears springing to her eyes. Despite everything she had learned, in the face of her elder sister's condemnation, she felt small. There was nothing more painful than to hear the things you hated most about yourself used as a weapon by someone you love. Tears dripped down her cheeks, and Celeste furiously wiped them away with the back of her hand. *They talked about her.* Celeste had always thought Sephone was the one on her side. The only one who let Celeste cry. All along she'd been talking about Celeste with their mother.

But then she thought of Kiyami. The strongest female, siren or human, she had ever met. She thought of the tears running down Kiyami's face as she helped her escape. Her hand on the hilt of the sword as she faced their captain.

"I lived with them, the humans. I know them," Celeste said calmly, despite the tears.

At first Sephone looked surprised, but it was soon replaced by anger. "Why would you do such a thing? What were you thinking? Celeste, you could have exposed us all! *Is that why you look like one of them?*"

Celeste took a breath, attempting to center herself. "I saved a human from a Chorus attack. The son of King Leonidas. I meant to kill him and make it right, but I—I misjudged the prince. And then... he used me to find this place. To find *you*. But the rest of his crew, they're no different than you and me. I swear it. They're—they're my friends." As Celeste spoke, her tears subsided. Her voice grew more certain. "The prince wishes to take the Voice—you—to his father. I assume the Pirate King wants to control the ocean. Please, Seph, we need to—"

"If we leave these sacred grounds before the ritual is completed, the Goddess's gifts will be lost forever," Gala said evenly, swimming toward Sephone and resting a hand on her shoulder.

Sephone's face was hard. The perfect copy of their mother. "Even if the humans have made it this far. The island only reveals itself to the Song of a siren under an eclipse," Sephone said, a note of finality to her voice.

She rejoined the ancient siren, gripping her wrists. The two sirens began humming together, searching for a thread to continue their work. As they found their note, their voices changed, becoming the unearthly sound that had lured Celeste to them.

Footsteps sounded on the stone steps of the temple, clanging like a warning bell. Celeste turned, reaching for her knife, only to remember its loss. She sank into her familiar fighting stance, wishing she had a weapon. Wishing her sister had listened to her. Wishing she'd done things differently.

The singers' voices joined together and broke apart in a haunting harmony. The doors pushed open. A silhouette appeared against the late-day sun. The familiar figure stepped over the threshold of the temple and stopped.

"Hello again, Princess."

Her hands sagged. Standing before her was the Sea Witch.

CHAPTER 39

"What—what are you doing here?" Celeste demanded. *And why do you have legs?* Nerissa still looked the same. The same dark hair, inky-blue skin, and bioluminescent glow. Just with—*legs*. Celeste eyed them warily.

With a laugh, the Sea Witch held up her empty hands. "Looking for you," she said, taking two long strides into the room. It was strange to see her walk.

"Why?" Celeste said, raising her fists.

At this, Nerissa stopped moving forward and crossed her elegant arms over her chest. "To give a warning. I have an interest in you, Princess. Have you forgotten?"

Celeste grimaced. If it hadn't been for the dark stain of the crescent moon on her wrist, she might have. Behind them, the two sirens watched, silent and wary. Celeste glanced back at her sister just long enough to see the anger in her eyes at yet another interruption.

"How did you find me?" Celeste asked.

"I followed you," Nerissa replied airily with a wave of her hand. "I arrived at the ship just as you jumped into the water. I admit—I was curious why you would leave the humans. You were so cozy with them last time I checked on you. Well—*with one of them*."

Celeste's eyes narrowed. "If you followed me, why didn't you help? I nearly drowned."

The Sea Witch's casual manner shifted into something more predatory. "You had nothing more I wanted. And I don't do charity."

"Wouldn't you want to protect your *investment*?" Celeste retorted, frustration simmering close to the surface.

"Perhaps," Nerissa hissed. "But by the time I *might* have stepped in, you did something—interesting." Her lips curled up into a smile on the last word.

"You made a deal with *the Sea Witch*?"

At Sephone's voice, Celeste turned, heart sinking in her stomach. "I did what I had to."

"And now you've brought her here! To this sacred island!"

Celeste took in a deep breath, her anger rising to boiling just under her skin.

"I am so very sorry to intrude, Your Highness," the Sea Witch's silken voice cut between them as she turned her attention to Sephone. "But I must warn you—when I arrived on the shore of this island, I saw a ship dropping anchor. The human prince's ship."

Celeste's face paled.

"You said they couldn't find this island without a siren's Song," Celeste said.

"I didn't think they could..." Sephone faltered, looking desperately at Gala. The ancient siren looked as though she was fading by the second.

"Enough talk." Nerissa's jaw tightened. "Celeste, you delay your prince. I shall help your sister and her companion escape."

"I will not leave before the ritual is completed!" Sephone insisted. "I will not be the one who loses the Goddess's gift."

"Then I suppose we will have to hold them off," the Sea Witch said.

Celeste straightened and fixed Nerissa with a suspicious stare. "I thought *you don't do charity*."

"I may be banished, but I am still a daughter of the Goddess."

The Sea Witch looked down her nose at her. Celeste bristled. She felt guilty for assuming the worst of Nerissa. "And I don't think it'll hurt to make a *friend* of our new Voice," she added with a sly smile.

Ah, there it was. Of course the Witch had some self-serving motivation for helping them. Still, Celeste wasn't in the position to turn down aid. Her fists weren't going to do much against a pirate and his crew.

"Quickly now, Your Highness," Gala croaked, her voice weaker than it had been mere moments ago. With one last worried look toward her sister, Sephone took a deep breath and let out a hum, syncing with her mentor. Their voices melted together, blending once again before opening into song. Without another word, Nerissa strode back through the temple doors, Celeste following behind.

"Why do you have legs?" the princess blurted once they were outside.

Nerissa blinked her large, inky eyes at her. "We are on an *island*, Princess."

Celeste felt her cheeks heat, and she fell silent. The painful process of forming legs burned in her memory. She couldn't imagine performing such a thing on herself.

The familiar song of the ritual drifted out of the temple on the wind, slowly building the momentum it had lost through its multiple interruptions. Of all the ways her reunion with her sister could have happened, she never expected this. It wasn't the island or even the revelation that her own sister had hidden her powers from her all this time that bothered her most. No, it was the way her sister looked at her. As though she were some blundering fool who could not help but make a mess of things. *Not that I don't deserve it*, she thought bitterly. Still, no cut was quite as deep as one from a sister.

Pressing down her feelings, Celeste looked over toward Nerissa. The Sea Witch was dressed in black fitted pants and top with a deep purple cloak framing her large pearl necklace.

"I don't suppose you're carrying a weapon beneath that cloak," Celeste said.

Nerissa cocked an eyebrow at her. "I am the weapon."

"Of course you are." Sure, a siren's best weapon was their Voice, but even the Chorus carried spears as a precaution. She fidgeted nervously, wiping her hands on her hips. After a moment, her curiosity flourished anew. "How—?"

"Ask one more question, Princess, and I'll throw you into the sea."

With a nod, Celeste fell silent. And that was when she heard them.

The humans.

She had hoped the others wouldn't have come. But from the sound of their footfalls, each as loud as thunder in the quiet of the island, Celeste could tell many were approaching. The Sea Witch glanced at Celeste. Above them, the afternoon sun slipped away from the moon, washing everything in golden light.

Captain Raiden Sharp appeared like a figment of her worst imaginings, framed in the bows of the trees above. Her heart stuttered at the sight. His face fixed into a grimace. Bastian stood at his left, sword drawn. And behind them, Kiyami, Nasir, and Torben wore expressions of discomfort or dread. A crew of ten strangers walked with them. Burly men with wide shoulders, roped in muscle. They were not as tall as Nasir, but they were twice as menacing.

"I hoped you wouldn't come," Raiden said.

Celeste lifted her chin. "Happy to disappoint." He took a step closer, but she refused to yield. "I see you brought new friends. I wonder when you had time to find them, considering how *busy* you were. Did you hide them in the brig too?"

Raiden's fist clenched at his side.

"Your captain here had plenty of time to call on his father's men after Velluno." The tallest of the strangers smirked. "And thanks to your wonderful navigation, *Wayfinder*, we knew exactly where to find your current."

Anger flared in her chest.

Raiden turned and glared at the man who'd spoken out of turn.

"Even then?" Celeste whispered. "Even then you were betraying me?" *So it was all a lie, wasn't it?* She blinked against the tears that threatened to fall. But Raiden still saw everything on her face. His hard expression faltered, but so quickly she couldn't be sure it'd happened at all.

"We only want the Voice of the Ocean," Raiden said, taking another step forward. "If you leave now, there will be no need for a fight."

"I'd rather like to fight." Celeste pressed down her grief to focus on the anger. "I've been *practicing*." A wicked smile played on her lips.

Raiden cocked an eyebrow, surprise and amusement dancing across his face. "Come on, Celeste," he said, his voice low. That same damn voice he used on her when they... when she had...

"Get used to disappointment, *Your Highness*," she seethed.

Raiden unsheathed his sword. "Step aside."

"No," she said.

"Step aside," he repeated, frustration mounting.

"No!" she spat, her resentment cracking through her calm. "I will not let you take my sister!"

Raiden's eyes widened. "Your *sister*?" He looked panicked as he glanced between Celeste and Nerissa, as if hoping for one of them to explain.

So he didn't know.

The tallest of the king's men had had enough of waiting. He unsheathed his sword, shouldering Raiden out of the way to run at Celeste. With a grunt, he lifted the blade high above his head, swinging it down in a deathly arc toward her. Heart pounding, Celeste spun out of the sword's path.

The other men sprang into action, Bastian among them. Half ran for Nerissa, while the others surged toward Celeste. A powerful alto poured from Nerissa, bringing three men around her to their knees. The melody was unfamiliar to Celeste, dark and mournful as it wrapped around the men, turning one against the other. The Song pulsed as she attempted to enchant more, but her powers only extended so far. Celeste opened her mouth, unsure how to join.

Bastian lunged at her.

Celeste leaped back, dodging his strike at the last second. But he was not deterred. He kept the pressure on her as other men joined him. She could hardly think, let alone focus long enough to pull at her magic, her gift from the Goddess given for this very reason—to protect sirens from humans. Outnumbered and without proper weapons, it was all Celeste could do to avoid their blows. They backed her toward the steps until she was pressed against the doors. She screamed in frustration, hoping to somehow tap into the same magic she had used to knock the crew unconscious.

Bastian and the men stepped back and plugged their ears, clearly warned about what she could do. But even if they hadn't, the magic didn't feel the same. It was as if it was locked behind a door, the key to which she did not have. Still, the break in their onslaught gave her just enough time to focus her energy and attempt to join Nerissa's song. The bodies of two king's men already lay motionless at Nerissa's feet.

A single note spilled from her lips before a knee collided with her stomach. She fell to the ground, gasping. When she looked up, Bastian towered over her, hatred burning in his eyes. This, too, knocked the air from her lungs. His chest heaved as he looked at her. He didn't see her. He saw only his pain. His loss.

Behind him, a call rang out. Celeste looked up in time to see Kiyami, flinging a sheathed sword toward her. She didn't know where it came from, given it wasn't Kiyami's, but could guess it hadn't been given freely. Celeste snatched the sword and pulled it free, pointing the blade toward Bastian and pushing him back. Suddenly, Kiyami was beside her, fighting back two of the king's men, who were trying to run into the temple. Nasir and Torben had joined the fight as well, both of them keeping Raiden busy.

They were helping?

Torben let out a battle cry as he charged, axe raised high. Bastian looked at his comrades, betrayal plain on his face. Celeste pushed herself to her feet and pointed the blade at his throat.

"I don't want to hurt you," she said.

He wheeled on her then, sword flashing. Celeste took a step

back, meeting each slash and jab with the clang of her own sword. His sword crashed against hers again and again, blow after blow, beating her away from the doors. Fury and pain fueled every strike. Celeste watched in horror as she made retreat after retreat. Her training from the Chorus and Kiyami were enough to keep her fighting, but his mastery of the sword was undeniable. He cut her across the arm. Shallow, but too close for comfort. She could not think. Could hardly breathe, let alone sing. And soon one mistake became many, and she'd given him an opening. It was only a moment, but it was enough. He raised his sword.

And then his eyes found hers. She watched him as he took in the blood, bright red and running down her arm.

And he hesitated.

A sword cut between them, knocking his weapon from his hand.

"Enough, Bastian," Kiyami said coolly, hovering the point of her sword inches from the soft skin of his neck.

But there was no victory in it. Not for Celeste.

"Go," Kiyami said, nodding toward the temple. "We'll take care of things out here."

With a thankful smile, the princess pushed through the doors into the temple. But she could see her sister was far from finished.

"If you give me your sister, I promise no harm will come to her."

Celeste spun around to face Raiden. He'd managed to get past the crew. Past Nerissa. She raised her sword. "As if I can trust anything you say."

A bitter smile played on his lips.

"I can't leave here empty-handed," he said, crossing his sword with hers.

"No." Celeste slid her blade down his until they were pressed against each other. "You'll leave here in pieces."

Metal rang between them as she pushed him with all her strength, sending him staggering backward. But he was quick. Much quicker than she expected. He regained his balance and advanced, his sword a flash of silver.

A rage of fire within her drove her forward. Kept her in the fight and him on defense, if only because she was so unpredictable. They were not training anymore. Their swords clashed as she threw blow after blow at him. But with one step of his impeccable footwork, Raiden regained control, advancing. He knew all her weaknesses. Knew that his long arms gave him an advantage, making it harder for her to get under his guard to land a blow.

And then she made her first mistake. She let her guard down, leaving her right side open. But he did not strike. Instead, Raiden tried to dodge around her toward the pool.

He's trying not to hurt me. The realization struck as she intercepted him, swinging her sword. He turned his wrist, attempting to disarm her. Somehow this made her angrier. She retained control of her weapon and lunged at him, but he parried easily.

Behind him, the battle pushed inside the temple. Kiyami, Nasir, Torben, and Nerissa continued to do their best to keep the king's men back, but they were losing ground.

The music rose. Water in the pool began to circle. Within it, tendrils of light circled the sirens. Celeste could see the power moving through them. The transfer was working. She just had to keep Raiden from reaching them. It was all Celeste could do to keep her body squarely between him and her sister as they circled closer and closer to the pool. But he was backing her into the base of the statue of the Goddess. If Celeste changed direction, he could push past her to the pool. *Hurry, Sephone. Please.*

Suddenly, Raiden twisted in his attack, and Celeste's sword sailed from her hand. It skittered across the temple floor behind him. There was no triumph in his eyes as he raised his weapon to her chin.

She still couldn't believe it. Couldn't believe that after everything they had been through he would take her sister from her. And what's worse, a part of her still felt for him. Still would take him back if he only stopped.

Swallowing, she retreated a step. The stone leg of the statue pressed against her back. There was nowhere for her to go. But she wouldn't let him win. Not while there was still breath in her lungs. With unearthly speed, Celeste kicked, aiming for his manhood. Raiden jumped back, anticipating the blow. But it was enough. She turned and scrambled up the base of the statue, setting her feet upon the head of the Hippokamp and pushing to reach the Goddess.

"I'm just going to borrow this," Celeste said, perhaps to the Goddess herself, as she grasped the golden trident and pulled.

Much to her surprise, it slid easily from the statue's hands.

The island beneath trembled. Stone fell from the temple ceiling. With a cry, the fight stopped. Celeste held tightly to the trident with one hand and clung to the Goddess's now open hand with the other until the shaking subsided. She turned to check on the others, praying the Song was finished. But she froze when she realized the trident in her hands was glowing. Pulsing. A once dead thing now alive.

"It has been claimed," Nerissa breathed just below her.

CHAPTER 40

"That can't be," Celeste said, looking up from the trident and meeting Nerissa's gaze.

"No, this isn't possible," Nerissa agreed. "The trident can only be removed by a siren touched by the Goddess."

Then only Sephone should have been able to move it. Celeste turned the trident in her hands. It was surprisingly light and perfectly balanced. Familiar. If she closed her eyes, she could almost believe it was the spear she had lost. *This wasn't meant for me*, she reminded herself. Sunlight glinted off its golden prongs. Celeste looked to her sister, whose Song had turned frantic. Sephone moved as though in a trance, her head rolling from side to side.

From the corner of her eye, Celeste saw one of the king's men barrel past Torben, sword held aloft, eyes trained on Sephone.

Celeste's body leaped of its own accord. Her feet slammed into the temple floor, knees buckling. And then she was running around the pool. But it was too large, and he was almost at the edge. Sephone, roped in light and still entranced, did not notice as his sword swung.

Kicking off the side of the pool, Celeste launched herself at him. Time slowed as she flew across the water, his blade cutting the air toward Sephone's neck. And then the teeth of the trident sank into his chest. Blood sprayed across Celeste's face as the man's body tipped backward. He slammed onto the temple's white floor with a smack, and Celeste landed over him, graceful as a dancer. For a moment, she watched as the color drained from his face. She felt no regret—no shame in taking this human's life. With a tug, she wrenched the trident free from his body. Three perfect holes were left in his chest, a red stain blossoming from them. With a flourish, Celeste brought the base of the trident down on the floor beside her. Its prongs dripped. Her wild eyes scanned the room, daring anyone to make a move.

No one did. Her gaze fell upon Raiden. She no longer felt like the lost little princess. Raiden looked from the body on the ground to Celeste. He took in her torn, dirty clothes and the blood splatter across her face and corset. And he saw it too. The change in her. Or maybe she was seeing what she wanted to see. Emotions warred in his expression. Fear, anger, and perhaps sorrow?

"Look at you," he said. "The bloodthirsty siren."

Tears pricked her eyes, but she did not falter. "And you, the backstabbing prince."

"How does the story end?"

"It's a tragedy," Celeste said. "It ends in death."

"Shame." A sad smile played on his face. "I do love a wedding." He took a step toward the pool but stopped as Celeste lifted the trident and pointed it to his chest.

"Leave," she said.

She didn't know what stayed her hand—why even now she could not bring herself to kill him, after everything he'd done. The pirate had betrayed her, manipulated her, locked her up in a cage. And yet her hands shook as she aimed the trident true. She still found him the most beautiful male she had ever seen. His brown eyes were on her face, a war raging within them.

"You know I can't," he said.

Grief ripped through her as she closed the distance between

them. They crashed together like gravity. Inevitable. Celeste thrust the trident toward him. Raiden met it with his sword. The impact echoed across the room. And then they were dancing. A terrible, horrible dance of death. And for once they were evenly matched. He may have trained with a sword since he was a boy, but Celeste had trained with a spear for just as long. Somehow the trident felt right in her hands. Like an extension of herself. She lunged, and he retreated, losing ground. And when his sword tangled between the trident's teeth, she knew she had him. With a flick of her weapon, the sword was out of his hands. She pressed the trident's prongs against his chest, his heart. Eyes wide, the captain raised his hands above his head. Her tears came unbidden, running down her cheeks as she prepared at last to finish her mission. She wondered if it would matter now.

A piercing cry filled the room.

She turned to see a sword sinking into Kiyami's side.

"No!" the scream ripped from Celeste's throat.

Celeste watched in horror as her friend fell to her knees. Color faded from her face. Beside her, Bastian's body lay on the floor, his limbs pointing at odd angles. To the right, Nasir and Torben raised their weapons, surrounded.

Raiden froze, his expression stricken. *The crew he promised to protect.*

It was Celeste who moved first. Raising the trident, she charged. A cry escaped her lips as she rushed to her friend's aid. But the Song of her sister and Gala had grown too loud to hear it. The two voices rose together, reaching the climax of their Song, which, at any second, would fall to its inevitable end. The king's man pulled his sword from Kiyami's side. Her body slumped, blood pouring from the wound across the white stone floor.

Raiden, his face tight with determination, raced the other way, toward the pool.

No...

There was no time. She had to choose: save her friend or her sister.

Her heart breaking inside her chest, Celeste turned her back on her crew. On Kiyami, lying still on the floor. On Nasir and Torben as they dropped their weapons in surrender. Celeste dove at Raiden. They collided, tumbling to the floor, a tangle of limbs. Celeste pinned the prince, trident pressed against his neck.

The final note rang around the temple. Sephone's voice sang alone, then stopped. Blinding white light exploded through the room in waves. Celeste buried her head in Raiden's chest, shielding her eyes.

When she looked up, Gala floated in the pool face down. Dead.

Behind the body, Sephone sat on the edge of the pool, a knife pressed to her throat.

A knife held by the Sea Witch.

"Kill him if you'd like," Nerissa said with a devilish grin. "His daddy won't mind."

Ice-cold dread crept down Celeste's spine as she gazed upon her sister. Slowly, Celeste pushed herself off Raiden and stood. But she kept the trident trained on him. She wasn't sure who her enemies were. She wasn't sure of anything anymore.

"Nerissa," she breathed. "What are you doing?"

"You poor child," the Sea Witch cooed. "So *naive*."

Celeste's grip tightened on the trident's neck. "I knew you couldn't be trusted."

"And yet you did everything as I planned." Nerissa smiled.

All color drained from Celeste's face. "What are you talking about?"

"Why do you think I left you at Port Romsey when you left your prince in Velluno?"

No... no, this can't be right. This can't be...

"How do you think the humans got on the island?" Nerissa's free hand idly pulled at Sephone's soft rose hair. Beneath the knife, Sephone stared unblinkingly at the dead body of her mentor. "When the Pirate King made a deal with me to retrieve the Voice of the Ocean," Nerissa continued, "I searched high and low for any sign of where *she* would be. When I learned she was in hiding on this sacred island, I knew *I* would never find it. Only a descendant of the Goddess herself could... or *her lover*." Nerissa winked at Raiden.

Celeste looked between them. How had she not recognized it before? The way he'd looked at Nerissa when he first arrived—not with confusion or surprise. He'd known her. But the expression on his face now made it clear he did not know this story.

"Don't you know what this island is? It is where the Princess of the Moon and the Prince of the Sun consorted with each other."

"Stop it," Celeste said, her voice a low warning.

Nerissa ignored her. "The king never thought Raiden would actually find it. It's why he came looking for me—tortured my location out of one of your pathetic Chorus scouts, and I was only too happy to help. Raiden always was a disappointment to him—a liability, in fact. And a costly one. Do you know what will happen when his father possesses the Voice of the Ocean? With the unification of the power of God and Goddess, the king will be immortal. And what need does an immortal have of an heir? Raiden was easy to sacrifice—useful if he could reach the island, but not for anything more."

Celeste's head spun. She had been a pawn in a much larger game. They both had been. Raiden stared blankly at the Sea Witch, a shell of the man she once knew.

"I have to thank you, Celeste." Nerissa drew Sephone's chin up with a turn of the knife. "If it wasn't for your information about the current, we never would have reached the island in time. Do you know, I almost thought you'd catch on that night I came to the ship to deliver instructions to Raiden from his father. But I shouldn't have worried. You were much too *in love* to suspect anything."

Sephone's gaze slid to Celeste, fear in her eyes. And defeat.

It was all her fault.

But this time tears did not come. Instead, something cracked within her. And pure, unadulterated rage blinded Celeste. Rage at Nerissa. At Raiden. At herself.

The room plunged into darkness deeper than a starless night. Screams and shouts filled the temple. As red anger rolled down her spine, Celeste looked at her hands and saw them glowing. It was as though moonbeams shone out from her fingers. Her eyes widened. Siren magic didn't work this way. This was something else. Something she had never heard of before.

A dull thud came from the darkness before her.

"Sephone!" Celeste cried, diving into the blackness. As she moved, the shadows parted, creating a path before her. Her sister lay unconscious in the Sea Witch's arms, a knife still pressed to her neck.

"Sephone," Celeste gasped.

"Stay back, or I'll cut her pretty little neck."

When the princess did not retreat, Nerissa pressed the knife into the soft skin below Sephone's chin. A line of blood trickled down her sister's neck.

Celeste retreated a step.

A smile curled the witch's lips as she took in Celeste's shining frame.

"You won't kill her," Celeste said, voice firm. "You need her. If she dies, all the power of the Goddess is lost."

"Oh, sweetie," Nerissa purred, running the blade of the knife along Sephone's chin. "She is clearly not the only one with the power of the Goddess."

A chill crawled down Celeste's spine. There were no stories about a siren with the power to create darkness, to put others to sleep with one note, to call the aid of the Hippokamp. It could be another trick. Nerissa had done nothing but lie to her. But the trident in her hands told a different story.

"I . . . How could I have the power of the Goddess?" Celeste stammered.

"You sirens think only of the Goddess's gift of Song, because that's what she gave to you. How to Isla, she gave her own Voice. But you've hidden away in your caves so long that you forget where you came from. Sirens are daughters of the moon, and your Goddess was also the Ruler of Night."

The Ruler of Night. Celeste's heart shuddered at the words. Just as the Land God ruled the day.

"I thought that power was lost. How...?"

"Even I don't know that, Princess," Nerissa said with a smile. "But you know, it's *funny*... after all this time, the Moon Princess and the Sun Prince fell in love all over again."

"But they weren't in love," Celeste said. "The Sun Prince killed her."

"No." The witch's voice turned melodic, sinister. "The human did not kill the fourth daughter. They fell in love. Hid themselves upon this island. A place where water and land met. She stole from her sisters to be with him forever in the human lands. Gave up her siren form. Betrayed her mother. Her *Goddess*."

Celeste felt sick. "You're lying." But in her heart, she knew this was no lie. "This war between sirens and humans—it started when he murdered the daughter of the Goddess. That's the foundation of everything we believe. If she didn't die by his hand, then... But the Goddess gave us the Song to protect us from humans, because of what he did to her."

"Did she?"

If the youngest daughter wasn't murdered; if she fell in love and was loved in return; if she betrayed her sisters, her mother, to be with him, then why did the Goddess give them the Song? If it wasn't to protect them from humans, then what was it for?

It hit her all at once. *Revenge.* Revenge for what the Sun Prince stole from her. Everything Celeste believed swirled, twisting into a new form. What was the truth? She couldn't tell anymore. She didn't know who to trust or what to believe.

"And it looks like the apple doesn't fall far from the tree, as the humans say." Nerissa's eyes lingered on Celeste's bare legs. "I'm not one to believe in reincarnation, but the mind reels."

Reincarnation? The Sun Prince. Raiden? But that would make...

"You said, 'With the unification of the power of God and Goddess, the king will be immortal.' King Leonidas—he's not just any human; he's the heir of the Sun God, isn't he?"

The Sea Witch laughed. "Very good. Got there all on your own, did you?"

The darkness around them wavered. Celeste tried to maintain focus, to force herself to hold it there. But she did not know how. The light radiating from her body dimmed. The darkness shuddered, then fell away.

"I'm afraid our story time is at an end," Nerissa said, inky-black eyes sliding to behind Celeste. "Take our Voice to the king. The rest of you ... kill the sister."

Celeste spun to find the remaining men moving toward her and Sephone, leaving behind the battered bodies of her crew, motionless and scattered across the blood-smeared floor. Trident raised, she leaped into their path.

"Oh! I almost forgot," the Sea Witch said. *"I'd like to call in my favor."*

Celeste's hands slipped on the trident's neck. A sudden heat bloomed from the crescent moon on her arm. It coiled around her, moving upward and out until the feeling encircled her body in a viselike grip.

"Don't fight," Nerissa said simply.

"No!" Celeste cried.

But it was done. Her knees buckled beneath her as the promise pulled her down, forcing her into submission. The trident fell from her hands, clattering to the floor.

"No, please!" One man continued past, and there was nothing she could do to stop him as he pulled Sephone's limp body into his arms. The other four surrounded Celeste.

She looked up and found Raiden still there. His dark eyes met hers, and she saw anger—a burning hatred she could not understand. He pulled his pistol from his hip.

"No one is going anywhere," he growled. "And if any of you touch her, *I'll kill you.*"

CHAPTER 41

The men hesitated, unsure which orders to follow: the prince or the Sea Witch. Celeste writhed beneath the spell's grasp, trying everything she could think of to move through it. But there was nothing she could do. And she could not allow herself to hope. Just because she couldn't see the game Raiden was playing, didn't mean there wasn't one.

Nerissa raised a perfectly arched brow. But as she opened her mouth to speak, the room erupted in Song. Nine voices rose in harmony, almost shrieking. Celeste's heart seized in her chest. It was the familiar voices of the Chorus of Staria. They were not singing the Song of longing, a gentle caress to beckon sailors to their watery graves. This was a Song of war. They emerged from the streams that wove through the temple, nightmares made real.

One by one, the humans submitted, their weapons clanking against the floor as they walked trancelike to the beckoning sirens.

Celeste waited for the magic to fall upon her, for the moment she, too, would be swept up into the song. But it did not come. *Are they not singing to me? Or is the power within me forming a sort of shield?* She looked at Raiden and found that he was unaffected. *Just as he always has been.* She should have known. Should have seen it. Celeste wondered what other gifts the Sun God gave his heirs.

Raiden looked up, meeting her gaze. He shouted something, fear plain on his face, but she couldn't hear him over the Song. Then he pointed.

The crew. They were moving. Getting up. The image was sickening, as though their limp bodies were pulled by invisible ropes. Their heads rolled on their shoulders, and their bodies swayed from side to side. Nasir took lumbering steps, while Torben shuffled behind. To their left, Bastian stumbled to the floor but picked himself back up. He took a few clumsy steps, before toppling back down. Kiyami was the worst of all. It was as though her injury made it impossible to stand. So instead she crawled, arm over arm, dragging herself toward the water's edge, a smear of blood trailing behind her. Her face was white as death. Eyes sightless.

Raiden holstered his sword and ran to Nasir, who was nearest to the water. He threw his shoulder into the cook's large stomach and shoved. But Nasir continued unencumbered. Raiden's feet slid on the temple floor as the large man pushed him toward Analora. Her familiar light purple hair flat against her cheeks, she didn't look like a nervous initiate anymore. She must have been made a full member. They all were. Which meant—

Celeste searched each siren's face until she found her. *Maeve.* The cecaelia bobbed in the stream, just behind where Celeste was pinned to the floor. Maeve's eyebrows pulled low over her eyes, lips tight as she sang. Relief broke like a wave upon Celeste. *She's alive. She made it home.* And Kiyami was crawling straight toward her.

A sickening splash sounded. A second not far behind.

Celeste turned, heart in her throat. But it was two of the king's men who had plunged into the streams. Long-clawed fingers tightened around their necks. They did not fight. They did not so much as blink as their bodies were dragged beneath. A fate her crew would soon share.

And all she could do was watch.

The Sea Witch's words—*Don't fight*—rang in Celeste's ears. She had to get them to stop before they drowned the others—her *friends.* But she couldn't move. The spell fixed her in place. And every second Kiyami crawled closer and closer to the water.

"Maeve!" Celeste cried out, screaming over the music.

The cecaelia's concentration wavered. Her eyes flicked to the side before returning to Kiyami's bloodied body.

"Maeve, please! Listen to me!" Celeste yelled, slipping into her mother tongue.

Again, Maeve faltered. But this time she turned, brows knit together. When Maeve recognized her, her eyes widened. She stopped singing.

"Celeste?"

Surprise moved across her face, then relief, and finally confusion. Though time had passed, Celeste could read her friend's thoughts as she once had. *What are you doing here?*

Tears rolled down Celeste's face. "Maeve, I'm so happy you're okay," her voice cracked. "But you need to stop."

Maeve's eyes hardened. "These humans kidnapped me."

"Please," Celeste begged, shaking under the weight of the promise. She looked to her friends, stumbling to their deaths inch by bloody inch.

"Save them yourself," Maeve spat, turning her face away.

"I can't," Celeste called frantically. "The Sea Witch enchanted me. *Please.*" Her vision blurred with tears. When Maeve still did not turn, she added, "I'll do anything."

"Why would you fight to save *them?*" Maeve accused, her voice climbing over the battle cries of the Chorus. "They do not deserve our mercy!"

Tears fell from Celeste's chin, dripping on to the temple floor below. She thought of Nasir teaching her to read. Of Torben giving her a dagger with a wink. Of Kiyami—*My sister is a dancer... I want to write to her before we leave tonight about how talented my friend is.* The pull on her body loosened as Celeste sank to the floor, surrendering to the spell.

"Because they are my *family.*"

Hurt flashed across Maeve's face. The cecaelia stared at Celeste, searching for some explanation. Some reason why Celeste would choose these humans over her own. Maeve frowned. And then she sang three jarring notes.

The Song stopped, the final scales of it echoing through the temple. One remaining king's man got to his feet, blinking as though waking from a dream. A look of horror crossed his face as he beheld the other men floating dead in the water. Then he ran from the room.

"What is the meaning of this?" hissed General Xandra in the siren tongue, her hands gripping another man's throat.

"The princess ordered it, General," Maeve responded curtly. Celeste's heart felt as though it could burst from gratitude.

Narrowing her eyes, Xandra followed Maeve's gaze to Celeste. But she was already racing to Kiyami's side. Raiden beat her to it. He tore a piece of cloth from his shirt and pressed it against the gash at her side. But Kiyami had lost too much blood already.

"Someone heal her," Celeste demanded, turning around to look at the general.

The sirens did not move.

"This is not a request." Celeste walked over to pick up the trident. She stood, fixing the general with a hard look. Silence fell.

"Yes, *Highness*," Xandra said bitterly. Distrust shone in her eyes. Celeste had never pulled rank before. But Xandra did not fight. The general turned and gave the order. A siren Celeste did not recognize swam forward, eyes as big as saucers. Had the siren ever seen a living human this close before? Touched one? Raiden looked to Celeste, uncertain what was happening.

"Move her to the water's edge," Celeste said in his language.

With a nod, Raiden lifted Kiyami in his arms, careful not to jostle her. He placed her gently beside the stream's edge before the siren. With shaking hands, the healer began to sing. Their voice was soft and soothing as they placed their hands against the wound.

And slowly, color bloomed in Kiyami's cheeks.

"She'll recover," the siren said, looking up to Celeste, who hovered as they worked. "But she won't be conscious for a while. She's lost a lot of blood."

Raiden let out a breath of relief and moved to check on the others. But Kiyami's unconscious body only reminded Celeste of one thing. One person.

Sephone.

Amid the chaos, she had lost track of her. But when she looked to where Nerissa last stood with her sister, there was no sign of them. Nerissa had used the Chorus's arrival as a diversion. She must have fled before the Song took effect. And now Nerissa would take the Voice to the king. Cold fear washed over Celeste. Heart hammering, her eyes fell to her wrist. The once black crescent had faded to white.

The deal was done.

"Did anyone see the Sea Witch?" Celeste asked in Starian, and then in the common tongue. "Anyone see where she went?"

"She'd have gone west."

Celeste whirled.

With shaking legs, Bastian pulled himself to his feet, his expression somber. Feeling Celeste's eyes on him, he lowered his gaze. "Where we docked our ships," he said softly.

"Thank you," Celeste said, uncertain. Was he ... *helping* her? After he tried to kill her?

"No," he said, meeting her eyes, "thank you for saving me. *Again.*"

Celeste looked away, unsure how to feel. Instead, she turned to the Chorus. "I know you have no reason to trust me—not after what I did." She thought of her mother, her plan to return to Staria once her mission was complete. Did she even belong in the siren realm anymore? But if she remained in the human world, would she have a place there? She pushed the thought aside.

"These humans are not your enemy. I can lead you to the humans who *are*. The ones who have Sephone and are taking her to King Leonidas."

The general looked upon the sacred weapon of the Goddess

in her fist. Her face hardened. "We shall follow you, Princess," she said, voice firm. Celeste's shoulders sagged in relief, her royal composure slipping. As if by habit, her eyes found Raiden's. His face was stony, unreadable. She wasn't sure if he was still here because he wanted to help them, or for his own selfish reasons. It would be just like him to play nice until he found a way to oust Nerissa and take the credit for himself.

But in the end, there wasn't a choice. Not with her sister's life in the balance. And it was time to accept whatever consequences awaited her.

"Swim west," she said to Xandra. "I'll meet you on the shore. Wait for my signal."

The general sang out a call, one short note and one long. And the Chorus disappeared into the water. All but Maeve, who lingered and looked at Celeste as though she did not recognize her. But then she, too, sank into the stream and swam away.

With a stab of relief, Celeste saw Torben and Nasir had awoken. Bloodied and bruised, but alive. They stared at Celeste, and she remembered she'd been speaking another language. None of them understood what was happening. But she did not have time to explain.

She turned, and with a thrust of her shoulder, she pushed through the temple doors to race west toward the setting sun. *Kiyami will be okay*, she told herself, heart squeezing in her chest. *The others will take care of her.* But it didn't make the decision to leave her friends behind any easier. Guilt racked through her with every step. The sky burned above her, washed in red and gold. But night was closing in. It crept at the sky's edge, purpled as a bruise.

"Celeste!" It was Raiden's voice.

She did not stop. She flew through the jungle, racing along the streams. Beneath the clear water, she saw the sirens, their tails shimmering under the soft glow of the floating lights.

Her legs burned. Her breath came in gasps. But she did not slow. Not until she saw a sliver of white sand between the trees.

She was almost there. But she did not have a plan. What would she do once she got there? Would Sephone be locked in the brig, like Maeve had been? What if they had already departed? What if she was already too late?

As she drew closer, she saw several large ships anchored just off the shore. The *Red Revenge* she would recognize anywhere, with its red-painted stripe and its black flags. The other two ships she did not recognize. Each one bore a large flag with the same sigil: a golden flaming sun. The same symbol she'd seen on the letter with the king's seal. Cold fear shuddered through her at the sight. Her feet slowed as she reached the edge of the trees. She wanted to get a look at the king's ships before giving away her position. Nerissa would be expecting her.

Footsteps behind her drew close, and Celeste turned to see Raiden. Whatever he wanted, it surely wouldn't be to help her get Sephone back. So she whirled, pressing the trident's prongs into the bare skin of his chest that showed through the opening of his black shirt. He did not move. Did not reach for his weapon.

"Go ahead," he said.

He doesn't think I'd do it. Anger burned in her as she closed the distance between them, sliding the trident up under his chin. She brought her face close to his.

"Do not test me, pirate," Celeste sneered.

Raiden laughed. It was nothing like the warm sound she knew. The sound was hollow. Mirthless.

"Trust me, Princess"—he pressed his chin down into the trident's teeth to meet her eyes—"you'll be doing us all a favor."

She searched his face and found a stranger. It was as though the flame that had raged within him had been stamped out. The only thing she saw in his expression was pain. A man who had played his last hand, and it had cost him everything.

"No." Celeste clenched her jaw. She pulled the trident down from his neck and pushed him hard against his chest, sending him stumbling back.

"What?"

"You don't get to do that."

"Do what?" He folded his arms across his chest.

"Give up! You don't get to hate yourself or switch sides or whatever you're doing right now," her voice rose. "I will not fall for your games again. You don't get to make me feel sorry for you! *You* betrayed *me*. You don't deserve my forgiveness! I don't forgive you!"

"I know." He lowered his eyes to the forest floor.

"No!" Celeste was shouting now. "No, you don't! Because I—I loved you, Raiden."

His back stiffened.

"And I was a means to an end." The truth pierced her, a double-edged sword.

Raiden looked up, his dark brown eyes empty. "I know," he repeated.

Celeste's heart shattered all over again. She held his gaze, watching as his walls rose around him. Until she could only see the mask of Captain Raiden Sharp.

"That's why you never trust a pirate," he said.

Celeste cursed under her breath. She didn't have time for this. Her sister was in danger. And she needed a plan. Gripping the gleaming trident, Celeste turned toward the beach.

"Hold it right there," shouted Torben between rasping breaths. Celeste stopped with a huff. She didn't know why she did. They weren't a crew anymore. She did not have to listen to their orders. The group emerged through the trees. Nasir cradled Kiyami, and Bastian brought up the rear. Celeste eyed the quartermaster warily. He avoided her gaze.

"What's the plan?" Torben asked, wiping the blood from his cheek.

"This isn't your fight," Celeste said. "I will not ask you to join me, not after I lied and—"

"A crew protects their own," Nasir said, taking his husband's hand.

Tears sprung to Celeste's eyes at his words, and the cook chuckled.

"I—I'm coming too," Bastian added.

The three turned to look at him. He shifted from foot to foot.

"I may not trust sirens, but I know the king. And if my sister was taken..." He broke off.

"Okay," Celeste said. Bastian looked at her, a grateful smile on his lips. The alliance was delicate, and Celeste still didn't trust him not to plunge a knife in her back, but she wasn't in a position to deny help. "Don't give me a reason to kill you."

Bastian grinned. "Of course, *Your Highness*."

The joke stung. She knew it was only his humor. A way for him to show he was on her side now that he knew who she was. And yet she could not stop her traitorous eyes from finding Raiden. He was watching her intently, reading her every move as always. *He knew I was in love with him. And he betrayed me anyway.* Her heart stumbled at the thought. But she did not have time to fall apart. So she shouldered her grief. She did not push it away or ignore it, but she carried it with her. A thing to be dealt with when the time was right.

"Do you know what they're planning?" she asked.

Bastian's smile faded. "I'm afraid not. All I know is, the Voice was to be delivered directly to the king."

Celeste nodded and turned back toward the beach. She scanned the great ships, searching for a sign of Sephone—a clue as to which ship she was on.

And then she saw him.

The Pirate King himself.

CHAPTER 42

Celeste had imagined King Leonidas countless times. A puzzle she had put together from the pieces she heard from those around her. But in all her imaginings, she never did him justice. He towered over his crew, standing above the others. But his height was not what set him apart. King Leonidas was resplendent. Thick waves of golden hair fell like a crown around his head, drawn into a knot at the nape of his neck. A large black hat with gold trim sat proudly atop his head, adorned with golden feathers. Blond stubble lined his square jaw, and above his warm smile was a small, trim mustache. Across his broad shoulders, he wore a long coat as red as the setting sun. This, too, was trimmed in gold. Leather belts with gleaming, ornate buckles hung across his hips, bearing a gilded sword at his hip. But far more dazzling than all this was his smile. It was as though the sun itself had turned its face upon her alone, showering her in warmth. Although Raiden clearly favored his mother in appearance, Celeste could see a striking resemblance. Not only in the square set of their jaws or their dazzling smiles but in their energy. Bright and burning.

This was the Pirate King? Captain Leonidas Sharp? The legendary King of Outlaws and self-proclaimed Ruler of the Seas? He looked nothing like the bloodthirsty pirate she'd imagined. With a laugh, Leonidas clapped his hand on the back of his helmsman, eyes shining as if he'd just told a joke. She almost couldn't believe this man would kidnap anyone.

Perhaps she had the wrong man.

But then Nerissa strode up from the lower decks, gait smooth and purposeful. No one batted an eye to her presence. *She's been with them this whole time*, Celeste realized bitterly.

She looked distinctly out of place with her siren features among the heavily built Ethorian male crew. Many of them were missing an eye, a leg, or a hand. Not a single human on their ship looked anything like Raiden, Nasir, or even Torben. Following in Nerissa's wake, two men appeared, each of them thick as tree trunks. And between them they held Sephone. Celeste's heart seized in her chest as she gazed upon her sister's gagged mouth and bound hands. The siren's tail lay limply on the deck, her eyes downcast.

At the sight of the Voice of the Ocean, King Leonidas clapped his hands together, beaming. He exchanged pleasantries with Nerissa, whose face remained expressionless. With a good-natured laugh at something the Sea Witch said, he turned at last to the siren princess.

Celeste's stomach twisted into a knot. There was no way for them to sneak onto the ship. The king's crew outnumbered them ten to one. And Nerissa would be expecting something. She knew Celeste was on the island. Even if she did not know of Celeste's precarious alliance with the Chorus, it would still be a risk to ambush the ship. But did she have another choice?

The king leaned in and spoke to Sephone, the proximity making Celeste's toes curl. She wished to move closer. To hear their conversation. But her feet remained rooted to the spot. She couldn't risk losing sight of her sister for even a moment.

Sephone nodded solemnly, and the king grinned. The Voice did not look afraid or even angry. She merely looked resigned. With fingers covered in golden rings, Leonidas carefully untied the fabric from behind Sephone's head and removed the gag from her mouth. With inhuman stillness, she stared unblinkingly at the king before her. He smiled, clearly pleased with her obedience. Did the man ever frown? But it was when Sephone turned to face the open ocean that Celeste saw the tears that shone down her sister's cheeks. Her eyes stared at the sea before her. Hollow.

Dusk fell around them as Sephone lifted her pale arms and opened her mouth. The voice that echoed forth was both hers and not hers. Despite the distance, Celeste could hear it as though her sister was beside her. A haunting melody, the song had no words, and yet Sephone painted an image of the ocean itself, embodying the water using only her voice. Each note moved with the rhythm of the sea beneath her, the once crystal-turquoise waters looking black in the fading daylight. Celeste turned to see the crew listening with similar expressions of amazement and trepidation. The Voice of the Ocean echoed off the waves, creating a sort of round.

Behind her, the Pirate King watched, reverence on his golden face.

"What's she doing?" Torben asked.

Suddenly, the waves that pushed gently against the shore began to swell. Water raced forward, covering more and more of the white sand. But the water did not ebb as it should. Did not return. It grew and grew until the beach was submerged. And still it did not stop. It rose rapidly, rushing toward the tree line.

"The ocean. It's *rising*," Bastian breathed.

Sephone jerked a hand, and a massive wave leaped from the ocean's surface, gathering water into itself until it looked swollen. Unnatural. With one brush from her hand, it careened toward the island, doubling in size. Then it crashed. Water rushed into the woods, covering the forest floor. It pooled around their legs, reaching above their ankles. Celeste stared down at the water. Something was wrong about it. It was warm. Uncomfortably so. Almost hot. Celeste tore her eyes from her sister and looked to the others.

"The island," she said, voice shaking. "She's drowning it."

"Get to the *Revenge*!" Raiden commanded.

The crew sprang into action. They stormed through the rising tide, water splashing around their knees.

"Sephone!" Celeste cried, waving her arm in a vain attempt to get her attention, all thoughts of a plan gone. But Sephone showed no sign of hearing. "Sephone, stop!" she repeated, racing toward the king's ship. A hand wrapped around her wrist, stopping her. She tried to resist, but the grip was too strong.

"Not so fast," Torben growled. "We gotta stick together."

Celeste blinked at him, shocked that Torben, of all people, held her back from a fight. And yet he was right. On the *Red Revenge*, they had cannons. Weapons. Even outnumbered, they stood a better chance on the ship. Yet what were they alone against the might of the king's ships?

But they weren't alone.

With a shrill cry, Celeste lifted her voice and sang out three notes. A summoning. And from the depths of the ocean, the Chorus emerged. The sirens were hardly discernible among the waves as night fell around them. But they had come all the same.

"Attack the crew! I think the king is immune to our Song!" Celeste shouted as she trudged toward the *Red Revenge*. The water had risen to her waist now.

Maeve appeared ahead of her, face pale.

"The sea is warming. If it continues, it will be too hot for us to breathe underwater."

"How far down does it go? She can't be heating the entire ocean," Celeste insisted.

"I don't know," Maeve said. "But if it spreads far enough—all of Staria could suffocate."

The blood in Celeste's veins ran cold. *Staria could suffocate?* Sephone would never do that. But even as Celeste thought it, she realized she didn't know what her sister would do. They hadn't seen each other in five cycles. Celeste didn't know this siren at all.

Torben swam up behind, pausing midstroke when he registered Maeve's words.

"How could a siren *suffocate*?"

"Hot water doesn't hold enough oxygen..." Celeste explained, numbly.

Torben's eyes widened.

"They might be trying to force the sirens to surface," Maeve said.

"You should go." Celeste gripped Maeve's magenta hands in hers. "Warn the queen."

She expected her friend to refuse. Maeve had always been a fighter, eager to prove herself. But she didn't. Instead, she nodded and looked at their hands, confused. The touch was human. Far too familiar for a siren. Surprised by herself, Celeste released their hands, and Maeve retreated into the water without another glance. And with a sweep of rolling tentacles, she was gone.

The waves were at Celeste's chest now. She pushed herself from the sandy floor and began to kick toward the *Red Revenge*. But the trident in her hand made progress slow. The rest of the crew swam ahead, Nasir carrying Kiyami's unconscious body upon his back. From somewhere near the king's fleet, the Chorus's Song began. The notes clashed against each other, twisting into a cacophonous melody. Celeste lifted her head as she swam, looking toward the ship. Nothing was happening.

The king's crew moved around the ship, entirely unaffected.

Celeste fell still. There wasn't any way humans could resist the sirens' magic. Any living creature with ears was defenseless against the Chorus's Song. Everyone except, perhaps, Raiden and the king. Unless... *unless they couldn't hear.*

"It's a trap!" Celeste cried, switching directions. She paddled furiously toward the sirens, but her voice was drowned in the noise. Panic rose like bile in her throat. But before she could reach them, strong arms wrapped around her waist, pulling her backward. She flailed in their grip, kicking her legs and swinging the trident.

"Let me go!"

"No," Raiden said, his mouth beside her ear. She bucked against him, but he pulled her closer, until her back pressed against his chest.

"Let me go, you bastard!"

A terrible noise ripped through the air, followed by a splash.

The Song was replaced by screams.

Celeste froze. She lifted her eyes to the king's ships. When the next blast came, she saw it. Saw the cannon fire from the ship. Saw the siren beneath as they were blown apart.

"No!" The scream ripped through her, raw and guttural. Tears stung her eyes.

"Celeste, we need to get out of the water."

The Chorus retreated.

Red stains bloomed in the dark water.

"Sephone!"

But her sister did not hear her. Her sightless eyes stared out upon the chaos. Beside her, the Pirate King still smiled.

Shaking, Celeste clutched the trident to her chest, cradling it like a child. But it did not bring her comfort. Raiden spoke in her ear. But she did not hear it. And then he was turning her away from the carnage, tucking her into his chest. She did not notice when he'd started to swim. But she could still see everything over his shoulder. Sirens dove into the water only to emerge moments later, gasping. The searing sea offered no escape. All the while, Sephone continued to sing, the angelic melody a sickening accompaniment to the horrors below.

Why? The word became a chant. *Why? Why? Why? Why? Why were they doing this? Why didn't Sephone fight?* Then a new thought moved through her like poison, shouting until it couldn't be ignored.

This is my fault.

The island sank lower into the rising sea, until the water smothered the glowing heart within. And then it was gone.

"Lower the rope!" Raiden shouted.

They had reached the *Red Revenge*. She hadn't even noticed. The great ship loomed above them in the darkness, a black silhouette against the moonless sky. The place she had called home for the last several months. Where she had played at being a hero.

But she felt so foolish now. It had all been a lie. She knew nothing about this war. About the humans. About *herself*. And it had cost everything.

Cold air needled her skin as her body was pulled from the searing water. She hadn't felt Raiden tie the rope around them. She couldn't even feel him beside her anymore.

"Just hang on," Raiden said. But his words sounded so far away.

Useless. You're useless, a voice inside her head said, achingly familiar. *Look at you. Falling apart when those around you need you most. Pathetic. They're paying for your mistakes.* It spoke in her own voice. *You're a liability.* She squeezed her eyes shut but could not silence it. After all, it had a lifetime of practice. Celeste's body fell onto the deck, but inside she continued to spiral down and down. Every new thought sent her deeper.

A wet nose sniffled in her ear. Little nails scraped gently against her arm. Insistent. She opened her eyes to see the Admiral staring at her, head tilted.

"Hello, you," she said, a weak smile on her lips.

Raiden kneeled beside the pup, dripping with salt water.

"You have to get me close to the king's ship," Celeste told him.

He stared at her, incredulous.

"We can't fight them," he said. "Even without the power of the ocean on their side, they outgun us."

"I won't leave my sister," Celeste insisted, using the trident for support as she pushed herself up onto her shaking legs. The image of that siren being blown apart flashed beneath her eyelids every time she blinked. Her stomach turned.

"Nerissa will have told the king what you are by now," Raiden said, gripping her by the shoulders. "What you can do."

"I don't care!" She pushed him, but he didn't move.

"Celeste?"

She whirled around, heart hammering. Kiyami was settled on the ground not far from her, propped up against a pile of barrels beside Nasir.

"Kiyami." The trident clattered to the floor. She ran to her friend's side. "Are you okay?"

Kiyami's eyes were bright, alert, but the rest of her moved sluggishly. She reached out, resting her hand gently on Celeste's cheek. And then smacked her.

"Ow!" Celeste yelped, more from surprise than pain. Behind her, Raiden laughed.

"Stop trying to get yourself killed," her friend snapped, before slumping back against the barrel, her energy leaving her at once. Celeste rushed forward, but Nasir stopped her with a hand.

"She's fine," he said, squeezing her shoulder. "She just needs to rest."

Celeste nodded, sinking back onto her heels. Then she noticed how quiet the night had become. Sephone's song had ended. The cannons hadn't fired again. Celeste pushed herself to her feet, walking across the ship to retrieve the trident from the floor. Its weight in her hand steadied her. With heightened vision, Celeste scanned the deck of the king's ship until she found her sister. Her breath caught. Sephone was staring at her.

Her sister's lips moved, forming words that looked like an apology—or a warning. The Voice spread her long fingers, lifted her hands, and pulled them down in a violent arc.

The world around Celeste exploded.

CHAPTER 43

Salt water crashed over her, sweeping her off her feet. No one had seen the wave coming. Her body twisted and turned at the mercy of the ocean. Splintered wood was everywhere. When she surfaced for a moment, she heard the strangled cries of her companions. Beneath her, the raging sea tore the ship apart. Celeste's body slammed into a railing. The impact left her gasping, bringing in a lungful of bitter water. It was all she could do to keep her grip on the trident. She couldn't tell where she was. Didn't know what was up or down. Her body shook with each cough, lungs desperately trying to remove the water from them. But with every exhale, more flooded in.

I'm going to drown. The thought appeared before her, clear despite the chaos. But it was unbelievable. Sirens could not drown. Yet she was no longer a siren. Not without her gills. Celeste kicked, looking for the surface. The sea was so dark. She saw nothing but endless night in all directions. Faced with her impending death, Celeste did not think of her past. Did not see her choices flashing before her eyes. Instead, she thought of what would happen next. She saw how angry Kiyami would be with her for "getting herself killed." She saw Sephone, a prisoner of the Pirate King, abandoned.

She saw her parents mourning her, despite everything she had done. She knew they loved her, even if they didn't understand her.

Then, inexplicably, she saw Raiden. His dark hair. His warm smile. And although everything told her to believe otherwise, she knew her death would hurt him. Even though he'd betrayed her and his crew for a father who didn't care if he lived or died. She could feel his arms around her. For the last time.

Darkness crept into the edges of her vision. Her body gave one final shudder. And then everything went blissfully dark.

Celeste awoke coughing. Her eyes blinked open to see the night sky spread above her. As she sat up, salt water poured from her mouth. The ground beneath her dipped and swayed. Each gasping breath was painful, raw. When her coughing subsided, Celeste looked down to see she was laid upon a splintered piece of wood. At her feet sat a very familiar, very wet dog.

"The princess awakens." Raiden floated in the water, his forearms crossed and resting on the piece of wood beside her.

"Oh, thank God." Kiyami sighed.

Celeste, at seeing her friend safe and awake, felt very much the same. Nasir, Torben, and Bastian treaded water next to her. But as Kiyami struggled a little, Bastian helped her to another piece of wood floating nearby. Celeste's shoulders fell in relief. She almost couldn't believe they'd all survived. She nearly hadn't. But when Celeste looked up for the king's ship, she saw that it was far away, fading into the night. Grief pressed like a weight upon her chest. *What's the point of having power if I can't protect the ones I love?* The king had her sister. And the power of immortality itself, if Nerissa was to be believed. But why did they sink Lunapesce? And why had they left them alive?

That question promptly answered itself when she took in what remained of their vessel. The *Red Revenge* was gone. The fragments of wood around them were the only sign a ship had ever been there at all. They weren't left alive. *They were stranded and left to die.*

"Celeste?"

She turned to see Maeve swimming toward her, the remaining Chorus members following behind. From their numbers, it seemed that three had fallen in the skirmish. The once jovial officer Io looked so small floating in the water despite their muscular frame. As Maeve neared, Celeste noticed there was something wrong about the way she moved. With every forward push, her right side dipped a little into the water. And then she saw the body in her arms.

The violet hair.

It was Analora. Their classmate. A siren who spoke little but worked hard. Gone. She hadn't known her well, but they had been initiates for four cycles together. The wood beneath Celeste tipped as her body swayed. She would have fallen into the sea, if not for Raiden righting her.

Maeve looked upon Celeste as a solider, no sign of the grief she surely felt. "I was intercepted on the way to Staria. A messenger was able to take your warning back," Maeve assured her. "The waters have also cooled. So we're safe for now."

"*Analora,*" Celeste breathed, scanning the body for the source of the injury. A glass shard protruded from the siren's stomach. "Was there no one to heal her?"

"The healer on our squad was killed as well," Io said softly.

And that's when Celeste realized the general should be the one delivering such news. "Xandra?" she asked, but for once she did not want the answer.

"Cannon," Io replied. "There is no body to return home with."

Tears fell freely down Celeste's cheeks as reality sunk in.

"Celeste," Maeve said, her soldier's demeanor softening slightly. "Crying isn't going to help, you know."

"I know," the princess replied, but the words were stifled by sobs.

"The human king has Sephone," Maeve said, a slight teasing in her voice despite everything, as though they were back in the training ring taunting each other. "Are you going to sit here and cry, or are you going to do something about it?"

Celeste smiled through her tears. "Bold of you to assume I can't do both."

It was as much comfort as she would get from her old friend, and far more than she deserved. Maeve nodded and straightened.

"Take care of her," the cecaelia said to the crew, voice stern.

"We will," Raiden replied. To most, he would have looked calm, stoic, but Celeste could see the pain in his eyes.

Satisfied with his answer, Maeve fell into line behind her superior officer. Together the sirens disappeared beneath the waves. And Celeste fell apart.

Three Chorus members dead. *Because of her.* And now the crew was stranded. Tears dripped down her chin. *It should have been me, not Analora. Not Xandra.* The Admiral moved closer, curling up against Celeste with his head atop her leg. She didn't feel it. Didn't notice when the crew gathered to her. They did not try to speak to her or stop her from crying. They merely listened, bearing witness to her pain. She didn't want them to see her like this. Didn't want the Chorus to see her like this. But she didn't have the energy to care. And, if she was honest, it felt good. It was a small comfort to know she wasn't alone.

She wondered if she'd ever stop crying. If this endless expanse of grief would ever ease. And although the grief did not, the tears eventually did. Her hands stopped shaking. And at last she was able to breathe.

In the water before them, rowboats emerged, each towed by two sirens. The princess's eyes widened in disbelief. Why had they returned? Why had they retrieved these from the wreckage of the *Revenge*? Leif, an initiate from her class, pushed one of the boats toward them.

"We take you to nearest human trade route," Maeve said in the common human tongue, her accent thick. "Perhaps you find a ship. Take you to land."

"Thank you," Kiyami breathed.

Celeste didn't know what to say. She lifted her head and found the two sirens helping each of the humans into a boat, Io steadying it as Oakes pushed himself over the edge. The process was awkward, and mostly silent. And although only days ago Celeste would have done anything to see humans and sirens working together, the victory was hollow.

Once they were all aboard, the sirens gathered behind the boats and pushed them east. The hours passed in silence. There was nothing to say. They swam through the night, until at last they saw the flickering lights of a ship on the horizon.

Nothing about the ocean felt safe anymore. For the next week, Celeste hardly went above decks, preferring to lay upon the hammock she'd been provided. The trade ship that had picked them up had been more than generous to the small group of survivors. Raiden had spun an easy tale about their ship being lost in a storm, and that was that. They were allowed to remain until the ship reached Velluno. The crew, in general, gave her space. Kiyami and Nasir were the only ones Celeste spoke to with any regularity. And only when they sat with her below deck.

It wasn't until the final evening that Celeste found herself stir-crazy enough to get fresh air. She stood along the railing, thoughts of her lost sister and the fallen Chorus members still plaguing her. What must her mother think? Her father? Had Staria been compromised? Surely, with Nerissa feeding the king information, it couldn't be safe for them to remain. But Celeste had no way of knowing. Of contacting them.

"Are you okay?" Kiyami sidled up to her friend, leaning against the banister as they gazed upon the endless ocean before them.

"No," Celeste said. It was perhaps the first time she'd answered the question in the many times her friend had asked. With a nod,

Kiyami wrapped her into a hug, squeezing tight. Celeste sagged in her arms, the last bit of fight leaving her body.

"Neither am I," Kiyami said into her hair.

They held each other together, until at last Celeste pulled away. When they did, Celeste saw Raiden standing behind them. Her heart thudded in her chest at the sight.

"May I have a word?"

They hadn't spoken for a week. He had visited her many times, but Celeste always turned him away. She accepted the Admiral's company, although the dog greatly disliked being placed upon a hammock.

Kiyami opened her mouth to argue, but Celeste quieted her with a hand. "It's fine."

With a glare in the captain's direction, Kiyami stalked away, leaving the two alone for the first time since the brig.

"What do you want?" she asked.

"I want to apologize." His eyes were red rimmed, as if he hadn't been sleeping, and his mouth was pulled into a permanent frown. "I don't deserve your forgiveness, but I want you to know I did not mean for all this to happen."

Celeste remained quiet, keeping her eyes trained on the ocean.

"I did not know the Voice of the Ocean was a siren, let alone your sister. I thought it was a necklace or a ring or—" He sighed, running a hand through his hair. "What happened was my fault. I should have told you everything. Should have trusted you with the truth. But you know what failure would have meant. I couldn't risk it with my crew's lives as forfeit. Your life."

Raiden drew closer, watching her carefully.

"You're right," Celeste said, turning toward him. "You don't deserve forgiveness." She hated him. Hated what he had done to her sister. To the Chorus. To her. She didn't trust him. And what's worse, she didn't trust herself around him. Not when he looked at her like that. As if all the world was darkness, and she was the moon.

"I promise I will help you make things right," he said, his voice a low rumble.

"Your promises mean nothing to me," she replied, and turned away.

She wanted to believe him. Wanted it so desperately it stole the breath from her lungs. But nothing had changed. Raiden betrayed her. All of them. And although something within him pulled at her like an invisible string, she couldn't bring herself to hope.

Raiden waited, searching her face. Then, with a sigh, he walked away. Good. She didn't want to speak with him anyway. So why did she feel such pain when he left?

"Land ho!"

Sailors crowded toward the railing, searching for sight of the port after weeks at sea. Relief washed over Celeste. It was over. She could finally escape the sea. Set foot on solid ground again and consider her options. But as the lights of Velluno came into view, the town looked different from when she last saw it. The lights were not from the festival's lanterns but fires. The long, sandy beaches she remembered weren't there. Nor were the docks. And as they drew closer, Celeste could hear shouts. Crying.

Velluno was in chaos.

Aboard the ship, the merchant sailors halted in their preparations to make port. There was nowhere to go. Their captain shouted orders, confusion erupting upon the ship. Celeste's heart thudded in her chest, and she tasted something bitter in her throat. Sephone hadn't only raised the sea around the island.

Half of Velluno was underwater.

The once colorful homes of the shoreline now looked like ghosts, distorted beneath the clear water. Streets they'd walked down now ran directly into the waves. Festival banners and flowers washed up along the new shoreline like trash. People cowered in the streets, displaced from their homes, while others plundered their neighbor's shops, the sound of breaking glass filling the air.

"What has he done?" Raiden was beside her now, his voice taut.

The former crew of the *Red Revenge* gathered along the bow, Bastian the last to arrive.

"The water must've risen across the entire coast. Maybe even as far as Port Romsey," he said.

"The Broken Compass—" Torben began, turning his eyes to his husband. The pub had been close to the waterline. If the water had risen in Port Romsey as much as it had here, his business would be underwater now. Nasir's expression darkened.

"If it's across Ethoria, it could have happened elsewhere too," Bastian added.

Kiyami's eyes widened. "My family lives near the coast."

"Did you know your father was planning this?" Bastian asked, turning to Raiden.

"No," Raiden said. "I didn't." The captain's eyes dropped to his hands. "But I guess now we know why that cargo ship was transporting my father's assets. His home was on the shoreline. He'd been planning this for a while."

The crew fell silent, watching Velluno with tired eyes.

"Captain said we can get you in our jolly boat and row you ashore," a sailor said, approaching. "Looks like that's the only way of getting to land at the moment." He gestured to a boat being lowered on the side of the ship.

"It's better than swimming," Raiden joked, but his smile didn't reach his eyes.

They gathered what little things they had and corralled the Admiral into the tiny boat. When their feet at last reached solid ground, the crew released a collective breath.

"I'm going to see if I can find a courier. Send a letter home," Kiyami said.

"I'll come with you," Bastian agreed.

Torben tugged at his husband. "We should write to Viktoria—see how the Compass fares with everything that's happened."

The group's eyes fell on Raiden and Celeste. Could Raiden send a message to his father? Would he? But the pirate merely shrugged.

"Go ahead," he said, patting the Admiral on the head. "We can meet in the square."

But Kiyami hesitated, looking between Celeste and her former captain. "Do you want to come, Cel? You don't have to stay with him."

Celeste shook her head. "It's fine."

The truth was, she didn't want to watch the others write to their families. To watch them as they poured their worries and fears on paper, knowing she was the cause of them. Perhaps that made her a coward. But she couldn't bring herself to go.

"All right, we'll see you both at the square, then," Kiyami agreed, before the group wandered off toward the shops.

When they disappeared, Raiden turned to her.

"I figured you'd want this back," he said, pulling a large cloth-wrapped object from his back and removing the fabric. The Goddess's trident glimmered in the city lights. How had she forgotten? She must have lost track of it in the aftermath of the wave. "I wanted to return it to you sooner," he continued, "But I didn't want anyone on that merchant ship seeing it."

Celeste accepted it, trying not to react as their fingers brushed, and sparks flew within her.

"Thank you," she ground out.

Raiden grinned. "I can think of other ways you can thank me."

Celeste fixed him with a glare. "I'd rather swim through jellyfish than do anything for you."

"Ah, Princess," he said, dark eyes dancing. "You know how I love a challenge."

The siren looked away, gazing over the endless expanse of sea. "Do you happen to know where your father is planning to go next?" she asked, purposefully changing the subject.

"I don't," Raiden replied, his smile fading. "But I might know someone who does."

ACKNOWLEDGMENTS

Storytelling has been my greatest passion for as long as I can remember. Whether it be in the form of a home movie, an online video, or the written word, something in me has always craved to tell stories. For me, the best part of storytelling is having someone to share it with. Someone who will sit with you and listen to find out how it all ends.

I consider myself an extremely lucky person to know a great number of such people. People who have sat with me throughout my life, who've listened to me cry during my own darkest nights, and who are—inexplicably—invested in how my story ends. So, if you'd lend me your time for just a few pages more, I'd like to thank them.

To begin, I'd like to thank my community on YouTube, Twitch, and TikTok. Without you, I wouldn't be here writing these acknowledgments. It is my belief that you are the best community on the internet, and I am so lucky to call you mine.

Thank you to my mom, who has believed since grade school that I was destined to be an author. You never doubted I'd succeed, even when I did. I hope you have enough space next to my previous "work" (or school writing projects) to fit this book.

To my dad, thank you for gifting me a solid foundation on which to build my life. Dreaming big was always easy knowing I had you in my corner. I know I got my passion for writing from you, and I hope I've made you proud.

To my brother, Chris, thank you for reading this book in book club. I hope you give it five stars. And to my big sister, Andrea, thank you for showing me romance movies and TV shows when I was too young to watch, and for always giving help when I needed it.

Thank you to Kaitlyn, who read this book first and assured me she liked it. We've come a long way from writing movies in my basement about fairies and evil queens.

To Liza, my book mentor, thank you for inspiring me to write again. You held my hand every step of the way, and this book would not have happened without you.

Thank you to my dog, Chewie, who not only provided inspiration for the Admiral but also kept me company through every writing session. Like Celeste, you cannot read this, but I hope you appreciate the sentiment.

To my friends—you know who you are—thank you for being my found family and forever crew. I'm sorry I never let you read the book until now. In my defense, I was scared.

Thank you to my managers, Tori and Lauren. My love for the two of you could fill oceans. Your unflinching belief held me together throughout this process. It's rare to have such wonderful managers, but I think it's even rarer to have them also be wonderful friends.

To my agent, Mark, thank you for choosing me and this book. I'd all but given up on getting it published, and you brought the dream back to life.

Thank you to my team at Blackstone Publishing, and to my editors Marilyn and Christina. From the moment I met you both, I knew Celeste was in good hands. I couldn't ask for a better crew to set sail with.

And last, to Taylor: You are better than any fictional character.

KELSEY IMPICCICHE is a professional YouTuber and Twitch streamer with over 1.5 million followers across various platforms, which altogether means she plays video games for a living. When Kelsey isn't making simulated characters fall in love online, she's writing about different characters falling in love in very difficult situations. *Voice of the Ocean* is her first novel – though she hopes to make it a regular thing. In the meantime, Kelsey can be found sitting beside her dog Chewbacca or making fun videos about books and games online @kelseydangerous.